I0640271

CODY HAWKE

AND THE LIGHT OF NIMBUS

BY
M. MIHM
Illustrations by R. Mihm

MoMo Publishing

For my writing buddies, Mozart and Molly.

Copyright © 2020 by Melanie Mihm
All rights reserved.

MoMo Publishing

ISBN 978-1-7324333-3-5

For more information about the Cody Hawke series, please visit:

www.codyhawke.com

CODY HAWKE

AND THE LIGHT OF NIMBUS

CODY HAWKE

AND THE LIGHT OF NIMBUS

Prologue: The Tome

Thousands of onlookers filled the National Mall, their patriotic voices echoing the Star Spangled Banner. Colorful bursts glittered across the night sky, gut-punching booms following close behind. Dignitaries, celebrities, tie-dyed hippies, and scores of dads bouncing little ones on their shoulders gazed at the spectacle.

A few blocks away an old tomcat crossed the deserted street, stopping to assess his kingdom by the glow of a streetlamp. A newspaper page borne by the spirited breeze, clung to the lamppost as if hanging on for dear life, its headline announcing the day's celebration: America's 200th Birthday.

The only sign of color amid the darkness was a spot of yellow emanating from the basement window of a non-descript brick building. Two men, faces partially hidden behind metal security bars, craned their necks to see the glittering display.

"George, it's time to make our rounds," a young security guard said firmly.

"Come on, kid, who's going to break in tonight?" The older man scowled. "The whole country is watching this, and you are making me miss it".

"But I think we should—" he began, straightening the embroidered name on his pocket: TIM G.

1

"Relax and drink your beer. How often do we celebrate a Bicentennial?" George mumbled, a frown creeping across his weathered face.

Thunderous booms permeated the small office despite the continuous whir of a desktop fan. Stacks of green-bar computer paper and elastic-band-wrapped punched cards dominated the surface of two utilitarian desks. Paper spewed from metal cabinets spanning the cinderblock wall. On the opposite side, a door leading to a vast warehouse offered the only escape.

"I hope Elaine and little Angie are watching this at home," Tim offered wistfully. "Angela may be too young to remember, but at least we can say she saw it," he added with obvious pride.

Tim glanced over his shoulder at the seemingly infinite warehouse. Boxes covered in thick dust filled rows of metal racks that disappeared into the distance. Florescent lights mounted high above cast long shadows across the thousands of assorted containers.

"What is that?" the young man murmured distractedly.

A greenish light lingered on the dusty air, swirling as if being stirred by an invisible spoon. He took a few hesitant steps into the warehouse.

"Where are you going, kid?" George called.

"There's a weird light coming from…"

As he headed down the corridor, Tim noticed a small box casting an eerie glow on the adjacent cartons. The box rocked slightly from side to side as if something inside was trying to escape.

"What the…" he mumbled.

A black cloud appeared farther down the aisle. Dusty rays of fluorescent light highlighted the nebulous entity as it rolled purposefully toward him. Tim backed up, peering cautiously around the corner.

"George?" Tim whispered into his walkie-talkie. "Something's going on out here."

"What? It's almost time for the finale!" George grumbled. "You're a pain in my—"

"Now!"

The dark cloud hesitated for a moment as if listening for an audience, then continued up the aisle, slowing as it approached the glowing carton. A cacophonous wail began to emanate from its center.

"Wow, did you see that one? It was huge!" Tim could hear the old man's distant voice despite the pounding in his chest. Turning suddenly, he raced back toward the office.

"GEORGE! COME, QUICK!"

The old guard took a gulp of beer. A swipe of his sleeve made quick work of the excess liquid.

"There's something strange going on over there," Tim whispered, breathless. "Do you smell that?" The young man wrinkled his nose.

"Wasn't me!" The older man turned, grinning broadly. The smile left his face. "It's a dusty, old warehouse, of course it smells! Some of this crap has been stored here for decades, maybe centuries," he added.

"No, it's like rotten eggs," Tim said, sniffing the air. "Come on!"

"You have an overactive imagination, kid." The old man said, ambling along behind. "You should get a job writing for the soap operas!"

They hid behind a metal shelving rack and peered down the corridor. The black cloud stopped, appearing to solidify as it hovered over the glowing carton. A tall cloaked figure became visible in the dim light. It opened the glowing carton and pulled out an ornate wooden box.

"What the—" George mumbled.

"Shush!"

Lifting the box's hinged top, clawed hands removed its contents, a dusty tome with a gilded cover. Light radiating from within illuminated the title's ancient script. Tim gasped as an eye opened on the cover and stared imploringly in their direction. Seemingly satisfied, the dark figure secured the old book under its robe, then headed back down the aisle.

"WHAT THE HECK IS THAT THING?" George cried in a choked voice.

The figure stopped. As it turned, a hideous face with burning eyes and a hooked nose came into view beneath the hood of its cloak. A growl echoed through the warehouse, as if the creature were angry at having been spotted. It leaped toward them with surprising quickness.

Tim glanced at his partner, fear apparent in the old man's eyes. He scrambled for his walkie-talkie.

"HELP! HELP US! IT'S TIM GARLOWSKI, WAREHOUSE 7. WE NEED—"

The two men turned to run, but the creature was too fast. Painful screams rang through the night, drowned out by fireworks reaching their final crescendo.

A few minutes later, the creature transformed back into a dark mist. As it headed down the corridor, a pile of bloody clothing scattered about the cold cement floor was all that remained of the two security guards.

Chapter 1: The Burglar

"What the *heck* are we doing at this hour of—"

"Shelby, shush!" Cody hissed as they crept down the stairs. "I saw lights coming up the driveway."

"Headlights?" Martin mumbled. "Nobody visits this haunted mansion in the daytime, much less the middle of the night."

The four peered down the curved staircase in anxious silence until a shadow became visible through the ornate windows surrounding Freya Manor's massive front door. The sound of someone fiddling with the lock was followed by the squeak of old hinges.

"Here we go again," Martin whispered. "Achoo!", he added, copper hair momentarily covering the splash of freckles on his cheeks.

Charlotte put her hand over Martin's mouth, Cody assumed to deter further sneezes.

"He has a *key?*" Cody muttered, lifting his cowboy hat to run a hand through the wavy blond hair that almost reached his shoulders.

Leaning out from behind the staircase's central pillar, he watched the door creep open. A dark figure emerged, his breath lingering on the chilly breeze. The imposing intruder closed the door slowly as if to not make a sound, then started across the room.

"Should we get Jack and Heather?" Charlotte whispered anxiously, twirling one of her many thin dark braids.

"What will *they* do, hug him to death?" Cody muttered. "Let's see what he wants first."

Even in the shadowy moonlight the man's stature was impressive, tall with broad shoulders. Dark denim jeans and a light T-shirt clung to his muscular body.

"Whoa," Shelby mumbled, flipping back her long dark hair. "Isn't he *dreamy?*"

Cody frowned. "We're getting robbed, but it's okay because he's good-looking?"

"Is no one else bothered by the fact that strange people are always creeping around here in the middle of the night?" Martin asked.

"More important, where did he get a key and how does he know his way around our house," Cody replied, watching him head purposefully across the foyer.

Stopping momentarily, the man turned his head. A quick smirk, visible under the brim of his western hat motivated Cody to wonder whether he sensed the presence of onlookers. Satisfied, the man approached the old elevator and pressed a button. As the metal doors opened, he disappeared inside, leaving no trace except for a slight chill in the air.

"Come on," Cody ordered. "Let's see what he's up to."

"Cody Hawke, it's one-thirty in the morning and I need my beauty sleep!" Shelby gave him her best pout and as usual a flood of emotions, including exasperation, amusement, and something he couldn't quite put his finger on, made him want to explode.

"Shelby, can you sleep while an intruder creeps around our house?"

"We've *seen* this movie," Martin frowned. "Last time, it involved an angry god who turned into a giant tarantula that nearly ate you for a snack."

"That was Loki," Cody replied. "This is just... some *guy.*"

"I believe you said that last time as well," Shelby said, pulling eight wads of cotton from between her toes and tossing them on the stair behind her. Slipping on her shoes, she added, "I better not ruin my pedicure!"

The four tip-toed silently down the staircase and headed toward the elevator.

"Did he go up or down?" Cody wondered.

"I'm guessing he went down," Charlotte replied. "Sounds like the elevator is coming back up."

"*That's* not good," Martin mumbled. "Not good at all."

"Tell me about it," Cody replied sourly.

"How could he know what's down there?" Shelby's asked as they stepped into the old elevator. "And how come it let him go down? It took months for us to get that to work."

Cody glanced nervously at his siblings, then pressed the button marked 'R'. When the elevator doors opened, one of Freya Manor's many subterranean tunnels loomed before them. The teens headed quickly down the stone corridor, hugging the wall for cover.

The intruder's lofty silhouette was barely visible about thirty meters ahead. He pulled on a sconce near the far end of the cave, clearly waiting for the hidden entrance to appear.

"How does he know about that?" Charlotte gasped, raising a cocoa-colored hand to her mouth.

"I don't know, but we're sure going to find out," Cody said gruffly, watching as the rock wall slid open and the man disappeared inside, as if he had done it many times before.

Who *is* this guy?" Shelby wondered.

"He's heading right for Rúndyrr," Martin said as they trailed along behind.

"Hurry, I don't want to lose him." Cody began to run.

The teens reached the rocky opening and lingered in the shadows. Cody stared in anxious silence as the intruder sauntered toward Rúndyrr, the supposedly *secret* doorway they had sworn to protect.

"Stay back," he ordered, ready to sprint after the man at the first sign of trouble.

"What's he doing? What do you see?" Shelby asked.

"Holy Hannah!" Martin whispered, peering around the rock wall.

"What?" Charlotte piped up.

"The Gatekeeper just walked up and *spoke* to him," said Martin with a gasp.

"He *knows* this guy?" Cody mumbled.

The two men engaged in a seemingly serious discussion. Their voices, initially restrained, grew increasingly animated.

"This is *foolish*! Thou know not what thou are dealing with!" Cody heard The Gatekeeper's distinctive voice.

"Listen old man, if we don't stop The Darkness now, we might not get another chance. It's growing more powerful each day. Now are you going help me or not? If not, get out of my way!"

"Who does he think he is, talking to The Gatekeeper that way," Cody said crossly.

"What the heck is The Darkness?" Shelby mumbled.

Cody tried to get a good look at the man's face, but he kept his back toward them. A few more angry words were exchanged. He couldn't shake the feeling these two were old friends, or perhaps old adversaries that shared a common cause.

What could this man want with Rúndyrr? How does The Gatekeeper know him?

Cody stared at the innocuous door they called Rúndyrr, its arched opening blocked by a seemingly permanent wall of stone. He wondered what this man wanted and how it involved the doorway they assumed was their secret.

"What are they saying?" Martin whispered. "I can't hear."

The Gatekeeper stroked his long white beard for a moment, apparently deep in thought, then retrieved the scepter from its gilded box. He uttered the words they had heard many times before. A brief but brilliant flash lit the cave as Rúndyrr's stone door transformed, illuminating the shimmering bridge. On the other side, Cody could see cactus surrounded by desert scrub. Darkness prevailed as the man disappeared through the door and Rúndyrr's impenetrable stone façade returned.

Cody hesitated, not sure what to make of this, when suddenly another flash of light illuminated the cavern. The intruder stepped back through the doorway, fanning himself with his hat in an apparent attempt to cool off. He dragged something heavy along behind.

"Help me with this," the man said, his gruff voice now unmistakable.

After a brief pause, The Gatekeeper obliged. Effortlessly transforming his usual black robe into clothing more suited to manual labor, he grabbed the handle on one side of a large wooden chest while the man took the other. They crossed the cavern and headed toward where the teens were hiding.

"GO!" Cody whispered.

Almost tripping over each other in their haste to get back down the hall, the four ran toward the elevator, stopping in one of the small alcoves off the main corridor. Cody directed them behind a large étagère that Jack used to store supplies for his internet business.

Why is The Gatekeeper helping this guy?

The two men had just reached the alcove when suddenly they stopped. A soft clunk echoed throughout the corridor as they set the chest down.

"What's the matter?" the man asked.

"*Resting*," The Gatekeeper said with a growl, "I'm not as young as I used to be."

"Yeah, *right*," the other man laughed. "What you *are* is pretty devious. I know what you're doing. Come on, old man, let's go."

As they lifted the chest, it shifted slightly, causing a small gleaming object to slip beneath the top and roll toward them. A few seconds later the two men were gone, disappearing into the labyrinth of dark caves hidden beneath Freya Manor.

"Is it just me…" Martin started.

"Or, was The Gatekeeper trying to make sure we saw what they were carrying," Charlotte continued.

Cody picked up the shiny object and glanced at the others.

"Looks some sort of ancient treasure," he said.

"A gold doubloon," Martin offered. "Where can we get a few more? I could use a new laptop… or maybe a new car. No, how about a trip to Hawaii?" he added with a cheeky grin. "Girls wearing those little coconut bras and grass skirts, dancing the hula—"

"Let's go Casanova," Shelby muttered, grabbing his arm.

Chapter 2: The New Arrivals

"Honey," Jack murmured, chewing a mouthful of pancake, "let's get that shipment of hand-made Indian baskets over to the store today. They sell better when people can touch them, see the quality. We've only sold a couple over the internet." He took another bite.

"Pancake stuck, can't breathe," Martin whispered to Cody in choking voice.

Cody tried not to bust out laughing. He saw Heather watching him and looked away.

Martin makes me laugh, then I'm the one who gets in trouble.

"When are we going to see the sun again?" Jack continued, glancing toward the window. "It feels like it's been dark for weeks."

"Maybe the end of the world is near," Martin said, impersonating a zombie. "The undead will soon be taking over," he added, grinning at the bemused faces.

Heather set another plate of pancakes on the table.

"On a lighter note," she redirected, "no pun intended. Don't forget, it's Sunday and we need to go grocery shopping, so don't go too far. I can't figure out where you four disappear to, but sometimes I swear you must be in another state."

"By the way," Jack added. "We'll be picking up Terrell and Gabby on Friday."

"Who?" Martin mumbled, chewing a bite of pancake then reaching for juice to wash it down.

Cody shook his head.

Every diner in the world can make good pancakes. How is it possible for these to be so bad? If I wasn't so hungry…

"Our new foster children," Heather replied.

Oh, joy and rapture.

"I can't wait, momma," Jessica said excitedly. "How old are they?" she asked.

Charlotte glanced at Cody, concern apparent in her eyes.

"Gabby Evers is a nine-year-old girl from Trenton, New Jersey and Terrell Connor is a twelve-year-old boy from Philadelphia," Heather replied.

"Whew," Cody whispered, glancing at his siblings while Jessica bombarded Heather with a slew of questions. They shared a silent nod, relieved to hear the new arrivals were not teens. The alternative could have meant trouble for their secret.

"Great news, honey," Shelby said, smiling at Jess. "I'm glad there will someone close to your age."

"That's right, Shelby," Heather said, then glanced reproachfully at Cody. "I know these kids are young, but please make them feel welcome. I'm not asking you to hang out, but at least talk to them."

"Yes, ma'am," Cody replied.

"I'm glad the new kids are little," Cody muttered, spinning himself around in Shelby's desk chair.

"Why is Meany Sweeny the only teacher who gives homework on the weekends?" Martin muttered staring at a textbook, then continued. "I agree, bro. We don't need any curious teenagers snooping around the basement. I hope they stay out of our business."

"Be nice," Shelby said. "We were the new kids once."

"Can you imagine them seeing the things we've seen?" Martin joked. "They'd run for their lives."

"The green ghosts," Cody said, "sucking us down through the ground."

"The unfinished roller coaster was a hoot," Martin quipped, sprawled across a beanbag chair.

11

"It's going to be a hassle having these kids around," Cody added. "We can only talk about Rúndyrr when we're alone. Hopefully, they won't want to hang with us."

"Put yourself in their shoes, Cowpoke," Shelby said briskly. "You finally get the chance to be part of a family after years in foster homes. Wouldn't you want a warm reception at your forever home?"

"Yeah," Martin added. "As if this house wasn't scary enough, you worry about fitting in, then you get here and people treat you like unwanted guests."

"You started it!" Cody frowned at Martin. "Besides, you know what I mean. We don't want them getting hurt or anything."

"Why do you suppose it's been so dark lately?" Charlotte wondered.

Cody joined her by the window, staring out at the drab countryside.

"We're in a pattern of bad weather," he replied, shrugging.

"It's *supposed* to be spring," Shelby said, grabbing a magazine and flopping down on the bed. "I may have to start transitioning back to my winter wardrobe."

"Shelby's right. The weather should be improving," Charlotte added, "but it's been cold and dark for days."

"Maybe the world is ending," Martin replied flippantly. "Eternal winter wipes out our food supply, followed by hurricanes, tornadoes, and forest fires. Then, a pandemic comes plus hordes of locusts."

"Aren't you just Mr. Gloom and Doom," Shelby said, then suddenly brightened. "Oh, my! Look at this burnt-out velvet tunic with lacy peplum and bell sleeves. It has such a lovely boat neckline and cute vents at the sides."

"What the heck are you *talking* about?" Cody grimaced.

Shelby held up her magazine.

"*Tunic? Peplum?*" he asked. "Why can't you speak English like the rest of us?"

"Cody Hawke, you oaf," Shelby teased. "They are terms to describe clothing."

"I don't see any boats on the neck or bells on the sleeves? And, why would someone burn their clothes?" he asked.

Shelby rolled her eyes at him.

"That *is* a cute tunic," Charlotte said, taking a seat on the bed next to Shelby.

"Don't encourage her, Charlotte," Cody said with a groan. "She'll suck you into her delusion."

Shelby went on for what seemed like hours describing peplums, tunics, boat-necks, and other things Cody had never heard of. Her southern accent seemed to get more pronounced when she spoke about clothes. He reached for the baseball and glove he'd left on her dresser.

She's such a nut. The way she talks about clothes, you'd think they're made of gold.

He tossed the ball in the air, observing his foster siblings with a combination of affection and amusement. Martin sang along with Shelby's music in a high-pitched voice, meanwhile trying to reach an apparent itch beneath his left leg brace. Charlotte stared at a book on her lap, clearly captivated, despite the braids blocking her view. She pushed them back at least ten times, but they'd just fall forward again.

They're such goofballs, but I couldn't imagine life without them.

The pending arrival of the new kids, reminded Cody of a time when those feelings were not so strong.

"KIDS!" Heather's crackly voice emanated from the old intercom.

"I guess they're here," Cody said, grimacing slightly.

Cody had to admit Shelby was right as the four made their way down the main staircase. He stared at the two orphans fidgeting nervously in the enormous foyer.

They deserve a chance at a normal life with people who care about them.

"Kids," Heather began, a breathy nervousness apparent in her voice, "meet Gabby and Terrell."

Their mom smiled warmly while pushing back a lock of her honey-colored hair.

"Hey," Cody offered, shaking each of their hands. "Welcome to Freya Manor," he added.

"Hi, sugars," Shelby said, giving each of them a hug. "It's nice to meet you both."

Charlotte and Martin added their greetings while the social worker carried in two small bags, one for each child. Jack and Mr. Cognetti, a short man with thinning dark hair and a kind face, shared a few words, then the man departed with seemingly unwarranted haste.

"Wow," Gabby said, breathless, as she and Terrell stared up at Freya Manor's frightening décor. "This place is pretty scary."

"You have *no* idea," Martin replied, chuckling.

"Don't listen to him," Shelby teased. "It's a lovely home . . . once you get used to it."

"Who built this place, King Arthur and the Knights of the Round Table?" Gabby wondered.

"It's not *that* old," Heather responded lightly.

"There's nothing to worry about," Martin added, a twinkle in his eye. "Just don't go wandering off alone. Oh, and try to remember the color of the hallway. Sometimes you find yourself in a different part of the house and it helps if you've memorized the décor."

"Now, kids," Heather said, "no need to frighten them. The house is perfectly harmless."

"Most of the time," Cody replied with a little grin.

"Please show them to their rooms," Jack directed, glancing at Cody, "the ones next to Jess."

Cody grabbed Gabby's small suitcase while Terrell picked up his duffel bag.

"I'm *so* glad you're here," Jessica said, nearly gushing the words. "Finally, someone to play with."

"Where have you guys been staying?" Shelby asked as they made their way up the stairs.

"A foster home in Boston," Gabby said. "It was okay. There were six kids, besides the two of us, a total of eight in all."

Gabby was the skinniest little girl Cody had ever seen. She reminded him of a newborn foal, all legs, knees knocking as she walked. The girl's straight, mousy brown hair, pulled back in a pony tail, did little to enhance her thin face and pale skin.

"Katie was a little kid who loved dogs," Gabby went on. "Joseph wore only blue and red. He was a Red Sox fan. Candy was a tall black girl who hated candy. The twins, Thomas and Gordon, had the most freckles you ever saw. Then there was Maria. She talked funny. I think she was from some other country, maybe Mexico."

Cody found himself zoning out. He quickly realized Gabby was appropriately named. It was like having another Jessica except her constant talking wasn't just a string of endless questions. He wondered who would win the battle of the mouths.

"How about you, Terrell?" Shelby interjected quickly as Gabby took a breath. "Did you like your foster home?"

Terrell seemed tall for his age with a slender build and skin the color of dark chocolate. He kept repositioning the blue baseball cap that left an indentation in his cropped afro.

"Yeah," Terrell said with a slight shrug. "It was alright. My father dropped me off because he travels so much and couldn't take me with him, but he'll be picking me up as soon as baseball season ends."

"He's a baseball player?" Martin asked.

"Andre Connor? You've never heard of him?"

"*That's* your father?" Martin asked, his mouth hanging open.

"The rookie with the Dodgers?" Cody wondered aloud, equally shocked.

"Yep. I'm going to be a baseball player, just like him," Terrell continued. "In another year or two, clubs will be scouting me."

Cody glanced at the others, looking for confirmation as to whether they were buying Terrell's story. The boy sounded very certain. Of course, Shelby still believed she had been kidnapped as a baby and her parents – the Coldswells of South Carolina – were out there searching for their lost child. Maybe Terrell had a similar delusion that helped him cope.

The teens got their new foster siblings settled into the bedrooms adjacent to Jessica's. Heather had succeeded in making the rooms look a bit less like Dracula's castle by replacing the dark velvet curtains and bedspreads. The décor in Gabby's room reflected the face of some popular doll. Terrell's room had been updated with a baseball theme.

As the young girls began a lengthy discussion on the doll in question, the teens took advantage of the opportunity to slip out quietly.

"Whew," Martin exclaimed, "if only we could harness the power of those two gabbers, we could light the entire state of Maine."

Cody laughed loudly.

"Oh, Cody Hawke, stop making fun of them," Shelby said reproachfully. "They're having fun."

"What did I say?" he asked indignantly. "It was Martin."

Cody and Martin helped Jack assemble two more kitchen chairs for the newcomers. Their father rolled up the sleeves of his flannel shirt, tied back his tar-colored hair, and hovered over the instructions like a mad scientist trying to build a time machine. Pieces of Styrofoam stuck to every surface within two meters. Cody tried not to laugh as their typically passive father muttered angrily under his breath.

"Stupid instructions!" Jack frowned. "Insert screw A into hole B using locknut C. Would it *kill* you to include a picture? What locknut? I don't see any nuts, except, that is, for the *nuts* you're making me!"

After an hour or so of periodic grumbling, Jack instructed the boys to set the finished chairs around the table. Their father's demeanor changed dramatically as he admired his work.

Cody and Martin joined the girls in the conservatory, watching as they watered endless rows of pots, each with a small stick in its center. Heather grew herbs along with various vegetables and summer annuals. Cody doubted any amount of spice could possibly help her cooking.

"I don't know why we bother watering these," Shelby said, frowning. "I think they're all dead."

"We water them because it's one of our chores," Charlotte replied with a grin.

"And because you don't want to be responsible for the murders of Mr. and Mrs. Plant and their offspring," Martin quipped. "Charlotte and Shelby did it with the watering can in the conservatory."

"I think I hear Heather calling us for dinner," Cody said.

"Where are my..." Martin anxiously checked his pockets, finally locating to objective of his search. "My tummy tablets," he said with obvious relief. "Never eat Heather's meals without one of these beauties. I was out of them last week and after one particularly greasy dinner . . ." He thought for a moment. "Ah, yes, the fried eggplant. It ran out of me like oil from a—"

"Okay," Shelby cut him off. "We get the picture." Cody glanced over as she wrinkled her nose and made a twisted face. "Yuck," she added.

He was still laughing as the four reached the kitchen. Terrell, Gabby, and Jessica were already seated on the built-in bench that ran along the kitchen wall. Cody's spot was on the end. Terrell was sitting in it.

"Uh, that's my seat," he said.

"Oh," Terrell replied. "Um, well, I have a condition that requires me to sit on soft things, it's called Pediatric Scoliosis," he added.

"What?" Cody frowned and sat down on one of the new wooden chairs. "I thought you were going to be a professional baseball player?"

"It's a mild case and the doctor says it should clear up before I start playing ball," Terrell added. "Unless I aggravate it by sitting on hard chairs."

Cody opened his mouth to respond, but never got the chance.

"I'd put navy blue cushions on those chairs. I like them, but they are very hard…"

He began to understand why Gabby was so thin. It's impossible to eat and talk *incessantly* at the same time.

"Gabby, honey," Heather offered with a heartfelt smile, "*please* eat your dinner."

"She's so skinny," Martin joked under his breath, "one meatball will be like a snake eating an alligator. You'll be able to watch it digest."

"I like spaghetti and meatballs," Gabby offered, barely skipping a beat. "Did you know that pasta originated in China? Most people think it came from Italy. Of course, the Italians made tomato sauce the perfect accompaniment to a bowl of spaghetti. Meatballs…" she continued. "Did you know they also originated in China? Most people think they also came from Italy, but the Chinese made them first. However, Chinese meatballs were larger than Italian ones."

Finally, Jack seemed to have had enough. "Cody," he said loudly, repeating it until Gabby stopped talking. "Saturday, I need your help. I'm picking up a new lawn mower. A guy I know in town is moving and he's selling it to me cheap. It's a ride-on mower and they cost a ton brand new."

"No problem," Cody replied.

"Mr. Storm hasn't been around much lately and mowing the lawn is going to be your job."

"Who's Mr. Storm?" Terrell asked absently.

"I like riding mowers," Gabby said before anyone could answer. "Did you know that if you cut grass too short, it won't grow?"

"The rest of you," Jack continued, slurping up a few strands of spaghetti, "can help me till the vegetable garden."

"Carrots," Gabby said, fiddling with the glazed slices on her plate. "Did you know carrots are root vegetables? Yep. Along with potatoes, yams, radishes, turnips, and onions."

Cody stared out the window, letting his new sibling's voice fade into the background. He thought about the start of summer and his plans to meet new kids, especially those of the female persuasion. His teenage sisters and brother were great, but the need to be alone with a girl was on his mind constantly. It was the only thing he could think about.

After dinner, Heather unveiled a pie she baked with blueberries from the bushes lining Freya Manor's western border. The pie was hot out of the oven and their mom added a scoop of vanilla ice cream to each plate. Cody devoured his in seconds. Either Heather's cooking was experiencing moments of inspiration or pie was hard to mess up.

"Shelby, honey," Heather said, "please dry the dishes and put them away. Charlotte, please wipe down the table and chairs. Cody, would you please take out the garbage? Oh, and dump this into the composter."

"How come *they* don't have to do anything?" he muttered under his breath.

"Because *they* are still getting used to our routines. They're time will come," Heather said of Gabby and Terrell. Cody frowned.

I need to remember to talk quieter. The woman's got bionic hearing.

Heather was like a deceptively sweet field general, barking orders while looking at you with those big persuasive eyes. Cody grabbed the over-stuffed garbage bag and bucket of table scraps. When he returned, the kitchen sparkled like new. Terrell was still sitting at the table, listening to Gabby ramble.

"Can I have the rest of the pie?" he asked.

"Well—" Heather began.

"No," Cody interrupted. "There are only two pieces left and I want one."

"We'll see," Heather offered, glancing reproachfully at Cody as she headed down to the fruit cellar, presumably to retrieve vegetables for tomorrow's meals. Charlotte and Martin went to play a game of chess in the living room. Shelby put the last of the clean plates on the shelf. Cody was hovering over the pie when suddenly Terrell began to gasp for air, hands grabbing at his throat.

"*Help me...*" he gasped.

"Are you *alright?*" Cody asked, his heart pounding.

"HEATHER?" Shelby screamed, running down the stairs after their mom.

"What can I do?" Cody cried.

Terrell's face was turning blue, his hand grasping Cody's arm.

"My . . . *inhaler,*" the boy managed to whisper. "It's in my room."

Cody sprinted into the foyer, then up the steps, taking them two at a time. He darted down the hallway as fast as he could, sliding into Terrell's room. Dumping the contents of the boy's duffel bag on his bed, Cody searched frantically for his inhaler, finally locating it amid the few articles of clothing and toiletries. When he returned to the kitchen, Heather was unloading potatoes from a basket. Shelby was nowhere to be found and neither was Terrell.

"Where *is* he?" Cody said, gasping for breath.

"Who?" Heather asked innocently.

"*Terrell!* I have his inhaler," Cody shouted.

"Oh, I think he, Gabby, and Jessica went to into the living room to play a game."

"A *game?* But he wasn't able to breathe!"

"I don't know." Heather shrugged. "He seemed fine . . . fine enough to finish off the pie," she added with a frown.

"He *what?*"

Cody stared at her, stunned.

Could this twelve-year-old kid have tricked me into leaving so he could eat the rest of the pie?

Charlotte and Martin gazed intently at the chess board. Cody was tossing a ball into the air and staring at the ceiling. He glanced over at Shelby, reading a magazine in the inglenook.

"Do you think he could be that devious?" he asked no one in particular. "Devious enough to pretend to be choking just to get the rest of the pie?"

"Really, Cowpoke?" Shelby chastised. "He's just a boy. Stop making a big deal out of it."

"You weren't the one who sprinted all the way upstairs, only to find out that you'd been duped by a twelve-year-old," he said irritably.

"I agree with Cody," Martin added. "I think he says whatever he needs to just to get his way. Like that load of crap about scoliosis so he didn't have to sit on the hard chair."

"Many children in the adoption system learn how to deal with not getting enough attention by creating situations to promote sympathy," Charlotte said, looking up briefly. "Even children who *have* parents learn to work things to their advantage. Foster kids can take it to a new level," she added.

"I suppose," Cody mumbled. "You make it hard to be mad at him when you put it that way."

"Of course, it is kind of funny that he seems to enjoy conning you the most," Martin offered with a chuckle. "I guess you're his *Chosen One* also."

Shelby laughed. "That's a good one," she said.

"Very funny," Cody replied, frowning. "I think the little vultures went to bed. I'm going to the kitchen to see if there's anything left in the house to eat."

"Wait," Shelby called. "We're coming."

They found a box of saltines with one package left. Shelby spread the crackers with peanut butter and jam. Martin made them each a glass of chocolate milk.

"This is so *boring*," Cody muttered.

"Oh, *excuse* me if we're not exciting enough for you, Cowpoke," Shelby grumbled.

"It's not..." he frowned. "You know how I feel about you guys, but every day it's the same thing. We get up, eat breakfast, go to school, do chores, do homework, and eat dinner."

"You forgot to include doing *more* chores," Martin quipped.

"Exactly. The next day it starts all over again." Cody sat back and folded his arms.

"What would you want to do, Cody?" Charlotte asked. "I mean, if you could."

"We need a car, then we could drive places, go to parties, meet girls," he replied.

"I don't care about high school parties," Shelby murmured. "I'm sure they're all lame. Now a party in New York City, perhaps one of the post-awards show parties, *that* would be something."

Cody smirked. "Obviously I could dream bigger too, if *any* of that was even a possibility."

After their snack, the four headed back to the living room. Charlotte curled up with a book in the inglenook. Shelby and Martin played a game of Go Fish. Cody continued tossing a ball in the air. He thought about what Charlotte said, how foster kids learn to manipulate people to get attention. As hard as he tried, he still couldn't imagine what it was like, growing up in the adoption system.

"Did you guys start your history midterm reports?" Martin asked.

"We need to do them at the library," Shelby said with a groan. "Remember?"

"We can use the internet," Cody stated with a smirk. "How would Shepard even know we didn't go to the library?"

"We need to cite references," Charlotte said, setting her book down and walking over to sit with Shelby and Martin. "Deal me in on the next hand."

"Me, too," Cody added. "Nothing else to do," he muttered.

"Oh, no!" Shelby cried suddenly, jumping to her feet. "Our little *friend* is back."

Skodar emerged from the door inside the fireplace, his round belly jiggling beneath a long thick beard. The dwarf's pointed hat had been replaced by a baseball cap. He glanced tauntingly at them from the inglenook, then opened Charlotte's book, holding it out as if trying to read.

"Is that Terrell's Dodgers' cap?" Martin wondered suspiciously.

Skodar dropped the book and skedaddled across the room, daring them to give chase.

"Give me that hat, you little thief," Shelby said, taking off after him. "It doesn't belong to you."

"Oh, no you don't," Cody added, sprinting after the little man as he ran down the hall. "You're not going to sucker me into getting caught in Rúndyrr a *second* time."

They chased Skodar into the foyer. Cody reached out to grab him, but the little man dropped to the ground and rolled up like a ball. He straddled the dwarf to keep from tripping over him, but by the time he could stop and turn around, the mischievous imp was gone.

"Where did he go?" Cody asked, glancing at each of his siblings as they gathered around him.

"I think he went that way," Shelby said, pointing toward the opposite side of the foyer.

"I don't see him," Martin replied, scratching his head.

The old radiators knocked and whistled incessantly, despite it being early May. Heather chose this chilly spring day to bake biscuits, presumably hoping the oven and its contents would warm their bellies. His mom's hair was pulled back in a pony tail, an apron tied about her waist. She tried to appear calm and cool, but nothing could hide the tiny beads of sweat glistening across her forehead as she bent over to pull a tray from the oven.

"Give me back my hat," Terrell said to Cody as the family gathered around the dinner table.

"I don't have it," he replied innocently.

Martin made a face and waddled in place, doing his best Skodar impersonation. It was all Cody could do to keep from cracking up.

"I saw you take it," Terrell stated.

"You couldn't have seen me because I didn't take it," Cody replied.

He watched Heather as she put a biscuit on each plate and ladled a heaping spoonful of chicken slop over the top. She picked up two plates and set one in front of Gabby and one before Jack.

"Come on, Cody," she said with a frown. "That's childish."

"I don't have it!" he protested, watching Heather serve the rest of the plates.

"Then why were you laughing?" Jack asked, shoving a forkful into his mouth, gravy dripping down his chin.

"Martin was being funny," Cody said, shrugging.

"We all know you love the Dodgers. Give it back to him right after dinner," Jack scowled, "or you'll be grounded."

"*What?* I *don't* have it!" he snapped. "And grounded from *what?* We don't *do* anything, just sit in this boring old house while the world passes us by!"

"That's just great," Cody said to Martin as they headed upstairs to do homework. "You *had* to make me laugh. Now I either have to get the hat back or I'll be grounded."

"That's what you get," Shelby said disapprovingly.

"For *what?*" he replied.

"For being mean to Terrell."

"When was I *ever* mean to him?"

"You don't show any understanding," Shelby retorted. "He can't help what he is. Terrell didn't have parents to fawn all over him like you did."

"I didn't . . . they never *fawned* all over me," Cody said testily. Even he had to admit it sounded lame. He hated it when Shelby made him feel childish. "I don't—" he began.

"When we peel back the outer layers of onion that protect it from damage, we get down to the heart. It's the same with us," Shelby said softly. "When we show understanding, people learn to trust, breaking down the walls they build to keep from getting hurt. Defense mechanisms like talking all the time or hurting someone before they hurt you, begin to fade."

"Maybe we can lure him out," Charlotte offered after an uncomfortable silence. "Skodar."

"Thank you!" Cody said. "Someone who actually *cares* about my predicament instead of always making everything *my* fault." Cody took a deep breath. "I'm open to suggestions," he added.

"Do you still have that gold doubloon from the treasure chest? Maybe we can use it as bait to flush him out," Charlotte added.

"Great idea!" Cody said.

"Yeah," Martin quipped. "That little thief won't be able to resist it."

The four waited in the living room until after midnight, their gold doubloon sitting prominently on the inglenook seat. Cody and

Charlotte played three games of chess while Shelby read her magazine and Martin played games on the laptop.

"It's no use," Martin said, rubbing his eyes. He's not coming and I'm tired.

"You're right," Cody mumbled, sitting back in the chair. "He knows we're trying to trap him."

The four teens got up and were heading across the room when Shelby turned abruptly.

"IT'S *HIM!*"

Skodar was standing in the inglenook, again trying to read Charlotte's book.

"Give me back that hat!" Cody demanded.

"*My* hat!" Skodar retorted in a nasally childish tone.

"It is *not* your hat. It belongs to a boy who has very little else in the world and you *took* it from him," Shelby said.

"My hat!" Skodar repeated defiantly.

"What can we give you in exchange for the hat?" Charlotte asked. "Would you like that gold doubloon?"

Skodar hesitated, continuing to stare at the old book.

"Book," he uttered. "I want book."

"So, you can have *that* book," Martin said.

"Hey," Charlotte whined. "That's mine. I got it years ago from an orphanage library."

Skodar pouted, shaking his head. "Need *different* book," he replied, almost ruefully.

"What's wrong with that one?" Cody asked.

"Too small," he said.

"If we get you a bigger book, will you give us the hat?" Cody asked.

Skodar thought for second, then nodded. "Bigger book," he muttered, then disappeared back though the wrought iron door on the inside of the fireplace.

"Fine! We'll meet you back here in an hour," Cody yelled, then turned to his siblings. "Does anyone have a big book?"

"I have my Chemistry textbook," Martin said with a laugh, "but I'm sure he doesn't want that."

"What do you suppose was wrong with this one?" Cody asked, examining the pages.

"I wonder," Shelby replied, taking it from his hand. "*Rumpelstiltskin*," she offered, perusing the cover. "It looks cute to me."

"That's a weird name. Who wrote it?" Martin asked.

"The Brothers Grimm," Shelby responded. "It says on the back they wrote lots of fairy tales."

"What's it about?" Martin asked Charlotte.

"A king locks a peasant girl in the dungeon because her father said she could spin straw into gold," Charlotte replied. "Her father was just boasting, but the king said if she doesn't do it, she'll be executed. The girl is running out of options when she gets visited by a little man, a dwarf, who does it for her, saving her life, but—"

"Who cares?" Cody said peevishly. "I need that hat by tomorrow morning, or *I'll* be executed. Where can we find a big book?"

"Does he want a bigger version of *this* book?" Martin asked.

"Maybe," Shelby said. "He seems to like it."

"If so, there's only one place to go," Charlotte said, "the library."

"How the heck are we going to get to the library? Besides, it's closed," Cody replied, running a hand through his hair.

Shelby frowned. "I guess if we want to save your behind . . . *again*," she said, "we have no choice but to go through Rúndyrr."

Chapter 3: The Library

"While we're there, we might as well get books for our midterm reports," Charlotte offered, stepping into the elevator.

"Who's your report on, Charlotte?" Shelby asked as the doors closed like metal jaws.

"Abraham Lincoln," she said. "What about yours?"

"I picked Ben Franklin," Shelby replied.

"I'm doing Thomas Edison," Cody added.

"Why did you choose him?" Charlotte wondered.

Cody shrugged. "I'll learn all about the humble light bulb. It doesn't get much more riveting than that," he added dryly, pressing the button marked 'R'.

"I don't understand why Old Man Shepard is making us go to the library to do our reports," Martin mumbled as they exited the elevator and headed down the rocky corridor. "Does anyone actually *use* them anymore? I mean isn't that why they made the internet?"

"I agree," Cody added with a scowl. "Especially since we have just one crummy old car, which by the way, Jack is *always* driving, and we live ten miles from the Dawnport library. How are we supposed to get there?"

"Well, kids," Shelby said, imitating a man's deep voice, "it's important that you understand the proper way to do research, not by using the biased and sometimes fabricated information you find on the internet, but by using *actual* research books."

Martin grinned. "You sound just like him."

"Who do you suppose came up with the idea of a library?" Cody asked.

Martin laughed. "Let's build a place with endless rows of books and people will come for miles to get the one little book they want," he quipped. "First, they have to *find* it amid the miles of shelves, then go through all the trouble of *reading* it, when in five seconds you can find exactly what you need on Wikipedia. I don't know how libraries have stayed around for so long."

Cody grinned as he pulled on the sconce and they made their way across the cave.

"What are you going to say to The Gatekeeper?" Charlotte asked.

"First, I want to know who that guy was and why he took gold from Rúndyrr," Cody replied. "Then I'll ask him to send us to the library so we can finish our history projects."

"I can wait to go through the doorway," Martin said, pointing to the braces surrounding his legs. "It's so nice to be able to keep up with you guys."

"Dost thou wish to enter Rúndyrr?" The Gatekeeper asked, appearing suddenly out of the shadows. No matter how many times they did this, Cody thought, the guy always made him jump.

It's like he enjoys scaring us.

The old man's pallid complexion and sunken eyes seemed a bit livelier than usual. He stroked the beard extending down to his waist and frowned, as if he already knew what they wanted.

"Uh, yes," Cody said, as sternly as he could muster. "But first, we want to know who that guy was, the one that broke into our house. You were talking to him, then he went through Rúndyrr."

"He is not your concern," The Gatekeeper said firmly.

"Then why did you go out of your way to make sure we saw what he took?" Shelby asked.

The Gatekeeper ignored her question, staring off into the distance.

"The Guardian made us honorary protectors of Rúndyrr," Cody said. "I think that entitles us to an explanation."

"Suppose the man does something to jeopardize Rúndyrr," Shelby asked earnestly.

"He will not."

"How do you know?" Martin added.

The Gatekeeper frowned at them as if to say this conversation was over.

"Dost thou wish to enter Rúndyrr?"

"We need to go to the library," Martin said. "To do our history projects. In the current year," he added quickly.

Cody whispered, "Everyone concentrate, like we planned."

The Gatekeeper hesitated for a second. Cody saw an almost imperceptible twinkle in the old man's eyes as he recited the first riddle.

"From Silence to Poor Richard,
He continued to astound.
Lightning rods and bifocals,
His genius still surrounds.
From firehouses to stoves,
His innovations abound."

"Why can't you ever give us a riddle about things teenagers do in their spare time, like video games or music, something we're experts on?" Martin asked.

Cody turned to the others. "Who the heck is Poor Richard?"

"And who invented bifocals? They must've been around for years," Shelby said.

"Could we be talking about the Ancient Greeks or Romans?" Cody wondered. "Or, maybe someone from the Knights of the Round Table?"

"I think the riddle specified a 'he'. That means we're looking for a specific person," Charlotte offered.

"Maybe the king of England, King Richard?" Cody asked.

"I'm not sure, but I thought that Ben Franklin was instrumental, pardon the pun, in creating the first lightning rod," Martin mused.

The doorway began to glow brightly, its thick stone suddenly replaced by an inky darkness whose lively breeze rustled the brim of Cody's cowboy hat.

"Uh-oh," he said, frowning.

"What does that have to do with the lib—" Charlotte begin.

As Cody was pulled across the bridge, The Gatekeeper's words rang through his head.

"I am a single fluid, both positive and negative.
It takes a charge, just for me to live.
Use me up and leave me for dead,
Or let me conduct the flow of fire, instead."

"What the *heck*," Martin said as he looked around. "I see streetlamps. Was someone thinking about money again?"

"Oh, no," Charlotte cried softly. "Where are we?"

"I'm going out on a ledge here," Martin muttered sarcastically, "but, I'm pretty sure this isn't the Dawnport library."

"Certainly not the twenty-first century," Cody said with a sigh. "Shelby, what were we talking about when we walked in?" he asked, trying to keep the snippiness from his voice.

"Our midterm reports," she replied. "Nothing that should've landed us here."

They stood on the outskirts of what appeared to be an early city. Candlelight flickered in distant windows as the group made their way toward town, a bumpy dirt road impeding their progress. The place seemed oddly deserted, as if its inhabitants had left in a hurry.

"It's so dark I can barely see the ruts in the road. Where are the sidewalks?" Shelby froze suddenly, then looked at Cody with wide eyes. "Oh, my. Is this *mud* I'm stepping in? *Please* tell me it's not something else."

"From the smell of things," Martin quipped, "I'd say it's..."

"Don't say it!" she said briskly. "I'm happier not knowing."

"At least it's not so cold that the snot is freezing in my nose, like during the Battle of Trenton."

"Ugh, that's gross, Martin Speck," Shelby said with a moan.

Brief flashes of distant lightning defied the darkness cloaking the landscape. They passed a non-descript stone building on the edge of town with the word 'Gaol' etched on the door.

"Who do you suppose lives in *this* spooky place?" Shelby asked. "These people weren't wanted. They made them live far from everyone else."

"I wonder if it could be a *jail*," Charlotte murmured.

Gusts of wind circulated the smells of the city as the four teens struggled ahead, finally reaching what appeared to be a small town. Shops lining the streets displayed wooden signs identifying their trade: tavern, milliner, silversmith, apothecary.

"What's a cooper?" Cody asked.

"Isn't it a car?" Martin asked with a twisted grin.

Charlotte pressed her face against the glass. "It looks like a cooper makes barrels. I suppose they were good for storage back then."

"What's an apothecary?" Shelby asked. "I see a mortar and pestle on the sign? Was it a restaurant?"

"I think an apothecary was an old-fashioned drug store," Cody offered. "They sold herbs as medicines." He looked around to see wide eyes staring at him. "What? I know some things. My mom used to grind stuff from her herb garden."

Cody winced. Just the thought of mom and dad made his stomach twist into knots.

"Uh, not to change the subject, but what's that *disgusting* smell?" Shelby asked.

"It smells like an outhouse, one that should be farther *out*, if you know what I mean," Martin said.

"Don't even *mention* an outhouse. We left in such a rush and I have to go to the bathroom!"

"Really, Shelby?" Cody said. "Good luck with that! You're going to have to hold it."

"I don't suppose they had indoor toilets and sewers hundreds of years ago?" Shelby frowned.

"I think they went in like bedpans or pots and I read somewhere that sometimes they threw the stuff out the window," Martin replied.

Shelby froze, her eyes as large as saucers. "Suppose you were *standing* there?"

"Don't forget," Cody added, "they rode horses. All that manure has to go somewhere, too."

"I can hardly breathe," Shelby said in a choked voice. "It's making me gag."

"How long do you think we would last, living here?" Martin wondered. "The smell of ripening poop is everywhere. No wonder they got sick all the time. I mean, every little thing that we do without a second thought would be a major task. Like, how do you clean yourself up after going in your little chamber pot?"

"Thank you for that visual, Martin Speck." Shelby said.

"Women probably spent hours cooking, sweeping, and doing laundry. There were no refrigerators, so I guess you had to go to the market every day, or eat dried foods," Charlotte said.

"And they all had lots of kids because some of them never made it beyond kindergarten. Not that they had kindergarten, but you know what I mean. Antibiotics are a beautiful thing. It's a shame they didn't have them," Martin added.

"What's up with this weather?" Shelby asked. "I hope there isn't a monsoon coming."

Martin lifted his arm to deflect a piece of newspaper, swirling like a projectile on the gusty breeze.

"I think we're about to get pummeled by a summer thunderstorm," Cody said. "Hey, let me see that newspaper."

"It's yours if you can catch it," Martin replied.

The newspaper toyed with Cody, prompting giggles from the girls. He would be about to grab it when a gust of wind blew it farther down the street. Finally, he stepped on the mischievous paper.

"Hmm." He kept them in suspense, justifiable retaliation for their laughter. "Very interesting."

"What?" Shelby asked. "What's interesting?"

"It's the *Philadelphia Gazette*," said Cody.

"We're in *Philadelphia*?" Martin asked. "Doesn't look like Philly to me."

"Well, that's because it's June 15th in the year 1752, over two hundred and fifty years ago." Cody frowned, folding the paper and sticking it into his pocket.

They turned down a street that showed some signs of life. The occasional colonist could be seen running for cover, trying to escape the pending storm.

"Wait! The answer to the first..." Charlotte's voice was drowned out by a boom of thunder so loud, it made them all cover their ears.

"We're going to get soaked or fried alive if we don't get inside," Cody said.

"Ugh!"

"What's wrong, Shelby?" Charlotte asked.

"I *really* have to go . . . bad."

Cody frowned. "So, go next to that building."

"I will not!"

"Come on, we'll keep watch."

"I will not!" she snapped, then seemed to reconsider. "Okay, fine."

"Hopefully no one throws their bed pan out the window while you're standing there," Martin offered with a mischievous grin.

Shelby frowned at him then headed down the narrow alley. Cody looked away until movement caught his eye. A group of young men and women appeared at the far end of the alley. He glanced over as Shelby jumped to her feet, straightening her clothes and trying to look nonchalant. One of the men turned and pointed.

"Look at that woman! What, pray tell, is she *doing*?"

"And look at her clothing?" another man added.

"Ugh," Cody whispered, trying not to laugh.

"She's probably red as a tomato right now," Martin added. "Thank God, it's dark out."

"Hello?"

A man approached from the street wearing typical colonial garb and carrying a lantern. After a few seconds of seemingly befuddled staring, he addressed Cody.

"What be your business here, sir?"

The two rows of shiny buttons adorning a navy coat led down to navy knickers with high white socks and dark buckled shoes. A ponytail draped down from the wig beneath his three-cornered hat.

"Uh." Cody looked at his friends. "Well, uh, sir, we're here to meet with an acquaintance of ours."

"What be his name, sir?"

"Uh, George Bush."

"I am not acquainted with Mr. Bush."

The man continued. "What be the matter of his profession, sir?"

"He's, uh, a politician."

The man hesitated a moment, seemingly unsure what that meant. "Well, sir, if you inquire within the Indian King tavern ahead on thy right…" He pointed, then continued. "There may be someone who can assist thee in locating thy acquaintance." He glanced at Shelby who had quietly rejoined them, clearly unsure what to make of these strange travelers.

"Dost thou wish to avail thyself of my services as a guide?"

"No, thank you. We'll inquire at the tavern. Thanks."

"Sirs," the man said. "And ma'am." He nodded toward Shelby.

"What the heck was that all about?" Cody whispered. "He treated Charlotte like she didn't exist."

"Welcome to the year 1752." Martin said, smirking. "George Bush, really?"

"It was the only name that popped into my head," Cody said. "Charlotte, sorry about that jerk."

They continued down the street in silence, checking signs for something that might indicate a tavern. Eventually, the area turned more residential.

"Maybe we should've let him be our guide," Shelby said finally. "I don't see it."

"Me either," Cody replied. "I think we missed it."

Ahead, voices carried on the humid air. A row of homes with shuttered windows dominated the right side of the road, abutting each other in typical city fashion. One large building loomed off to the left, a towering steeple suggesting it was some sort of church.

"Do you hear someone yelling?" Martin asked. "I hope we're not heading toward another battle."

Cody determined the voices belonged to two men standing in a field adjacent to the church. A discussion of obvious importance monopolized their attention as they lingered near a small wooden shed. The men had to yell to be heard above the frequent rumbles of thunder.

"We must hoist it up," the first man yelled.

He appeared to be middle-aged with spectacles resting on the tip of his ski-slope nose. Although his hairline had receded, it still allowed for shoulder-length hair that danced atop the neck of a frilly shirt and dark vest. The latter appeared a bit tight in the stomach. His pants were gathered below the knee, like those of the man they had seen earlier.

"One deep breath and the buttons on that vest will become lethal weapons," Martin mumbled.

"That older guy looks familiar," Cody added pensively.

The second man was dressed in similar clothing, but appeared to be much younger than the first. It was obvious Mr. Spectacles was in charge.

"We shall verify at once the sameness of electric matter with that of lightning, William," the man yelled. "A kite will provide access to the necessary regions of thunder, and thereby this matter be completely demonstrated."

The older man lifted something large into the air.

"What are they doing?" Shelby asked.

"Thus prepared, a large silk handkerchief and two cedar cross-strips of a proper length on which to extend it, provide the body of a kite," the spectacled man continued. "To the top, we then affix a sharp pointed wire, extending a foot above the wood. To the end of the hemp twine below, a key must be fastened. When rain has wetted the twine so that it can conduct the electric fire freely, we will find it streams out plentifully from the key at the approach of a knuckle."

"There, I hath suspended the key," the younger man replied.

"We now take the opportunity of the approaching thunderstorm to verify the hypothesis," Mr. Spectacles continued. "The person who holds the string must stand under cover, perhaps within this doorway, and good care must be taken that the twine does not touch the frame of the door. As soon as the thunder clouds come over the kite, the pointed wire will draw the electric fire from them."

The older man watched with obvious anticipation as the younger one released the kite into the stormy sky.

"Is he flying a kite in a thunderstorm? Does he want to get fried by lightning."

"I think that's the point, Cody!" Charlotte said excitedly.

Martin, Shelby, and Charlotte yelled at the same time, "Ben Franklin!"

"*The* Ben Franklin?" Cody asked. "I thought his claim to fame was the Declaration of Independence."

"Ben made the discovery that lightning is actually electricity," Martin said.

"What's the big deal? Everybody knows that." Cody made an unimpressed face.

"Not back then," Charlotte said. "People thought lightning came from divine intervention, like God was angry or . . . It was *me*," she uttered suddenly. "Ben Franklin is on the hundred-dollar bill. I was thinking about the money Jack gave me to pay when we went shopping."

"No, it was *me*! I was talking about my history report project," Shelby said with a gasp.

"Well, whoever's fault it is, we need to figure out how to get home," Cody said. "What was the return riddle again, Shelby?" he asked.

"What do you suppose it means?" Charlotte wondered, once Shelby finished.

"Well, if *you* don't know, the rest of us have no chance," Cody replied.

A flash of lightning was immediately followed by a few large raindrops, quickly erupting into a downpour. The dry, dusty street transformed into a mud river, wafting the smells of the city up into the humid air.

"I'll tell you one thing for sure, *he* would know." Cody motioned toward Ben. "Come on."

"UGH!" Shelby whined. "My shoes are going to be ruined from all this mud."

"Mr. Franklin, sir?" Cody yelled to be heard above the downpour.

Ben looked up from the doorway, his gaze lingering on the four approaching youths, obviously pondering their strange appearance.

"Mr. Franklin, could we speak with you for a moment?"

"Sir, I shall endeavor to gratify you with any particulars, but it is of dire importance that this experiment be performed undisturbed. Avail yourselves of this dry shed and I will attend you forthwith."

He seemed a bit miffed. Cody suspected that Mr. Franklin had hoped to perform his experiment without an audience. Maybe he felt a bit foolish standing in the rain with a child's kite, doing something he wasn't totally sure would work. They entered the small shed and waited quietly while Mr. Franklin stood in the doorway.

Shelby leaned over and whispered to Charlotte, "He didn't set fire to the shed during the experiment, did he?"

"I know he lived for a while after this day, so I think it's safe."

Mr. Franklin yelled to his companion. "Considerable time has elapsed with no appearance of it being electrified. I begin to despair of my contrivance."

Suddenly, a bolt of lightning lit up the night sky, followed closely by a loud boom.

"I'll bet the clouds directly above are electrically charged," Charlotte whispered.

"The loose filaments of the twine stand out in every way!" Ben blurted excitedly. He ran his finger up and down near the twine. "They are attracted by an approaching finger!"

Heavy rain pummeled the yard, soaking the string. Ben reached up and held his knuckle near the key. Cody assumed electricity must've passed through to the dangling key, providing a small spark. The bespectacled man jumped for a second, then threw his head back, laughing heartily.

"I *knew* it would be true! It is *not* God's anger!"

He picked up a jar of some sort that had been left near the shed door. The jar contained a clear liquid and a submerged wire coming out through its metal cap. Foil covered part of the jar's exterior. Ben held the protruding wire up to the key.

"What in the name of Kitty Hawk is *that*?" Shelby spoke louder than she planned.

"Why this, young miss, is a *Leyden* jar. This device will collect and store the electric fire, thus allowing for later use."

"Mr. Franklin, sir?" Cody began.

"We have verified the sameness of electricity with that of lightning, young sir. Is that not of great magnitude?" He paused for a moment, the smile leaving his face. "Where are my manners. This is my son, William," Ben said. "What be your names?"

"I'm Cody Hawke and this is Shelby Long, Charlotte Cower, and Martin Speck."

"It's so nice to meet you, Mr. Franklin." Shelby nearly gushed the words.

"The pleasure is mine." Ben nodded. "The oddity of your clothing vexes me. Where does one obtain such garments?"

"We, uh, come from far away, sir," Cody replied.

"What matter of state or country avails themselves of such attire? If one exists, I have not seen such a place." He hesitated again. "Miss," he addressed Shelby. "Such garments, although quite pleasurable, do not hold a suitable place in this society. Perhaps I can avail myself of the consideration of an acquaintance who will provide you proper attire, lest this prove dangerous."

Cody glanced out the shed door. The storm was beginning to subside. In the distance, he saw a group of lanterns bobbing up and down as if being carried. They appeared to be heading their way.

"Hurry," Ben said, apparently noticing them as well. "Follow me to my home before the town busy-bodies arrive. We shall attend to our wet clothing and to your inquiries."

They followed Ben and William down the street, away from the approaching townspeople.

"I can't imagine what he must be thinking," Cody whispered.

"Yeah," Martin replied, "Put yourself in Ben's buckled shoes. He's celebrating his success, but at the same time wondering whether he was struck with enough electric fire to toast his marshmallows."

Cody heard a distant voice yell, 'They went that way.'

"It appears you four are causing quite a stir," Ben said with a chuckle.

"He walks pretty fast for a guy his age," Martin murmured.

They had followed Mr. Franklin for few minutes when a man emerged from the darkness of an alleyway. He was leading a team of horses hooked up to a carriage. Ben seemed to be expecting him.

"Sir," the coachman said, nodding in Ben's direction. The Founding Father nodded back, then glanced at the teens, eyes twinkling.

"I was hoping to avoid an audience, in case my contrivance was unsuccessful," he said with a wide grin. "So, I planned to arrive and depart undetected by my fellow Philadelphians."

The coachman held the carriage door open.

"Be careful, ladies, watch your heads," Ben directed, then turned to the driver. "The corner of Race and Second Streets," he said. "Make haste!"

While Shelby and Charlotte climbed up, Cody took in the carriage's glossy black finish and red-trimmed doors perched atop a chassis with large spoked wheels.

"It will be a bit congested, I'm afraid, six in this small carriage," Ben said, positioning himself between Shelby and Charlotte. "Come close, ladies," he added playfully.

William, Cody, and Martin sat on the opposite bench while the driver took his place in front. As they pulled away, Cody could see the townspeople running along behind, yelling for them to stop.

They traveled down what Ben referred to as appropriately-named *Ridge* Road. Cody found himself missing modern pavement and suspension systems.

"My aching coccyx. I'm not going to be able to sit down for a week after this," Martin murmured.

Mr. Franklin's home was quite comfortable. Everything the eye could see was made from wood, brick, or fiber. There were no plastics or even metals, except for the iron in the fireplaces. Mr. Franklin directed the boys toward the parlor's warm fire, while the girls waited in the hall. Cody noticed the uneasiness on Shelby's face as Mrs. Franklin's chambermaid fastened a long skirt over her regular clothes. A few minutes later, Shelby and Charlotte joined them by the fire.

"Will you partake in a libation?"

"I don't suppose you have a nice cold glass of milk?"

"That's not a good idea," Martin whispered.

"Cold *cows'* milk?" Mr. Franklin seemed perplexed.

"Ixnay on the ilkmay," Martin warned. "No pasteurization," he muttered under his breath. "You need to drink it within a few minutes of milking the cow: otherwise, can you say *food poisoning?* And, *trust* me, you don't want their doctors so much as standing near you!"

"Uh, on second thought, I'm fine, but thank you anyway," Shelby replied anxiously.

"Perhaps you would care for a cup of Madeira or a sip of brandy?"

"Uh, Madeira, thanks. That would be great." Cody leaned toward Charlotte. "What's Madeira?" he whispered.

"I'm not totally sure, but I think it's something we shouldn't have, like wine."

Cody enjoyed the cozy feel of Ben's home. It was simple, but solid. The floors were made of natural wood planking. A small hallway led from the front door to the stairs in back with entrances to the parlor and dining room on either side.

The parlor was painted a bright shade of green with what Shelby referred to as white crown molding at the ceiling. In the far corner, a serving cart displayed bottles of brandy and Madeira, along with blue stemmed glasses. A small table, a few chairs and a 'harpsichord', as Ben called it, represented the only other furniture in the room.

"A chess set," Cody said, pointing.

"Why, yes, Master Hawke. Do you play?"

"I-uh, yes, but I'm sure I wouldn't be much competition for you. Charlotte beats me almost every time." He motioned toward his foster sibling, then noticed Ben's strange look.

After pouring the wine, their host led them to an area beyond the dining room he called the 'common room', but added he used it for his experiments.

Ben's laboratory elicited a few seconds of awestruck silence as Cody stared at contraptions whose function was anyone's guess. An iron stove dominated the left side of the large room while chairs lined the far wall.

"*Cool* stove!" Martin exclaimed. Then, after seemingly noticing Ben's confused look, he continued, "I mean nice, *warm* stove."

"It's an old design of mine," Ben replied. "It allows more air to be warmed by the fire, thus producing more heat."

Tables covered with various jars and bottles of liquid spanned the room, many containing metal plates with wires emanating from the middle, like the one they had seen at the shed. Mr. Franklin seemed pleased, describing his experiments with obvious pride. The odd collection made Cody smile, but also appreciate the technology he took for granted.

"Uh, Mr. Franklin?" Charlotte began. "What's this glass container for? Is it another one of those Leyden jars?"

Ben sighed. "I have never been engaged in any study that so engrossed my attention as with electric fluid," he said with a rueful smile. "Last summer we planned an electrical party on the banks of the Schuylkill River to end our experiments for the season. We proposed to shock the turkeys for dinner," he said, laughing, "but the use of electric fire is best at keeping a man humble. I came quite near to joining the turkeys in their demise."

"Oh, my," Shelby responded. "That must've been quite a shock."

He laughed again then continued. "These Leyden jars..." He held one up. "Will store an electric charge, for electricity will be attracted to points such as the top of this rod. The electric fluid exists in two states, positive and negative, always remaining in balance. The charge can be held and used, as an example, to expire turkeys."

"How long does it last?" Martin asked.

"Long enough," Ben responded. "I assembled panes of glass with thin lead plates and used lead wire to bind them together. I call this device an electrical *battery,* as it is a *series* of storage devices, thus allowing for more electric fire to be save at one time."

Cody was stunned. He glanced at his foster siblings to see if they shared his revelation.

"Thank goodness they get *much* smaller!" Martin whispered. "Otherwise, we would need to carry our phones on our backs!"

Ben sighed again. "I do often lament though that my experiments are for naught. It seems this electricity will never benefit humanity in the way I had hoped."

"Mr. Franklin, please don't . . . *lament* long over that." Shelby smiled. "*Trust* me on this. I am absolutely sure that your experiments in electric fire will be *very* useful in the not-too-distant future."

"In phones, cameras, gaming devices and much, much more!" Martin added.

Ben wrinkled his brow. "Gaming devices?"

"I'm guessing, of course," Martin replied, shrugging his shoulders. "Who knows what things will be invented in the future?"

Ben smiled, though it was obvious that the joke was beyond his knowledge or experience.

"Where do you call home?" he asked earnestly. "It is clear as a full moon in July that your home is not here in Philadelphia." Ben mused for a moment while the friends tried to think of an appropriate answer. "Could it be you are from another *time?*"

An awkward silence ensued.

"Uh, well, it's a *long* story." Cody grinned, then changed the subject. "This is *very* impressive work. You have an incredible mind, sir. With all our technology, we never even *think* of these things."

"Mr. Franklin?" Charlotte had been quiet for a while, but could no longer contain her curiosity. "Who are Silence and Poor Richard?"

"Poor Richard Saunders was a character in my annual almanac, an astrologer. Silence Dogood was an outspoken widow created by me for the purpose of writing anonymous essays to appear in my brother James' *Boston Courant* newspaper. James was unwilling to further my position, in fact quite the opposite. His tyrannical treatment of me is in part the reason I left Boston."

"So, you wrote articles under the assumed name of Silence Dogood to get them published in your brother's newspaper?" Charlotte asked.

Ben nodded, staring thoughtfully in her direction. "Your eloquence and high-spiritedness are truly admirable," he offered. "You make me question my negative stance on issues of abolitionism."

"That's our Charlotte," Shelby responded perkily, "the smartest person we know."

Cody watched Ben's reaction with interest. It seemed to reflect an epiphany of sorts.

"By any chance," Cody asked, breaking the awkward silence that followed, "did you open the first library? You know, where you keep books for people to read."

"The *first* library?" Ben repeated. "Are there *others?*" He hesitated for a moment. "Books offer so much. Unfortunately, they are costly. Through the Library Company of Philadelphia, we make books available for all to share. The members pay dues collected with the intent to buy more books. It has been well-received. The existence of the library has improved the general conversation in Philadelphia. It is with great industry we endeavor to recruit new subscribers. Is this of interest to you?"

"Books were so expensive and hard to get only certain people could afford them," Charlotte said. "But you made it possible to share books, making them available to others who might not have the opportunity," she added, nearly gushing her admiration.

Cody felt a wave of pride flush over him. Not only was Charlotte the smartest person they knew, but she was also so admirable. Who else would behave with such class under these circumstances? He wondered if *he* would be as gracious around someone who clearly saw him as inferior. The answer, he feared, was probably *no*.

"Boy, does that make me feel sheepish," Martin whispered, baaing like a lamb. "The comments I made before, saying libraries aren't important. Obviously, they were, and still are important to people who can't afford to buy books and to anyone who wants to learn things."

"It also makes you appreciate the opportunity to get an education." Charlotte added. "Something previously afforded only to the rich."

"It's true," Shelby said ruefully. "Sometimes . . . no, *all* the time, we forget how lucky we are to be able to go to school. A lot of people in the world don't have that chance."

Cody nodded, turning back toward Ben. "What about a fire station? Did you have something to do with that?"

"Fires are an engaging concern here in Philadelphia," Ben said. "We have many spirited volunteers, but they lacked order and method. I therefore recommended organizing fire-fighting clubs. We founded the Union Fire Company in 1736 and met every month to communicate such ideas as occurred to us on the subject of fires. An ounce of prevention is worth a pound of cure," he added.

"*Amazing.* You just *think* these things up?" Cody continued. "That's enough ideas to last a lifetime, and I'm sure there are many more."

Ben smiled, clearly enjoying the accolades.

"Talking about your accomplishments makes me feel…" Cody hesitated.

"Inadequate?" Martin offered. "Useless? A waste of time?"

"Okay, we get the idea," Cody grinned sheepishly. "You've done so much to make the world a better place. I hope we can do the same someday."

"I am certain you will," Ben replied. "Clearly there is much more to do."

"Uh, Mr. Franklin?" Charlotte asked. "Are these your glasses?" She picked up the pair lying on a table nearby.

"Yes," Ben replied. "Do you need them? If so, please take them. Those glasses correct far-sightedness, difficulty in seeing up close. I've so many pairs everywhere, I forsake them at every opportunity." He chuckled. "Perhaps someday, I will create bi-focal glasses to correct vision for seeing both near and far at the same time, thus requiring only one pair.

Charlotte smiled, then her eyes opened wide. "A *battery*!" she almost yelled. "The answer to the riddle is a battery."

The Gatekeeper awaited them across the shimmering bridge. The four teens waved goodbye to Benjamin Franklin. He had impressed them with his genius, wit, and candor. And maybe, just maybe, they had left Ben with something as well, an opportunity to see a future that had moved beyond the prejudices and shortfalls so prevalent in 1752.

Cody took a last fleeting glimpse at Ben's makeshift laboratory, then let out a gasp. There he was again, that man staring at them through a nearby window.

"The man with the one eye! I've seen him before," he mumbled.

Odin?

"Just great," Cody said as they crossed the foyer. "So much for going to the library."

"And," Martin added, "we never got to do research for our projects."

"It was great meeting Ben and all, but unless someone can conjure up a big copy of *Rumpelstiltskin*, we'll never get the hat back. I'm going to be grounded for days," Cody continued.

"Charlotte, honey," Shelby asked, "what did you want with Ben's glasses?"

"You'll see," Charlotte offered playfully as they followed her into the living room.

"Skodar?" she called. "I have something for you."

They waited a few agonizing minutes until finally, the little man emerged from the fireplace.

"You have book? Big book?" he asked.

"No," Charlotte replied.

Skodar hung his head sadly, then turned to go.

"But I have something better," Charlotte said.

She walked over and handed him the glasses.

"Try these on," she said, opening *Rumpelstiltskin* to page one.

Skodar fumbled with the earpieces until Charlotte helped him get them on straight. He stared at the page, glasses resting on the end of his nose. Suddenly he glanced up, eyes wide with delight.

"You *did* it! You got bigger book!"

Charlotte smiled and nodded. "In a way," she said.

Cody glanced at Shelby and Martin. "He wanted a bigger book because he couldn't read the small print on this one," he exclaimed. "Charlotte, you're a genius!"

"Thank you, Miss Charlotte," the dwarf said shyly.

Skodar hung his head and removed the baseball cap. He hesitated, then handed it to Cody.

"Uh, thanks," Cody mumbled.

"Thank you, Skodar," Shelby said, bending to kiss his head. "That's *very* sweet of you."

Skodar shrugged bashfully, turning as dark a shade of purple as Cody had ever seen.

"You welcome, Miss Shelby."

Chapter 4: The Handyman

"We're learning about the color wheel in art class," Gabby stated with the same enthusiasm one would exhibit if they were announcing the end of world hunger.

"That's very important information, honey," Shelby replied. "It will teach you how to correctly match pieces in your wardrobe and someday match the furnishings in your home."

"Mrs. Murphy says colors near each other on the wheel go together and ones on opposite sides..."

Gabby's voice faded into the background as Cody stared out the expansive window bordering their kitchen banquette. Spring rains had thawed any remaining pockets of snow dotting the Maine landscape. Color was slowly creeping back into the previously monochrome world.

"Please make sure you guys are around this afternoon. There's someone I want you to meet," Jack mumbled absently, squinting as he glanced up from an open newspaper. "Honey, have you seen my glasses? I left them somewhere, I just can't remember—"

"These glasses?" Heather asked, removing a pair from her apron pocket.

"Ah," Jack said, beaming, "my bifocals". He reached for the glasses with obvious urgency. "Now I can actually *see* the newspaper."

Chapter 4: The Handyman

Their father's black hair, now strewn with the occasional strand of white, was tied back in a long ponytail. He reminded Cody of a bumbling Wizard perusing a spell book, his lips moving as he scanned each page. Heather interrupted Cody's vision with a platter of scrambled eggs, bacon, and toast.

"Did you know Ben Franklin made the first bifocals?" Gabby asked.

Cody grinned at his teenage siblings, then scooped up a large pile of eggs and shoved them unceremoniously into his mouth. Martin and Charlotte both reached for the ketchup. Shelby was busy checking her makeup in a small compact.

"Guess what?" Charlotte inserted quickly while Gabby grabbed a piece of toast. "I read Ben opened a school for slaves in Philadelphia, not long after we left—"

"Ahem," Martin offered loudly, pretending to choke on his eggs.

Charlotte's hand flew up to cover her mouth, her eyes open wide.

"Left where?" Jack wondered.

"Who is it?" Cody interjected, noticing their father's confused expression, "The guy you want us to meet? Is it someone from town?"

"It's a handyman I met through a mutual friend in Dawnport," Jack said, writing an answer on his crossword puzzle. He looked up and continued. "I've been spending most of my time at the store and projects are starting to mount up around here. Sam's in town for a few months and he's going to help with chores in exchange for a place to stay."

Cody shrugged absently. "Whatever. We'll be here."

The afternoon sun filtering through a leaded glass window above Cody's bed made strange shapes on his wall. He sat on the floor, alternately curling weights with each hand. Charlotte and Shelby were sprawled across the bed, reading a book and magazine respectively, while Martin played a video game.

"I'm sorry, guys," Charlotte offered abruptly.

"About?" Cody asked.

"I was so engrossed in my thoughts I nearly spilled the beans about Rúndyrr at breakfast this morning," she said.

"No biggie," Martin mumbled. "Jack is easily distracted."

46

"Did you guys hear Joe Mason is selling his truck?" Cody asked.

"Huh?" Shelby looked up absently.

"Joe's selling his pickup. He only wants eight hundred. I figure if each of us could save two hundred dollars, we could afford to buy it."

"Why would I want a pickup truck, Cody Hawke? How about a nice late model Cadillac with soft, leather seating and an eight-speaker sound system instead?"

"Yeah, Earth to Shelby. Where would we get the money for an expensive car? At least with the truck we wouldn't need to depend on Jack to drive us everywhere like a bunch of little kids." Cody grimaced at the thought. "We could share it. Each of us would get one Saturday night a month… and I could actually go out on date without you three tagging along."

"Kids, please come down here," a crackly voice called from afar.

"Maybe that guy is here," Martin said.

"I hope Jack checked this loser's references. He's going to botch things up around here," Cody muttered as the four headed down the main staircase, "and we're going to have to clean up the mess."

"Or, get blamed for it," Martin whispered.

"Charlotte, Shelby, Cody and Martin, I'd like you to meet Sam Sharkey," Jack said.

Each of them reached out to shake the man's hand. "Sam will be staying with us for a while."

"Why, how do you do, Mr. Sharkey?" Shelby's accent seemed to get thicker when she was around attractive men. "That's a cool outfit," she added.

"*Cool?*" Cody whispered in her ear. "And you call *me*, Cowpoke?"

"Are you some sort of Dr. Jones or something?" Martin asked.

The man offered a somewhat aloof grin. "Maybe a deep-sea version," he replied.

Sam Sharkey was a tall, muscular man. One look told Cody he was all business, nothing frivolous or flashy about him. Cropped reddish-brown hair was predominantly covered by a well-worn Stetson. The sleeves on his shirt were rolled up, seemingly to free his arms for whatever emergency might transpire. Dark denim jeans fit tightly around his legs with a pair of serious work boots visible below.

Brown suspenders lent a somewhat scholarly look to his decidedly rough attire.

"I'm an oceanographer – a geological oceanographer," Sharkey explained. "From our ship, *The Independence Ten*, we explore the sea floor as well as the processes that formed it. Sometimes we are fortunate enough to locate shipwrecks."

"A treasure hunter?" Martin asked.

"On occasion," he added, eyes twinkling with amusement.

"That sounds exciting," Shelby said, nearly swooning. "You must be *very* brave."

Cody tried not to make his frown too obvious.

"How did you become interested in oceanography?" Charlotte asked.

"Being an oceanographer requires an understanding of biology, chemistry, geology, and physics. Basically, you need to be good at science."

"Well, that leaves me out!" Shelby declared, crossing her arms.

Everyone laughed, except Cody.

"Anyway, I'm currently between expeditions. Jack here, was kind to enough to offer me a place to stay in exchange for tackling some projects around the house."

"And, when school ends in a few weeks, I'll be offering up *your* services as worker bees," Jack added. "So, Sam will be your boss for the next few months."

Cody looked at Jack. "Do we get paid for this? There's this truck—"

"We'll see." Jack cut him short. "Now you guys go back to whatever it is you do while I get Mr. Sharkey settled in."

"Sounds good," Sam said with a nod. "I could use a hot shower after two months at sea."

"Alright, let's get you—"

Suddenly Charlotte gasped, eyes flying open, a trembling hand covering her open mouth.

Everyone froze, apparently awaiting some sort of explanation. An uneasy quiet followed as none was offered. Charlotte just stared at the ground, clearly squirming with embarrassment.

"Well, nice meeting you all," Sam said, breaking the awkward silence and grabbing his duffel bag.

The teens mumbled a reply as Jack escorted Sharkey up to his room.

"Charlotte, that was a bit weird," Cody said as they headed down the hallway.

"Yeah, sugar, what was that all about?" Shelby asked.

"She was probably picturing him in the shower." Martin grinned. "I guess it got the better of her."

"Martin Speck!" Charlotte chastised. "I can't believe you guys. That *man*..."

"Mr. Sharkey?" Shelby asked as they reached Cody's room. "It's alright, honey. I'm sure a handsome man like that probably has women swooning over him all the—"

"No," Charlotte turned, staring at them with big eyes. "You missed it . . . his boots."

"Charlotte, what are you talking about?" Cody asked, picking up the weights he left on the floor. He glanced at Martin and Shelby to see whether they had any idea what she was getting at. All appeared equally confused. "Missed *what*?" he asked.

"Mr. Sharkey!" Charlotte nearly gushed the words. "Am I the only one who noticed?" She looked around the room. "He's the man who broke into the house that night!"

Chapter 5: The Light

Jack's face was hidden behind the morning paper. Heather intently perused a circular from a local furniture store while Shelby read the latest issue of Elle. Gabby and Jessica's incessant voices melded into a blurry backdrop, mixing with the whir of an old fan. It was an otherwise uneventful June morning. Cody observed his family with a combination of embarrassment and amusement.

Jack, don't you ever get tired of those crossword puzzles? And, good luck with that furniture ad, Heather. There's nothing in there that will fit this house. You'd have a better shot finding something at the Museum of Ancient History. And, do these girls ever breathe? All they do is talk, talk, talk.

He took the last bite of a syrup-laden waffle and pushed his plate to the middle of the table. Martin and Charlotte covered their few remaining bites with crumpled napkins.

"I don't understand the world today," Jack roared suddenly. "A gang of kids beat up the curator at a Native American museum not far from here, then vandalized the displays. They urinated on them and set fire to a priceless display of Indian artwork." He hesitated, shaking his head. "Why would anyone *do* such a terrible thing? If you're not going to respect the world around you, why take it out on priceless Indian treasures that are clearly irreplaceable," he added, shaking his head.

"Yeah, that's bad." Cody nodded somberly. "Definitely not cool."

For once, Gabby and Jessica were quiet, clearly not wanting to provoke Jack's anger.

"I just don't understand it," he continued. "We're in a downward spiral. No one cares about anything or anyone, except themselves."

"Why would they do something so mean?" Shelby asked dolefully.

"I've always thought Native American history was cool," Martin added. "How could you be mad at them when we're the ones who stole their land."

"I don't know," Jack said, rubbing his forehead, "Back in my day..."

"At Woodstock?" Cody quipped, trying to add a bit of levity.

Jack ignored him. "We respected other people and cultures. Everyone has a place in this world."

"It's The Light," Sam Sharkey mumbled matter-of-factly as he glanced up from his National Explorer magazine.

"It's the *what?*" Cody scowled at the man sitting alone on the opposite side of the room. He'd been treating Mr. Sharkey with extreme suspicion since Charlotte's revelation.

"The Darkness began stealing The Books of Light back in the mid twentieth century. Since then the world's been heading down a path of intellectual darkness."

"What the heck does that mean?" Cody said testily. "And who's The Darkness?"

"The Darkness is destroying the world's goodness and repressing any attempt at enlightenment. As a result, humanity remains stagnant. People are no longer building their essences. In fact, the power of their collective conscience is fading."

Cody glanced at the other teens.

How does he know about our essence? We know because Radianna explained it during our visit to Nimbus. How does he know?

Everyone had now looked up from their respective reading material, curiosity appearing to get the better of them.

"Humanity has become intellectually stagnant – just like back in the Dark Ages – because The Light of Nimbus is dying," Sam continued absently. "Once the Light goes out, The Darkness will be all-powerful and humanity will be at its mercy."

Cody glanced at his siblings. It seemed Sharkey *did* know about Nimbus.

But how? Who is this guy?

"We've had some pretty great thinkers since then," Cody replied. "What about a couple of *clearly* unimportant guys like Gates and Jobs?"

Sam smiled condescendingly. The more Cody let on he didn't trust the man, the more Sharkey seemed to enjoy confronting him.

"Yes, there have been a few individuals who carried the world, but as a whole, we've become narrow-minded and shallow." Sam took a last bite. "Case in point: How many people read books these days?"

"I wait for the movie to come out," Martin joked.

"Exactly," Sharkey responded. "The numbers have decreased exponentially. All you kids do is play video games and watch reality shows or movies. All of those represent someone *else's* reality... or fantasy. There is no imagination or effort required. You don't challenge your minds; you just sit on your sofas and watch someone else's creation."

Cody could feel his face getting flushed.

"I—" He was fired up and ready to argue, but before he could get the words out, Sam continued.

"A hundred, two hundred years ago, people lived their *own* reality, always on the edge of life, trying to improve their circumstances. There were many great thinkers: Franklin, Tesla, Bell, Edison, just to name a few. They accomplished amazing feats, designed innovative new inventions, or packed up all their worldly possessions and headed someplace new, trying to make life better for themselves and everyone around them."

"Where would we go? We've already colonized the all major parts of the world," Charlotte replied.

"There are other worlds," Sharkey said. "And, that's not the point. People nowadays want things handed to them. Instead of reaching for the stars, they just complain, or make fun of those who are different. 'He called me a bad name', or 'she was mean to me'," he squeaked in a whiny voice.

"We do not!" Cody frowned, knowing his response sounded childish.

"Who cares if some closed-minded fool doesn't see your potential?" Sharkey continued. "If you want to show them what you're made of, do great things! But no, you would rather watch some movie director's vision, rather than create your own.

"That's not true!" Cody snapped. He struggled to come up with something clever, a cerebral retort that would make this smug man eat his words. But all he could add was, "not true at all."

Sharkey smirked and shook his head as if the icing on the cake was Cody's lame and disappointing response to the intellectual stimulation he'd provided.

"Very few people experience the magic and inspiration one gets from a good book, because reading is too much work," the man added.

"What gives *you* the right to give us advice on life?" Cody retorted, "A guy who steals treasure for a living and needs to do odd jobs just to have a place to sleep?"

"Cody Hawke!" Heather said reproachfully.

Sharkey calmly got up and set his dish in the sink. He appeared to enjoy the power he had over his rapt audience. It bothered Cody that the man didn't seem the slightest bit fazed by his insults, as if his opinion was too meaningless to matter.

Finally, when the moment seemed to be just right, Sharkey turned. "This is not about *me*, Mr. Hawke. I'm not the one who'll be affected." Again, he smiled condescendingly. "It is *you*. When The Light finally goes out, humankind's worst enemies – apathy and ignorance – will take over. It's happened before."

"So, what are you saying?" Cody growled.

"I think he's saying things are going to get worse before they get better," Jack muttered.

"That is correct." Sam hesitated before stepping through the doorway. He ran a hand over his jaw, contemplating the reddish-brown stubble. "Much worse!"

"I don't trust him," Cody muttered, lying on the foot of his bed and tossing a ball in the air.

"Yes, we see that," Shelby replied in an annoyingly disapproving tone.

"There's more to him than he's letting on." Cody got up and stared out the window, pondering the elaborate maze below.

"Your concern over Mr. Sharkey's intentions doesn't justify your hostility," Shelby stated.

"Shelby, if Charlotte's right and he's the one who broke into the house that night, he obviously knows about Rúndyrr. He also clearly knows about Nimbus. That makes him very dangerous. Who *is* he? And what does he want?"

"Why does he bother you so much?" Shelby continued, not even looking up from her copy of Elle. "Maybe it's because he's handsome and successful."

Cody scowled. "How is he successful? Because he steals treasure from ancient shipwrecks?"

They don't understand how bad things could get if this guy makes our secret public. Being a handsome man doesn't make him a good guy.

"Well," Martin offered, "he's clearly hiding something. I mean, what do we know about him?"

"He says he's a treasure hunter. Maybe he wants to use Rúndyrr to make money," Charlotte added.

"Yeah, and Jack unknowingly hired that *thief* to work in our house," Cody roared.

"Why don't we search the internet. Maybe we can find out more about our Mr. Sharkey?"

"Good idea, Charlotte. Let's start with a search for his name," Cody said, grabbing the laptop. He typed while the others peered over his shoulder. "Well, let's see. We have a Sam Sharkey Trucking Company in Oklahoma, a few social site entries, none of which appear to be him."

"Why isn't he coming up on social media?" Shelby asked.

"He doesn't strike me as a social media kind of guy," Martin said, shaking his head.

"Strange," Charlotte mumbled. "It's like he doesn't even exist."

"How is it possible to not have a social media presence in this day and age," Shelby said. "Wait! What did he say was the name of his ship, The Independence Ten?"

"Good job, Shelby," Cody responded, typing the name into the search area. "Hmm, this could be it." He leaned forward to get a better look.

"This says Independence X," Shelby said.

"X means ten in Roman numerals," Charlotte offered.

"What does it say?" Shelby asked.

"It talks about the voyages of the deep-sea exploration ship Independence and the team of scientists on board mapping the ocean floor. The ship belongs to wealthy financier and thrill-seeker Thorvald Drynurr," Cody said.

"Sounds Icelandic or Norse," Charlotte added.

"Click on *Excursions* and see where they've been." Martin leaned in and pointed at the link.

"It says they map the contour of the ocean floor and are always looking for sunken treasure. They just returned from a voyage to the Norwegian Sea," Shelby read aloud.

"Click on Ship's Logs," Martin said, pointing.

"It launched the NOAA site – National Oceanographic and Atmospheric Administration," Charlotte stated.

"And the ship's logs are password protected. Interesting," Cody added.

"What does that mean?" Shelby asked.

"Sounds like they're hiding something," he said, feeling somewhat vindicated.

"Keep trying," Charlotte said, clearly intrigued. "Why didn't he mention the wealthy financier or his affiliation with NOAA?"

Cody clicked on various menu options and links searching for details on the elusive Sam Sharkey, but the information was all scientific in nature. "This is getting us nowhere," he said.

"I wish we could just climb aboard his ship and see what he's hiding," Shelby said.

"Do you think he could be planning to steal the scepter?" asked Martin.

"I doubt it," Charlotte said. "He could've stolen it when he entered Rúndyrr that night."

Suddenly Cody looked up. "What did you say?"

"I said, he could've stolen—" Charlotte began.

'No, Shelby."

55

"Me? I said I wish we could climb aboard his ship—"

"That's it!" Cody jumped to his feet. "Rúndyrr! We'll board his ship to see what we can find out."

"Remind me not to open my mouth." Shelby muttered with a grimace.

"Why do you suppose his ship is The Independence Ten," Martin asked as they reached the cave.

"I guess there were nine ships before it with the same name," Charlotte offered.

"What could've happened to the other nine ships?" Shelby wondered.

"Dost thou wish to embark on a journey?" The Gatekeeper emerged from the darkness.

"Everyone, concentrate!" Cody whispered, then turned to face the old man. "Yes. We need to learn more about this Sharkey guy. Since you won't tell us anything, we did a search on the internet—"

"*What* didst thou search?" The bearded man stared at him like he had two heads.

"We searched the internet on our computer. Don't you know what the internet is, or a computer?" Cody asked, getting only a steely stare in return.

"I'm not surprised," Martin quipped. "You guys need to get out more."

"Anyway," Cody continued, "The search results for Independence Ten on our computer didn't add up to anything, so we'd like to—"

"It's based on the number of fingers or toes,
And, how many we have of each of those.
We use it to add, subtract, multiply, and divide,
Ones in the first column, tens and hundreds beside.
Ten is the name, but in the column won't fit,
Only the numbers that are one digit.
So, although ten tells the whole story,
Zero through nine get all the glory."

"That sounds like a math problem. What the heck does that have to do with Sharkey?" Cody frowned.

"Fingers and toes? We have ten of those," Martin offered.

"He said 'ten' in the verse," Charlotte said, twirling her braids.

"I heard something about adding, subtracting, multiplying, and dividing. Is it math? Arithmetic?" Martin asked.

Cody ran a hand through his wavy blond hair. "How about counting or numbers?" He asked, glancing at the solid doorway, but it did not illuminate.

"Our number system," Charlotte offered softly, "is based on ten because we have ten fingers that, at some point in history, we used for counting. It's the decimal number system."

Cody turned as the rock doorway began to swirl, shimmering with light. Beyond the bridge, however, darkness prevailed.

Chapter 6: The Bug Byte

Cody's first sensation was a warm breeze passing over him. There wasn't much to see in the overwhelming blackness, not even a single star in the sky, thus he assumed they were inside.

"Well, this is lovely!" Martin exclaimed, glancing around. "There's nothing like an abandoned warehouse in the middle of the night to make you feel warm and cozy."

"Could this be the cargo hold of his ship?" Cody asked.

"I don't think so," Charlotte murmured. "Unless the ship is in dry dock, it's not moving."

"This is so creepy. Where *are* we?" Shelby asked.

"You know," Cody sighed, shaking his head, "We plan. We prepare. We work out the smallest details. We go over it together, numerous times. Can someone explain to me **why** it *never* works out?"

"There was that *one* time," Martin added sheepishly, "when they let us go to the concert for Shelby's birthday."

"Yeah, and almost burned us alive afterward," Shelby replied.

"They give a little, they take a little," Martin muttered, aiming his flashlight around the room.

"Any ideas?" Cody asked briskly.

"This reminds me of a supermarket after a nuclear blast," Charlotte mumbled distractedly. "It's completely empty – no people, no produce, no soup cans or cereal boxes – just empty aisles and stands illuminated by the green glow of a distant generator light."

"Oh, my, honey," Shelby exclaimed. "That's a lovely thought."

"Let's follow the backup generator light and see where it leads," Cody said. "Following the light usually gets us to something helpful."

"Maybe we're inside a power plant," Martin said, wiping his brow. "It's sweltering in here."

"At least there's a bit of a breeze," Charlotte added, fanning herself.

"What in the name of Kitty Hawk is that buzzing sound?" Shelby asked.

"Maybe it's a fly that mutated in Charlotte's nuclear blast. The green light is his nest," Martin said.

Shelby glared at them. "There better not be any big bugs in this place! I *hate* bugs."

"What's *that*?" Martin yelled. "Oh, no! It just landed in your hair!"

"Get it off!" Shelby cried, swatting at her head.

"Look at the size of the beetle burrowing into your scalp," Cody teased.

"Knock it off, Cowpoke!" Shelby smacked him.

The floor began to angle downward. It was slippery, like black linoleum. They walked for what felt like miles, but nothing changed, just endless rows of black cabinets looming in the greenish darkness.

"What was the return riddle again?" Cody asked.

"I'm not telling you," Shelby said testily, presumably still sore at him.

"Do you want to be trapped here forever?" he asked.

Shelby sighed loudly, then recited The Gatekeeper's words.

"Zeroes and ones, it's all you'll find,
In a math problem of this odd kind.
Just two unique digits in all there'll be,
A two or a three you'll never see.
By using this, one can still add,
Though writing it might make you mad.
Take a one, one, and zero, zero,
And add the reverse to be a hero.
But be sure to recite it in a form you know,

Or stay in this world with a greenish glow."

"It's a simple math problem," Charlotte said. "How can this creepy place help us with that?"

"Simple?" Cody rolled his eyes.

"It sounds like he wants us to add 1100 and the reverse, 0011," Charlotte replied. "But that would be 1111." She glanced around. "Clearly that's *not* the answer."

"But be sure to recite it in a form you know, or stay in this world with a greenish glow," Shelby added.

"What does that mean?" Martin asked.

"No idea," Cody said. "Let's keep moving. Maybe something down there can provide answers."

The breeze picked up until it began to impede their progress.

"This wind is *ruining* my hair. I spent two hours this morning getting it just perfect!" Shelby whined loudly, trying to be heard above the buzz.

"You spent two *hours* on your hair?" Cody asked. "You wash it, run a comb through it, and go. It takes five minutes, tops."

"And it *looks* like you spent five minutes," Shelby retorted.

"Why? What's wrong with my hair?" Cody asked indignantly.

"It's bright down there," Martin said, clearly trying to change the subject. "Maybe that's the operating room where the insect aliens are waiting to run tests on us."

"It looks like rows of little light bulbs, thousands of them," Cody offered, craning his neck to see down the hill. "Where *are* we?"

"What does this mean?" Shelby asked, pointing toward an emblem on the corner of one black cabinet covered with metal dots.

"It appears to be a company trademark." Charlotte perused it for a moment. "If I'm not mistaken, they manufacture…"

Cody watched Charlotte's eyes roll back, her expression reflecting a realization of some sort. The subsequent loud chortle bursting from her lips echoed through the darkness.

"Manufacture what?" Cody asked, unsure what was so funny.

"They manufacture silicon chips just like this one, just like *all* of these," she replied.

"Silicon chips?" Cody asked.

"Silicon chips as in the inside of a computer?" Martin added.

Cody frowned. "When I said nothing 'added up on the computer', I didn't mean *literally*," he yelled to The Gatekeeper.

"Great job figuring that out, Charlotte. But, what about the riddle?" Shelby asked. "We still don't know how to recite it in a form we know."

"Let's keep walking and see if we can find some help," Cody said.

"Watch out for the fan," Martin said. "We don't want to get chopped to bits."

Ahead was an enormous bank of lights made up of seemingly unending rows of tiny white dots, turning on and off intermittently with no discernable pattern.

"Reminds me of those electronic signs," Martin said as they approached, "like the one in Times Square, except with millions of bulbs. Maybe it's saying something but we're too close to read it."

"Did you see that?" Shelby whispered abruptly. "It looked like a snake made of lights."

"Let's go, Miss South Carolina. You're imagining things," Cody mumbled, heading back toward the main aisle.

"No, I saw it, too," Charlotte added. "The lights created a pattern. It wasn't random like the rest."

"There it goes!" Martin yelled, pointing.

As Cody ran down the ramp, the snake of lights scooted in the opposite direction, lighting new bulbs and turning ones off as it moved.

"Wait! I won't hurt you," he said, walking more slowly.

This time it moved, but just far enough to be out of Cody's reach. "Come closer. I promise, I won't hurt you."

The snake slid along, slowly illuminating a string of lights until it was right next to him.

"Aw, it's so cute," Shelby chuckled.

She reached down as if to tickle its ear. Two lights near the head went half dark, like eyes closing. Another group below lit at an angle, like a grinning mouth. Two perpendicular sets of lights emanated out from the main body, like arms trying to hug Shelby.

"What do you suppose it is?" Charlotte whispered.

"Who *are* you?" Cody asked.

"It's okay, don't be afraid," Shelby said softly.

"Come on, we're wasting time," Cody mumbled. "These lights are just playing tricks on our eyes and we need to figure out how to get home."

He turned to walk away. The others hesitated, then followed. They had only taken a few steps when Cody heard something.

"Da da da dummm."

"Was that you?" he called.

The creature giggled and repeated, "Da da da dummm."

"So, you *can* talk," Shelby said.

"So, you *can* talk," the creature repeated.

"What's your name?" Cody asked.

"What's *your* name?"

"I'm Cody."

"I'm Cody."

"Stop repeating me."

"Stop repeating me."

Charlotte and Shelby giggled.

Martin grinned. "I like this guy!"

Cody was not amused. "Come on. He can't help us. All he does is repeat everything."

"Come on, sugar. Can you tell us your name?" Shelby asked sweetly.

The creature hesitated, then replied shyly, "Bug . . . My name Bug. Bug B-Y-T-E. Bug Byte. Ha, Bug-bite, get it?"

A series of lights lit up in a half circle to show his big grin.

"Nice to meet you, Mr. Bug Byte." Shelby smiled.

"Nice to meet you, Miss South Carolina." He smiled back.

"What *are* you?" Cody asked.

"I – I Bug Byte."

"Yes, we established that. But *what* are you?".

Bug looked at Cody, confusion apparent on his face. He started to inch away.

"Wait! Don't go," Shelby said, frowning at Cody. "Don't pay any attention to that grumpy Gus."

"Grumpy Gus. Grumpy Gus," Bug said to Cody.

"I'll bet you are very smart," Shelby said. "And, I'll bet you know *everything* about computers." Bug grinned shyly. "Do you know how to add 1100 and the reverse, 0011, in computer talk?"

Bug dimmed his lights except for the four in the middle. The first two became very bright and the last two went dim. "One, one, zero, zero," he said. Then, he did it again, but this time they were reversed. The first two lights were dim and the second two were very bright. "He said, "Zero, zero, one, one. Add together, you get four lights on: one, one, one, one."

"Bits!" Charlotte yelled suddenly.

"Who?" Cody asked.

"Bits! Binary digits! Binary is a number system – like decimal – except it's based on the number *two* instead of *ten*. It has only two possible digits, zero and one. It doesn't include the number two – like our decimal system has zero through nine but doesn't include ten. In binary, you get numbers like 1100 and 0011 instead of 1234."

"That seems a bit dumb to me," Shelby said. "Pardon the pun, but what do you use it for? I mean, why write all those ones and zeros when you can just write decimal numbers."

"Binary is unique because the two digits – one and zero – can represent on and off – just like these little lights bulbs. That way, you can write numbers electronically. It's the basic premise of how computers work."

Martin looked at Charlotte, his mouth hanging open. "Wow! I actually understood that."

"Okay, this is all great, but we still don't know the answer," Cody muttered. "Bug said 1100 and 0011 add up to be 1111, but I don't see the bridge opening."

"We still need it in a form we know," Shelby said, turning toward Bug. "Decimal! We need the answer in decimal."

"Exactly, Shelby." Charlotte retrieved a pen and paper from her purse. "The question is, how do we change it to decimal format?" she added.

"Mr. Bug Byte," Charlotte asked, "Do you know how to change the number 1111 in binary to a decimal number, so it can be written?"

Bug's eyes opened wide. "*Output* format? Why you not say so? You need to extend out," he said.

"What does that mean, extend out?" Cody asked.

Bug seemed frustrated, searching for the right words. Suddenly he brightened.

"Binary notation! It will be like Decimal Notation, except instead of columns for ones, tens, hundreds, and thousands, it has columns ones, twos, fours, and eights."

"Charlotte, what is he talking about?" Cody asked.

"You know how in decimal we have the 'ones' column at the right, then the tens column, hundreds column, thousands, and so on. Each column is ten to a power, or ten times itself some number of times. Then you multiply that answer times whatever number is in that column. It's called Decimal Notation."

"So, 987 is a hundred times nine, plus ten times eight, plus one times seven," Martin offered.

"Exactly. So, if I do the same thing in binary for 1111," Charlotte said excitedly, "we get eight times one, plus four times one, plus two times one, plus one times one. The answer is fifteen!"

"Charlotte," Cody said, grinning broadly, "we'd be *so* screwed without you! Come here."

He walked over and planted a kiss on her forehead. Charlotte stared at the ground, clearly embarrassed. The Gatekeeper appeared amid the glowing doorway, five meters from where they stood.

"Thank you, Bug," Shelby called over her shoulder. "Goodbye!"

Chapter 7: The Jezebel

"Why don't we just *ask* him?" Shelby mumbled, legs dangling over the arm of Cody's chair as she thumbed through a magazine.

Cody frowned. "He'll just throw his hands in the air and say, you caught me, I'm a thief."

"And, I'm planning to use Rúndyrr to locate sunken ships so I can steal the bounty. Please call the authorities and save me from myself," Martin added, grinning.

"That's an interesting idea," Cody said. "It may be exactly what he has planned."

"Maybe this *darkness* he's referring to is actually *him*," Charlotte murmured. "Maybe he's the one causing trouble and promoting apathy, trying to use Rúndyrr to take over the world. I mean, it started around the same time he arrived."

Cody sat up for a moment, contemplating her words.

"Hmm, I wonder," he mumbled breathlessly. "I think you may be onto something."

"Charlotte, honey, don't *you* start. It's bad enough we have to hear all of Cowpoke's crazy conspiracy theories," Shelby said.

"No, that's a great point. Maybe he's trying to fool us into thinking he's got the answers, when in fact he's the *real* threat to our world," Cody said, lying back on his bed and tossing a ball in the air. "Shelby's got a point, too. Clearly The Gatekeeper is not going to help us, why not ask Sharkey what he's up to. If he knows we're onto him, maybe it'll force his hand."

"Cody, do you think a guy like that is scared of four penniless teenagers? We don't even have a car," Martin said. "What are we going to do? Ground him? Pummel him with toilet paper?"

"We could tell Jack and Heather," Charlotte replied.

"Picture *that* conversation," Martin said. "Jack, you know the guy you randomly hired to help out around the house? Well, he's actually trying to access a magical doorway to other dimensions in the caves below our house and use it to destroy the world."

"Fine, so we're not the FBI. But, we're still four people watching him very closely," Cody said. He got up and began to pace. "We'll keep a close eye on him, starting with his room. Let's go through his stuff, see what we can find."

"That's against the law," Shelby said.

"Hey, he's in *our* house. We have a right to know what he's keeping here," Cody replied.

After much prodding, the others finally agreed the treasure hunter's possessions might provide a clue to his intentions. They also agreed to track Sam Sharkey's comings and goings, making note of when he left and for how long. Even Shelby had to admit it was fun playing private eye. Besides, school was over. It should've been a time for celebration, unfortunately, there wasn't much else to do.

Cody lifted himself onto the stone wall surrounding the fountain on the west side of their property. The smell of freshly cut grass carried by a warm spring breeze, filled his senses. He opened a notebook and read to his siblings as they relaxed on the lawn below.

"Okay, so he leaves every Friday afternoon and doesn't return until Saturday morning," he said, staring absently across their property, the shimmering bay stretching out beyond.

"I wonder where he goes," Shelby said.

"He also leaves for a few hours early Monday or Tuesday, and sometimes Thursday mornings. It's like he tries to be back before we wake up."

"Maybe he knows we're watching him," Martin said. "I wonder why he doesn't leave on Wednesday or Sunday?"

"Jack goes to the bank every Wednesday morning," Charlotte offered.

"Yeah, and Heather takes the car to go grocery shopping on Sundays. Maybe he doesn't want to run into them in town," Martin added.

"Interesting," Cody mumbled. "Maybe he—"

"Do you see that bird?" Shelby interjected, pointing upward. "It's huge!"

"Is that a pterodactyl?" Martin quipped. "It just blocked out the sun."

"It must be an eagle, or maybe an owl," Charlotte said.

Cody became obsessed with uncovering Sharkey's true intentions.

Maybe Charlotte is right. Maybe he wants to make everyone think he's all righteous while he takes over the world.

Shelby said he had an unhealthy preoccupation with the man. But for Cody, it was a game of wits, and there was too much at stake to lose.

"Next time he leaves the house, we're going to find out what he's hiding in his room."

"Cody, I must protest. I think this is a bad idea."

"Shelby, I don't trust this guy. He tries to sound so high-and-mighty. Maybe he uses those lofty words as a front to throw us off the trail while he steals the scepter and uses Rúndyrr to rob us, or worse, perpetrate some evil on the world. Do you want to just sit back and let him do it?"

"Stop being so dramatic, Cowpoke," Shelby said, rolling her eyes at him. "I love our home, but unless he collects junk, there's nothing here to steal. If it's the scepter he wants, I'm sure The Guardian and Gatekeeper are far better suited to protect it than any of us. Besides, he could've taken it that night we saw him in the Rúndyrr cave."

"But he didn't," Charlotte added.

"Whose side are you on?" he mumbled.

Cody woke the others early Thursday morning, just after Sam Sharkey left the house. They crept up the back staircase, being careful not to make any noise. The last thing Cody needed was one of the big-mouth twins, Gabby and Jessica, asking a lot of questions.

The fourth-floor stairwell felt very inhospitable with its dark wood paneling and total lack of natural light. It wound to dizzying heights, finally disappearing into the darkness. The four teens were panting when they finally reached the top, a crescent-shaped landing with three hallways, one to the left, one right, and another straight. Smelly gas lamps flickered their meager illumination.

"Any reason we have an aversion to electricity up here?" Shelby mumbled.

"It probably can't reach this high," Martin muttered, gasping for breath.

The bust of an old man wearing a dark tuxedo, filled a semi-circular alcove between two hallways. The statue rested atop a stone column, mostly hidden behind a half-dead sapling in a large pot.

"Whoa," Shelby said. "Look at the eyes on that guy. He almost looks . . . alive."

The bust's stern gray face, set off by a dark crown, reminded Cody of the devil. He shivered, feeling its eyes burning a hole in him as they passed.

"Where do these guys buy their furnishings," Martin whispered, "Satan's rummage sale?"

The straight hallway leading toward the back of the mansion was wide enough for them to walk four abreast. They followed the dimly lit corridor lined with gold wallpaper in what Shelby referred to as a jacquard pattern, until reaching an intersection.

"I think it's this way," Cody said, pointing down a western hallway that disappeared into darkness.

They passed more than a few closed doors, many with framed pictures hanging nearby. Cody wondered if, at some point, the pictures had been used to identify the room's owner.

After a right turn down another long hallway, they arrived at what Cody believed to be Sharkey's room. Jack called it the Golden Axe Room because the painting hanging beside the door was of a Norseman holding a shiny axe.

"This is it," Cody whispered. He slowly pushed the door open, peering anxiously into the dimly lit room. In its center, a massive stave supported the vaulted peak, typical of an old Norse-inspired structure. Light filtered between the velvet curtains, highlighting a bed, dresser, and small seating area.

"Hello?" A woman's shrill voice echoed about the shadowy room. "Who's there?"

The four teens must've resembled a comedy act, Cody thought, as they scrambled for the door.

"Great job, Cowpoke!" Shelby hissed. "He's got a *woman* in there!"

"Uh, I'm very sorry. We were looking for Sam," Cody called, feeling sheepish.

"Sam?"

"Yes, Mr. Sharkey," Cody called nervously. "I'm sorry to bother you. Are you a friend of his?"

"Hello?" she repeated.

"We, uh, live here, and uh, we just wanted to talk to Sam."

"Sam Sharkey?"

"Yes. Sam Sharkey."

"Hello?"

"Wait a minute," Charlotte said, a smirk gracing her lips. "There's something funny about that voice."

She stepped forward and, much to Cody's surprise, pushed past them.

"Charlotte, what—" he began.

"Shush!"

Cody stood frozen as she entered the room. Charlotte was usually the last to make a scene and the first to run from trouble.

"Hello?" the voice repeated.

"I certainly hope that's not his hundred-year-old mother relaxing in a muumuu as she massages her bunions," Martin whispered. "Or, Charlotte could be scarred for life."

"Just as I thought," Charlotte said, reappearing in the doorway. "What self-respecting shipwreck treasure hunter, aka pirate, doesn't have a parrot?"

Martin laughed. "Polly want a cracker?"

"Hello?" the bird offered.

"Whew! That was close!" Cody grinned. "Okay," he said, feeling even more sheepish. "Now, let's see what he's hiding."

Cody stepped in and pushed the curtains open. The room seemed almost inviting, despite the thick, dark molding and heavy furnishings.

"We have a duffle bag!" Shelby held it up in seemingly breathless anticipation. "Filled with…?" Her animated voice mocked him. "Could it be? *Clothes!*" she said, rolling her eyes at him.

"Fine," Cody muttered. "Let's keep looking."

They checked Sharkey's dresser and closet but found nothing out of the ordinary. Cody was beginning to get frustrated. He was so sure there would be something to confirm his suspicion this man was trouble.

"Come on, Cowpoke. This is a waste of time!" Shelby said reproachfully.

"Come on, Cowpoke," the parrot mimicked.

Cody was beginning to agree when he saw the strap from another duffle bag protruding out from under the bed. He bent down to take a closer look. The bag was heavier than expected. Something shifted inside as he lifted it onto the bed. Cody unzipped the bag, then glared at his siblings.

"Okay, so every scientist we know packs a weapon, right?" he said, feeling somewhat vindicated.

"Cody Hawke put that thing down before you shoot somebody," Shelby said with a groan.

"Wow. If I'm not mistaken," Martin offered, staring transfixed, "That's a *Peacemaker.*"

"A what?" Cody asked.

"A Peacemaker. A Colt single action army gun from the late 1800s." Martin stared in apparent awe. "I'll bet it's worth something."

"Maybe it's just a collector's piece," Charlotte added.

"Yeah, except he's got ammunition for it," Cody said.

"Still, that's not a thief's gun," Martin responded.

"Come on, Cowpoke!" the parrot repeated.

"I agree with Polly. Let's go," Shelby said.

The four stepped out into the corridor and began retracing their steps. Cody was relieved when they reached the main hall. Something about this part of house felt unnatural, like it existed in some other dimension. He wondered briefly whether the long flight of stairs could be a pathway to another world, one much older than now. Cody shook his head to clear the wild notions swimming inside.

"I was so sure we'd—" he began. "HOLY—"

"YIKES!" Martin yelled.

The four teens dropped to their knees as something the size of a human flew overhead.

Shelby and Charlotte screamed and covered their heads. The creature landed about ten meters down the hall, then flew back in their direction. Cody could hear the whir of enormous wings flapping as it passed overhead. A few seconds later, silence returned to the dark corridor.

"What *was* that?" Cody asked. "Come on," he added. "Let's see where it went!"

"Cowpoke?" Shelby gulped. "You're going to *follow* that thing?"

They ran down the hall, stopping at the top of the stairs.

"I think we lost it," Cody mumbled, scanning the area. "How could it have just disappeared?"

Cody turned toward the alcove. The bust stared ahead in frozen silence.

Is that an old man? It's so odd-looking, almost like some sort of demon. Wait. Did it just move?

"That's no bust of an old man!" Shelby screeched. "It's alive!"

"Could that be what flew down the hall?" Charlotte whispered in a choked voice.

As his eyes adjusted to the light, Cody saw the statue's head cock slightly to one side, its piercing eyes moving from one teen to the next. Shelby's scream reminded Cody of a tomcat on the prowl as she took off down the stairs. Charlotte followed close behind. Martin began to back up, then he, too, scrambled down the stairs. Cody couldn't move, he just stared at the bust as it stared back.

"Is there something I can help you with, *boy*?" The creature hissed, then spread its enormous wings until the tips extended from one side of the alcove to the other.

Cody shook his head, then took off down the steps as fast as his feet would carry him.

Heather set two plates on the kitchen table, a platter of sliced ham and a rectangular dish filled with potatoes, peppers, and eggs in some kind of sauce. Cody was hungry after their alarming trip to the fourth floor. He grabbed two slices of ham, then scooped a pile of potatoes and eggs onto his plate.

"Cody," Jack said curtly. "Put the second slice back until everyone's had at least one serving."

"I don't know how you can even *eat* after that," Shelby whispered. "My stomach's still in knots. I thought we were going to get murdered by that evil thing."

"And, it's still up there," Charlotte moaned.

"Anything you four want to share with the group?" Heather asked sweetly.

"Uh, no," Cody said briskly, "Just something that happened—"

"So," Sam Sharkey said, taking a seat and eying the teens with amusement. "I see you met Jezebel."

Cody stared at the man in dumbfounded silence. "That . . . *thing* is yours?" he said finally.

Sharkey nodded. "Jez is a harpy eagle."

"I am sorry, Mr. Sharkey," Shelby said, "but I thought it was the devil."

"She has a very unique look, even for harpy eagles," Sharkey replied.

"Where did you get her?" Charlotte asked.

"I-uh," Sharkey began, taking a plate of food and returning to his chair, "found her during a trip to South America. She was injured. I nursed her back to health, but wasn't sure she'd make it in the wild."

"You could've warned us about your pet raptor," Martin said with a frown. "I nearly had a stroke."

"The bigger question is what were you doing outside my room?" Sharkey asked.

"We, uh, we were just exploring," Martin replied.

Sharkey nodded knowingly. "I'll *bet* you were."

"But I could swear sh-she . . . *spoke* to me," Cody stammered.

"Mr. Hawke," Sharkey said smugly. "Maybe we've been working you too hard."

"Yeah," Jack chuckled, shoving a forkful of potatoes in his mouth, "it *spoke* to you? Really, Cody?"

Cody realized how ridiculous it sounded and decided to let it be.

"Look at this thing," Cody said, holding up the laptop for the others, "it's a harpy eagle".

Shelby lifted her head off her pillow. Charlotte and Martin gathered around him.

"Imagine seeing that in the wild," Charlotte said. "I'd have a heart attack."

"And I *swear*, it spoke to me," Cody added, shaking his head. "I just didn't want to get into it in front of Jack and Heather."

"I wouldn't be surprised by anything around here," Shelby said.

"Did anyone notice Mr. Sharkey's response when I asked where he got her?" Charlotte asked.

"Yeah," Martin replied. "It was as if he was making it up."

"He's hiding something, as usual," Cody fumed. "What could he be up to?"

"Maybe it was actually The Guardian," Martin mused.

"Interesting thought," Charlotte added. "We've seen his shape-shifting capabilities."

Chapter 8: The Tide

Late Friday afternoon, Jack was heading back into town. Cody convinced him to let the four come along, saying they'd been invited to a friend's pool party. Cody was very clear about the impact on their collective social lives if anyone saw the VW bus, so Jack let them walk to the kid's house from their store. He sternly reminded them they needed to be back by 9 p.m. when he closed up shop.

The bad weather had finally cleared out, bringing unseasonably warm temperatures for the end of June. Cody wasn't sure whether he was more excited about the prospect of tracking Sam Sharkey or just walking around town without parental supervision. Either way, they were free, away from Freya Manor, even if just for a few hours.

"It's almost six o'clock," Cody said. "We need to be back here by nine, so watch the time."

Chatty tourists explored the various shops and attractions dotting Dawnport's quaint streets. Bunting flags already lined porch roofs in anticipation of the July Fourth holiday. Petunia-filled window boxes nearly burst with a bounty of red, white, and blue flowers.

"We should do this more often," Cody said, taking a deep breath of salt air.

"I agree. Even if we don't find Sharkey," Shelby added, "this is great."

Old brick buildings lined the waterfront, signs like Whalen Sardine Factory and Peavey Shellfish Processing identifying their trades. Scallop boats bobbed in the oncoming tide, resting from a flurry of earlier activity. Seagulls perusing the warm currents, scanned the salty expanse for a tasty morsel.

"What was that?" Shelby cried suddenly, stopping in her tracks.

"What?" Cody asked.

"Something just landed on my shoulder," she said with a moan.

"Uh, it's just a little stain," Charlotte said, wincing as she retrieved a tissue from her purse.

"It's bird poop!" Cody yelled, as he leaned in to take a closer look.

"*What?* On my new jacket? Get if off!" Shelby shrieked.

"I'm trying," Charlotte said, trying to sound calm. "Hold still."

"Hurry!" Shelby cried. "Get it off me!"

"It's gross, but you're not going to die," Cody muttered.

"You know, in some cultures, having a bird defecate on you is considered good luck."

Charlotte always found the positive in everything.

"They just say that to make the poor sucker feel better!" Martin joked.

"Is if off?" Shelby whimpered.

Maybe the blob of bird excrement on Shelby's new jacket is an omen, Cody thought. Lying to his parents always seemed to get him in trouble. Even if there was zero chance of them finding out.

They scoured the town, but there was no sign of Sam Sharkey. It was early evening and Martin was clearly exhausted, his arm around Shelby's shoulders for support. Suddenly Cody heard a loud snap and Shelby dropped to the ground. Martin landed near her.

"What happened? Are you okay?" Cody asked, helping them up.

"My heel broke," Shelby said with a pout.

"You and your stupid shoes," Cody murmured.

"Oh, be quiet, Cowpoke," Shelby said testily, limping along on a shoe without a heel.

Maybe Sharkey hadn't come to town. Maybe he was far away or worse, back at the house, having his way with Rúndyrr while they weren't there to protect it.

"Let's check out the last street on this block, then we'll head back. We must be looking in the wrong area," he said with a sigh.

"I'm so tired. My feet feel like stones, I'm limping on one heel, and I have to pee!"

"I'm with you, Shelby. If I take one more step or I'm going to drop like a rock," Martin muttered.

"Whose idea was this anyway, Cowpoke? I mean, Dawnport is no New York City, but did we honestly think we'd find him just walking around?"

"Let's head back to that diner in town. We'll get a soda and Miss South Carolina can pee."

Three cheeseburgers, a chopped salad, a slice of cheesecake, and four sodas later, they felt renewed.

"That'll be thirty-four dollars and seventy-nine cents," the waitress stated absently, leaving the check on the table.

"Thirty-four dollars? What did we eat?" Shelby asked.

"With tip, it will be about forty bucks. How much money do you have?" Cody asked.

As the teens amassed their collective fortunes, the burn in his stomach got worse.

"We're short eight dollars and seventy-nine cents! And, that doesn't include the tip," Cody said with a groan.

The four spent the next embarrassing half hour carrying dishes into the kitchen. The girls scraped them and loaded them in the dishwasher, while the boys wiped down and set the tables. Finally, after filling all the ketchup bottles and salt shakers, the manager let them leave, yelling 'get out and *stay* out' as they started up the sidewalk.

"Yikes! What is wrong with people these days?" Martin muttered. "Everyone's so angry."

"That was mortifying," Shelby added. "What happened to boys paying for a lady's lunch?" She frowned at Cody.

"Anybody up for a little more walking?" He asked, ignoring Shelby's comment. "We've got over an hour and there are some areas by the docks we haven't covered. Maybe we'll get lucky."

The words no sooner left his lips when the sky grew dark. Large raindrops began to pelt the sidewalks. Shelby hobbled down the street, taking shelter on the covered porch of a nearby home.

"Another outfit ruined," she muttered.

After the rain subsided, they headed down one last street, following it along the water until the road became a path. Patches of fog blanketed Passamaquoddy Bay, fostering an eerie vibe.

They reached the end of the dirt road with no sign of Sharkey. One house remained, barely visible in the distant mist. Everyone wanted to turn back, but Cody insisted they check it out. He ran ahead to get a better look. About fifty meters down the road, he waved them on, unable to hide his satisfaction.

"Sharkey's red Jeep!" He pointed, shouting with excitement. "I *knew* we'd find it!"

They crossed a narrow land mass covered with pebbles and shells. The house sat on a small atoll, enjoying a spectacular view of the bay in almost every direction. As the teens approached, the golden rays of a setting sun peeked through the mist.

"Wow, the tide is pretty high. I wonder if this place ever floods out," Charlotte wondered aloud.

"This doesn't look like a pirates' hangout," Martin said.

"Maybe it's where they plan their smuggling runs," Cody said. "It's certainly isolated enough and has easy access to the bay."

Shelby frowned at him. "It looks charming to me," she muttered.

The attractive home was tan-colored with a large front porch and burgundy shutters surrounding two 2nd floor dormers. The soft glow of an inside lamp radiated through a side window. Cody crept quietly toward the house.

"Now what?" Shelby whispered.

"We need to find out what's going on inside."

"And how do you propose we do that?"

Cody looked around and located a lobster trap. He positioned it below the living room window and climbed on top. The others waited in silence near the edge of the driveway.

"Well, what do you see, Cowpoke?" Shelby asked impatiently.

Cody stared in through the window for a few minutes, then stepped down, feeling disgusted. He shook his head and began walking back up the path.

"Come on," he said.

"What? What did you see?" Martin asked.

Cody kept walking.

"Cody Hawke!"

He stopped and frowned at his siblings. It was almost too painful to admit he was wrong.

"Sharkey's in there with quite possibly the most beautiful woman I've ever seen," Cody said.

"What? Are you *kidding* me, Cowpoke?" Shelby snapped. "Criminal activity? I broke a shoe, had to wash dishes, got soaked, and got bird poop all over my new jacket for *this*?"

"And, don't think for one little red-hot minute we are leaving here without me getting a look!" Martin called.

"Shush!" Shelby admonished. "He'll hear you."

Martin ran back and tried his best to climb onto the lobster trap. He had finally made it up when Cody heard male voices emanating from the backyard.

"Martin! Get down! Someone's coming!" Cody whispered.

"How did they get here?" Shelby asked. "We should have seen them coming up the path?"

"Maybe they came by boat," Charlotte said.

The four peeked around the corner of a nearby shed, squinting anxiously in the growing dark. Finally, Cody finally saw what he had expected to find all along. Two men wearing dark pants and T-shirts with chains around their necks approached the house. It was apparent this place – or something in it – was of interest to them. Their swarthy complexion, hoop earrings, and tattooed arms gave them a pirate-like appearance, but something about them wasn't right.

"Do they look…" Shelby began.

"Almost like zombies?" Martin replied.

One of the men climbed atop the lobster trap and looked inside, just as they had. He spoke roughly to the other man. The two ducked down and headed around to the back of the house, as if casing the place for a way in.

Uh-oh. This can't be good. Should we warn Sharkey? If we do, he'll certainly want to know what we're doing here.

"Are they going to break into the house?" Charlotte whispered?

"You guys stay here. I'm going to follow them."

"Cody Hawke, you are not going anywhere without us," Shelby declared.

The sound of breaking glass was followed by dark shadows visible through a back window. The shadows headed toward the front of the house where Sam Sharkey and his woman waited, unknowing.

"We should do something," Martin urged, "but what?"

Cody picked up a couple small stones and lobbed them at the living room window. He wondered if Sharkey heard the warning, and if so, what he would do. A scuffle erupted inside. Shadows lunged, darting back and forth. Suddenly the front door opened and one of the men came flying out as if he had been thrown. The second man followed.

Sam Sharkey stood in the doorway. "Go back to the hole you crawled out of and stay there," he growled.

The men ran toward the backyard, presumably to a waiting boat. Sharkey surveyed the area from the side porch until the pirates disappeared down the hill, then went back inside. Cody could make out the outline of the woman through the window as she ran into his arms.

"Oh, my, what a strong and virile man." Shelby whispered, nearly swooning.

Cody hoped his smirk let her know how he felt about that. He tried to think of a clever comeback, but nothing came to mind.

"Oh, no, it's almost time to meet Jack!" Charlotte cried, glancing at her watch. "We only have a few minutes to get back to Dawnport."

The four looked at each other, clearly realizing they were in trouble. Cody took a moment to assess their limited options. They could talk to Sharkey, let him know they had followed him to Dawnport. Maybe he would drive them to town. They could head back to the center of town on foot, a seemingly impossible task in a few minutes, especially with Shelby and Martin limping.

"Let's try to get back to town," Cody ordered. "We'll call Jack's cell in a few minutes and let him know we're on our way. Think of a story that sounds convincing."

"Why don't we just call Jack and have him pick us up here?" Martin asked.

"Because, then we have to explain what we're doing in the middle of nowhere, a couple miles from where we said we'd be," Cody replied briskly.

They headed back down the path in silence, Cody leading the way. A quarter moon provided scant light in the looming darkness.

"For once, I'll be happy to see that smelly old v—" Shelby began.

"Oh, *no!*" Cody yelled.

"What?" Shelby stopped next to him. He grabbed her arm, pulling her back.

Cody turned to face Charlotte and Martin. "Do *not* move."

"Cody? What's wrong?" Charlotte asked.

"We're *dead.*"

He picked up a stone and tossed it into the darkness.

Kerplunk.

"In answer to your question about whether it floods here, Charlotte, it does. The tide came in and the path is under water. We're stuck here until morning."

Chapter 9: The Incarceration

After an agonizing call to a furious Jack, a humiliating knock on Sharkey's door, and an hour-long rant from Martin on how much he fancied Sam's lady friend, the teens finally passed out. Sharkey had wanted them to sleep on the living room floor, but Aluria insisted they use the spare bedrooms.

The following morning, the four devoured the stuffed-French-toast breakfast their hostess made like it was their last meal. They thanked Aluria profusely for her hospitality and Sharkey drove them home, an arrogant smirk gracing his expression the entire way.

"What were you doing snooping around my friend's home?" he asked as they passed Dawnport.

"The bigger question," Cody said irritably, "is why you told Jack you needed a place to stay when you obviously have a *friend* in town?"

"That, Mr. Hawke, is none of your business."

The uncomfortable silence that followed, lasted until they reached Freya Manor's long driveway.

"Mr. Sharkey?" Charlotte piped up. "Who is Thorvald Drynurr, the wealthy financier funding your missions on the Independence X?"

The man's head turned abruptly and the smirk left his face.

"So, you've been snooping online also," he replied.

Suddenly Charlotte gasped. They all looked at her, waiting for an explanation, but none was forthcoming.

Jack met them at the door and confirmed they were grounded for a month. To say his siblings were sore at him would've been an understatement. Cody tried to convince their father taking a walk to the far side of town had been his idea and the others shouldn't be incarcerated, but Jack wasn't buying it. He said they should all be old enough to know right from wrong.

"Families don't lie to each other," he said.

Cody stopped to lean on the handle of his mop. As he wiped the perspiration from his forehead, a quick scan of the foyer told him he wasn't even halfway done. He slammed the mop back into the bucket causing water to spill over the sides.

"Charlotte?" he asked, watching her wring out the mop she was using to dry the floor. "Yesterday, when you asked Sharkey about the Independence, it sounded like you realized something."

Shelby and Martin stopped washing the windows and looked over as well.

"I-uh…" Charlotte glanced around to see if anyone was nearby. Satisfied, she went on. "I realized Drynurr is just an anagram of the word Rúndyrr," she said quietly. "It's almost like he made up the whole thing. Maybe it's all a lie, working with NOAA and mapping the ocean floor."

"Cody?" Heather called. "Dinner's ready."

He quietly joined the rest of the family at the table. Keeping to himself meant fewer angry stares. They were having something called Swedish meatballs over egg noodles. He wasn't sure what Swedish meatballs were supposed to taste like, however, if it was rock-hard little balls swimming in a pool of canned beef gravy, then Heather's rendition was spot on.

"Are we going to do anything now that it's summer vacation?" Jessica asked perkily.

"Do you mean go somewhere?" Jack asked. "Honey, you know I can't leave the store," he added before she could respond.

"I might take you kids on some day trips," Heather offered warmly.

We, on the other hand, will be doing chores, lots and lots of chores.

Cody winced slightly, reaching for the bowl of noodles. His arms felt like jelly after spending the last few days cleaning and chopping wood, with Sharkey as his dictator boss. Martin, Shelby, and Charlotte were charged with stacking the wood in neat piles. It was a bitter pill to swallow, being this man's flunky when Cody was just trying to protect the family from his sinister plans.

"Oh, my! Have you ever seen a more beautiful outfit?" Shelby said, holding up a magazine.

While he savagely attacked the buttered noodles, Shelby rambled on about the outfit social media celebrity, Kala Bennington wore to some party. Then, Gabby took over and it was ten minutes on the virtues of Q-tips to remove ear wax. Their words washed about in Cody's head like ocean spray hitting the rocks, but couldn't douse the fire burning in his gut.

"Who took my Dodgers pennant?" he asked somewhat curtly, pushing back his empty plate. He already knew the answer, but was waiting to see whether there would be a confession.

"It wasn't me," Jack mumbled. "Did anyone take Cody's pennant?"

Cody watched as Jack scanned the table. No one offered an answer.

"I see one that looks exactly like mine hanging in *your* room, Terrell," Cody said evenly.

"Terrell, did you take Cody's pennant? We don't take things that don't belong to us in this family."

"Me?" Terrell asked innocently. "No, I had one of my own, right Gabby?"

"Huh?" She gave him a deer-in-the-headlights stare. "The Dodgers…" Gabby thought for a moment. "Weren't they in the World Series?"

"You know they were," Terrell said, rolling his eyes at the girl. "That's when my dad sent me the National League pennant."

"Did you know the Dodgers used to play in New York City?" Gabby offered.

"Really?" Jessica asked.

Don't encourage her.

"Brooklyn, to be exact. They moved to L.A. like, sixty years ago or something." Gabby opened her mouth to continue. "But, I—"

"My pennant was from 1988," Cody interrupted. "It was my *dad's*."

"Yeah, mine, too," Terrell replied. "It was my dad's, also."

"No, you have *mine*," Cody said crossly. "Your dad wasn't even *born* in 1988."

"Oh, yeah? Well, it was *his* father's pennant, my grandfather," Terrell explained absently.

Cody could feel his face redden. "You change your story every time I say something. You *know* that's my pennant."

"Cody," Jack mumbled, "let's discuss this later."

"But, he's—"

"Later, Cody."

Sam Sharkey had been staying with them for a few weeks and Cody still had no idea what he was up to. It was clear Sharkey had sought Jack out in the hopes of arranging this situation. But why? And where did he go during his frequent trips? Was it always to visit that same woman?

Cody climbed into bed and pulled the covers up to his chin, but he couldn't quell the thoughts echoing in his head. Sharkey certainly seemed to know The Gatekeeper. What was their relationship? He tried asking The Gatekeeper again, but the old man dismissed him with a wave of his hand.

"Cody?" Jack was standing in the doorway.

"Jack? What's wrong?" he asked, propping himself up on his elbows.

"Listen, son," Jack said, taking a seat on the edge of Cody's bed. "I'm sorry about the pennant. I know it's yours—"

"So, tell him to give it back!" he said irritably.

"Cody," Jack said softly, running a hand through his thinning hair, "I know it means a lot to you and I promise it won't leave this house," his father added, "but, I'm asking you to let it go for now."

Cody scowled. "So, it's okay for them to just get away with anything they want?"

"No. No, it's not." Jack looked down, apparently trying to find words that would make Cody understand. "But think about it from his perspective," he said. "His father's in jail and probably not getting out any time soon. He was taken from his mother years ago and put in foster care because she was an addict and couldn't take care of him. She finally contacted him last year, said she was doing better, but the day she was supposed to pick him up, they found her body."

"Whoa," Cody said in a choked voice. "That's awful."

"Yes, it is," Jack said.

"I didn't know."

Cody thought he saw his father's eyes glisten. It occurred to him how incredible his new parents were. He didn't appreciate how much Jack and Heather gave of themselves, how much they sacrificed to show these kids love, maybe for the first time in their lives. He always looked at them as oddballs, but maybe he'd been wrong. They were the strongest and kindest people he knew.

Cody stopped to take a fragrant breath of summer air as he carried Jack's bucket of tools to the bay side of Freya Manor. The zinnias Heather planted were in full bloom, creating a bright pink circle around the base of the obelisk that towered over their front yard.

He and Martin helped Sam Sharkey repair the wood planking on the deck by their side door. It had been damaged during a spring thunderstorm. They removed the old boards, cut new pieces and nailed them to the stringers beneath. Cody stood back and admired their handiwork, thinking they were done.

"Martin, want to throw a ball around?" he asked.

"Not yet, Mr. Hawke," Sharkey interjected. "We still need to put a coat of stain and sealer on this wood or you'll be replacing it again next year." Sharkey rubbed the stubble on his chin. "Go down to the basement storage room and find the paint cans I left in the far corner."

"Where are *you* going?" Cody wondered.

"I'll be right here."

"No, I mean after you leave Freya Manor."

"I told you, we'll be mapping the North Atlantic and hopefully locating that elusive shipwreck..." Sharkey hesitated, checking his watch. "Now go see if you can find that stain. The brushes are in the bag next to it."

Cody and Martin stepped through the screen door into the coolness of the shaded hall. "And bring a screwdriver!" Sharkey yelled.

"Something's going on," Cody said, stopping to peek back out the door.

"Cody, give it up. Let's just find the paint," Martin muttered tersely.

"Why did he check his watch?" Cody hesitated. "It's 2 o'clock. He's got something going on, I know it. Wait here."

Cody tiptoed cautiously outside with Martin grumbling behind him.

"He's not here," Cody called over his shoulder.

"Where could he have gone? We just left him ten seconds ago," Martin replied from the doorway.

"The maze!"

Cody ran to the other side of the house, past the two seemingly dead trees guarding the hedge labyrinth's entrance. Navigating his way through the turns, he reflected on all the times the old maze had beaten them. Now it seemed so easy. He heard Martin behind him, breathing loudly.

"Cody, slow down, I can't—"

"Ssh! He's in there."

Cody peered into the cave, then hid behind the foundation wall. The Guardian and Sharkey were walking toward them.

"Get back," he whispered to Martin.

"…I only have a minute. The kids are getting some paint."

"Let's go, before they see us," Martin whispered with obvious urgency.

"I think they stopped," Cody mumbled. "Hang on a second."

"…Obviously, I'm familiar with the area," Sharkey declared. "You said it's about an hour from Reykjavik? Hopefully I can triangulate the location."

"Yes." Cody recognized The Guardian's gravelly voice. "And, it must be at least a thousand years old because that is when I recall seeing it last. Is that of help? I just can't remember anymore."

"Hmm." Sharkey added. "I'll bet its Buri. It's been closed for a few years now. Inconsiderate tourists were damaging the cave."

"Perhaps. When will you leave?"

"Thursday."

"You must save it, otherwise…" The Guardian sounded uncharacteristically shaken."

"No worries, old man. Have I ever let you down before?"

Chapter 10: The Voyage

"Try to remember, Cody. What were his exact words?"

"Charlotte, we didn't have Miss Total Recall with us," Cody said, pacing the bedroom floor. "It was the name of a place. I've heard it before.

"Sharkey said it was an hour from there," Martin said, biting his lip. "Wait! Ray something…"

"Reykjavik?"

"That's it, Charlotte!" Cody yelled excitedly.

"It's the capital city of Iceland," Charlotte added.

"Sweet!" Cody said. "But there was another name. He said, 'Must be Bur-ree', or, something like that."

"I've never heard of that. If it's a town, I guess it's a small one," Charlotte replied.

"So, he's leaving in a week. But, what does it all mean? Why Iceland? And, why did The Guardian seem so worried? Something about 'saving it'. Save what?" Cody wondered aloud.

"Sharkey said he wouldn't let him down," Martin added. "Sounded kind of serious to me."

"Obviously, he knows The Guardian also," Cody said, deep in thought. "Hey, maybe we should use Rúndyrr to try and figure this out."

"Oh, no, Cody Hawke! I don't think so! Every time we go on one of your stupid adventures, I ruin an outfit or a pair of shoes," Shelby grumbled.

Cody stopped pacing. "Aren't you totally crazy over this? How can you just let it go?"

"It's healthier that way!" she replied.

"Cody, The Gatekeeper clearly doesn't want us involved," Charlotte declared. "He's given us absolutely no help. What makes you think he's going to send us there."

"We'll make sure to concentrate. Sharkey's not going to another time or someplace dangerous, just Iceland in the current year. How bad could it be?" Cody turned to his siblings. "Besides, if there is bad stuff going on, he could use our help."

"I doubt that," Martin said. "But, if everyone else agrees, I'm in."

"Fine, Cowpoke. I *know* I'm going to regret this," Shelby said with a deep sigh. "I just don't know how *much* yet."

Cody rolled over in bed wondering what might be in store for them and for Sam Sharkey. Could the man be trying to protect their mysterious secret or endanger it? And, why was The Guardian concerned about Iceland? Should they be worried as well? Did it all have something to do with Rúndyrr? There were lots of questions and very few answers. He had just closed his eyes when suddenly he felt a hand on his arm.

"Cody!" The voice whispered hoarsely. "Cody, wake up!"

He bolted up, glancing around in a panic.

"Jeez, Charlotte, I just fell asleep." Cody rubbed his eyes. "You almost gave me a heart attack. What the heck is so urgent at one in the morning?"

"I got it, Cody. I think I figured out what Sam Sharkey will be looking for. I mean, I'm not actually sure, but I *could* be right."

"I'm listening."

"It's The Light of Nimbus!" She could barely contain her excitement.

Chapter 11: The Wizard

Cody couldn't quite put his finger on exactly what Heather's cheese omelets tasted like, however, he knew it wasn't eggs or cheese. He reached for the ketchup then glanced at Terrell, scooping up forkfuls like it was his last meal. Cody thought about what Jack had said. The boy put on a brave face, like he didn't care, but Cody knew it was a defense mechanism to help him cope.

Jack finished his breakfast then folded the cartoon section of the newspaper under his arm and headed toward the hallway. Jessica began a five-minute dissertation on which came first, the chicken or the egg. Gabby started in on the difficulties of a foster home with six kids and only one bathroom.

Cody was trying to tune them out when he saw something that made him gasp. Charlotte, Martin, and Shelby all looked up, clearly expecting some sort of explanation, staring at him in anxious silence. Cody reached for the newspaper. He hesitated for a moment then turned it so the others could see.

TWO PIRATES FOUND DEAD IN PASSAMAQUODDY BAY – Police confirm foul play.

Sharkey! But why? He threw them off his porch, but they were definitely alive. Why would he kill them? Did they come back after we left? Who are they and what did they want from him? Are we living with a murderer?

"Maybe they were involved in something illegal," Martin said, as they crossed the lawn.

"You know how Dawnport is with their pirates and that crazy pirate festival," Charlotte offered. "It could just be a coincidence. Maybe these are not the same guys we saw. Maybe it's just two townspeople who dressed up as a gag and ended up drowning in the bay."

"Okay, but the pirate festival isn't for another month and how about drowning in the bay with a hole in their chests!" Cody said testily. "I'll bet it was the *Peacemaker!* We need to find out what's going on with this guy. Enough fooling around, we need answers."

Cody headed into the maze, his unzipped parka fanning out behind. He knew he was going too fast for the others to keep up, but the angrier he got, the faster he walked.

"Stop jumping to conclusions, Cowpoke," Shelby called to him.

"I'm not jumping to anything," he said testily. "You guys are so taken with him you can't see reality."

"Like I said, maybe it has something to do with The Light," Charlotte called.

Cody waited briefly at the cave entrance, then disappeared into the darkness.

"Dost thou wish to embark on a journey?" The Gatekeeper's deep voice reverberated throughout the cavern.

"Yes, yes we do," Cody began, waiting for the other teens to join him.

"Art thou planning on snow?" the man asked, his voice edged with amusement as he glanced at their parkas.

"We would like to visit Iceland," Cody said.

"And learn more about the Light of—" Charlotte's words were abruptly cut off by The Gatekeeper's riddle. Cody thought it almost sounded intentional.

It makes up the band our eyes can see,
Moving in waves all about thee.
Infrared extends beyond our red,
Ultraviolet beyond violet instead.

Appearing to us as totally white,
Breaking down into colors ever so bright.

"Lovely, another dark, dreary place," Shelby said, then turned toward Charlotte. "Honey, how did you know 'visible light' was the answer to the riddle?"

Charlotte shrugged and added, "Visible light makes up the section of light waves humans can see. Infrared and ultraviolet are outside our range of vision."

"This place looks more like the *absence* of light," Martin quipped.

"Yeah," Cody said with a frown. "We asked to learn more about The Light, so either he completely ignored our request or things should brighten up soon."

They made their way through a grassy field toward what appeared to be a narrow road. A sliver of moon hovering above the horizon created long shadows at their feet.

"Now which way?" Shelby asked.

Cody looked up and down the dark street, lifting the hood on his jacket.

"Any ideas?" he said.

"You know, a neon sign with the words, 'This Way' would be helpful." Martin looked up as if talking to The Gatekeeper, then blew on his hands for warmth.

"I think I see a spot of light over there," Cody said, pointing to the right. "Let's head that way."

Zippering his jacket to combat the chilly wind whipping through leafless trees, Cody stepped onto the gravel road. He noticed a house on the opposite side of the street, barely visible in the inky black.

"It looks like we're in a small town," Martin offered.

"Do you think it's the current year?" Shelby asked. "The homes look similar to those in Dawnport."

"It's hard to tell," Charlotte replied. "It could be an old town with new houses or a present-day town with old houses. It's hard to tell in the dark. Perhaps the bigger question is, are we in Iceland."

"Would it kill them to install a streetlight?" Martin muttered, stumbling over some debris in the roadway.

"Do you suppose we can *die* here?" Charlotte wondered.

"Well, that's certainly an uplifting thought, honey," Shelby mumbled.

"I mean, is it *possible* for us to die here, or is this just a façade?" she added.

"Not sure what façade means, but it feels real enough," Cody muttered, especially the cold wind.

"Could we contract smallpox, the Black Death, or even get lice from someone?" Charlotte asked.

Shelby stopped abruptly. "Lice? Cody Hawke, if I get lice in my hair from one of these stupid trips, you will *never* hear the end of it!"

"Shelby, out of those three, you're concerned about *lice*?" Martin exclaimed.

"As Radianna indicated, we're visiting alternate dimensions," Charlotte said. "Time is just another dimension. It's explained in physics, specifically quantum theory. Despite the fact that The Gatekeeper selects the dimensions for us, I'd say they are still real, at least real to us. They're all part of the fabric of infinite paths we can take in life."

"I don't understand a thing you just said," Martin quipped.

"So, is that a yes or no?" Cody asked.

"I'm not certain," Charlotte said, flashing a silly smile. "Maybe it's best we not know."

They reached a cross street sprinkled with old homes. Cody glanced up and down, but all were dark and quiet.

"Keep heading straight," he said. "That area seems to hold the only sign of life."

"Don't you find that a bit strange?" Charlotte murmured. "No one's home in *any* of these houses."

"It's like they all left in a hurry," Shelby replied anxiously. "I hope something bad isn't about to happen."

"Like what?" Cody asked.

"Like maybe war is coming," Shelby said. "We've seen that movie. Or, perhaps there's a terrible disease going around."

"Or, maybe they're just all at church," Martin mumbled.

They walked for a few minutes in silence. Cody hoped the reason for their journey would soon become apparent as he contemplated Charlotte's concerns.

Could they be susceptible to some awful disease? What would happen if one of them got shot? Could they die here?

"I hear voices." Shelby's voice broke the silence.

"Maybe it's a little league game," Martin said.

As they drew closer, Cody saw a large group of people gathered in the compound ahead. Men, women, and even children stared in rapt silence, something on the field captivating their attention.

"These lights are propped up on makeshift poles," Cody said as they passed.

"Looks like they put this event together in a hurry," Charlotte added.

"Love the outfits," Martin said with a chuckle. "I'm guessing this is *not* the current year."

To their left, a middle-aged man stared intently ahead. His dark necktie highlighted the white shirt and dark vest beneath what Shelby referred to as a double-breasted coat. As if sensing his fascinated audience, the man pulled out a gleaming watch attached to a chain. After a quick check of the time, he flipped it closed, dropping it back into a waiting pocket.

Many people in the crowd stood on tiptoe, apparently to get a better view. The men to their right were dressed more casually, sporting baggy denim jeans with suspenders and well-worn coats. Cody wondered if perhaps they were farmers.

"What are they all *staring* at?" Shelby said, jumping up and down. "I don't see anything."

"Yeah, it's just a few buildings in an empty field." Cody added. "Whatever they're waiting for must not have arrived yet."

Cody glanced at a woman to his right, trying to determine the direction of her awestruck gaze. The fitted jacket she wore extended most of the way down a long, ruffled skirt. She fidgeted nervously with the lace scarf tied in a bow around her neck.

"Doesn't anyone around here own an iron?" Martin chuckled. "Their clothes look like they've been slept in for months."

The woman glanced in their direction. Cody winced, wondering if she had heard Martin's comment.

"The Wizard has yet to appear," she offered excitedly, nodding in their direction. "How could one even *imagine* such a triumphant display?"

Shelby smiled and nodded back. "*Very* triumphant," she replied, then glanced at the others, her face contorted in obvious confusion. "What wizard? What display?" she whispered.

"I guess there's going to be a magic show," Cody replied.

"The *Wizard?*" Charlotte mumbled pensively. "This looks to be around the turn of the twentieth century. No one believed in wizards. What could she be talking about?"

"*Achoo!*" Martin sniffled then added, "I don't see any display . . . triumphant or otherwise."

"Excuse me, ma'am," Shelby said, as she leaned in the woman's direction. "Might I ask, exactly *what* triumphant display are we looking at?"

The woman stared at Shelby like she had two heads, momentarily speechless. "I think perhaps you need spectacles!" she said crossly. Seemingly appalled, she walked away making huffing noises.

"I'm sorry," Shelby called, "but I don't see anything."

"You're not the only one," Cody said, frowning.

Suddenly the crowd of onlookers began to surge forward, converging into a line that ran alongside a nearby fence. Cody and the teens waited at the back of the line.

"I'll bet it's a Christmas display they're looking at," Shelby added. "I see boughs of greenery hanging on the doors and windows."

A boy, perhaps ten years old, darted about behind them, clearly uninspired by the long wait. He grabbed a stick and ran it along the fence, making whirring sounds. His clothing was akin to that of the men, long pants with a dark coat, but knitted mittens and a muffler were added to combat the crisp air.

"Hello, young man." Shelby called.

"'Allo." He eyed Shelby up and down then looked at the other teens. "You look funny. Are you circus performers?"

Shelby giggled. "Kind of."

The boy grew serious, suddenly taken with the front of Shelby's jacket. "What is *that?*" he asked, his mouth hanging open.

Shelby glanced frantically downward. "What? Is there a *bug* on me?"

"Nah," he said with a laugh. "But there's a shiny thing that looks like it has teeth."

"This?" She pulled down on her zipper. "Ah! You don't have these yet?"

"No, ma'am! Does it bite?"

"No." Shelby laughed. "Well, maybe, if you get your finger caught in it."

He grinned, looking up at her. "You're pretty."

Shelby smiled, showing him how the zipper opened and closed. As he stared in silent fascination, she moved closer so the adults couldn't hear.

"So, tell me. What's all the fuss about?"

"This?" he turned toward the main building and waved his arm. "It's the Wizard... and his show."

"Is *he* a circus performer?" Shelby asked.

"Ha! That's funny! That's what my mom thought. She didn't believe it," he said, grabbing the stick and running it along the fence. "That's why we came to see it for ourselves," he called over his shoulder.

"What year is this?" Shelby asked.

"You don't know the year?" He laughed. "Girls are dumb. It's New Year's Eve! Tomorrow begins the year 1880."

"Hey, I am not dumb."

Cody stood behind Shelby. Pointing at her head, he grinned and nodded. The boy laughed.

Shelby gave him a smack "So," she continued, "does this Wizard have a name?"

"Yeah, The Wizard..."

"Henry!" A woman's shrill voice cut through the night. It sounded insistent.

"I gotta go," he said, running off.

After waiting in line for about ten minutes, they were channeled through an open gate. It led to a compound containing various buildings. Everyone seemed to be heading toward the largest one. Anxious to get out of the cold, the teens followed the crowd inside.

"I hope they're not making Frankenstein in here," Martin quipped.

The building contained a laboratory of some sort. Soft lights illuminated many strange looking contraptions scattered across long wooden tables. Shelves on the walls displayed various jars and glass items, reminding Cody of an antique museum.

An assistant, standing in front of an elevated podium, barked information to the crowd. He described the dynamos, vacuum pumps, and various other gizmos on display. An oddly-shaped glowing bulb immersed in a jar full of water, seemed to enthrall many of the spectators.

"LOOK!" A man yelled suddenly. "It's *him*! It's The *WIZARD!*"

"Oh, my! The Wizard!" a woman added. "It's really him!"

A throng of eager followers ran in the man's direction, shouting questions in unison.

"That's the *Wizard?*" Cody mumbled. "He doesn't look like a wizard to me, just an average guy in his thirties wearing a wrinkled suit."

"Yeah," Martin added. "I thought at least the guy would be wearing a cape and top hat."

"He's quite handsome," Shelby declared. "I wonder who he could be."

"Handsome?" Cody frowned. "He reminds me of the Wizard of Oz."

The man answered a few questions in simple language that seemed to appeal to the masses. They hung on his every word. It reminded Cody of a celebrity doing a photo-op, though the Wizard did not seem to relish the attention. His demeanor gave the impression he saw it as the price of fame.

"We will make it so cheap, only the *rich* will burn candles," The Wizard yelled, much to the delight of his fans, who cheered and clapped their appreciation.

The four teens made their way to a table containing what appeared to be a replica of the compound. Lab assistants surrounded the exhibit, trying to protect it from overzealous fans. Suddenly a man in a dark suit slipped through, carrying a jar filled with liquid. He dumped the liquid onto the display, managing to short-circuit the lights.

Everyone stared as the assistants forcibly removed him from the building. All except Cody. He couldn't take his eyes off the Wizard, who used the distraction as an opportunity to make a quiet getaway.

"Come on!" he whispered, rushing down the main aisle.

Cody ducked out the back door with the others close behind. He followed the Wizard across the compound to another building. Inside was a cozy living room with a fireplace.

"That way," Shelby whispered, as The Wizard disappeared through a door in the far corner.

Cody made his way across the room and cautiously opened the door. It led to a narrow hallway. Soft light illuminated a room at the far end. They tip-toed down the hall, entering what appeared to be an office. The Wizard looked up from his desk.

"Hello, sir. I'm Cody and this is—"

"Please," the man interjected, "the demonstrations are back in the other building. I do not allow visitors in my office." He seemed tired.

"I-uh," Cody struggled to find the right words. "I-I know, and I'm sorry. We are not here to bother you." He took a breath. "We just need your help with a question. It's hard to explain, but I think we need the benefit of your knowledge to help us get home."

The Wizard sat back, appearing genuinely suspicious.

"Are you another one of those *spies* sent by the gas company to sabotage my work?" he snapped. The aggravation left his face as he gazed at the teens, clearly trying to make sense of their strange attire.

"Definitely *not*," Charlotte replied.

"Are you reporters?" he asked, regaining his composure.

"No, we just need your help with a scientific question," Martin added.

"Why are they trying to sabotage your work?" Shelby asked.

"They are afraid of the success we have achieved and how it will affect the gas company's future."

"Is that why you are having this demonstration?" Cody asked.

The Wizard nodded and sighed. "One year ago, this past September, I informed the *New York Sun* I had succeeded in achieving the subdivision of light."

"What happened?" Martin asked.

Again, he sighed. "I told them we were ready with the perfected outcome, one that will not pain the eyes, stay lit for hours, and be of good utility to the general public. I had the correct principle however the accomplishment was not as straightforward as expected," he added with a grimace. "My comments were premature and my reputation damaged.

98

"I'm sorry," Shelby said softly.

"Plus, William Sawyer is claiming I have infringed upon his patent, yet *he* is unable to make it work." Fire danced in The Wizard's eyes. "He and others are saying my announcement was just a ploy to raise money in the capital markets," the man added.

"It doesn't sound like they're playing fair," Shelby said.

"No, they are not. But I have *finally* done it," he exclaimed, a wide grin suddenly pervading his weary expression. "I've put to rest the naysayers. Hitherto, the public will know it is here at last!" His animated voice exuded passion. "Soon I will be able to install my light centers in lower Manhattan," he rambled excitedly. "There will be power stations providing current to businesses and homes. It will be magnificent! *And...*" The man hesitated, shaking his head.

"Are you okay, sir?" Shelby asked as The Wizard paused to stare at the group.

"I am sorry, carrying on about myself. How can I assist with your scientific question?"

"How does it work, sir?" Charlotte asked.

"It is *so* very simple," he said, picking up an odd-looking object from his desk, beaming like a man introducing his children. "Electric current coming from the dynamo flows along this wire," he said, running his finger along a length of copper wire dangling from the bottom.

"What's a dynamo?" Cody wondered aloud.

"A dynamo generates electricity. It converts mechanical energy – you know, movement – to electrical energy using a magnetic field. That's a fancy way of saying it rotates a big copper wire between two magnets to generate electricity."

"How do you get the electricity to flow?" Shelby asked.

"Why it flows in everything, but it *especially* likes copper wire. You see, copper has very little resistance, and electricity *wants* to travel along the wire. The carbonized filament, however, has *much* resistance." He pointed to the wavy part of the wire inside the glass. "So, the electricity dances happily along the copper wire until it reaches the filament, at which point it has to huff and puff to get through."

The four teens laughed.

"The energy created from that effort," he continued, "makes the filament glow."

"I actually understood that," Shelby said. "You have a great way of explaining things."

"So, making it shine is just having electricity do what comes natural?" Charlotte asked.

"Precisely! Although, we do create a vacuum inside to increase its longevity," The Wizard added, "and, finding the right filament material took time, but it is *such* a simple concept."

"As we were walking up the street, we didn't see any lights on in the houses—" Shelby began.

"Because there *are* none," Charlotte interrupted excitedly. "We were trying to understand what everyone outside was *staring* at—"

"They were staring at the *lights*," Martin exclaimed. "*That's* what had them so excited."

"The Wizard of Menlo Park," Charlotte said, seemingly awestruck.

Suddenly it all made sense to Cody. The houses were dark because there were no lights. Until now, the only nighttime illumination came from the moon or dangerous gas lamps. The lamps smelled foul and gave off irritating smoke. There were no transformers, no power lines, no outlets or toaster ovens and no electric lights. None of that had happened yet.

The public was entrenched in a frenzied obsession with something that would become so commonplace Cody couldn't even imagine a time when it was not around – the lightbulb.

"Now people will be able to do things at night," Martin said, "like read or do homework." He glanced at Cody, then frowned. "Maybe we should keep this thing quiet," he joked.

"No wonder the gas companies are mad at you," Shelby added. "What will they do when everyone has electric lights in their homes instead of gas lamps?"

"They'll go out of business," Martin added.

"Exactly," The Wizard replied. "That is their fear."

"Uh, Mr. Wizard? What does this mean?" Shelby asked, then recited the second riddle.

"Electrons jump along its atom train,
In copper, they move with minimal drain.

But when they reach the carbon so resistant,
They shine like a star that's not so distant."

Cody watched as Shelby's eyes flew open wide. "The electric light!"

"Mr. Edison," Charlotte spoke softly, "It has been *such* a thrill to meet you! And, you said it Shelby, the answer to the riddle, the electric light bulb."

"The *Light*," Cody said with a grin. He could see The Gatekeeper awaiting them on the other side.

Chapter 12: The Demon

"Mr. Gatekeeper, that was cool, but we were trying to learn about The Light of Nim—"

"Shh!" he replied briskly.

"Yeah, not the light *bulb*," Shelby added with a smile.

"It is best you not know," the old man said fretfully, then turned to walk away.

"Why? After all we've been through, you don't think you can trust us?" Cody asked.

The Gatekeeper stopped and glared back at them, fire smoldering in his eyes.

"Thou doth not understand the danger! Sometimes, thou must trust others."

"What does that mean? Sharkey broke into our home, went through Rúndyrr, and stole a chest full of treasure! And you allowed him!" Cody retorted. "You seem to trust *him*."

"Things are not always as they seem."

"Okay, so explain it to…" Cody began, then became distracted by movement across the cave.

A dark cloud approached, its eerie moan filling the air. The Gatekeeper turned abruptly, then looked back, his face losing all its color.

"RUN!" he hissed with obvious urgency. "HURRY!"

"What . . . what *is* that?" Cody murmured.

The Guardian emerged hastily from an opening on the opposite side of the cavern. The Gatekeeper yelled something in another language. A scraping sound filled the grotto as one of the cave doors slid open. Pitaskog, The Horned Serpent, emerged from the darkness, encircling the veil of black with its slithering body. As Pitaskog squeezed, the shadow began to solidify.

"*RUN!*" The Gatekeeper repeated.

The cloud began to transform into what appeared to be folds of black fabric swinging from a long cloak. Pitaskog opened its mouth, preparing to attack. As the entity solidified, an ashen face with glowing eyes became visible under the dark hood. Clawed hands emerged to push back the cape.

"Oh, *my*," Shelby croaked.

The creature was tall with a hooked nose and horns sweeping up from its head. As Pitaskog closed its massive jaws, the creature let out a blood-curdling shriek, revealing black pencil-like teeth that quickly took a chunk out of Pitaskog's neck. The serpent reeled back, blood gushing from its wounds.

"CODY!" Shelby screamed. "WHAT IN THE NAME OF KITTY HAWK *IS* THAT THING?"

The Gatekeeper turned toward them. It was the first time Cody had seen fear in the man's eyes.

"The Darkness controls three demon sisters," he croaked. "The Icelandic people call this one Grýla. The Slavic people refer to another as Hala and the Greeks call the third Lamia. He glanced at Grýla then back at Cody. "Answer, quickly," he said, whispering a riddle.

"These three terms describe the way;
Travel is navigated every day.
For pleasure, for work, or a trip to a star,
No matter how high, no matter how far;
Up, down, tilt, or side to side,
Control is maintained using this as a guide."

"I know this one!" Martin offered in a strangely distracted tone. "A guy at one of my foster homes was into gas powered model airplanes. He explained to me about roll, pitch, and yaw. They describe the directions a plane can move: nose side to side, up and down, and rolling side to side—"

"Martin, who *cares* about roll, pitch, and *whatever!*" Shelby cried. "Do you *see* that thing?"

Pitaskog and the demon continued their bloody dance. The Gatekeeper touched the wall, then lifted his staff, as if preparing for battle. Cody opened his mouth, but before he could speak, the four were drawn into the doorway, the return riddle echoing in his head.

"It raises an object straight up, so high,
Then forces it along, across the sky.
Tie a rope and watch the object hover;
Draw two lines, one straight up and one over,
Perfecting the formulas takes a logical mind,
But the results will soar for all mankind."

Cody looked back as they crossed the bridge. His last glimpse was of Pitaskog's bloodied form lying on the ground and the demon's evil eyes as she turned toward The Gatekeeper.

"*NO!*"

Chapter 13: The Mathematicians

A chilly wind whipped Cody's face. His numb hands were clutching the wing of a biplane as it hovered above a sandy beach. Cody assumed the muffled yell he heard came from Martin, desperately gripping the wing on his right. The rushing air made it difficult to breathe. He could hear Shelby and Charlotte's distant screams and assumed they were on the other side.

"Are you alright?" Cody yelled to Martin.

"I am *not* letting go. I am *not* letting go…" the teen repeated, his eyes closed.

Their added weight began to pull the plane down after a journey lasting only about ten seconds. It felt like a lifetime. The plane thudded heavily into the sand and came skidding to a halt. Martin lost his grip and flew off the wing, landing in the sand about five meters ahead.

"Buddy?" Cody yelled. "Are you okay?"

A man Cody estimated to be in his early thirties climbed down from the control area. His dark hair had been pushed back by the wind, revealing a slightly receding hairline. The man's moustache twitched with frustration as he approached Cody, still tightly gripping the front edge of the wing.

"May I ask, sir, what you are *doing* on the wing of our aeroplane?" He spoke sternly, unable to hide his disappointment, presumably over the shortened flight.

"I-uh..." Cody rolled off the wing and stood, brushing off his clothes.

"You could build a castle with the amount of sand in my shorts," Martin called as he climbed to his feet.

"I'm-uh, sorry, sir," Cody replied, trying not to laugh.

Another man, about the same age, but with far less hair approached from up the beach.

"Is there much damage?" he yelled to the first man.

"It does not appear so."

The two men stared at the teens, their confusion regarding how the four got onto the wings of their plane seemingly outweighed by the oddity of their attire. Finally, Martin broke the silence.

"You . . . you're Orville and Wilbur Wright!"

"Yes, sir. Have we met?"

"I-uh, no. That is…" Martin said. "Wow, it's the early twentieth century!"

"December 17th, 1903," Orville offered.

"And this is *Kitty Hawk*," Shelby called as the girls approached, "Kitty Hawk, North Carolina!".

"What they mean," Cody said, "is that we have been reading about your work. I hope we have not damaged your experiment, but we're fascinated by your, uh, aeroplane."

"Why, much obliged, sir." The man with the moustache, introducing himself as Orville, appeared to soften. "Now if you would be so kind as to wait at a safe distance, we would be happy to discuss our experiments with you once we have completed the test flights."

"Uh, sure," Cody responded sheepishly. "We'll wait over there."

The brothers' voices carried on the gusty wind as they returned to their aeroplane, discussing plans for the next flight.

The biplane looked to be less than fifteen meters across. Cody estimated the top and bottom wings were two meters apart. The pilot lay across the center of the lower wing where the controls were accessible. Two large, flimsy-looking rudders on the back apparently provided maneuverability.

"Remind me, when I fuss, not to mention anything real," Shelby said with a frown.

"You mean like 'what in the name of Kitty Hawk'." Martin joked.

"What was that *thing* back there?" Charlotte asked, eyes still wild with fear.

Her words brought Cody back to the reality of the world they left. "I don't know," he replied.

"It was *eating* Pitaskog. What's going to happen to The Guardian and The Gatekeeper?" Shelby cried. "We need to help them!"

"Wish I knew," Cody said shakily. "But we're stuck here until we solve the riddle."

"What if it does the same thing to them it's doing to Pitaskog?" Shelby added, her voice quivering.

Cody just shook his head. He felt terrified and helpless at the same time.

"Hopefully between The Guardian and The Gatekeeper they can stop that thing," he mumbled.

How can I protect them when I'm stuck her? What should I do? What would Sharkey do?

The four teens watched as Wilbur and Orville took turns launching their airplane. Although this aircraft was clearly an engineering marvel for its time, Cody thought how little it resembled a commercial jet.

Wilbur flew next, proceeding a bit farther along the beach. Then, it was Orville's turn again. Cody estimated his flight to have covered about seventy meters. Wilbur's final flight easily passed all other attempts. It lasted about a minute, ending up a few football fields down the beach.

"Wow, that last flight went far," Shelby said.

"Did the plane land? I can hardly see it," Martin mumbled.

A short while later, Wilbur and a group of men, hauled the plane back to its starting location. The Wrights seemed pleased with the final flight as they inspected some minor damage to the front rudder.

"Where's the media? Where are the television cameras? This is an amazing feat!" Shelby looked perplexed as she stared at the small group of onlookers.

Cody nodded. "I guess they didn't realize the importance of this day until later."

Martin shivered. "Why couldn't they do this in Hawaii or at least in July?"

"I believe they selected this location for the wind and probably the soft sand," Charlotte offered.

"I hope The Gatekeeper and Guardian are okay?" Cody mumbled anxiously.

Shelby shook her head and frowned. "They seemed truly frightened by that thing."

"Wouldn't you be?" Martin said.

"Cody, we need to figure something out before we solve the riddle," Charlotte stated. "As we know, time in Rúndyrr doesn't impact time in our world," Charlotte said.

"What are you getting at?" Cody asked.

Shelby replied, "Charlotte is saying that thing will probably still be there when we get back."

"Exactly," Charlotte responded. "And, based on the easy time it had defeating Pitaskog, we will pose no threat whatsoever."

"We need to be prepared for anything," Martin added.

"Maybe Nidhogg can defeat it," Cody said.

"Now, sirs and madams." They looked up to see the Wright Brothers approaching. "How may we be of assistance?"

"Congratulations on the spectacular flights," Shelby said, gushing charm.

"Why, thank you, ma'am," Wilbur replied, appearing to blush.

Cody stepped forward to shake their hands.

"I'm Cody and this is Shelby, Charlotte, and Martin."

The brothers nodded, introducing themselves.

"We're trying to understand the forces that raise an airplane and allow it to glide for extended lengths of time." Cody didn't know what he was asking, but it seemed like a good starting point.

"Sir, the calculations of true lift and true drift are the basis of our research in determining glide times."

"Come again?" asked Martin, wrinkling his nose.

"Sir?"

"I mean, could you please clarify."

"True *lift* is the force directly opposed to gravity. True *drift* is perpendicular to it." He held one hand straight up and the other pointed straight at his palm. "These forces form the legs of a right triangle. All the parts of the triangle are related mathematically. The size of the triangle does not matter. We use algebra and trigonometry to determine the impact these values have on our wing design."

Cody shook his head. "I'm sorry, but I don't understand."

"You seem like an educated man. Have you not studied algebra or the Pythagorean Theorem?"

"Uh, well, actually we *have*," he replied sheepishly, "but we're not sure what it means."

"The Pythagorean Theorem states that all the parts of a right triangle – a triangle with a ninety-degree angle – bear a special relationship to one another, and they don't change, no matter how large or small the triangle. Algebra is incredible!"

Wilbur seemed so excited, Cody thought he might spontaneously combust.

"Mr. Wright," Shelby said gruffly, "it seems pretty clear to me that when God was sitting up in the Kingdom of Heaven creating stuff, He came up with algebra while He was sleeping. It's the only way to explain something so *boring*!" She crossed her arms.

Wilbur smiled briefly. Sad eyes reflected the emotions of a man who viewed the opportunity to advance previously held foundations of mathematics and science as an honor.

"No, ma'am," he said softly. "Algebra is only boring to those who don't understand its *magical* power, the ability to solve complex problems through the simple, elegant beauty of an algebraic equation . . . beauty much like yours."

Cody thought he saw Shelby blush. "Why, sir!"

"But what does that have to do with flying an aeroplane?" Cody asked.

"Without it, we could not have achieved these improvements to our glider design."

Wilbur ran his hand through what remained of his thinning hair.

"Hmm," he mumbled, seemingly trying to formulate an answer they would understand. Locating a grassy reed on the beach nearby, he began to draw in the soft sand.

"Let us say I am standing on the beach holding a long rope." He drew a small circle to represent himself. "I'm using the rope to fly an aeroplane," he said, drawing the plane in the sky, then an angled line from himself to the plane.

"Flying it as if it were a kite?" Charlotte asked.

"Exactly! The rope represents the long side of the triangle, called the hypotenuse. If I draw another line straight up from where I am standing to the point even with the height of the aeroplane, that indicates *lift*. Then, all I need to do is draw a line connecting the two, indicating what we call *drift*, and I have a right triangle."

"So, you've created a big right triangle in the sky," said Shelby.

"Perfectly correct!"

"How does that help you?" she asked.

"We need to measure the characteristics of our designs, to record how design changes affect lift and drift. Of course, we cannot fly up there to measure the triangle, but the beauty of mathematics tells us the following. If we know the length of one side, and either angle between the hypotenuse and any other side…" Wilbur said, pointing to the two ends of the 'rope.' "It allows us to find any part of the triangle."

"With you so far, I think," Martin said.

Wilbur nearly took flight, flapping his arms like wings. Orville grinned at his brother's enthusiasm.

"Once we established the requirements for our triangle and defined the forces of true lift and drift, we use that knowledge to improve our glider," Orville added.

Wilbur looked directly at Shelby. "Behold the *power* of mathematics!" He smiled warmly. "I can create an *enormous* triangle in the sky and determine its size without ever leaving the ground! And *this* has aided us in determining the optimum glider capabilities of our aeroplane."

"So, you could change your designs, record the values for lift and drift, and based on those values, make improvements to your designs," Charlotte offered.

"Yes, ma'am! It seems that a high 'lift to drift' ratio will result in a shallow gliding angle which helps extend the length of our flights."

"Very ingenious," Martin said.

"Thank you, sir," Wilbur said, eyes shining proudly. "I know it's a dream," he sighed. "But perhaps someday the opportunity to travel long distances will be available to average folks. The world will be able to share cultures and experiences without enduring weeks or months at sea or difficult overland travel. It is still just a dream," he paused ruefully, "but maybe *someday...*"

"Oh, sir, I do believe you will prevail," Shelby said warmly.

"Why, uh, much obliged, ma'am."

"Yes, *trust* us on this," Martin offered. "Your dream *will* become a reality. They'll be packing folks into 'aeroplanes' like sardines in a metal can. It'll be *awesome*. For a mere week's pay, one can endure hours in a straightjacket filled with crying babies, tiny bags of peanuts, and seats the size of a postage stamp," he added, grinning impishly. "From what I've heard."

Ignoring the Wright brothers' frozen stares, Shelby broke the silence.

"Perhaps you can tell us what this means." She took a deep breath and faced the two men.

"It raises an object straight up so high,
Then forces it along, across the sky.
Tie a rope and watch the object hover;
Draw two lines, one straight up and one over.
Perfecting the formulas takes a logical mind,
But the results will soar for all..."

Shelby's words trailed off. The surprise on her face was apparent to all. "Why, sirs! I do believe the answer is true lift and true drift!"

The Wright brothers' faces beamed with delight as the four teens waved goodbye. But Cody's smile was short-lived. His mind returned to the cave, contemplating what they would find upon their return.

Chapter 14: The Hero

A choked scream filled Cody's head as the four stepped off the bridge. His eyes darted about, trying to adjust to the dim light. What he saw made his heart pound. The Gatekeepers' limp body, staff still in hand, was propped up against the cave wall. The demon stood over him, a clawed hand around the old man's neck.

"LET HIM *GO!*" Cody growled.

Grýla hesitated, slowly turning her head in Cody's direction. She licked her lips, then tightened her grip on The Gatekeeper's throat, lifting him off the ground. Cody noticed a shaded form slumped against the opposite wall, barely visible in his black robe.

"Is that The Guardian?" Shelby cried.

"Oh, *this* is not good," Martin whispered solemnly.

"Get the girls out of here," Cody ordered, glancing at Martin and seeing fear in his eyes.

"Come on," Martin grabbed Charlotte's and Shelby's arms.

"Cody—" Shelby began.

"GO!"

He turned back toward The Gatekeeper. The old man was fighting back with all he had, but Grýla was too strong.

"NIDHOGG!" Cody yelled. "HELP HIM!"

The stone wall on the far side of the cave began to slide heavily open. Each second seemed like hours. Finally, the dragon's enormous

112

shadow appeared, prancing across the cavern. Nidhogg paused briefly to sniff Pitaskog's body, its old adversary sprawled motionless across the cave floor.

Cody glanced over his shoulder to make sure Shelby, Charlotte, and Martin had reached the other side of the cave.

"GET OUT OF HERE!" he yelled, as they watched from the apparent safety of the entrance.

Nidhogg moved toward the demon, drawing in a fiery breath. Grýla dropped The Gatekeeper, the old man's beaten body falling to the hard ground, and turned to face Nidhogg. Cody heard Charlotte's terrified gasp from across the cavern.

The demon hissed, her eyes burning like hot embers as the two creatures circled each other. Finally, Nidhogg seemed to have had enough. Using his spiked tail for leverage, a long stream of fire erupted from the dragon's mouth. Grýla hissed and moaned, clearly enraged. She hesitated, as if trying to regain strength, then launched herself toward Nidhogg with surprising quickness.

"LOOK OUT!" Cody yelled.

Nidhogg extended his wing to keep her away, but the demon vaulted over it. Grabbing the dragon's neck, she sank her teeth into flesh. Nidhogg shook his head to free himself from the demon's grasp, but Grýla held on. Cody was afraid the dragon was at a disadvantage as flight wasn't possible within the confines of Rúndyrr cave.

Nidhogg brushed up against the cave wall in an apparent attempt to extricate the demon, but with no success. Cody grabbed The Gatekeeper's staff off the floor nearby. He pointed the end toward Grýla, not sure what to expect.

"HEY! UGLY DEMON! GET YOUR CLAWS OFF MY DRAGON!"

Come on, staff, do something!

A sudden flash illuminated the cave as lightning arced from the staff's end, striking the demon in the side. She screamed, glaring at Cody with wrathful surprise.

You're not nearly as surprised as I am.

The demon let go of Nidhogg and scurried toward Cody with outstretched claws.

"Children are so *plump* and *tasty*," Grýla growled in a non-human sounding voice, dragon blood dripping down the sides of her gray face.

Cody tried to maneuver the staff between them, but she pushed it aside.

"CODY!" Shelby screamed.

The demon grabbed him and sank her long teeth into his shoulder. Cody stood frozen for a moment, watching as she licked the blood oozing from his wounds with a black tongue. He had never felt such pain. Glancing briefly at his bloody shoulder, Cody's legs gave out and he dropped to the ground. Grýla leaned over him, preparing to take another bite.

"*CODY!*" Shelby cried. "NO!"

Suddenly Grýla screamed, hissing with rage. Nidhogg had unloaded a blast of fire, scorching her back. The demon turned, a long stream of red light erupting from her mouth. Nidhogg backed up, but was unable to get out of the line of fire. The dragon growled then responded with fire of his own. The two blasts met in the middle, creating a large fireball. Cody stared in desperation as it slowly pushed back toward Nidhogg.

"STOP!" he cried.

The fireball engulfed Nidhogg, setting the dragon ablaze. Its body seemed to be burning from within. Cody's heart broke watching his friend drop to the floor.

"*NO!*" Cody let out a choked scream.

He crawled over to The Gatekeeper's staff and grabbed it with his good arm, sending another arc of white light at Grýla's back. The demon growled, then leaped toward him, grasping his neck with a hooked claw.

"You've taken your last breath, *Chosen*," she hissed, squeezing his throat.

Can't breathe.

Cody punched the demon's face with all his might. She threw him against the cave wall like a toy. He gasped for air, waiting for death to come, but nothing happened. Glancing up, he saw Grýla scowl. His siblings were throwing stones at the demon, trying to distract her.

"You're *next*, juicy children," she wailed, glancing toward them.

"GO! Get out of here," Cody tried to yell, but he didn't have the strength.

"*LOOK OUT!*" he heard Shelby's voice.

The demon hovered over him, her nasty breath in his face. Again, wrapping a claw around his neck, she lifted him off the floor, preparing to take another chunk of flesh. Cody fought with all his might, but it had no effect. Then, suddenly Grýla froze. Cody wriggled free then dropped to the ground. The demon stood motionless, ice crystals forming throughout her body.

Sam Sharkey pulled a long ice sword from the demon's back.

"Get out of here!" Sharkey ordered, offering Cody a hand and lifting him to his feet.

"What *is* that?" Cody asked, staring at Sharkey's weapon.

"An ice sword," the man replied. "Now go! It won't hold her for long."

"Get a *real* weapon," Cody growled. "Take her out while you have the chance!"

"It doesn't work like that," Sharkey said condescendingly. "She can't be killed that way."

Grýla was already beginning to thaw, red eyes glaring at Cody as the ice around them melted. She snarled briefly at Sharkey, then transformed back into a dark mist. Rolling along, she quickly disappeared through the cave wall.

"Let me see that shoulder," Sharkey said.

Cody looked down at his blood-saturated shirt. Sharkey reached out and touched his arm. A light seemed to emanate from the man's hand as soothing warmth permeated Cody's body. He felt strangely renewed as Sharkey headed to The Gatekeeper and reached down to touch the old man's forehead.

"What are you *doing*?" Cody asked, feeling the pain in his shoulder subside.

Sharkey ignored him and headed across the cave to touch The Guardian's shoulder. The old man slowly sat up, leaning heavily against the rock wall.

Cody glanced over at The Gatekeeper, breathing a sigh of relief as the old man's eyes opened. He rushed over to help him up.

"He's still *bleeding!*" Cody yelled.

"Let me take a look at that old man," Sharkey said, returning to The Gatekeeper and placing his hand on the man's torso.

"Are you *healing* them . . . healing *us*?" Cody asked, stunned.

"Well, Mr. Hawke," Sharkey said with a frown, "I don't see *you* doing anything to help."

"Let the boy be," The Gatekeeper muttered, wincing slightly. "You weren't exactly skilled at his age."

"Maybe now he'll learn to mind his own business when he's told to." Sharkey smirked at Cody, then appeared to soften. "How's that shoulder?"

"I-I-uh, it seems okay," Cody mumbled, lifting his arm. "I'm not sure how." Then Sharkey's words struck him. "What's he talking about? *What* should I have done?" he asked, turning toward The Gatekeeper.

"I told you to stay out of this," the old man responded, ignoring his question. "There are many things you don't yet understand."

Shelby and Martin helped The Guardian to his feet. The old man put his arms around their shoulders for support as they joined Cody and Sharkey. An awkward silence followed.

"Are you . . . from Nimbus?" Charlotte asked Sharkey, her eyes wide.

The man appeared to smile but said nothing.

"What about Nidhogg?" Cody cried suddenly, running to the dragon's side. "Can you help *him*?" he asked, staring sadly at the burning beast.

"I'm not sure," Sharkey replied.

"What do you mean?" Cody cried angrily. "*Do* something! He'll die!"

"He may already be dead," Sharkey said softly, "I'm not sure how much more I've got to give."

"What does that mean?" Cody asked.

"It means," The Guardian offered as he gazed down at the burning dragon, "our power has its limits."

"Can *you* help him?" Cody asked The Guardian.

"I cannot. My power has been depleted by my own injuries."

Sharkey took a few steps closer and crouched down, his hand about a meter from the burning dragon's head. The man appeared to wince, as if from some supreme effort.

"That's all I have," he said sadly, then headed back toward The Gatekeeper.

"You have to do *something*!" Cody yelled. "You can't just walk away."

Cody turned his head toward Nidhogg, tears welling in his eyes. When he looked back, Sharkey, The Guardian, and The Gatekeeper were gone. Pitaskog's body was also gone.

He stared at the burning dragon in despondent silence. Suddenly, and with great effort, Nidhogg stood and lumbered back to his lair. Cody's heart sank as the dragon glanced over at him. He wondered whether the pain in the beast's eyes emanated solely from the fire, or from disappointment as well.

Was there more I should've done? What did Sharkey mean when he said I did nothing? Could I have saved them?

The stone wall protecting Nidhogg's lair slid shut behind him and suddenly all was quiet. With the exception of some blood spattered across the cave walls, all indications of the massacre Grýla had perpetrated, were gone.

Chapter 15: The Lecture

Cody kept to himself for a while, struggling with his perceived inadequacies. He had let everyone down. They seemed to expect big things from him. There was just one problem. He had no idea what. Grýla had come into their home and hurt them. Cody let it happen and the disappointment he felt from Sharkey, The Guardian and Gatekeeper, even Nidhogg, weighed heavily on his mind.

He tried to talk to Sharkey, but in typical form, the man offered no help. He seemed to hold Cody to his own standards, standards so high there was no way Cody could deliver. When asking Sharkey what he should've done differently that day in the cave, all he got was, 'if I have to tell you, then there's no point in discussing it.' It was as if he was so pathetic, it wasn't worth the effort.

Cody sat on the wall surrounding Freya Manor's impressive fountain, searching for answers amid the dancing spray. The morning sun warmed his shoulders.

"Hey, bro," Martin called, climbing onto the wall next to him. "What's up?"

"Nothing, I guess," Cody replied distractedly.

"Want to throw a ball around?" he asked.

"Uh, sure. I-I guess." Cody should've jumped down, but he just sat there.

"You're quiet lately," Martin offered.

"I'm just dealing with some stuff," Cody mumbled.

"Like what?" Martin pressed.

"I don't know." A voice in Cody's head told him to let it go, but he didn't listen. "I'm just feeling lost and useless, like everything I do is wrong."

"Want to switch places?" Martin smirked, then added. "Look, don't be so hard on yourself."

Cody sensed the edginess in his brother's voice, but he couldn't contain himself.

"You have no idea what it's like to live with this burden, everyone constantly treating you like you're incompetent and hopeless," he said irritably. "I don't know what they *want* from me."

"Seriously?" Martin jumped down and turned toward him. "No, I don't understand anything about feeling like I'm not as good as everyone else, like I'm just a burden to everyone around me. You've got a lot of nerve sitting there feeling sorry for yourself, Mr. *Chosen*."

Cody thought he saw tears well up in Martin's eyes.

"Hey, bro, I didn't mean—"

Martin turned and headed back toward the house.

The pressure building inside made Cody feel like an overfilled balloon, ready to pop at any moment. He didn't know what to do to make himself feel better. Cody was angry a lot of the time, at what he wasn't sure. All he knew was, he felt completely alone, almost as alone as the day he first arrived at Freya Manor, trying to deal with the sudden and mysterious death of his parents.

At least depression hasn't affected my appetite, he thought, rubbing a too-full belly and staring out the library window as a passing thunderstorm pummeled the ground.

"How do you think Sharkey knows them?" he wondered aloud as the teens perused their respective summer reading books, sprawled across four over-stuffed chairs.

"I guess they're friends," Shelby offered absently.

"No, it's more than that," Cody said, shaking his head.

"It's almost like he's one of them, but he's not tied to the cave like they are," Charlotte replied.

"Maybe he's just got special powers because he's from Nimbus," Martin added. "Obviously he can *heal* things, he seems to *know* things, and he can jump around from place to place."

"There's more to it," Cody mumbled. "They've got history together."

While Charlotte, Shelby, and Martin read their books, Cody just stared at the fireplace, hoping to find answers amid its scattered ashes. A few minutes later, he stood and tossed the book onto his chair.

"I can't..."

"Can't what?" Shelby looked up.

"I-I can't just sit here reading this stupid book when that demon is lurking around somewhere and I've got no idea what I'm supposed to do about it."

"What are you going to do?" Shelby stood.

"I-uh, don't know," Cody stammered, lifting his hat and running a hand through his hair. "It's probably a waste of time, but I'm going to talk to them."

"What do you expect to find out?" Charlotte asked.

"I don't know," Cody said, "but I've got to try. You guys wait here."

"We're coming," Martin called after him.

Cody could feel his face get warm as they stepped outside, but it wasn't just from the humidity. He was on the verge of exploding, a firestorm of pent up feelings waiting to come out.

"Those Belgian waffles Heather made for breakfast weren't bad," Cody said, trying to regain some composure as the four zigzagged through Freya Manor's meandering maze.

"Yeah," Martin replied. "I didn't even need to drown them in syrup."

"What are you hoping to find out, Cowpoke?" Shelby asked.

"First, I want to see how The Guardian and Gatekeeper are doing, and make sure that *thing* hasn't tried to come back, then I'll ask them to clarify my role in all this," Cody said, frowning.

"I wonder why that demon came to Freya Manor?" Shelby asked.

"When we returned from Edison, we were asking about The Light of . . ." Charlotte began, then appeared to rethink mentioning its name. "Maybe we somehow lured it here."

"They told us to mind our business," Martin said. "Maybe it *was* our fault."

Cody frowned. "The demon didn't seem very interested in us. It seemed to be after The Gatekeeper and Guardian. Sharkey just used that as an excuse to make it sound like our fault."

Cody silently fumed over how little the three men confided in him.

If I'm supposed to eventually take on the role of Guardian, you'd think they would mentor me and help me learn. How can I grow if they won't trust me?

"I'm thinking about changing, or at least delaying, my choice of professions," Charlotte offered lightly, breaking the strained silence.

"I thought you wanted to be a middle school teacher?" Shelby asked.

"I do, but there's something I would like to do first," she replied.

"And that is…" Cody waited for a response. He had little patience for games lately.

"I think I'd like to go into space, be an astronaut," Charlotte said.

"With your fear of heights?" Martin laughed.

"I know. It sounds strange, but these trips through Rúndyrr have given me a confidence I didn't have before," Charlotte replied with a demure smile.

"Wow, honey, that's awesome!" Shelby exclaimed. "We can all say we knew you when."

"An astronaut," Martin said. "Charlotte in space. I love it!"

"What do you think, Cody?" she asked softly.

"Uh, yeah, that's great," Cody replied with muted enthusiasm.

Cody knew the insecurities brewing inside were coloring his response.

"You don't sound so sure."

"It's just dangerous, that's all," Cody said.

He heard the words coming from his mouth and knew he was heading down a slippery slope, but out it came anyway.

"What are you trying to say, Cowpoke?" Shelby asked.

"First, it'll be extremely competitive. Even someone with Charlotte's brains might not get in. You might be setting yourself up for disappointment. Second, it's going to be very rough and scary, especially for a girl."

"Cody Hawke!" Shelby said crossly, crossing her arms. "What is *that* supposed to mean?"

"Uh! Why did I open my mouth?" Charlotte mumbled.

"Shelby, why would they send a woman to do something so difficult?" Cody asked.

"Listen, Cowpoke, there are many amazing women in this world . . . women much smarter and more capable than you!" Shelby put her hands on her hips. "And, Charlotte's a perfect example."

"Leave me out of this," the girl offered, grinning shyly.

"I'm not saying they're not smart, what I'm say is, they're . . . *fragile*."

"Who are you calling *fragile*, Cowpoke? Why I ought to punch you right in the kisser," Shelby roared. "The things I've seen in my life..." she snapped. "There are *all* kinds of monsters."

"Girls *are* fragile," he repeated.

"Bro, I'd quit while you still have all your teeth," Martin muttered.

"Cody," Charlotte said, "there have been quite a few women in space already and they've performed well at their jobs."

"Can you honestly tell me girls can withstand the same physical torture that men can?" Cody continued. "I mean, what if it's that – you know – time and you're feeling cranky or bloated."

"So, what are you trying to say, Cowpoke?" Shelby nearly hissed the words.

"I'm saying there are dangerous times when a person needs all their faculties. They can't be sniffling over somebody's offhand comment or worried about whether their jeans are too tight. That's why space travel should be done by men."

"Oh, boy," Martin murmured, rolling his eyes. "Here we go."

"Cody Hawke," Shelby growled, her eyes on fire, "I will take you on at *anything, anytime, anywhere*, and I will kick your—"

"Dost thou wish to enter Rúndyrr?"

"Yes," Cody replied quickly, relieved by the interruption. "I'm glad to see you've recovered from your injuries. Is everything okay?"

The Gatekeeper nodded curtly. Cody had come to expect limited emotion from the man.

"What did you mean when you said there are things we don't understand? What things?" he asked.

"There is still much thou needs to learn," the old man replied.

"Like *what*?" he demanded. "How am I supposed to help if I don't know what thou . . . I mean, you, want from me?"

The Gatekeeper frowned. "It is not something that can be taught in the blink of an eye. Many eons are required to amass the knowledge and experience needed to effectively defend Rúndyrr. Learning all about The Darkness and The Light is just one aspect."

"So that's it?" Cody said angrily. "Go home, kid, there's nothing you can do?" he lifted his hat, trying to regain the composure that eluded him. "We *saw* what Grýla can do," he said with a scowl. "I don't need to know any more about her than she needs to be stopped. And, I've *asked* you about The Light repeatedly. You never give me a straight answer," he added.

"You do not understand The Darkness," The Gatekeeper replied, frowning. "It is complicated."

"How?" Cody asked.

"Are you talking about The Darkness, meaning Grýla, or are you referring to something more intangible and abstract," Charlotte asked.

"This young lady," the old man said, smiling disarmingly at Charlotte, "understands much more than thee."

"About *what*?" Cody roared, feeling his face get red.

"The Darkness is an entity fueled by apathy and ignorance," the old man replied.

"I don't understand," Cody said.

"Hence the reason thou need to learn," The Gatekeeper replied briskly.

"Where is Grýla now? Will she be back?" Shelby asked.

"The demon is gone for now, but she is growing ever stronger. She *will* be back," the old man said with a sigh. "As will they all. Now, wouldst thou like to go on a journey," he repeated.

"Yes," Cody replied firmly. "I want to visit Radianna. Maybe *she* will answer my questions."

"Very well," the old man said pensively, a devious look suddenly permeating his previously foul expression. "You will meet a woman who can help you learn."

Much to Cody's surprise, as well as the apparent surprise of his foster siblings, The Gatekeeper began to laugh. It started as a snicker but magnified into a gut-wrenching belly laugh.

"What . . . what's so *funny*?" Cody asked, unsure whether to be furious or laugh with him.

The Gatekeeper stopped suddenly, clutching his still-healing chest and winced, driving the smile from his face. He turned and headed toward the doorway, reciting the riddle as he walked.

"Curie, twice won science's greatest prize,
It was the 1840s when Lovelace started the computer's rise,
Leavitt measured the brightness of stars,
Providing insight into exactly how far.
Hopper's program converted words to code,
Howard's advances furthered robotic mode.
Carson's work led to the EPA and more,
Apgar saved babies with her newly defined score.
Nightingale, Blackwell, and Parks pushed social shifts,
With their strength, passion, and tireless gifts.
Joyner, Rudolph, and Kersee used their speed,
Opening doors for many others to succeed.
This provides just a very short list,
But without a doubt, thou get the gist."

Cody frowned at the others. "Any ideas, because I don't 'get the gist'?"

"Of course, you don't, Cowpoke," Shelby said testily.

"Could it be great women in history," Charlotte asked, smiling at The Gatekeeper.

Rúndyrr illuminated, the bridge shimmering its readiness. On the far side, a loud whirring sound emanated from something that seemed to be moving.

Chapter 16: The Superstar

Charlotte, Shelby, Martin, and Cody immediately crouched down to keep from falling. The floor shook slightly as the whir of powerful engines filled the space. A number of people wearing orange jumpsuits squatted around them. They seemed to be waiting for something.

"Oh, my!" Charlotte said with a sudden gasp, her eyes wide open. "It's Mae James."

"Who?" Cody asked. But he was immediately distracted as they began to rise . . . fast.

"Get down!" a voice yelled.

They were inside some sort of flying machine, presumably a large airplane, ascending at such a sharp angle that if the back door had been open, they might have slid out. Cody's heart pounded.

What's happening? Have we lost control?

There were no seats, no handrails, nothing to hold onto. He glanced around at three sets of wild eyes, all apparently wondering – as was he – whether this trip would be their ultimate demise.

Maybe we'll get our answer as to whether we can die here.

Suddenly, the plane leveled off.

Whew!

But Cody's relief was short-lived. He panicked, grasping for something, *anything* to hold onto, as his bottom came off the floor and he began to float. Shelby, Charlotte, Martin, and the orange jumpsuits did the same.

"WHOA!" Cody cried. "What's *happening?*"

"Weightlessness," a lovely, dark-skinned woman replied.

Cody heard her voice, but all he could focus on was his stomach and the three Belgian waffles he'd eaten for breakfast. It wasn't long before a stream of partially digested waffle erupted from his mouth, floating in front of him. It hung there, suspended in air, taunting him until the plane began to drop and it splattered all over the floor. The sight only made him more nauseous.

Cody wiped his mouth, eyes darting about in panic as they went into a powered dive. Again, he tried to hold on, glancing at his siblings. He wondered if this would be the end, but a few seconds later the plane began to level off. He glanced at Shelby's wide grin as he again began to heave.

How is she able to handle this? I'm going to die.

Again, the plane angled sharply upward, then after about a half minute of floatation, went into another powered dive. Finally, after a dozen more agonizing ups and downs repeated with sickening precision, the plane descended. Cody had nothing left in his stomach as the wheels touched down. His hands were shaking so he could barely control them.

Cody wished the mess he'd made on the floor would just disappear, taking with it any reminder of the last hour. He glanced at his siblings. Martin looked a little green, however, he had managed to keep from losing his breakfast. Shelby appeared exhilarated. Even Charlotte seemed fine.

The pretty woman smiled at him as they taxied in. "That's why they call it the 'Vomit Comet'," she said with a sympathetic grin. "It's common for about half the people who experience weightlessness to also experience some degree of nausea."

Cody nodded as the plane came to a stop, his embarrassment only outweighed by the sick feeling in his stomach.

"It's okay," Shelby replied, as Cody stood on shaky legs and began to disembark the plane, "he's just a little *fragile.*"

He frowned at her but was still too nauseous to speak. The group headed across the tarmac to a nondescript white building. Cody was glad for the fresh air and slight breeze. Inside was an office and debriefing area with a long table and numerous chairs. He stopped at the rest room to splash cold water on his face.

A few minutes later, everyone took a seat as the orange jumpsuits discussed the experience in depth. Cody kept his hands in his lap so no one could see them shaking. After the review concluded, Charlotte, eyes wide with awe, approached the pretty lady.

"Ms. James," Charlotte said, the words nearly gushing from her mouth. "You are my *idol*. It is such an incredible honor to meet you."

"You are too kind," Ms. James replied with smiling eyes. "Please, call me Mae. Are you here as part of a training program?"

"Uh-uh, well, sort of," the girl stammered. "I'm Charlotte, this is Shelby and Martin. The unhappy guy in the corner is Cody."

"Nice to meet you all."

"Are you preparing for your Space Shuttle flight?" Charlotte asked.

"Yes," Mae replied. "Weightlessness is part of NASA's training program.

"You work for NASA?" Shelby asked excitedly.

"I do, yes. I'm actually a medical doctor and I just returned from a few years in the Peace Corps," Mae said. "But going into space has always been a dream of mine."

"Wow! Talk about your overachievers," Martin declared with an envious grin, "a doctor, the Peace Corps, and now an astronaut. I need to work on building my resume," he said emphatically.

"Yes, such an incredible list of accomplishments," Shelby stated.

"I already had a lot of respect for astronauts," Martin added, rubbing his tummy and grinning sheepishly, "but it just increased *exponentially* over the last hour."

Everyone laughed, except Cody.

"Why were we floating?" Shelby asked.

"The plane flies in a six-mile parabolic arc," Mae said. "We climb fast, then go into a powered dive. During the arc, there's about a twenty-two-second window of weightlessness that mirrors the effects of space flight."

"Have you always wanted to be an astronaut?" Charlotte asked.

"Yes," Mae replied, "since I was a little girl."

"I've heard people say women shouldn't be astronauts," Shelby uttered loudly. Cody glanced up to see a smirk permeating her face. "Imagine that!"

Mae laughed. "It takes a lot of training and hard work, but I've never been one to listen to the naysayers. Unfortunately, I've run into some men along the way who felt I didn't belong, especially during my undergraduate studies."

"Well," Shelby said, "you certainly proved *them* wrong." Cody frowned as she glanced over at him again. "Charlotte is thinking about getting into the space program," Shelby added enthusiastically.

"That's music to my ears," Mae said, smiling broadly.

"I could never hope to do all the great things you've done . . . but I'd like to try to become an astronaut someday," Charlotte replied. "Then perhaps go into teaching afterward."

"I am absolutely certain you can do anything you set your mind to," Mae said.

"Mae, can you help us with this riddle?" Shelby asked.

"This common force is all around,
Even in space it still abounds.
Some think it exists only on Earth,
Because satellites orbit above her girth.
But it's speed that keeps satellites high,
As they fall along the horizon's sky."

"Hmm, well, I'm not a physicist, but I believe it's saying gravity still exists in space. It's a misnomer that, because we experience weightlessness, there is zero gravity. Satellites remain in orbit because of their speed. They are pulled to earth by gravity, however, because of the curvature of the earth, they fall over the horizon, thus remaining in orbit."

Cody stood, still feeling a bit green. After taking a moment to steady himself, he joined the others.

"Ms. James?" he said, reaching out to shake her hand. "I apologize . . . to you and the other women in the room," he glanced at Charlotte and Shelby, "for my ignorance. Women have plenty to offer the space program, and," he turned to Charlotte, "would make exceptional astronauts."

"Hmm," Shelby said, beaming with delight. "I do believe we are defying gravity right now."

Chapter 17: The Healing

Cody got up early and headed to the barn, a warm sun baking his shoulders as he crossed the yard. He lifted his hat, allowing the minimal breeze to tussle his hair. Sharkey's harpy eagle was assessing her territory from atop the barn roof. The eagle stared at him as he passed below, her gray face appearing eerily human.

Sharkey lets her out? Doesn't he worry Jezebel will fly away?

"Hey, girl," Cody whispered, hugging his beloved chocolate and white pony.

Gypsy Storm eagerly took the pieces of carrot he retrieved from his pocket. Cody gazed adoringly at her rascally-look while she ate. It felt good to be with someone who expected nothing from him, only his affection.

He saddled Storm and went for a leisurely ride around the property. They trotted to the eastern ridge and stood there for a while, ogling at an azure bay. As they headed across the front yard and passed the towering obelisk, Cody noticed Jezebel gliding high above. He made sure his hat was secure, then gave Storm some rein.

The old VW had left ruts in the driveway after last week's thunderstorm, but it was the only treeless area on the property. He urged Storm on as they galloped down Freya Lane, her long mane and tail streaming out. It was liberating, the bond between them highly therapeutic.

Suddenly Storm took a tumble. Cody was thrown from the saddle, hitting the fence on the far side of the driveway so hard, it knocked the wind out of him. When he opened his eyes, Cody saw Storm laying in the grass about ten meters away.

"STORM! *NO!*" he cried, climbing groggily to his feet.

Cody stumbled to his beautiful pinto. "Storm? What's wrong, girl?"

She struggled to her feet and took a few steps toward him, but was unable to put weight on her right front leg.

"YOUR LEG!" Cody yelled, feeling tears well up in his eyes. "WHAT HAVE I *DONE?*"

He wrapped his arms around the horse's neck, then dropped to the ground like a sack of potatoes, his face hidden in his hands.

"I'm *cursed*," he sobbed. "Everything I care about gets hurt . . . or worse."

He cried for a few minutes until he felt Storm nudge him with her muzzle. He looked up at the horse he loved.

"I'm so sorry, girl. It's my fault. I shouldn't have run you like that. I should've left you back where you belong, with the Passamaquoddy."

He sat there for a moment, so heartbroken he couldn't move.

What if her leg is broken? What will I do? I love her so much.

Storm held out her leg, as if showing it to him. He hesitated for a moment, then gently ran his fingers up and down. To his horror, he felt a bump just above the fetlock.

"NO!" he screamed. "NO! *Please! Please,* someone *help* me!"

A lump formed in his throat making it difficult to breathe. He stared at the ground in agonizing silence, as a shadow passed overhead. It was Jezebel, landing on a nearby branch.

"What have I done?" he cried.

Suddenly Cody began to feel strange. His arm got warm and started to shake. He wondered briefly whether he'd broken it in the fall, or maybe he was having a heart attack. The blood flowed to his fingertips as if being drawn from the rest of his body. Cody stared at his hand, afraid it might explode, when suddenly the image of a burning dragon appeared on his palm.

You're losing it, Cody. You must've hit your head harder than you thought.

He didn't know why, but something compelled him to touch the bump on Storm's leg. His arm felt like it was on fire from the shoulder down to his fingertips. A few seconds later, the burning subsided and the dragon tattoo disappeared.

Suddenly Storm pranced back and whinnied. She rose up on her hind legs, pawing at the air. After a few seconds she came down hard on her front legs and took off, galloping and frolicking in circles around Cody.

"*WHAT...*" he stared at his horse, then at his hand. "What just *happened?*"

Was that me? Did I heal her? Could it be?

He hurried over and felt Storm's leg. The bump was gone. Cody hugged his precious pinto, tears of joy filling his eyes. A few minutes later, he rode Storm back to the barn. By the time they got there, he was feeling like a new man.

Chapter 18: The Shadow

It was a muggy and cloudless Saturday. Cody, Charlotte, Shelby, and Martin waited atop the stone wall spanning Freya Manor's front border. Sam Sharkey was away on one of his mysterious trips. No one knew where he went. At first, they assumed he was visiting the same woman they'd seen him with in town. That was, until the day Aluria came to Freya Manor looking for him.

The Quitmeyers didn't seem to mind. As long as the chores got done, he could come and go as he pleased. This time, however, the teens were waiting. The summer was coming to a close and they still had no idea what Sharkey was up to. The trips to Rúndyrr were not providing answers and Cody had become resolute in his efforts to learn more about the man. He no longer believed Sharkey was trying to steal the scepter, but his true intentions were still anyone's guess.

Finally, Sharkey's Jeep pulled up the rocky driveway. Cody jumped off the wall and jogged along behind. As the dust cloud settled, the man's muscular form emerged from the vehicle. Flinging a backpack over his shoulder he turned toward the house.

"Mr. Sharkey," Cody called. "We would like to talk to you."

Sharkey waited as the teens approached, amusement apparent in his eyes. He looked at each of them, rubbing the stubble on his chin. Cody had the disturbing feeling he was reading their thoughts.

"Well, it certainly took you long enough. You've finally worked up the nerve to mention the trip I made through Rúndyrr. Obviously, you've been snooping around for weeks, following me to town, searching my room."

Cody frowned, but couldn't think of anything insightful to say.

He obviously knew about everything, but let us think we were doing it in secret.

"So, what questions are burning a hole inside you?" he continued flatly.

"What are you doing here?" Cody asked. "According to Radianna, your people aren't allowed on Earth anymore, assuming you are Nimbusian." He wanted Sharkey to know he was very familiar with Nimbus, just in case he tried to feed them more of his lies.

"Mr. Hawke," Sharkey said gruffly, "I am here to defeat The Darkness and help restore The Light."

"What does that even mean?" Cody asked, grimacing.

"I'm not sure I can state it any clearer."

"Then why didn't you kill the demon when it was in the cave?" Martin wondered.

"It cannot be killed in that manner," Sharkey replied.

"So," Charlotte asked pensively, "then how do you plan to defeat it?"

"It is a process, Miss Charlotte."

"Did you steal from Rúndyrr?"

"Steal, Miss Shelby?" Again, the light in his eyes conveyed amusement. "I guess it would appear that way. However, had I been stealing, I would have been stealing from myself. Besides, whatever benefits the greater good is acceptable."

"Oh, so was it acceptable to kill those two pirates?" Cody said crossly.

"Kill them?" The twinkle left his eyes. "I didn't kill them. They were already dead."

"Stop talking in riddles. What does that mean?" Cody could feel the anger creeping into his tone.

"As I said, I am concerned about The Light and what will happen to your people when it goes out."

"Are we, Earth's people, in danger?" Charlotte asked.

"I believe I made that clear, Miss Charlotte."

"We could help you, if you'd tell us what's going on."

"Mr. Hawke, this is not a game and I have no more time for your petty questions."

Sharkey turned and headed toward the house. The fact that he didn't even look back, further aggravated Cody. They were just a trivial nuisance. He didn't think enough of them to confide a single detail.

"How is that possible?" Martin shrugged. "I know less now than before we started asking him questions. I mean, he spoke . . . I heard words . . . but he said nothing."

Cody stared in the direction the man had gone, anger seething inside.

Warm sunshine filtered in between Cody's drapes. He began to stir, sensing something had disturbed the stillness. It was early, perhaps shortly after dawn. A finch from the nest outside his window, warbled anxiously. He rolled over, trying to recapture the sleep that now eluded him, when the flicker of a shadow momentarily blocked the sunlight. Cody's eyes flew open.

"Get up."

"What? How did you get in here without me hearing you?"

"I have no time for discussion. You wanted to be a part of this, now you have your chance. Get up. And, wake the others. Meet me downstairs in ten minutes," he said. "Bring water and sunblock."

Cody sat up and rubbed his eyes. Sharkey was gone. There were no footsteps, no creaking of the old wooden floors, not even the rustle of clothing. Not a sound.

How is that possible? Who is this guy?

Ten minutes later, four sleep-deprived teens stood quietly in the foyer. Martin muttered something about the lousy wake-up call and Shelby whined about the lack of time to get ready.

Sharkey appeared suddenly through a door on the right. With barely a glance in their direction, he headed down the basement steps, the teens following close behind. After traversing various stone passageways, they arrived at the Rúndyrr cave.

"Mr. Sharkey?" Charlotte asked, running alongside. "Where are you taking us?"

"Weaver's Needle, Miss Charlotte."

"What's that?" Shelby asked nervously.

"You'll see, Miss Shelby."

The Gatekeeper emerged from the dark, apprehension apparent in his eyes.

"Let us in," Sharkey commanded.

The two men exchanged long glances. Cody was sure they were somehow communicating during the awkward silence that ensued. The Gatekeeper grew suddenly annoyed, perhaps at Sharkey for bringing the teens.

"It is too dangerous," the old man whispered.

"They'll be fine. Now, the doorway, if you please."

"Thou art unreasonably rough on him," the old man mumbled loud enough for Cody to hear, then pointed the scepter with obvious reluctance.

"Somebody needs to be," Sharkey muttered.

The bridge began to glow its readiness, bright sunshine apparent on the other side.

"How come he doesn't have to answer some long-winded riddle about science or history before they let *him* in?" Martin whispered.

"Because, Mr. Speck, *he* is worthy. And, there is no question he cannot answer," the old man responded curtly.

"What are you saying exactly?" Martin cocked his head. "That we're dumb or we're not worthy."

The Gatekeeper gave him a quick glare, prompting Martin into uncharacteristic silence. Cody grinned in spite of the knot in his stomach.

Where is Sharkey taking us? Can he be trusted?

They were pulled across the shimmering bridge and Cody immediately felt a scorching sun bake his shoulders. He scanned the dramatic landscape stretching for miles in every direction. Jagged ridges surrounded a rocky canyon, sparsely dotted with vegetation. The occasional cactus extended into the blue sky like a sun worshiper paying homage to the desert heat.

Cody pulled down on the brim of his cowboy hat to block the afternoon glare. At once, his gaze focused on a pointed mountain, a pinnacle towering high above the landscape.

"Weaver's Needle," Sharkey said matter-of-factly.

"What?" he muttered.

"That cliff," he pointed. "It's part of the Superstition Mountains, the only remnant of an ancient volcano."

Sharkey surveyed the area. "This way."

Cody's mind focused briefly on the prudence of blindly following Sharkey to some unknown danger. Could he be trusted? He *had* instructed them to bring water, sunblock, and some snack bars. If he planned to let them die, he could've said nothing. But still, he was leading them through a hostile place, and providing no clue as to why. They were completely at his mercy.

After walking for almost an hour, they stopped for a water break. Sweat trickled down the middle of Cody's back. His eyes focused on the ground ahead, searching for rattlesnakes, scorpions, or some other deadly creature that could take one of their lives in the time it would take to gasp out loud.

"Why don't any of these adventures require a trip to Hawaii, or even Florida?" Martin mumbled.

Cody assumed they were heading north, motivated by the occasional glimpse of a burning sun hovering to his left. They continued along a canyon, the pointed peak looming to their south, until reaching a sharp ridge.

"Uh, Mr. Sharkey? Where are we?" Martin's tone reflected his anxiety.

"Arizona, Mr. Speck."

"I lathered myself with SPF 50, but I better not find one little sunspot on my pearly white skin," Shelby muttered.

"I believe just ahead we'll find the tributary canyon we need to follow. Unfortunately, it is deep and rocky with fairly dense vegetation, so stay close. We'll head south, back toward Weaver's Needle, until the Black-Top Mountains are due west of us."

The scorching sun was beginning to sink lower in the sky. Cody knew when the sun went down a whole new set of problems would face them. One slip of the foot could mean a broken leg... or worse. Plus, he was sure mountain lions, bobcats, and coyote would be lurking in the darkness, waiting to make a meal out of some unsuspecting traveler.

"Oh, my," Shelby said with a gasp. "What is *that?*"

"That, my dear," Sharkey replied, "is a skull, a human skull. The Apache hold this land sacred," he called over his shoulder. "Many prospectors and treasure hunters – lured to this place over the possibility of unfathomable riches – have been beheaded here over the centuries. The Apache believe their thunder god dwells in these mountains, protecting this sacred land from intruders."

Shelby gulped loudly. Charlotte's water bottle hit the ground with a thud.

"And, we are here *why*?" Cody made sure his tone was not lost on anyone.

"The gold, Sir Hawke, gold from the Lost Dutchman Mine."

"Gold?" Martin said perkily. "Why didn't you say so."

"What gold?" Cody asked.

"It began with Francisco Vasquez de Coronado in the mid-1500s. He came from Mexico, looking for the legendary Seven Golden Cities of Cibola," Sharkey offered nonchalantly. "Coronado remained until various members of his team ended up headless. In the mid-1800s, it was the heirs of Don Miguel Peralta, with clues handed down from their forefathers, heading into these mountains looking for a gold mine just north of La Sombrera."

"The sombrero?" Shelby asked.

Sharkey nodded toward the towering hat-shaped peak. "Weaver's Needle. They returned from occasional trips to the mine with saddlebags of gold nuggets until the Apache decided it was enough. Four hundred men were ambushed and massacred not far from here."

"That's lovely," Martin muttered flippantly.

"Then a man called 'the Dutchman', Jacob Waltz – who was actually German – and his partner Jacob Weiser, came to the aide of one of the Peralta sons a few years later and were shown a map for their trouble. They apparently made a few trips to the mine and returned with copious amounts of ore from the large gold vein, that is until Waltz left one day to get supplies and returned to find Weiser cooked over his own campfire."

"This just gets better and better," Martin added sarcastically.

"And, it has continued for centuries, the lure of unimaginable riches and the unexplained murders. Legend says ghost prospectors still roam these mountains trying to find – or perhaps protect – the mother lode. Attempts by treasure hunters to locate the mine have resulted in many headless skeletons scattered across the Superstition Mountains."

Sharkey stopped and pulled a worn piece of paper from his pocket. Cody almost laughed as he glanced at his siblings, staring at their guide with wide eyes and mouths hanging open. Carefully unfolding the paper, Sharkey revealed a faded map detailing mountain peaks and winding trails. A large circle in the center seemed to be the focus. Rubbing the stubble on his chin, Sharkey perused the map.

"And *this*…," he muttered absently, "is the Peraltas' map."

"Are the Apache still guarding this place?" Cody asked. "Do you know what you're doing?"

"Not really," Sharkey replied. "To the first question. Without question, to the second."

"What does that mean, not really? And, just so I'm clear," Martin added cynically, "did you just say *beheaded* and *cooked over his campfire*?"

"I did."

"Just checking," Martin replied.

"Why did you bring us here?" Cody asked scornfully. "Are you trying to get us killed?"

"No one's going to get killed. We just need to procure some gold. I can only carry so much."

"Gold? For what?"

"All in good time, Mr. Hawke." Sharkey looked around. "The sunset should reflect off the mountainside in a few minutes, revealing the mine's general location so keep your eyes open," he added. "Come on."

They traveled along the ridge in uneasy silence. The blistering heat was beginning to take its toll. Frequent gulps of now warm water were not enough to quench a growing thirst. They had headed just a short distance along the west side of the canyon when Cody stopped.

"Look!" he yelled, pointing at the mountain.

The setting sun reflected off a towering cliff, illuminating the area with a golden glow.

"There it is Mr. Hawke, the legendary Lost Dutchman gold mine. We need to continue along this ridge. These cliffs form the northern slope of Needle Canyon. That massive rock atop the ridge," Sharkey said, pointing, "makes up the southern slope."

"Then what?" Martin asked.

"It's hidden right now, but from up there, we should be able to see Weaver's Needle. There's a path that leads to a large rock with a very distinctive face. The years and the elements have helped carve the rock into an important sign. Once we get close, we'll find a pointing tree that shows the way."

Really? And Mary's little lamb will pop up and lead us to the treasure.

Cody had given up asking questions. Sharkey told them exactly *what* he wanted them to know, exactly *when* he wanted them to know it.

The group headed southeast for what Cody estimated to be another half hour, then climbed up a cliff toward the rocky outcropping they had seen from a distance. It was a difficult climb, but doable without any special equipment.

"Hurry! We don't have much time. If the sun sets, we will need to stay here overnight."

Shelby looked at him with wide eyes. That was all the incentive they needed. The four climbed as fast as they could, trying to match Sharkey's blistering pace.

"Finally, level ground. Thank goodness," Shelby said, breathless.

They reached a small plateau that narrowed to a worn path. Numerous trees surrounding the rocky outcropping provided some relief from the late afternoon sun. Cody wondered why Shelby wasn't spewing a list of complaints like she always seemed to do when he was in the lead.

"Hold up," Sharkey said suddenly, pointing. "See that rock over there? What does it look like to you?" Holding Shelby's shoulders, he turned her body in the direction he was pointing. Cody felt his face redden and it wasn't from the heat.

"Oh, my! Why it's a horse's face," Shelby blurted out.

"You see it?" Sharkey asked with uncharacteristic joviality. "That's where we're headed."

They reached a small clearing and stopped for a moment to catch their breath. The temperature began to drop rather dramatically as the sun continued to dip below the mountain ridge.

"Look, over there!" Martin yelled.

A branch stuck out of an old tree stump. It resembled an eerie looking arm with a finger pointing ahead.

"That's it, Mr. Speck," Sharkey replied.

The worn path wound along the face of the ridge, leading behind the horse monument. The others followed in silence, not wanting to disturb his heightened state of focus, a man on a mission.

Just then, the whinny of a distant horse echoed throughout the chasm. Sharkey hesitated for a moment. Cody heard it again. The sound appeared to be getting closer.

"Go!" Sharkey blurted suddenly. "Continue on this path! Remember what I told you! Just beyond the rock that resembles a horse, look for the entrance to the Thunder god's realm." Sharkey turned and headed toward the clearing. "NOW!" He yelled over his shoulder.

"*What?* What is he doing?" Shelby asked, staring at Cody with wide eyes. "He's *leaving* us?"

"This isn't good," Martin mumbled.

"Could that be the Apache?" Charlotte asked, her voice choked.

The four ran ahead until they were far enough away to observe the clearing below, but not be seen. A group of men approached on horseback.

"I hope they aren't the guys who like to behead people," Martin said curtly.

Cody saw one of the men dismount and approach Sharkey. He was clearly of Native American descent. The two seemed to be exchanging greetings that quickly escalated into a heated argument.

Suddenly, the Native American drew a blade from the leather pouch at his waist. He and Sharkey circled each other in an apparent war dance. The Indian lunged, but Sharkey easily avoided his attack, holding his hands in the air as if saying he wouldn't engage. The man was clearly angry over something as he continued trying to draw Sharkey into a fight.

"Oh, my!" Shelby moaned. "What should we do? Should we try to help him?"

"I'm quite sure he doesn't need our help," Cody mumbled.

"Is that motivated by confidence in Sharkey, or a lack of concern," Shelby asked.

"The other man has a knife," Charlotte piped in. "And there are five of them."

"He'll be fine. I'm sure of it. Come on. Let's see if we can find this supposed gold mine. Sharkey said we need the setting sun to locate the entrance so we better hurry. I'm sure he'll catch up when he's finished."

"I *really* do not want to be stuck here another day," Shelby added.

"I'm sure he was just toying with us," Cody replied.

They traversed a small, wooded area next to the big rock that resembled the face of a horse. The monument jutted from the ground like a sacred testament to an earlier time. After a brief look back at Sharkey, the girls joined Cody.

"Uh, guys?" Martin yelled from ahead. "I think I found something."

Cody followed Martin's voice along an overgrown path at the base of the mountain. A rocky outcropping loomed in front of them. He stared ahead, silently questioning the soundness of his quest to learn more about Sharkey's exploits.

"Well, this is lovely," Shelby said nervously.

"Do you think someone's trying to tell us something?" Cody asked.

A crudely constructed wooden fence held the skulls of various unfortunate souls who had clearly not heeded the various warnings during their hike through the Superstition Mountains. The fence stood auspiciously in front of an area covered in brush, spanning the distance between two large rocks.

"That fence is almost comical," Cody muttered. "Such a wobbly thing isn't going to keep anyone out. I could probably push it over with my foot."

"It's just there to remind prospectors what happened to the last idiots who passed by," Martin replied.

Cody walked back and forth between the rocks, trying to assess the hidden danger. Finally, he got down on his knees and crawled through a gap under the fence.

"Where are you going, Cowpoke?" Shelby cried.

"Stay here. Let me see what's on the other side," he called back.

The rocks formed a sort of tunnel covered with tree branches. He made his way up the rocky incline. Light filtered through the branches above, leaving dappled shadows on the ground around him. Finally, he reached the cliff face.

Well, that was fairly harmless. It can't be that easy.

"Uh, you guys might want to see this," he called.

The others joined Cody on a ledge that ran along the rock wall. The cliff created a cathedral-shaped backdrop with an old wooden door at its center. Trees and dense scrub surrounded the doorway, making it nearly impossible to head in any other direction. The door was made from thick boards bound so tightly together the seams were barely visible. Round columns carved into the surrounding rock, flanked each side.

"Well, doesn't that just look inviting?" Shelby moaned. "I am hot, sweaty, and tired. I don't suppose there's a nice bubble bath inside where I can soak my aching feet."

"Shelby, I'd think less about bubble baths and more about the various ways we could get mutilated in there," Martin said bluntly.

"I don't suppose it opens," Charlotte uttered.

"Nope. I tried," Cody said. "Maybe together we can do it."

The four teens pushed, leaning into it with their combined weight, but the door wouldn't budge.

"Well, now that I have a herniated lower intestine, are we all in agreement it's locked?" Martin muttered.

"Maybe we need Mr. Sharkey's muscles to help us," Shelby said.

"I'm sure even the great and wonderful Sam Sharkey can't open this door." Cody replied.

"So, now what?" Martin shook his head. "Do we go back and find Sharkey?"

"Wait," Charlotte said pensively. "Look at that shadow on the door. There's something interesting about it."

"Where's it coming from?" Martin wondered aloud.

The four turned back toward the west. Cody could see the worn path and old fence below and the horse head outcropping looming just beyond.

"The horse head is blocking the sun," Shelby said.

"The sun is sitting right at the horizon, shining around the horse rock and creating this shadow on the door," Charlotte offered. "Shelby, what did Mr. Sharkey said about the horse being important?"

"He said, the years and the elements have helped carve this rock into an important part of our journey."

"I assumed he meant as a landmark," Charlotte said, "but maybe there's something more."

"So, it's making a shadow on the door," Cody said briskly.

"It almost looks like a person, doesn't it?" Charlotte asked.

"I always do poorly at those inkblot tests," Shelby said with a chuckle, "but, it looks to me like a Native American."

"Yeah," Martin chimed in. "He's wearing a long tunic. His arms are raised up and his back is to us, like he's chanting."

Charlotte murmured, "His upraised arms and the flowing sleeves of the tunic are the horse's ears."

"The forelock is the Indian's head and the animal's face, his body," Cody added. "Okay, so we see it," he said, "but what's the significance?"

"Cody, that cannot be a coincidence. Can it?" Charlotte asked. "Is he pointing at something?"

"Well, maybe it's not a coincidence, but I don't see how it helps us open the door."

"Look at that smooth piece of rock next to the door. Are those scratches, or could they be some sort of writing?"

"Martin, you're right!" Charlotte moved in to take a closer look. "Unfortunately, it's really worn. It doesn't appear to be English. I would guess it's Spanish."

"What do you suppose these columns are for?" Martin asked.

"Could be just for decoration," Cody replied.

"Wait! There's a channel below the door with moss growing in it," Charlotte said. "There's been no sign of water the entire way, then suddenly we have trees growing around us and moss."

"What are those openings in the front of the columns? They look like vents," Cody said.

Charlotte smiled. "Good question. Maybe the plaque will tell us how to get the door open."

"Why can't any of this stuff be easy and just say, 'enter this way'?" Martin muttered.

"I wish I had my notes from Spanish class," Charlotte said, squinting at the plaque.

"Unless the words are numbers, colors, or days of the week, I'll be no help," Cody offered.

"Mr. Sharkey mentioned Francisco Vasquez de Coronado coming here in the 1500s," Charlotte added, "so this is probably not the same Spanish we learned."

"This is hopeless. We can't read Spanish, old or otherwise," Martin said.

"Oh, for Pete's sake, get out of the way." Shelby stepped gruffly past them, folding her arms as she reviewed the inscription.

"What do you think you're doing?" Cody said peevishly.

"Guerrero? Hmm, warrior?" Shelby mumbled. "Esencia que da vida? Essence of life?" She thought for a moment. "There are parts missing, but as best I can tell it says something like this."

For a warrior to be truly great,
And enter through this treasure gate,
He should be brave but also smart,
And continue with a stout heart.
Only the mirrored reflection of the life-giving essence,
Holds the power to unlock the sacred entrance."

Cody stared at Shelby in stunned silence. "How the heck did you do that?"

"It's not *that* different from regular Spanish," Shelby replied.

"You girls don't even need us around," Cody said, grinning. "Between Miss Genius and Miss Total Recall, you two are unstoppable."

"Why, Cody Hawke, is that humility? That's unusual, coming from you. And, it doesn't suit you. I like you better when you're being pigheaded," Shelby teased.

"Very funny," Cody said. "So, what does it mean?"

"Only the life-giving essence has the power to open the entrance," Charlotte repeated. She bent down to examine the moss-filled trough. Cody joined her. He pushed some of the debris aside and found smaller plaques near the bottom of each column.

"Shelby, take a look at these."

"The left one says 'tesoro' or 'treasure' and the right, 'esencia que da vida' or 'essence of life'."

"Well, we know the treasure is supposed to be gold, right? The 'essence of life'…" Cody hesitated, "what could that be?".

"Could it relate to religion, like your soul, or maybe something you love?" Charlotte asked.

"Or, maybe it's something that keeps us alive, like air, or food and water."

Charlotte's eyes lit up. "I think you are onto something, Cody. Life-giving essence, could it be water? That would explain the moss. But where would we get water from out here?"

"Well, let's say the answers are 'gold' and 'water'," Cody said. "If I remember my Spanish – help me out, Miss Total Recall – I think they are 'oro' and 'agua'."

"That sounds right."

Cody bent down to get a better view of the little plaques. "There is something else below."

"They almost look like little buttons…" Martin chuckled. "Hey, maybe this is like playing Jeopardy except instead of money, you get gold. The plaque said you need to be smart."

"Okay, what do the letters say?" Charlotte asked.

"The plaque on the left looks like it has the buttons 'o' and 'r'. The right one has three letters, 'a', 'g', and 'u'," Cody said.

"Those are the letters in 'oro' and 'agua'," Shelby replied excitedly.

"Try pressing the buttons in the right sequence and see what happens," Charlotte suggested.

"Shelby, you do the right one and I'll do the left," Cody said. "Okay, here goes."

They waited anxiously, anticipating a grand spectacle, but the door did not move.

"Well, that was anticlimactic," Martin said.

"Maybe it's broken," Charlotte added.

"Maybe," Shelby said. "Or, maybe we need to press them both at the same time. The clue said 'mirrored reflection of the life-giving essence'."

"Not bad," Cody said with a grin. "Okay, let's try."

They pressed the buttons at the same time and waited in silence.

"Nothing," Martin said.

"Hold on, I think I hear something," Cody mumbled.

"It almost sounds like running water," Shelby replied.

"Exactly," Charlotte said excitedly. "I believe it's filling those columns with water, and perhaps something blocking the door from opening is now floating to the top."

"Look," Cody said, "the shadow Indian's hand shows how high the water needs to get to open the door."

"And those vents are there to drain the water back down to the trough. Clever!" Martin added.

"We did it!" Shelby yelled.

Their excitement faded as the door swung open and stagnant air wafted out. The four teens stared into the waiting gloom. As his eyes adjusted, Cody could see the silhouettes of skeletons, scattered about the rocky floor.

Chapter 19: The Goldmine

"Cody, maybe we should wait for Mr. Sharkey."

"I'm sure he'll be here soon, Charlotte," he replied, taking a few cautious steps into the inky black.

Martin, Charlotte, and Shelby joined him though he could sense their apprehension.

"Lovely! The remains of all the poor souls who did exactly what we're doing," Shelby said with a moan.

"Let's just find some of Sharkey's gold, then get out of here. Look, if you see anything dangerous, just run for the door," Cody replied.

"One question," Martin muttered with obvious cynicism. "Why didn't these poor chaps just run for the door?"

Cody examined the walls, expecting some visible signs of gold, but nothing. Suddenly, a loud thud rocked the small room. The massive door swung shut, leaving them in total darkness.

"Oh, just great! What's your plan now, Mr. 'Let's run for the door if we see anything dangerous'?" Shelby cried.

"Sharkey stuffed a flashlight in my backpack," Martin whispered shakily, as he fumbled through the bag. "I should've known we were in trouble right then."

"Ugh," Shelby whimpered, "I feel something in my hair and…"

"And, what?" Cody asked. "We're fine. No need to cry," he mumbled.

"I'm *not* crying," she said petulantly. "It's just, I-uh…"

"*Again?*" Cody said. "You've got the weakest bladder on the planet. Find a dark corner," he added. "There are plenty of them."

"Cody Hawke, you are a mean, inconsiderate oaf," Shelby muttered. "I don't want to go on one of these poor fellows."

"I'm sure they won't mind," he replied curtly.

"Martin, shine the light on the door," Cody directed. "The bar blocking the door fell back into place. We should be able to lift it up."

He pushed on the thick wooden slab with all his might, but it wouldn't budge.

"Now what?" Martin mumbled.

"There must be a way out, otherwise how would anyone get the gold," Charlotte said.

"Looks like there's another door over here," Martin called.

Cody surveyed the large slab of smooth stone. He tried to push, but it wouldn't budge. "Let's try sliding it," he said.

The four were able to roll the door just far enough to squeeze through the opening. A blast of cool, stagnant air blew out from the adjoining room.

"It smells like your old gym shoes in here, Cowpoke."

They entered a silo-shaped room about ten meters in diameter. Light filtered through a few openings in the rocky ceiling, providing limited visibility. Cody took a few steps then stopped.

"Don't move!" he yelled, lifting his arms as a barrier. "It's like the crossword puzzle all over again. We're on a ledge."

"I can't even see the bottom," Martin mumbled. "Do you think the gold is down there?"

"How are we supposed to get to it? I don't see any stairs," Charlotte asked, hugging the wall.

Cody and Shelby were peeking cautiously over the edge, when a scraping sound broke the silence. The door began to roll shut. Shelby let out a choked scream.

"Give me something to block it!" Cody yelled.

They tried to hold the door, but it just kept moving. Cody wedged his backpack into the opening, but the force crushed it against the jamb. He heard a pop and water began dripping from the backpack.

"I hope we don't have to hike back," Martin said. "The door just massacred your water bottle."

"Just great! Now what? We're stuck in here." Shelby cried. "We'll either die of starvation or fall to our deaths! The Coldswells of South Carolina will never find me inside this mountain!"

"Relax. No one's going to die. There has to be a way down." Cody tried to sound confident.

"Why can't we just stay in our rooms, watch stupid TV shows and eat junk food, like other teenagers. It may kill us, but at least it'll take twenty or thirty years," Martin said with a groan.

"There must be an opening or hidden pathway around here somewhere," Cody mumbled. "Let me see that flashlight for a second."

"What are those things on the wall behind you?" Charlotte asked anxiously.

"More weird letter buttons, like those outside," Shelby replied.

"Why would they be in here?" Martin asked.

"Maybe there's another door we need to open," Cody said.

"Okay," Shelby muttered, "but how are we supposed to answer a question, when there's no question?"

The words no sooner left her lips when another heavy, scraping sound filled the room. One of four stone panels began to slide, revealing a worn metal plaque.

"Wonderful! We need to answer more questions," Martin quipped. "Goldmine Jeopardy: get rich or fall to your death. Good times!"

"Well, might as well get started." Cody sighed, lifting his hat and running a sweaty palm through his hair. "Miss Total Recall, what does it say?"

Shelby was trying to translate the plaque, when a sudden lurch made them drop to their knees.

"What's happening?" Martin asked nervously.

"The ledge appears to be receding," Charlotte whimpered.

"What happens when we run out of ledge. Don't answer that," Martin mumbled.

"It's moving pretty slowly," Cody said, trying to sound calm.

"The sign outside said the warrior needs to be 'brave but also smart, to continue with a stout heart'," Shelby offered.

"If you have a point, better make it quick," Cody replied.

"She's saying we need to answer the question before the floor recedes," Charlotte added.

"Okay. Shelby, what does the sign say?" Cody asked

"I-uh, I'm not sure—"

"Shelby!"

"Okay! Roughly translated, I think it goes like this:

I fly above the ancient world,
Mythical wings of scarlet unfurled.
When my golden plumes are set afire,
I sing with grace upon the pyre.
I live just five-hundred human years,
But do not shed any mortal tears.
Because when my time on Earth is through,
A rebirth will come and I will rise anew."

"A riddle? I'm shocked. I'm so shocked, I'm going to have a heart-attack," Martin muttered.

"We've got to figure out the answer, then hope Shelby can translate it," Charlotte said.

"A bird of some kind? I heard something about flying and wings," Cody offered.

"You can't just speak it. It must be typed in," Charlotte replied.

"Anyway, that's not the answer." Shelby looked at the buttons. "I think 'bird' is 'pájaro' in Spanish. We don't have those letters."

"Wonderful. Charlotte, if you have any ideas this would be a good time," Cody said.

"The buttons are 'e', 'f', 'i', 'n', and 'x'," Shelby offered. "WAIT!" she exclaimed. "I think…"

"Shelby?" Cody said. "I'm open to any ideas that keep us from falling to our deaths."

"I-uh, I'm not sure," she whined. "I don't know how to spell it in Spanish."

"What happens if you enter the wrong answer?" Charlotte asked nervously.

"Nothing good, I'm sure," Martin replied.

The ledge had receded to less than a third of its original width. Cody leaned against the wall and tried to slow it down with his feet, but it wasn't possible.

"Wings of scarlet," Cody said. "Could it be a cardinal?"

"I-uh," Shelby said with whine. "I think it could be…"

"Guys!" Charlotte screamed. "My toes are almost off the ledge!"

"SHELBY!" Cody yelled. "NOW!"

"OKAY! UGH…"

Shelby quickly pushed five buttons. The ledge stopped then slowly began to extend back out.

"Shelby," Cody said, trying to catch his breath, "I take back *every* bad thing I've ever said about you. You're a genius! What did you enter?"

"The answer was Phoenix. I thought it might be spelled fénix in Spanish. Lucky guess, huh?" She grinned. "Good thing I could type it with my hands shaking."

The four teens laughed, but their happiness was short-lived as another sound echoed throughout the silo. Cody thought it sounded like a blow torch firing up. The room grew warm.

"Uh-oh!" Martin peered over the edge. "Fire!"

"I *really* don't want to burn to death. That would hurt!" Shelby said with a whimper.

"It's getting closer," Cody muttered, wiping his brow. "What's the next question?"

Shelby stared at the second plaque.

"Uh, Shelby, we don't have a lot of time."

"STOP RUSHING ME, CODY! This one is more difficult. Some of these words are a total guess."

"A guess is far better than us becoming the gooey center of a smore," Martin cried.

"Cristóbal Colón plans to head the wrong way,
Seeking spices and wealth, no matter what they say.
The king finally relents to Colón's pleas,
And he sets out by ship to reach the East Indies.

His hopes were high, but navigation imperfect,
And he ended up in a place he didn't expect.
He dubbed the locals 'Indios' as a fake,
So as not to admit his big mistake.
Instead he said his trip went as planned,
But he called the place his 'savior' land."

"Whew! That's a mouthful!" Martin said.

"Shelby, could 'Indios' be the Spanish word for 'Indians'?" Charlotte asked.

"Then Cristóbal Colón could be Christopher Columbus," Martin added.

"What letters are available to us?" Charlotte asked.

"It's a pretty long list. I see 'a', 'd', 'l', 'o', 'r', 's', and 'v'," Shelby replied.

"Uh, it's getting warm in here," Martin added.

"Well, if it's Columbus, then shouldn't the savior land be America?" Cody hesitated. "What's the Spanish word for America?"

"Cody," Charlotte answered softly, "it's a misnomer Columbus discovered the United States. He actually landed on the Caribbean islands off North America. And, he never admitted he had not arrived in Asia as planned. So, America is named after Amerigo Vespucci, not Columbus."

"Okay. Okay. I don't need a history lesson!" He softened. "What islands did he get to?"

"I believe he reached the Bahamas," Martin replied, "but it doesn't fit. We are about to become crispy critters!"

"Wait!" Shelby cried. "His 'savior' land was in quotes. I think savior in Spanish is like 'salvador' or something. Is there a Salvador island? It fits the letters."

"Yes, Shelby. It is called San Salvador and its part of the Bahamas," Charlotte said, excitedly.

"Guys! I'm getting a suntan on my feet!" Martin exclaimed.

"Type it in, Shelby!" Cody yelled, peering over the edge. "Yikes!" He jumped back from the edge as one of his sneakers ignited. He quickly kicked it off and stomped on it with the other foot.

"Oh, my. Oh, my…"

"*NOW*, SHELBY!"

Cody watched as she typed the letters. "Please stop," she said, turning toward them.

"LOOK! I think it's going down!" Martin yelled.

"That was close." Cody mumbled, using his sleeve to wipe the sweat from his forehead. "There are two left. What do you suppose the next fun adventure will be?" he muttered. "And, where the heck is *Sharkey* as we hover on the ledge of death?"

"Uh, I think I hear trouble," Charlotte cried, peering over the side. "Do you hear water rushing?"

"What does it say, Shelby?" Cody shouted. "Quickly!"

"You know, this is not the Spanish I learned. We've been lucky so far because I've been able to deduce the essence of these little riddles. But who knows—"

"Shelby!" It was Charlotte this time.

"Okay!"

Cody stared at the swirling water filling the silo, its spray rising up to splash his face.

"Okay. I think it goes something like this," Shelby yelled.

One Easter Sunday in days of yore,
Ponce De León set out to explore.
He came upon an island, paradise for sure,
And sailed around it for a three-month tour.
Though, it was not an island he soon discovered,
But a large peninsula that was lushly covered.
The Feast of Flowers he called this place,
And so, established a lasting base."

"What did Ponce De León discover? And what is the Feast of Flowers?" Cody asked.

"The whirlpool is so loud!" Martin yelled. "I can hardly hear myself think!"

"Did he discover Puerto Rico?" Cody asked.

"I thought Columbus discovered all those islands around 1492," Charlotte cried. "Ponce De León made his discovery after Columbus. I believe it was the early 1500s."

"Besides, Shelby said 'peninsula' so it's not Puerto Rico," Martin added.

"Come on guys! It's almost to the top!" Cody yelled.

"What are the letters?" Charlotte asked, her voice cracking.

"They are 'a', 'd', 'f', 'i', 'l', 'o', and 'r'."

The swirling vortex was beginning to wet their shoes. It spun so quickly Cody had no doubt it could easily wash them from the ledge. He looked around for something to hold onto but there was nothing.

"Stay back against the wall!" he shouted.

The water was let than a meter from their feet.

"Fiesta de las flores," Shelby repeated, sounding strangely calm. "Discovered a peninsula on Easter Sunday." Suddenly, she gasped. "I think I'm translating wrong! It's not literally a feast of flowers."

"SHELBY!" Cody yelled as the rushing water covered their shoes.

The force of the water pushed against them, making it difficult to stand still.

"I can't hold on," Charlotte cried. "WAIT! SHELBY, THE ANSWER IS—" and she was gone.

"CHARLOTTE!" Shelby screamed.

"MARTIN, HOLD MY FEET!" Cody cried.

"Sure, and who's going to hold mine?" the teen muttered.

Martin sat with his back to the wall using his legs as leverage. Cody dropped down onto all fours, extending his legs backward so Martin could hold him steady. The water splashed in their faces making it difficult to breathe. Suddenly, Charlotte's face emerged from the foam. Cody reached as far as he could into the spinning eddy.

"CHARLOTTE! Grab my hand!"

She tried, but it was too far. The force was pulling her toward the deadly center. She coughed and splashed, trying to keep her head above water. Cody knew in another second she would be sucked into the vortex, lost forever. He could feel Martin losing his grip. The force of the water was too strong.

"LET GO!" he yelled to Martin.

"Let go? Are you—"

"YES!"

Cody immediately went spinning out into the whirlpool.

"CODY!" Shelby screamed.

He tried to reach his foster sister, but she disappeared into the foam. Suddenly the whirlpool stopped spinning. The water grew calm and began to recede. Cody dove under and pulled Charlotte to the surface. He swam to the ledge with her in tow and climbed up while Martin held her hand. As he turned to reach for her, the water began to recede quickly. Charlotte was now dangling from the edge.

"Help me!" Martin shouted.

Cody tried to reach her other hand, but she slipped from Martin's grasp.

You will not fall. Reach up to me, Charlotte.

Charlotte screamed, then seemed to grow calm. Her body rose as if by some unseen force. She and Cody locked hands.

"Don't *ever* say we don't need you guys," Charlotte cried, flopping down on the stone, shivering.

"Whew! That was close!" Shelby said.

"I think I peed in my pants," Martin added, dropping to the floor.

"I can't believe the whirlpool just stopped like that," Cody exclaimed.

"It stopped because I typed in the answer," Shelby replied, grinning broadly.

"Thank you, Shelby!" Charlotte said emphatically. "I thought I was done for!"

"Me, too." Cody grinned. "What was it?"

"Florida," she replied.

"Yes," Charlotte added. "Ponce De León discovered Florida."

"I was translating it literally. Pascua Florida refers to the feast of the flowers."

"That's right! And, he discovered Florida during Easter season," Charlotte added.

"Well, we have one more riddle to answer. I hope this one's easy. I'm not sure I can take much more excitement," Martin said with a deep sigh.

The ledge heaved and began to turn, slowly at first then picked up speed. The sound of scraping rock filled the room. Three spinning blades jutted out from the wall to their right. One blade was about shoulder height, the second waist high, and the third was the level of their ankles. The blades swung intermittently out from the wall in a random, horizontal pattern that made them difficult to predict.

"Shelby!" Cody yelled.

"I'm on it."

The four walked in the opposite direction, trying to maintain their position.

Shelby twirled her hair nervously. "How am I supposed to read this and walk at the same time? Oh, my! I do not want to get cut into pieces," she said with a whimper.

"So, this is how so many treasure hunters lost their heads," Martin muttered.

"Thanks for the visual," Shelby cried. "Okay, I think this is it."

"Their metal armor furthered domination,
Any thought of defiance brought quick rumination.
Swords forged from Toledo steel,
Inspired the fiercest enemies to kneel.
Their message encouraged honor and chivalry,
Their literacy and horses helped clinch victory.
These men from Extremadura's land,
Conquered all brave foes arising at hand.
One warrior searched for the Golden City,
But was unsuccessful and gained no pity."

"That sounds to me like a Spanish Conquistador," Martin said, breathing heavily.

"How many letters do we have?" Cody asked.

"Quite a few but there's no 'Q', so I don't think it could be Conquistador," Shelby replied.

"Guys! Think! We're losing ground!" Cody yelled.

"Stop that, Cowpoke! We clearly see the importance of thinking!" Shelby snapped.

"It sounds like they want one particular Conquistador. The only one I can think of is Cortés. He conquered the Aztecs," Charlotte said.

"No, I don't think it will fit. We have letters 'a', 'c', 'd', 'n', 'o', 'r'," Shelby whined. "Oh my, we are getting close! Cody! Do something!"

"I can't think of any other Conquistadors!" Charlotte cried. "Wait! Pizarro conquered the Incas. Does that fit?"

"I don't think so. Ugh!" Shelby replied, panting. "I'm having a hard time staying near the buttons."

"We need to run!" Cody yelled.

By jogging they were able to reach the far side again. But just as Shelby approached the letters, the ledge began rotating faster. It became increasingly difficult to maintain their position.

"Where is *Sharkey*! I knew he would get us killed!" Cody roared.

"He took the gold and left us here to die," Martin muttered. "He's home having a cold beer."

"The guy rambled on for an hour with all that useless information about everyone from Coronado to the Dutchman," Cody growled, "then, when we need him, he leaves us."

"Now they can add our names as the latest bunch of idiots to die here," Martin added.

"Cody!" Charlotte yelled suddenly. "THAT'S IT!"

"WHAT'S IT?"

Running as fast as they could, Charlotte and Martin were just a few meters from the blades. Shelby was a meter behind, but all were losing the battle.

"I can't run in these stupid shoes!" Shelby screamed. "Cody, it's up to you! You need to reach the letters!"

"WHAT DID I SAY?

"CORONADO!" His foster siblings yelled in unison.

He bolted as fast as he could, quickly reaching the ancient keypad.

"The blades . . . I hear them. They're right behind me." Martin sounded so winded he could barely finish. "It's been fun, guys," he mumbled.

Cody was having a hard time hitting the correct letters while running. 'C', 'O'..." He held one hand with the other, trying to stabilize his index finger.

"HOW DO YOU SPELL IT?"

"CODY!" Shelby screamed.

Suddenly the blades stopped swinging and receded into the wall. The ledge began to slow down as the teens dropped to the floor, gasping for air.

"Talk about your motivational exercise plan," Martin muttered, panting.

Cody started to laugh and the others joined in. Their chuckle turned into hysterical laughter until they were almost crying. Suddenly, the floor began to move.

"Oh, no! *Now* what?" Shelby said as they all jumped to their feet.

"There aren't any more plaques," Charlotte added nervously.

The ledge began to recede for a second time, methodically disappearing into the wall.

"LOOK!" Cody yelled, pointing to a rock formation emerging just below.

"Where did that come from?" Martin asked.

"I'm not sure but run for it!" Cody said.

He made his way around the ledge and jumped down onto the rocky outcropping protruding from the silo wall. Another appeared just below the first, forming a crude set of steps.

"I-uh," Charlotte whimpered, staring at the steep drop from atop the ledge.

"HURRY!" Cody yelled, letting Shelby and Martin pass. "The step above recedes as soon as the next one appears. JUMP! Charlotte, I've got you!"

She jumped down into Cody's waiting arms. The narrow steps swung out and back quickly and there wasn't time to go single file, so they had to descend two abreast. It was more like controlled falling, Cody thought, leaping onto the next step.

"We're almost halfway! Keep moving."

A sudden scream echoed about the chamber. Shelby was leaning over the edge, trying to regain her balance.

As he reached for her hand, the step disappeared. There was only room for two on the next step and Charlotte and Martin were already there. Martin reached out his hand, but it was too far. Cody wrapped his arm around Shelby's waist and held tight as they plummeted into darkness.

"CODY! SHELBY!" Charlotte screamed.

He tried not to focus on Shelby's scream or his racing heart. In his mind he pictured the cave floor below and the two of them landing softly like leaves floating down from an autumn tree.

"Do you *see* them? Where *are* they?" He heard his siblings' frantic calls.

"CODY? SHELBY?"

"We're over here," Cody called, as Charlotte and Martin emerged from the darkness.

"How did you…" Martin began.

"Don't ask," Cody replied.

"My hero," Shelby said with a grin, planting a kiss on his cheek.

Again, his heart raced, but this time for a different reason. Relax, Cody chastised himself.

As his eyes began to adjust to the dark, he surveyed the funnel-shaped mine. Human skulls littered the floor along with the bones that probably went with them. A door swung open revealing the dim light of another chamber.

Cody stepped cautiously into the next room, ancient moist air filling his lungs. Meager light filtered in from somewhere above.

Just then, a voice broke the silence. "Glad to see you made it."

Cody could see the outline of a man approaching.

"Sharkey! Nice of you to show up!" Cody growled.

"We almost *died* up there!" Shelby said crossly.

"But you didn't. I had every confidence you would prevail." Sharkey's eyes twinkled with amusement.

"Are you *kidding*?" Cody yelled. "We were *this* close to getting burned, drowned, hacked to pieces and falling to our deaths! And you! You were just *waiting* here?" Cody's face burned. "I ought to punch you in the—"

"Relax, Mr. Hawke. I would not have allowed anything to happen to you."

"What would *you* have done? You weren't... You were *watching*?" Cody's mood went from anger to disgust. "You let us go through that? Do you know what could've happened? We almost lost Charlotte!"

"But you didn't. Now, you have the confidence that comes from knowing what you can do when tested." Sharkey grinned nonchalantly. "I did it for *you*."

Cody wanted to reply but all he could do was scowl.

"How did you get down here?" Charlotte asked.

"There's a side entrance."

Cody frowned. "You couldn't have *said* something?"

"I didn't know until I got here. You four were so preoccupied with the columned doorway – as you were meant to be –you never bothered checking the underbrush to the right. The shadow was pointing that way. I told you it was important."

"That's just great," Shelby muttered. "Charlotte said something about him pointing. We should've listened."

160

"Never assume anything without first making certain you've considered all options.

"Well, aren't you just a *genius*," Cody said sharply.

Regardless, he felt sheepish, knowing Sharkey had outsmarted them *again*.

Cody noticed Shelby scanning the room, her mouth hanging open. Charlotte and Martin also appeared to have forgotten their anger as they stared in stunned silence. The chamber was covered in a breathtaking façade of what Sharkey referred to as rose quartz. In addition, shiny containers of various sizes and shapes reflected the light from a single ray of sunshine as it angled through the cave. Golden nuggets filled many of the vessels, the rest brimming with shiny gold doubloons.

"Oh, my," Shelby said in apparent breathless awe.

"Is this where you came to get the gold?" Charlotte asked.

Sharkey shook his head. "I left the old chest in a chasm along the ridge. It was filled with nuggets and doubloons. I knew the actual mine was nearby but never had the chance to look for it until today."

"So, exactly *why* are we stealing this gold?"

"Technically, Mr. Hawke, we are *not* stealing. And, we need this gold to fund various expeditions."

"What expeditions?"

"All in good time, Mr. Hawke. All in good time."

"But isn't this a state park? Charlotte asked.

"It is in our time."

"This isn't the current year?"

"No. Waltz, before his death, perhaps aided by some seismic activity, hid the mine entrance, making it more difficult to find. So, we came back to the late 1800s."

"Who was responsible for the chamber of horrors up there?"

"Mr. Speck, you can thank the Conquistador and his men for that. And, you can thank the Aztecs for storing their treasure here. Now, fill your backpacks and let's go home."

"We lost one," Cody said with a smirk.

"Great job, Mr. Hawke." Sharkey muttered. "How did you let that happen?"

"It got crushed in the funhouse doorway."

Chapter 20: The Fool

"Please hang your new outfits in your closets," Heather called from the kitchen, "I do not want to find these expensive clothes on the floor. When you're done, come down for dinner. We're eating a little early today. We have to be at the store by six a.m. to prepare for the Labor Day crowds."

"Yes, mom," Shelby and Charlotte replied.

"It's hardly worth the effort," Cody mumbled as they climbed the stairs, bags in hand. "I only got two shirts and two pairs of pants. And, in what universe are these *expensive*?"

"Anything that didn't come from good will is expensive to her," Martin replied.

"I could teach you to sew your own clothes," Shelby offered with a cheeky grin.

Cody frowned at her with a look he hoped would nip that discussion right in the bud.

"I hope we're in some of the same classes, like last year," Charlotte said.

"Unfortunately, honey, I doubt we'll be in any classes with you," Shelby responded.

"Yeah," Martin quipped, "unless you want to come down a few notches to our level."

The first day of school was easier than previous years, but they were still known as the 'Addams Family Orphans'. Thus, the four kept mostly to themselves. Many of their classmates knew where they lived and stayed away. Those that didn't, would become scarce as soon as they found out.

Cody thought about the girl Shelby ran into while they were school shopping. They teens exchanged hellos with Marissa while Heather called a friendly greeting to the mom. As they were walking away, Cody overheard the girl's mother ask if those were the kids from the orphanage. Marissa replied they were. The mother chided her daughter, urging her not to hang around with such kids.

Things like that motivated Cody to begin distancing himself from the others. A voice in his head prompted him to focus on his reputation. As much as Cody cared about his foster siblings, sometimes he felt they dragged him down, kept him from realizing his potential on the popularity food chain. And popularity would certainly improve his status with the young ladies.

What's the harm in branching out a bit? I'll still be around most of the time, but seeing other kids might be good for me, for all of us. Instead of being together every second, we'll have more quality time. Once I make kids from school see this old place is basically harmless, things will get better for all of us.

"I need you guys to make yourselves scarce on Friday," Cody said as they headed up to do homework. "Go to town with Heather and Jack or stay in your rooms."

"And why is that?" Shelby asked.

"Because I have a date coming over and I don't want this to be a group effort."

"Who is it?" Shelby asked edgily.

"None of your business."

"I'll bet its Kim Cornell. I saw you talking to her in school," Charlotte said.

"No, it's not Kim."

"How about Jamie Finch?" Shelby asked.

"No, I know who it is. It's Shena Corelli!" Martin offered excitedly. Cody glanced up, noticing his foster sibling's eyes glowing with envy.

"Shena?" Shelby sneered. "No way Shena would go out with you. You're not high enough on the food chain or anywhere near rich enough."

Cody was silent, but he knew his grin told them all they needed to know.

"I can't believe she would agree to go out with you! What did you promise her?" Shelby asked.

"I didn't promise her anything."

"Come on, Cowpoke. A girl like that wants something. If it's not expensive gifts, and I know you can't afford those, then it has to be something else." Shelby gasped suddenly. "Cody Hawke!"

"What? What is it?" Charlotte looked at her friends. "What is he giving her?"

"Just stay in your rooms and do *not* come out!"

The smell of cheap perfume wafted up the stairway as Cody watched his mom check her look in the mirror. Jack helped Heather with her shawl, then headed out to start the van.

"Be good, honey," she called over her shoulder.

"Of course," Cody said, grinning slightly. "Aren't I always?"

She grabbed her purse, gave Cody a crooked smile, then closed the door behind her.

Heather and Jack had been invited to a party in town and it was all Heather could talk about for days. She met Joan Guzman at the grocery store and they became fast friends. Joan and her husband, Carlos, own a metaphysical shop in Dawnport, selling items used for magic and witchcraft.

The party theme was The Roaring Twenties. Heather was supposed to be dressed as a flapper, whatever *that* was. Cody thought the Guzmans were a bit strange, but his adoptive parents didn't have many friends. People would find out where they lived and never return their calls. Unlike everyone else, however, the Guzmans were fascinated by the old manor.

He watched his parents through the foyer window. Jack held the car door for Heather, then ran around to the driver's side with an uncharacteristic spring in his step. The old VW rocked back and forth as it navigated the bumpy driveway.

Chapter 20: The Fool

As soon as they were out of sight, Cody stepped out into the evening chill and ran down the driveway. Car exhaust fumes lingered on the slight breeze. It was a bit hypocritical of his parents, with all their hippy tendencies, driving a polluting vehicle. But even that had not motivated them to buy something newer... and less embarrassing.

A few minutes later, a car came screeching down Freya Lane. It skidded to a stop near where Cody waited and a female passenger got out. The driver immediately sped off.

This could be a great night, if the house doesn't scare the living daylights out of her.

"Shena?"

"Hey, Cody."

"I see you made it okay. Any trouble finding it?" he asked as they headed up the driveway.

A nearly full moon illuminated the highlights in her long black hair.

"No, but I might be regretting my decision."

"Don't be a baby," he teased.

Shena was silent for a moment, staring ahead at the old manor with obvious apprehension. She shook her head as if to rid it of some evil premonition.

Cody caught movement out of the corner of his eye. He glanced up just as Jezebel flew overhead. He hoped Shena didn't notice. One look at that face and she would go screaming into the night.

"My brother carried on the entire way about having to come so close to this place", Shena declared with a nervous giggle. "I told him I would tell our parents about the night at Sweeny Point unless he agreed to drive me."

"What happened at Sweeny Point?"

"Let's just say his *boys* had to carry him from the car to the house. They left him sprawled across the chaise on our front porch."

"Rookie," Cody said, laughing. "What did he tell your parents?"

"Please," she replied with a smirk, "a pitcher of extra dry martinis and they never even knew he was gone." Shena's eyes lit up as she took his arm. "So, did you get the stuff?"

"Yep, it's in my basement. My dad got it as a Christmas gift, but he won't even know it's gone."

"This is *some* house," Shena offered distractedly as Cody tugged on the front door. "Don't you ever worry about getting murdered in your sleep? There are rumors about this place being haunted?"

Cody laughed and shook his head. "There aren't any ghosts," he lied. "And, if any do come out to play, I'll protect you," he added with a cavalier swagger.

"Move over!" Shelby said testily as they peeked around the back corner of the staircase.

"But I can't see!" Martin whined.

"You're on my foot," Shelby grumbled.

"Well, stop hogging the view," Martin said.

"They're coming in the door," Charlotte whispered. "He's going to hear you."

"Get your head out of the way," Shelby mumbled.

"Unless you want him to see us, we better get back behind the stairs," Charlotte said.

"Look at her! She's all over him like white on rice!" Shelby sniffed as they stepped back. "I knew I didn't like that girl!"

"I've been looking forward to this," Shena said, grinning playfully as they crossed the foyer.

"Me, too."

"Interesting decor," the girl added, her voice echoing throughout the foyer. "Are those *faces* carved into the molding?"

"I know, it's a little creepy, unless you're a fan of medieval mahogany," Cody said, opening the basement door, "but there's nothing to worry about. I'll protect you."

"Have you ever come across anything gross, like bats or skeletons?"

"Not really," Cody lied. "Nothing dangerous anyway. Come on, this way."

"So, um, how is it . . . living with that girl, Shelby? You aren't really her brother, right? Isn't that a little weird? I mean, being in a family with someone who means nothing to you."

"Be careful," Cody said. "The steps are kind of steep."

"Yeah, and dark. I feel like I'm walking into a horror movie." Shena held onto Cody's arm. He liked the way it felt. "Yikes! Is this your basement or a cave? How many steps are there?"

"Just a few more," Cody mumbled.

As they reached the bottom, he put his arm around her shoulders.

"Is that a *gas* lamp?" Shena shook her head. "So, where's the stuff?"

"Over there," he said, heading to a table in one of the alcoves. "I have cups and some soda to mix with it. *And,* I brought some popcorn."

"Wow, you thought of everything."

He poured them each a glass, having no idea how much to mix.

I'll fill half the cup, then add the soda. Might as well get the biggest bang for the buck.

"Well, here's to us." Cody said, handing Shena a glass.

"Hmm," she took a sip, then coughed a bit.

"What's the matter, too strong for you?" he teased.

"No, it's fine." She took another sip. "You never answered my question. That girl, Shelby, you don't *like* her, do you?"

Cody shrugged. "She's okay."

"You aren't attracted to her or anything?"

"No," he replied quickly. "I mean, we're just friends."

"I hear she's like a wacko, thinks she's from some rich family."

Cody hesitated. He thought he heard voices.

"Well, she's... I mean, she's alright."

He felt a pang of guilt wash over him.

"So, there's nothing's going on between you?"

"No, of course not." Cody grinned, the liquor beginning to take effect. "I'm all yours," he said, putting his arm around her and moving in close.

"You agree she's a wacko—"

"Enough about Shelby," Cody interjected. "Let's talk about us. I've heard you're quite an experienced girl. How many boyfriends have you had?"

"Well, quite a few, if I do say so myself," Shena said haughtily. "Of course, I don't get too involved with any of them. I'm a free spirit, if you know what I mean."

"You have beautiful eyes," Cody whispered, "But, I'm sure you hear that all the time."

"I do? I mean yes, of course." Shena took a step closer and grabbed Cody's hand. "What about you? How many girlfriends have you had?"

"Enough," he said evasively. "What's that cologne you're wearing?"

"It must be my cherry lipstick," she giggled. "I didn't wear any perfume."

Cody gulped the rest of his drink, then pulled her close until his arms were around her waist.

"Slow down a bit," she said wriggling free, finishing her drink as well. "Let's have another, shall we?"

Cody made them two more drinks. He filled the glasses so full, some of the liquid splashed onto the floor. His vision was beginning to get blurry. He didn't want to appear inexperienced so he drank the second glass with the same enthusiasm as the first. Shena did the same. Again, Cody put his arm around the girl's shoulders.

"So, where were we?" he mumbled.

"You know, I usually only date rich men who can buy me things. Of course, I know *you're* not rich." Cody winced, looking away to hide his reaction. "So, the only reason I'm here," she continued, "is because I think you're cute."

"Did I mention you have beautiful eyes?"

"Uh-huh. So, what do you use this creepy basement for?" She moved closer.

"My parents run an internet business down here."

"I would be too scared to hang out down here alone. But I'm sure you're not scared." Shena smiled then looked around. "I'll bet if this old house could tell stories…"

"Oh, trust me… there is more to this house than you could ever imagine."

"Do tell!"

"Well, I'm just saying, there's like hidden treasure and stuff. I mean, we pretend to be poor, but we could buy expensive things any time we want."

He now had Shena's full attention. "Cody Hawke! Tell me more. Could you buy me, say, an expensive ring or something?"

"Of course! What would you like?"

Cody heard voices, an angel on one shoulder telling him to stop and a demon on the other, driving him on.

"Can you show me? The treasure, I mean."

"It's well-hidden and dangerous to get to," he replied.

Shena's look reflected her skepticism.

"It's true," he said. "I mean, I could show you if you want but—"

"Let's go!" She jumped up and down like a kid wanting a lollipop. "I want to see it!"

Cody took her hand, pulling her close. "Later, first let's…"

He leaned down until their lips touched. Her eyelids drooped provocatively. His head was swimming.

"Come on, Cody. Show me," Shena said abruptly, stepping back.

"Well, it's actually a doorway…"

"What's happening?" Martin moaned. "I can't see!"

"Shush," Shelby said testily. "It's hard enough to hear from a hundred steps up. Thankfully everything reverberates around down there like a concert hall."

"What are you three *doing*?" The man's prickly tone imparted something between amusement and impatience.

Shelby slammed into Martin as she backed up. He slipped and almost fell, dropping his glasses. Charlotte held her hands to her face, seemingly flushed with embarrassment. Shelby would've laughed at how ridiculous they looked, except for the realization they were all in trouble.

"Hello, Mr. Sharkey," she said.

"Why are you listening at the top of the steps? And, where's Mr. Hawke?"

They stared at him, momentarily frozen.

"Uh, well, we were actually just looking for something," Shelby said.

"Yeah, Shelby lost her earing," Martin added quickly.

"Looks like you've got both to me," Sharkey said. "Again, where's Mr. Hawke?"

"I-uh, mean *ring*," Martin responded. "Did I say earring?"

"Uh, Cody's not feeling well," Charlotte offered.

Chapter 20: The Fool

"Let's try again, shall we?" the man muttered, clearly not buying their story. "Where's Mr. Hawke?"

The sound of female laughter echoed from below. Sharkey didn't hesitate. He bolted past them, taking the steps two at a time. Charlotte, Shelby and Martin lagged behind, not wanting to be seen.

"What kind of doorway? Come on, Cody! Let's go see it!"

"In a minute."

"I'll bet you showed it to that loser, Shelby!"

"Uh, well..."

"Mr. Hawke? What are you doing?" Sharkey said reproachfully.

"Huh?" Cody turned abruptly. "What? Uh, well, we were just—"

"Drinking?" Sharkey asked, frowning.

"Uh, we were..."

His mind squirmed, trying to come up with a viable excuse.

"Why, hello." Shena approached Sharkey with obvious interest. "Are you his Dad? What are you like... Dr. Jones or something?"

"Get down here," Sharkey yelled up the stairway.

Shelby, Charlotte, and Martin came down the stairs like little kids about to be scolded.

"You ratted me out?" Cody snarled.

"We did no such thing!" Shelby retorted. "You managed that all on your own."

A large rat appeared out of the shadows and raced across the basement floor. Another followed.

"EEK!" Shena screamed. "Get it out of here! Get *me* out of here!"

"Did I just make those..." Cody began, scratching his head.

A brief recount of his conversation with Shena flashed through Cody's mind. He tried to replay it in his head to determine whether he needed to do any damage control, but it was hard to focus.

How much did they hear? What's wrong with me? Why can't I concentrate?

"Mr. Hawke, what do you think you're doing?" Sharkey said crossly.

"I'm, uh, just talking with a friend," he replied, knowing his words weren't coming out right.

"Cody was just telling me about the hidden treasure in this house," Shena said, nearly swooning. "We were just going to see it when you guys came down. I *love* treasure."

Cody glanced at his foster siblings.

"Is that true, Cody?" Charlotte asked, disappointment apparent on her face.

"No, uh, I…"

"I know you. You're that geeky genius girl," Shena said, pointing to Charlotte. "And you, you're that nerd, uh, Martin." She turned to Cody. "How many loser kids do you have living in this place?"

Cody took a few wobbly steps toward Sharkey and pointed his finger at the man's face.

"This does not concern you. Now, all of you, get lost!"

"It does concern me, Mr. Hawke. Your safety and the safety of this girl concern me." Sharkey dramatically lifted the half-empty bottle of whiskey.

"Hey, put that down," Cody said, his words slurred.

"What about the treasure?" Shena pouted, stumbling slightly. "I want to see it. I love treasure."

"There isn't any treasure," Sharkey said snappily. "He's got an overactive imagination. Now, let's go, young lady. I will see to it that you get home."

"But we—"

"Mr. Hawke, I suggest you drink a few tall glasses of water and get yourself to bed." The man shook his head, glancing down at the bottle. "Oh, and I'd bring a bucket. Let's go, young lady." Sharkey headed for the steps. "You two," he ordered, pointing to Shelby and Charlotte, "you're with me."

As he climbed the steps, Sharkey called over his shoulder, "Mr. Speck, help Mr. Hawke upstairs. And see to it he wipes that lipstick off his face."

"Hi kids, we're home!" The crackly intercom speaker echoed throughout the hall.

It took a supreme effort for Cody to lift his head off the toilet seat.

"Hi, mom," Shelby called.

Uh-oh.

He couldn't hear Heather's response, but she must have asked where everyone was because, a minute later he heard her coming down the hallway.

"Everything's fine. He's in the bathroom," Martin called.

"Is he alright?" Heather asked, concern apparent in her voice.

"Yeah, he's just got a touch of the flu," Shelby replied.

"Does he need anything?" Heather asked. "Should I make some soup?"

"No, it's okay, mom. He doesn't need anything. I'm sure he'll be fine."

Heather pushed the door open.

"Cody, honey? Are you okay?" she asked, feeling his forehead. "Wait. What is that smell?"

He heard his mom walk away and yell, "Jack? Jack, can you come up here?"

Uh-oh.

Then he heard Shelby's voice again. "Are you going to be *fine*, tough-guy?" she taunted. "I'm *so* sorry to see you barfing up your guts. It's nothing you don't deserve."

Cody was pretty sure he heard enjoyment in her reproachful tone.

"When I'm feeling better," he groaned, "I'm going to—".

He never got to finish his threat, turning quickly back toward the toilet.

Chapter 21: The Darkness

The haphazard creaking of rocking chairs, pitching back and forth with mindless repetition on Freya Manor's front porch, mixed with the chirp of crickets hiding in nearby bushes.

"What do you think he plans to do with that gold?" Cody asked, breaking the prevailing silence.

"Cowpoke, don't even talk to us!" Shelby said crossly.

"Look, it's not my fault you all got punished," Cody replied.

"How is it not your fault? Every time you get in trouble, we get punished with you," Martin added.

"I *told* them you had nothing to do with it. I can't help it if they gave us the 'when one of us lies and the others cover for him, then we all lie' speech," Cody declared.

"We should have just let you sink with the other rat and not tried to protect you. Now we're all suffering for your stupid mistake!" Shelby grumbled.

"Like I said, it's not my fault you got punished," he responded.

"How—" Martin began, but never got the chance to finish.

"*Excuse* me, Cowpoke? Wow, you live in a fantasy world . . . one where you can't possibly do anything wrong." Shelby stood, crossing her arms defiantly. "It's not your fault? If you hadn't been such a total jerk in the first place, doing what you *clearly* knew was wrong, then none of us would be in this predicament!"

"Look, I'm sixteen years old. It's not a crime to want to be alone with a pretty girl."

"No?" Shelby stood over him, her eyes on fire. "Well, how about not drinking yourself into intoxication and telling a total stranger – one who would turn on you in half a second, I might add – our most important secret. You nearly ruined everything! All your big talk. 'The secret stays in this room'," she said mockingly. "And you let us down at the first opportunity."

"But I—"

"Dude, I'd let it go," Martin mumbled.

"And, it's comforting to know you'll turn on us like a rabid dog, just to please some girl you've known for all of *five* minutes!" Shelby stared at him, hands on her hips. "I trusted you, and I opened up to you."

"Shelby, I'm—"

She cut him off, her voice quivering. "All your *talk* about friends don't let friends down. Obviously, *that* was a load of—"

"KIDS?" Heather's voice sounded far away.

Cody grimaced. Hearing the emotion in Shelby's voice, he knew she'd heard at least some of what was said, and she was absolutely right. He had been weak and so easily manipulated. He'd let Shelby down and come so close to doing exactly what she said, ruining everything. Her words dug deep.

I should have told Shena to leave right after she insulted Shelby – but I didn't. What does that say about me? I almost told the girl about Rúndyrr, just for a kiss. Getting drunk and lying to Heather and Jack, what does that say about my character? What would mom and dad think? Would they be disappointed in me also?

Cody didn't want to know the answer. A lump so large he could barely swallow filled his throat. Lowering the worn cowboy hat to hide his face, he wondered whether Shelby would ever forgive him.

"Where *are* they?" Heather mumbled. "Kids! Dinner!" she called through the open window.

Shelby, Charlotte, and Martin got up and headed inside. Cody hesitated, preferring the solitude of an empty porch. The hangover was just the beginning. Everyone he cared about was furious with him. Oddly enough, the only one who didn't give him a lecture was Sharkey.

"Cody, get in here!" Jack yelled, clearly disappointed in him also. "Your mom said dinner's ready."

Cody played with his macaroni salad, still thinking about what Shelby had said. All I wanted was an evening with a pretty girl, he thought ruefully.

"The annual pirate festival is going on in town tomorrow," Shelby murmured between bites of a hotdog. "It would be fun to go. *Everyone's* going to be there. Oh, wait," she added, frowning at Cody, "that's right, we're not allowed out of the house."

"Momma?" Jessica asked. "Is my costume ready?"

"Jess, honey," Heather whispered. "It's not nice to talk about it in front of your brothers and sisters when they can't go."

"I'm sorry, mommy."

"Mr. Sharkey needs your help tomorrow," Jack said. "He'll be painting the front porch and you four, will be helping."

"Yes, sir," Martin mumbled.

"Yes, dad," Charlotte added.

"Do we have any gloves?" Shelby asked. "Last time, it took days to get the paint off my hands."

"Your hands," Martin quipped, "were the least of your worries. There was paint in your hair and even on the back of your legs. How is that even possible?"

After dinner, Shelby, Martin and Charlotte went upstairs to play a game in Shelby's bedroom. Cody went back to the porch. It was clear his siblings didn't want him around. The chilly atmosphere spoke volumes, and deservedly so. He rocked back and forth in silent reflection. How had life had gotten so complicated? He seemed to be constantly disappointing everyone he cared about.

All I want is to be treated like an adult. Is that too much to ask?

Cody noticed something lingering in the air west of Freya Manor.

"What is going on?" he wondered aloud, then bolted upstairs to Shelby's room.

"Has anyone looked out the window recently?" he asked, catching his breath.

"I'm not sure that's within the confines of our punishment," Shelby said with a smirk.

Cody ignored her, parting the curtains. Charlotte and Martin joined him at the window.

"What *is* that?" Charlotte whispered.

A black cloud had engulfed the woods. It appeared to go on for miles, consuming everything in its path. Curiosity appeared to get the better of Shelby as she got up to take a look.

"Could it be a cloud?" Martin asked.

"It looks more like smog," Shelby said.

"It's The Darkness," a male voice replied.

Cody turned to see Sam Sharkey leaning against the door jamb, arms crossed.

"What? That's a real thing?" Cody asked.

"The Darkness is gaining power. It's starting to take on a physical presence."

"What does that mean?" Shelby asked.

"I guess it means we're in trouble," Martin said.

"Very true, Mr. Speck," Sharkey said, rubbing the stubble on his chin.

"What will happen when it gets even more powerful?" Charlotte wondered.

"We will plunge into perpetual darkness, similar to nuclear winter. Crops will die. Food will become scarce. People will get sick and fight for whatever limited resources remain."

"Where do you come up with this stuff," Cody said, frowning. "It's just a cloud."

"Ignore it if you want," Sharkey turned to leave, "but the world as you know it will become a very unpleasant place."

"How can we stop it?" Shelby asked.

"I'm leaving early tomorrow morning to try and do just that."

"Where are you going?" Cody walked over and looked directly into the man's eyes, hoping for a straight answer.

"Ireland, first anyway."

"What's in Ireland?" Martin asked.

"One reason for the gold we procured," Sharkey said. "And hopefully answers on how to locate The Darkness, or at least its stronghold. Then, it's off to search for some old books."

"Can we come?" Charlotte asked suddenly.

Cody turned toward Charlotte, knowing the surprise on his face must've been obvious.

"You *want* to go?" he asked.

"Actually, I could use the help," Sharkey said. "These guys can be tricky to find . . . and even trickier to capture."

"Will there be any deadly Jeopardy games?" Martin mumbled.

"What guys can be tricky to find?" Cody asked.

"Be downstairs, six a.m. sharp," Sharkey said, then disappeared down the hall.

Chapter 22: The Rainbow

They paced about the foyer for nearly an hour, but Sharkey never showed. Cody grew increasingly annoyed. It was as if their time didn't matter to him, as if *they* didn't matter.

Shelby grumbled more than once about going back to bed. Just when they were about to do so, one of the many doors lining the foyer's western wall swung open and a bent figure emerged.

"Cometh," the gravelly voice uttered.

"Guardian?" Cody called. "How did you get that door open? I swear I've tried—"

"Dar . . . Mr. Sharkey hath been unavoidably detained. Cometh. Thou can begin without him."

"What were you about to call him?" Cody asked.

The Guardian stepped briskly back through the doorway.

"Just ignore me," Cody muttered. "That's fine."

They followed the man down a stone staircase and along an underground corridor. At its end, a thick wooden door with a crossbar spanned the opening. Cody lifted the bar while The Guardian pushed the door open, stepping out into cool morning air.

Cody gazed upward as dawn's orange fingers highlighted the dark clouds blanketing their property. They stood in a small, isolated garden surrounded by hedges. Flower beds, bulging with crimson daisies flanked a wrought-iron bench. He glanced at his siblings to see if they shared his confusion.

Where did this come from? Has it always been here?

The Guardian made his way through a narrow hedge opening, turning down a brick path that ran along Freya Manor's western wall. The hedgerow ended, revealing their home's rocky foundation. To Cody's surprise, they soon reached the area at the end of the maze.

"How is it possible we never saw this—" Martin began.

"Keep up," the old man interrupted.

They followed The Guardian across the cave toward the Rúndyrr doorway.

"Take these," he said, pointing to four leather backpacks scattered about the dusty floor.

Shelby grabbed one, wrinkling her nose and frowning. "This filthy old thing is going to ruin my lovely pink shirt."

"They're heavy," Martin added, flinging one onto his back with a clank. "What's in them, rocks?"

"Maybe it's the gold we took from Weaver's Needle," Charlotte said.

The Gatekeeper emerged from the shadows. He grabbed the scepter and recited their riddle.

"Visible are the waves our eyes view,
With different lengths for each colorful hue.
Red is the longest while violet is not,
At the end one may find a golden pot.
They cannot be seen from two different places,
And when raindrops are gone, they leave no traces.
Ancient lore tells of treasure to be found,
From folks who, to its end, are eternally bound."

Charlotte gasped, as the doorway pulled them through its shimmering center. "Where *are* we?"

"If I could see something," Martin mumbled, "I'd let you know."

Cody stared at the thick white mist surrounding them. It was as if they were suspended in the center of a cloud. Flashes of light briefly illuminated the cotton candy air, followed by thunderous booms that punctuated the sky's anger. One boom was so loud, Cody had to cover his ears.

"Did that seem…" Shelby began nervously.

"A little too close for comfort?" Cody replied.

"What did you say?" Martin yelled. "I think I'm deaf."

Cody felt his body get all tingly. He glanced down at the hair on his arms standing at attention. A sudden beam of sunlight poked through the foggy center, generating a slippery swath of bright colors.

"Is anyone else feeling—" he began.

"Electrified?" Charlotte cried anxiously.

"Uh-oh," Martin said with a moan as Shelby let out an ear-splitting scream.

"Hang on!" Cody yelled, sliding downward.

But there was nothing to hold onto. Brilliant hues lined the swath beneath them. On and on they slid, winding through light so bright, it was nearly blinding. Once Cody realized they were not going to drop to their deaths, he began to enjoy the thrilling ride, like an unearthly roller coaster with no cars. The wind hit his face with such force, it was difficult to breathe.

After a few terrifying minutes, the four teens dropped to the ground, landing in a pile atop a bed of leaves. Cody quickly sat up, realizing his head was on Shelby's butt. He was too embarrassed to look at her, trying to appear unphased. Charlotte also sat up, patting her torso and legs with trembling hands, as if making sure they were still attached.

"Ugh," Martin mumbled, pulling what appeared to be a feather out of his mouth. "I think I just swallowed a swallow."

"My hair!" Shelby sat up, running a hand through her locks. "Is it a mess?"

Cody had to look away so he wouldn't laugh. He was already in enough hot water with Shelby. Martin, however, broke out in a high-pitched cackle.

"*WHAT?*" Shelby demanded.

Martin laughed and pointed. "Not only is it decorated with sticks and leaves, it looks like you stuck your finger in an electric socket!"

"Great! Just great!" Shelby responded with a sniff, busily trying to fix the mess. "And just *look* at my lavender capris," she added, wiping debris from her pants.

"Where *are* we?" Cody mumbled, climbing to his feet.

He stared out at a seemingly infinite forest filled with trees planted in rows of symmetrical perfection.

"Hey! Who *are* you?" A high-pitched voice squeaked. "I said, who *are* you? You're not after my gold, are you? You better not be after my gold."

Cody glanced at his siblings to see if anyone else was hearing this. Martin looked around, apparently trying to locate the source.

"I-uh," Cody mumbled. "Where are you? No, we're not after . . ."

His words trailed off as he noticed the contents of a wrought iron pot gleaming brightly on the ground in front of them. It was bursting with gold coins. Just then, a head popped out from behind a nearby tree. A little old man in a green suit and black hat grinned impishly at them.

"You *better* not be after my gold," he said.

With surprising quickness, the little man darted toward them, picked up the pot and disappeared into the forest, hesitating only for a second to call gleefully over his shoulder, "Hope you like it here! You'll never get the answer without me!"

"What did he say?" Martin mumbled. "Is he referring to the riddle?"

Cody jumped to his feet and took off in hot pursuit. He spotted the sprite zigzagging through the woods, emerging a few seconds later from behind a tree about ten meters in the opposite direction.

"There." Cody whispered, pointing.

Shelby tiptoed around the far side while Martin and Charlotte waited in front and Cody crept to the right. One minute he was there, hugging his pot, the next he was gone. Cody dove after him but came up empty, planting his face in the dirt.

"Over here!" Shelby yelled.

Cody ran in the direction of her voice. Behind a tree, he found Shelby and the little man staring at each other. He was still clutching his pot of gold.

It's another dwarf. Like those living in the tunnels under our home.

Shelby reached for him, grabbing his black hat instead. Light twinkled in the man's lively eyes, as if the mere thought of the chase was more fun than he could handle. While the teens stared in obvious wonder, the little fellow grabbed his hat and took off. Shelby leaped after him, landing empty-handed on her knees.

"Just great! Another outfit bites the dust!" she muttered, climbing to her feet. "Just let him go."

"But he may be right," Charlotte whispered. "We may not be able to get out of here without him."

"Spread out!" Cody ordered. "He's a tricky little thing. Martin, you head about twenty meters that way. Shelby, you go that way. Charlotte, you and I will cover the middle. Stay in your respective lanes. We'll converge on him from opposite sides.

Cody dropped his backpack for added maneuverability. The others did the same. A few minutes later, Martin flushed the dwarf out from behind a tree. He chased the little man toward Charlotte as she approached from the other side.

"Got him!" Martin yelled, leaping forward. "Don't got him." he added, landing roughly on the ground. "He's pretty spritely for a plump little fellow."

Charlotte held her position on the far side. Martin scrambled to his feet, approaching from the right. A rocky outcropping marked the edge of the forest, blocking the little man's escape.

Martin yelled, "We've got him now!"

Shelby arrived and reached for his arm, but he ducked down and scooted between her legs. She did a summersault trying to grab him.

"Ten!" Martin yelled.

Cody laughed for the first time in days.

"Very funny!" Shelby grinned sheepishly, pulling pine needles from her hair.

The dwarf took off back into the forest, turning to circumvent a small pond surrounded by reeds. He looked over his shoulder as he ran, giggling with delight. Just as it seemed the little man would get away, his foot got tangled in an outstretched root and he tumbled to the ground.

"Get him!" Cody said.

Martin and Charlotte approached from either side, the pond blocking his escape ahead. As Cody and Shelby came from behind, Shelby grabbed his pot of gold.

"I'll take that if you don't mind!" she said.

"I *do* mind! I *do*!" he cried.

"Slippery little fellow, aren't we?" Cody grinned. "Nice work, guys!"

"You can't have my gold."

"It looks to me like we already have it," Cody said.

It appeared at first as if he would put up a fight, looking around to weigh his options, but then he shrugged as if giving in to the inevitable.

"I will grant three wishes in return for my pot of gold."

"We don't want your gold, but we're going to keep it until you help us."

"Everyone wants my gold. Help you how?" He walked in circles like a child hyped up on sugar.

"Are you a *leprechaun*?"

"What do you want?" he asked, ignoring Charlotte.

"Did you say three wishes?" Shelby piped up.

A lime green jacket covered most of his round belly, surrounded by a belt with a large buckle, and matching knickers below. Green eyes darted mischievously about, his red-orange beard dancing as he spoke.

"Those are handsome shoes," Shelby said.

The little man's demeanor changed immediately.

"Aren't they? I made them," he replied, holding his buckled shoe out for them to see. "That is what I do. I am a shoemaker." The leprechaun rocked back and forth with delight then looked down. "Your shoes are quite handsome as well."

"Why, thank you," Shelby said, beaming. "You are obviously a man of exquisite taste. They're Thierry Dunhill knock-offs, but you can hardly tell, right?"

"Okay, enough about shoes." Cody said. "You said we can't leave here without your help. What did you mean by that?"

"You can't leave."

"Why?"

"Is that a wish?" He jumped up and down.

Cody looked at the others. "Yes, that's a wish."

"You need my help."

"Yes, you said that. Why do we need your help?" Cody frowned.

"Because," he sneered, "you don't understand the riddle."

"You know about the riddle?" Charlotte asked.

"Of course," the leprechaun replied.

"Who told you?" Shelby asked

"I just know, that's all. I know everything."

"So, what does the riddle mean?" Charlotte asked.

The little man added, "You also want to know about The Darkness."

"You know about The Darkness?" Martin asked, glancing at the others.

"I know searching for it is very dangerous."

"Why?" Cody asked.

"Because it will come after you," the little leprechaun stated.

"Who?" Cody glanced at his siblings. "Grýla?"

"Shush! Do not speak her name! I can say no more."

"We need to know everything you know . . . *now*," Cody said crossly, getting irritated with the little fellow's games.

Shelby looked at Cody and frowned.

"Ignore him," she said, nodding toward Cody. What's your name, honey?" she asked sweetly.

"I am Patrick," he said proudly.

"Patrick, we need to know more about The Darkness," Shelby added.

"Fine. You use another wish?"

"Okay, we will use another wish. Who is The Darkness?" Cody asked.

"The Darkness is that which has The Light," he said.

"The Light of Nimbus?" Cody asked.

The sprite seemed uncomfortably with the conversation. He was no longer smiling. "The Darkness wants to keep the Light hidden away."

"Why?" Charlotte asked.

"When The Light is not free to inspire and spread love, the world is in shadow. People are without hope or dreams, ignorance and apathy abound. Desperation gives him power. He feeds off it."

"What does that mean?" Martin asked.

"I can say no more?"

"That's it?" Cody scowled. "You've told us nothing."

"What is the answer to the riddle?" Charlotte said.

"You need to use your last wish."

He seemed to enjoy stringing them along.

"You haven't told us anything. We are not..." Cody hesitated, looking around.

The wind had suddenly pick up, black clouds swirling above. Patrick gripped his hat tightly. The forest was growing darker by the second. Treetops bent over as if trying to get away from something.

"She's coming!" the little man cried. "She eats children . . . and Patricks."

As quickly as it had begun, the wind stopped. Everything grew still. The dark, however, remained.

"What just happened?" Cody looked around. "It's like something blew in for a visit."

"Yeah," Martin whispered. "And, not a friendly visit."

"Do you smell that?" Shelby asked nervously.

"Yeah, old gym socks," Martin muttered.

"And what is that moaning sound?" Cody asked, not really wanting an answer.

"Hey! Where did he go?" Charlotte yelled.

They looked around, but the leprechaun was gone. Shelby had set his pot of gold on the ground and he had managed to slip away while they were focused on the storm. Cody scanned the trees, but he was nowhere to be found.

"Great, just great!" Cody said testily.

"And we didn't even get our last wish," Shelby said with a moan.

"I don't like this," Martin said. "How are we going to get out of here?"

Let's grab the backpacks," Cody muttered. "I think they're on the opposite side of the pond."

"Why do you suppose The Guardian gave us these?" Charlotte asked absently.

"Who knows," Cody muttered. "Shelby, give us the riddle—"

"Obviously, to give to Patrick," a male voice offered briskly.

Sharkey stood behind the four backpacks with his arms crossed.

"You lost the leprechaun and now The Darkness knows you're here," he said with a frown. "Did any of you bother to think about why you brought the backpacks?"

"I-uh, assumed it was to keep them safe," Cody said.

"Well, you assumed wrong." Sharkey shook his head. "And, what did I say was the whole point of this exercise? To locate The Darkness' stronghold. Did you even listen?"

Cody frowned at Sharkey. "We were just getting to that when—"

"Patrick?" Sharkey called. "I have packs filled with gold nuggets and they're all yours," he said. "Patrick? Come on out."

Suddenly, the little man emerged from behind a nearby tree.

Ugh! I should've realized that's what the gold was for.

"Hello, Darwon," the leprechaun's high-pitched voice called out.

"It's good to see you, Patrick," Sharkey replied.

"What did he call you?" Cody asked, but was ignored.

"I need to find The Darkness' stronghold. Where is it keeping The Light?"

The leprechaun took a few steps forward.

"Buri," he whispered.

"I searched Buri from one end to the other and I couldn't find it."

"It is not *at* Buri however, *they* can tell you what you need to know."

"Alright, my little friend, I will go to Alfheim, but if they can't help me, I'll be back. I'm keeping one of these packs, just in case. Until next time," he said, flinging a backpack over his shoulder and tipping his hat. "Enjoy your gold."

"Goodbye, Darwon," the leprechaun said excitedly, scooping nuggets into his pot.

"Sharkey, where are you going?" Cody called as the man turned to walk away.

"You're not leaving us," Martin said.

"Answer the riddle," the man yelled over his shoulder. "But you better hurry. The Darkness is coming."

Cody frowned. "Nice," he muttered.

"How are you doing that?" Charlotte asked Patrick, leaning over to get a closer look at the pot. "Your pot was full before, but you keep adding more gold and somehow it fits."

"Magic," he replied.

"It's like Santa's sack," Martin said with a grin. "It has no bottom."

"Shelby, give it to us again," Cody said, "the riddle."

"A physical phenomenon that explains why,
Waves get redirected in the human eye.
Rainbows and prisms divide white light,
Into colorful displays to please our sight.
The science appears in things all around,
From glasses to cameras, it can clearly be found."

"Hey, where did Patrick go?" Martin yelled.

"Great! That's the last we'll see of him," Cody muttered. "Any ideas on the riddle?"

"I don't even have a guess," Charlotte replied.

"Uh, guys? Do you see that?" Martin asked.

"There's something over there," Shelby cried.

An entity became visible between the trees, a shroud of material becoming darker than the surrounding fog.

"Get together in a circle, facing out. Just like the night in the Dead Forest. That way, nothing can sneak up on us."

"It'll still sneak up on us," Shelby whined. "Now we'll be able to see what's about to kill us."

"I can't believe Sharkey just left us here," Charlotte cried.

The forest became deathly silent, even birds and squirrels hid in their nests. A rolling darkness approached, dissolving the daylight as it moved. The pond seemed to freeze, resembling a sheet of cracked glass.

"Is anybody else seeing this?" Martin cried. "What happens when it reaches us?"

"It's almost here," Charlotte whimpered.

"Cody?" Shelby cried. "*DO* SOMETHING!"

He spoke calmly. "Nothing is going to happen, I promise. Now, focus on the riddle."

A lone sparrow flew toward The Darkness. Cody watched as it approached the murky black, then dropped to the ground, a stiff corpse. Suddenly, he felt far less confident.

"It mentions colorful displays from light waves," Charlotte said shakily. "That sounds like rainbows or prisms, but those words are already used in the riddle. Plus, he wouldn't give us two riddles with the same answer," she said.

"It describes some sort of phenomenon," Shelby added.

Cody's attention was suddenly drawn to the motionless pond. Stiff marsh reeds lining its edges reflected off the silver surface. A single ray of sunshine poked down between the clouds, permeating the greenish liquid. Below the water, the unbending reeds jutted off in strange directions. He saw Shelby staring at it also.

"It's almost like someone is trying to show us the answer," she mumbled.

Cody could only see a meter or two into the forest. He knew in a few seconds they would be immersed in the choking black grip of The Darkness, its bone-chilling mist surrounding them. A hideous figure became visible amid the trees, its burning eyes cutting through the darkness.

"Charlotte, honey," Shelby asked edgily, "why do the reflections of those reeds seem to bend right where they meet the water?"

"When light passes through two mediums of different densities, meaning air and water, it gets deflected, making the object appear to bend," Charlotte said.

It's getting so cold. Gatekeeper bring us home.

Cody could feel himself beginning to lose consciousness. He tried to focus on going home, but nothing happened. Pressure was building around him, squeezing the life from his body.

"Wait! It's also the science behind rainbows, prisms, and the lenses in our eyes," Charlotte yelled from behind, "as well as in glasses and cameras! Shelby, that's it! It's called *refraction*!"

Chapter 23: The Hexagons

"Did Sharkey go to Buri without us?" Cody asked, still coughing up black mist.

The Gatekeeper glanced at them, as if to confirm they were fine, then turned to walk away.

"Perhaps," he replied over his shoulder.

"Why didn't he wait for us?" Cody asked.

"Thou hast no idea how dangerous such a trip could be."

"We want to go to Iceland," Charlotte said firmly.

The Gatekeeper stopped. "Dost thou wish to go on a journey," he asked sharply.

"Yes," Cody replied. "Buri."

"Great," Shelby said with a smirk. "Iceland? We don't even have our coats. It'll be brrr-y alright."

"You know," Charlotte offered, "It's a misnomer Iceland is always covered with ice and snow. Greenland – a place you'd think was lush – is actually colder and more frozen than Iceland."

"Charlotte! Focus on Iceland," Cody whispered, as the four were pulled through the doorway.

"Cody, are you there?" Shelby's muffled voice sounded far away.

"I'm here," he replied. "Charlotte? Martin?"

Martin yelled, "I'm frozen speechless, but I'm here."

189

"I'm fine, just shivering." Charlotte added.

"Where *are* we?" Shelby asked.

"Hold on tight. Don't let go." Cody yelled.

"Oh, *trust* me," Martin cried, "not even Thor could pry my fingers off this thing."

Cody stood on a frozen cross, desperately clinging to its icy framework. The hunk of ice, more than twice his height, floated slowly downward. Hundreds, or maybe thousands of similar structures drifted around him, making it difficult to hear his siblings and impossible to see them.

"Wow, this is…" Cody mumbled, his voice trailing off.

"Incredible?" Shelby said.

"That works," he replied.

"I'd call it breathtaking," Charlotte offered.

"Everyone okay?" Cody called out.

"So far," Martin muttered. "But the day is young."

Cody stared at the white world highlighted with a glistening silvery glow.

"Are any two exactly the same?" Shelby asked.

"No, they're all different," Charlotte confirmed.

"Uh, Cody?" Shelby began, nervousness apparent in her voice. "I think it's…" she hesitated.

"Uh-oh!" Martin added. "*Disintegrating?*" he cried.

"JUMP! Jump to the next one!" Cody screamed as he leaped across, grasping another frozen pole. "DO IT! NOW!"

He glanced back as the previous structure disappeared.

"Got it," Shelby yelled.

"Me, too," Charlotte added.

"That was scary," Martin mumbled. "My shorts are soaked. Hope I didn't wet myself."

"I *liked* this," Shelby said, "until that little episode. Now I'm not so sure."

"It's our body heat causing it," Charlotte called out.

"Just make sure you jump every few minutes. There are plenty of them nearby… shouldn't be a problem."

"Cody?" Shelby called softly. "This is the most amazing…"

"Yeah, I know," he replied, his throat choked with emotion.

For the first time in weeks, Cody felt on top of the world – literally and figuratively. From this lofty vantage point, anything was possible. Excitement pulsed through his veins. He felt invincible. Somehow, The Gatekeeper seemed to know not only their thoughts, but their feelings as well.

How could he have known this was exactly what I needed to make me feel whole again.

Cody's crystalline structure alit onto a soft bed. He jumped off and called to the others.

"That was awesome!" He yelled.

"Again! Again!" Shelby cried.

"Martin? Charlotte?" he called.

He heard their muffled replies as the silvery creations continued to blanket the earth. They kept coming, accumulating until Cody couldn't see anything above. A sudden uneasy feeling came over him.

"Keep moving up!"

He climbed as fast as he could, but the structures were falling faster than he could scramble. Fear began to grip him as he became disoriented. It was difficult to tell up from down, or right from left.

"I can't keep…" Charlotte began, her voice fading.

"Charlotte? Are you okay?" Cody called.

"I'm getting so tired." Martin sounded distant.

"KEEP CLIMBING! FOLLOW MY VOICE!" he yelled, but silence ensued. "SHELBY! GIVE US THE RIDDLE!"

"Crystalline arms swirl with grace,
As delicate and unique as hand-sewn lace.
Hexagons land softly atop a bed of white.
Then disappear when the sun shines bright."

Her voice sounded weak and distant.

"SHELBY? MARTIN? CHARLOTTE? ANSWER ME!"

Cody searched frantically, but soon lost his sense of direction. Then he saw something, a patch of lavender amid the frosty whiteness. Working his way over, he reached out his hand.

"*SHELBY!* Are you alright?"

She tried to nod, gasping for air. Shelby's face and hands were bright red and her body trembled. Cody took her hands in his, then held her close, hoping body heat would warm them both.

"Shelby, I'm so sorry about that whole thing with Shena," he whispered in her ear. "I was *such* a jerk. Can you ever forgive me?"

They were completely engulfed now. The air was getting thin. Shelby's eyes closed and her body appeared to go limp. Panic filled him, fearing they would suffocate amidst the breathtaking . . .

Wait! That's it! How could I be so stupid! Just say it!

"Snowflakes!"

Chapter 24: The Princesses

Cody and Shelby slid across The Shimmering Bridge and collapsed onto the cave floor.

"Boy, am I glad to see you guys," Cody said.

Martin and Charlotte were stand nearby, hugging each other for warmth.

"Come on," he said, standing and extending a hand to Shelby. "Let's get a cup of hot chocolate."

"It's eighty degrees out," Shelby murmured with chattering teeth.

"Eighty degrees sounds pretty good," Martin quipped, rubbing his hands together.

Cody took a few steps then stopped.

"We wanted to go to *Iceland*, *Buri* to be exact," he called gruffly to The Gatekeeper, shaking his head, "not *ice* land or brrr-y or whatever!"

The four sat around their kitchen table, the chocolatey aroma of hot cocoa lingering on the air. Shelby's face was hidden in the latest edition of Cosmo. Charlotte was finishing an assignment for school. Martin and Cody hovered over the laptop, playing a video game. For once, Cody was fine with the fact the old manor had no air conditioning, a warm breeze rustling the curtains.

"Oh, my," Shelby said in a breathy voice, "it says here Kala went shopping on 5ᵗʰ Avenue and spent a quarter million dollars in one afternoon. Can you *imagine*? That's like a dream come true."

"What is it with you and the Benningtons?" Cody asked.

Shelby glanced up and shrugged. "They're totally awesome."

"They're just *people*," Martin added.

"No, they're people, just better," Shelby offered. "I mean, look at them. They're perfect. That outfit alone probably costs more money than Heather and Jack make in a year." She thumbed through a few more pages. "Here's a picture of Kala, Kyrie, and Kensie at an exclusive night club in Manhattan," she said, pointing. "I would give anything for just *one* of their outfits."

"Having money and expensive clothes doesn't make you better than everyone else," Cody said.

"They don't just have money." Shelby dropped the magazine on the table and dreamily closed her eyes. "They have *tons* of money. They're like . . . *royalty*. Besides, how is it any different than the way you talk about Brett Starr, that quarterback guy you like," she added curtly.

"It *is* different," Cody said. "He's *good* at something, something that makes people respect him."

"The Benningtons are good at lots of things," Shelby replied.

"Yeah? Name one?"

"They're good at . . . being the Benningtons."

"It's all part of The Darkness," a man's voice added.

Cody looked up to see Sharkey coming through the doorway. He set his worn hat on the counter and began to wash up at the kitchen sink.

"What's part of The Darkness?" Cody asked.

"People living vicariously through celebrities instead of following their own dreams," the man replied.

"Well, I don't hear anyone asking *me* to be part of a hot TV show," Shelby quipped.

"Is that what you want?" Sharkey asked, drying his hands on a towel. "If so, then make it happen. I can't imagine why, but trust me, there's not too much stranger than the things that go on around here."

"You know we can't talk about—" Cody began.

"I don't mean that," Sharkey said. "I mean the Four Musketeers and the trouble they get into."

"Very funny," Cody said.

"You could have your own show, focusing on the things that make you such special people."

Cody glanced around the table at the other bemused faces.

Did he just say something nice about us?

"Your point?" Martin asked lightly.

"Shelby designs and sews her own clothes. I'm certainly no fashion expert, but in my opinion, *nice* clothes. Charlotte has a good shot at becoming the youngest astronaut in space, definitely no small achievement. Martin faces the world with a smile each day, despite the difficult hand he's been dealt. Those things are far more impressive than any TV show."

"Nothing about me?" Cody rolled his eyes. "Can't say I'm surprised."

"Mr. Hawke, let's not wallow in modesty. You have many talents, not the least of which are your leadership skills . . . when you're not being an idiot."

"Well, those were very nice compliments," Shelby said, apparently fighting back a tickled grin, "from someone we didn't even think liked us."

"Miss Shelby, I don't have time for friendships. However, if I wasn't fond of you all, we wouldn't be having this conversation right now," Sharkey replied.

"So, what are you saying, that we should get our own reality TV show?" she asked.

"I'm saying you should be proud of the people you've become and focus on realizing your own dreams, not immersing yourself in someone else's."

Chapter 25: The Light Elves

"We've been sent to help you," Cody called ahead as the four teens crossed the yard.

Removing his hands from warm jeans pockets, he zipped up his jacket. The heat wave broke and a chilly front had moved in. It was cool for September even by Maine standards. Sharkey glanced up, then set down the enormous log he was carrying.

"Grab one of those garbage bags and start picking up debris," he said.

"Doesn't this seem a bit ridiculous," Cody muttered, "worrying about a downed tree when, by your own admission, the world is ending?"

"Life goes on, Mr. Hawke, for now."

Sunday's violent storm had caused widespread damage all along the northeastern coast. Freya Manor had been fortunate to escape with only a few downed trees however, the power was still out in Dawnport, and as a result, schools were closed.

"You never told us what happened at Buri," Cody asked. "We tried to come help you," he sighed, "but The Gatekeeper wouldn't let us. He sent us to *ice land* instead of Iceland." Cody frowned.

Sharkey looked away, as if to hide a grin. "Unfortunately," he said, rubbing his chin, "something came up and I was unable to complete my mission."

"What happened?" Shelby asked.

"The Darkness is rapidly gaining power. These frequent storms are an example," he added. "There were many people in need of help."

"You were rescuing people from the storm?" Charlotte asked.

"So now what?" Cody mumbled.

"I'll be going tomorrow," Sharkey replied. "As you heard, Patrick believes they can provide the location of The Darkness' stronghold."

"Who can provide?" Shelby asked.

"You'll see," he replied dismissively.

"We're coming with you?" Cody asked, glancing excitedly at his siblings.

"If school is still closed."

After a short and uneventful hike through some beautiful but rugged country ending with a lecture about the inherent dangers of spelunking, the group arrived in the middle of nowhere. Their leader instructed them to search the ground.

"For what, rocks?" Cody asked flippantly. "There are lots of those."

"You'll know it when you see it, Mr. Hawke," Sharkey replied.

"Great," Martin muttered under his breath. "He can't just *tell* us."

They searched for nearly a half hour, but all Cody could find were rocks and grass.

"This is like an Easter egg hunt but with invisible eggs," Martin mumbled.

"I found it!" Charlotte called out, pointing downward.

"Ah, good job, Miss Charlotte," Sharkey responded.

"Teacher's pet," Cody mumbled, winking at Charlotte.

He leaned forward and stared into what could've easily been the entrance to hell, a black hole surrounded by rocks. He wondered what would be waiting for them inside.

"You're not thinking of going in there?" Shelby asked, her eyes wide.

"Yes, Miss Shelby," Sharkey said. "Once you get through the opening, it gets easier."

"Here," the man said, removing items from the backpacks. "Each of you take a helmet and gloves. And, zip up those parkas. You're going to need them."

"Nothing like a thirty-second rest to make you feel refreshed and invigorated," Martin mumbled.

"We'll rest when we get there. Right now, we still have a little hike ahead of us."

"Get where?" Cody frowned as his question was ignored.

Sharkey tossed him a hat with a flashlight on top. Cody attempted a cavalier catch, but the hat slipped from his grasp. He watched helplessly as it hit a rock and rolled about on the ground. The only thing he was able to catch was Sharkey's disapproving glance.

"I don't have any spare equipment so let's be careful," the man said testily.

"I just know my outfit is going to get ruined," Shelby mumbled.

"At least you're wearing the right shoes this time," Cody said.

"I had no choice," she replied. "Dr. Jones made me go back and change."

Sharkey climbed down through the small opening with his back to them. Cody wondered if it was another attempt to hide a smile.

"Help everyone down, Mr. Hawke," Sharkey's muffled voice ordered.

"Shelby, you're first," Cody said, taking her hand. "Charlotte, you're next, then Martin."

"I-ugh," Martin croaked, looking at Cody with anxious eyes. "I'm a bit claustrophobic."

"I hear you, bro," Cody mumbled. "He says it's *better* inside."

Martin hesitated for a second, then climbed down. Cody took a deep breath and followed his siblings into the dark hole. A quick sniff of the musty cave, heightened his uneasiness.

"Buri is a five-thousand-year-old lava tube cave," Sharkey offered, his words echoing about the chamber. "The floor will be rocky for about seven hundred meters, so you'll need to be careful. The rest is pretty flat so it should be easier to traverse."

"Did he just say seven hundred meters?" Martin grumbled. "Two thousand feet of rocky surface. What are we, bighorn sheep?"

"How does the air get down here?" Cody mumbled, scanning the other-worldly landscape.

"You'll be fine, Mr. Hawke," Sharkey replied, "Just relax."

"Is there some reason we can't know what we're looking for?" he asked.

"Ljosalfar."

"Who?" Shelby asked.

"Ljosalfar. That's where we're going, or at least, who we're going to see," Sharkey replied.

"Well, that certainly clears things up," Martin muttered.

"Enough conversation," Sharkey said. "Let's go."

Taking a last glimpse up at the outside world, Cody stepped into the rocky tomb. His body responded to the immediate chill with a slight shiver. A few seconds in, he realized the necessity for the gear they carried. Filtered sunlight faded, as if the sun knew this was no place for its warmth. The initial ceiling height meant walking bent over.

"It feels like we're praying to whatever spirits rule this dark place," Charlotte whispered.

"Yeah," Martin added, "like forced penitence."

If he can do this, I can too. I certainly hope there's air in here.

As they made their way through the darkness, the tunnel opened up enough to walk upright. In places, it was less like walking and more like balancing from rock to rock. The air was dank and numbing, the echo of their voices a bit hypnotic, however Cody had to admit he felt very alive. One thing he could say about Sharkey, time spent with him was never boring.

Eventually, they emerged in an open chamber, its alien moonscape surrounding them. Long icy stalactites reached down from the ceiling like sharp teeth ready to chew them for dinner. Round stalagmites covering the outcroppings reminded Cody of frosty seals sunbathing on a rocky beach. Groups of taller, rounded stalagmites resembled frozen church-goers, some standing and others kneeling, but all holding hands.

"Everybody okay?" Cody murmured.

"There had better not be bats in this cave," Shelby said. "I had enough of them in the caves beneath Freya Manor."

"The bats won't hurt you," Sharkey called back. "I'd worry more about cave trolls."

"Did he just say *cave trolls*?" Martin asked, his eyes wide.

Chapter 25: The Light Elves

Sam Sharkey led the group in resolute silence, using his senses to guide him through the rocky darkness. A few times Cody wondered if he even remembered they were following.

"Keep up!" the man yelled, apparently noticing the distance between them.

"I wonder how many people have breathed this air in the five thousand years since the cave was created. It's hard to believe it was formed by a lava flow," Charlotte said.

"Keep up!" Sharkey repeated. "I don't want to have to tell Heather and Jack I lost a couple kids."

"We have names, you know," Cody muttered.

"Yeah," Martin whispered under his breath, "and we're not all Norse gods like you, with your perfect physique."

Cody grinned but his expression was short-lived.

"Did you see that?" Martin froze, his eyes open wide.

"I saw something, too," Charlotte whispered, "like a shadow racing along the cave wall."

"Wonderful," Martin muttered. "We're being tracked by cave people who've been craving taste of meat for centuries. That one just went off to fire up the barbeque."

"It was probably one of the Ljosalfar . . . Light Elves," Sharkey called matter-of-factly.

"Lovely," Shelby said with a moan. "What's a Light Elf? Do they eat people?"

"Hardly. Light Elves are beautiful people," Sharkey said, clearly trying not to chuckle. "They won't hurt you, they're just curious."

"So, *where* are we going?" Cody asked again.

"Alfheim. The home of the Elves."

"Alf who?" Cody muttered.

"It's not so easy, is it Cody Hawke?" Shelby said. "Blindly following someone when you have no idea what to expect. It's something we've gotten used to, something you are not.

Sharkey stopped, waiting for them to catch up. A short distance ahead, the floor dropped off into a huge lava pit about fifteen meters deep. Cody noticed the fear on his siblings faces as Sharkey pulled a rope from his backpack and secured it to some rocks.

"He's not thinking..." Martin began.

"Oh, I think he is," Shelby replied.

"Do you want to see what we came for or turn back?" Sharkey asked absently. "Alright, then.

The man pulled on the rope, presumably to make sure it was secure. He retrieved a second rope and made a noose on one end.

"Are you planning to hang someone?" Martin asked.

"Mr. Hawke, you go down first and help everyone as they reach the bottom. I'll get them started."

"Uh, Mr. Sharkey?" Charlotte's voice sounded fearful. "Assuming we get down, how will we get back up?"

"We will climb the rope, Miss Charlotte."

Sharkey wrapped the lasso around Cody's waist and held the other end.

"Just in case," he said.

Grabbing the first rope with gloved hands, Cody climbed over the edge and lowered himself to the ground. He heard Sharkey ask who wanted to go next. Silence ensued.

"Just hold the rope and walk backwards down the wall. Were you watching Mr. Hawke?" he asked.

"Oh, nuts," Shelby replied finally. "Out of my way."

As he watched Shelby lower herself over the edge and descend into the cavern, Cody smiled, imagining Sharkey staring at Charlotte and Martin, waiting for one to step forward.

It took a bit of coaxing, but once they had all reached the bottom, Sharkey began to survey the area. He located something that seemed to be of interest, a narrow rock protruding from the wall. He pushed on it and the sound of scraping rock filled the lava pit. A stone slab slid to one side revealing a small opening in the wall. Sharkey ducked down and climbed through.

"Let's go," he commanded.

Cody glanced briefly at the others, then followed him into the narrow tunnel about a meter long. They entered another lava tube, this one smaller, but still large enough to stand erect. After passing through a rocky chamber, Sharkey instructed them to get down on all fours. They followed as he crawled through various tunnels that made Cody nauseatingly claustrophobic.

"Shush," he heard Shelby whisper behind him, apparently directed at Martin.

"What's wrong," he asked over his shoulder.

"Shelby was trying to sneak a granola bar and she lost part of the wrapper," Martin mumbled.

"I don't want Mr. Perfect to yell at me for littering," she whispered.

Cody wondered if the rope would still be there when they got back to the lava pit. And, he wondered if – when Sharkey abandoned them –would he be able to lead them back out. All these concerns just made him more nauseous.

They wriggled through a small doorway into an open area. As Cody stood, he stared in awe at the scene before him. A dark forest stretched out for what seemed like miles.

"How can trees grow underground?" he mumbled.

"There's something odd about this forest," Shelby added.

"A forest in a cave? What's odd about that?" Martin asked.

"It's too . . . symmetrical," Charlotte added softly.

"Very observant," Sharkey said. "There's only one tree. We just need to find it."

Cody stared at the trees until he became dizzy. They definitely all looked the same, like a series of mirrors reflecting images of the tree in all directions. Sharkey meandered through the midst, assessing each tree.

Martin approached one particular tree and stared into a narrow hole in the center of its trunk. Suddenly, a small animal lunged out of the hole. It screamed at him, baring its teeth. Martin jumped nearly a meter into the air and fell back. Cody laughed in spite of himself.

"What the flying squirrel *was* that thing?" Martin asked shakily, climbing to his feet.

"It's called a quidder," Sharkey said. "And, thanks to Mr. Speck for identifying the real tree."

The quidder glared at them from his hole while Sharkey recited a poem Cody had heard before:

"Ó Valfǫðr í nafni þínu biðjum vér,
Seiðar til þess at opna Rúndyrr,
Gefðu oss kost at ná vísdómi,
Sem þú namt at Mímisbrunni."

"That's The Gatekeeper's secret poem." Shelby said. "How do you know it?"

"It unlocks the door to any bridge," Sharkey replied.

Suddenly, a small wooden door appeared on the front of the tree. Sharkey pulled on the brass doorknob, ducked down, and stepped inside. As Cody followed him across the shimmering swath, he felt something soft, like gossamer cobwebs surrounding him. One by one, Shelby, Charlotte, and Martin appeared next to him.

Cody stared ahead, in frozen silence. Maybe the lack of oxygen had affected his brain. Or, maybe they'd been drugged. He glanced at his foster siblings, their mouths hanging open in disbelief.

"Is this . . . paradise?" Shelby whispered.

Chapter 26: The Utopia

The first thing Cody noticed was light, tons of it. It's source however, was unclear. Second, was fresh air, nothing like the dank caves they had just left. He filled his lungs, taking a deep, floral breath.

The view was lush. Weeping willow trees, made even more beautiful by heaps of draping moss, permeated the landscape. Floral climbers in shades of red and pink blossomed everywhere. Ahead, a rocky waterfall splashing into a clear pool was nearly overcome with tropical blooms.

"Where *are* we?" Charlotte asked.

"I don't know, but I think I'll stay," Shelby whispered.

"If I had known we would end up in Eden, I wouldn't have complained so much during the trip," Martin mumbled.

"Follow me," Sharkey ordered.

He headed purposefully down a nearby path flanked by peaceful woodlands. Cody and the others followed, trying not to trip over a tree root or vine as they gaped at their surroundings.

On the far side of the wooded area, verdant rolling hills interspersed a rocky landscape. Tudor-style facades dotted the emerald hills as if Mother Nature herself had put them there. The structures were reminiscent of the Viking longhouses Cody had seen with Jack.

Sharkey approached one house set off by itself and knocked softly. A god-like man answered the door. He was tall with shoulder length hair and a noble beard. His brown pants, green tunic, and vine-like sash about the waist, seemed to fit with the natural setting. A brown cape covered his broad shoulders.

"My friend," the man said, his voice deep.

He stepped forward and gave Sharkey a brief hug.

"Andola," Sharkey replied. "So good to see you. These are my friends," he added, turning to the teens, "Martin, Charlotte, Shelby, and Cody."

The man nodded and smiled a hello then turned his attention back to Sharkey.

"What brings you to Alfheim, Darwon?"

"The Light of the Æsir," Sharkey let his words weigh upon the man. "I must find it."

Cody couldn't help but notice the man's sobering reaction.

"Come inside," he said softly, eyes darting about as if to confirm no one was nearby.

The inside of Andola's home was even more cozy-looking than the outside. Arched doorways of thick oak accentuated tan walls and warm oak flooring. Following their host to the parlor, they each took a seat in one of the over-stuffed chairs surrounding a large wooden table.

"I have three of the books," Sharkey said softly, reaching into his backpack.

"How did you get them?" Andola marveled as Sharkey set them on the table.

"It wasn't easy," he replied, grinning.

Cody glanced down at the old leather tomes, a metallic dragon eye adorning the center of each cover. He was about to look away when one of the eyes opened. It looked anxiously around the room as if assessing the danger, or lack thereof. Shelby nudged Charlotte and Martin and they all stared at the eye until it closed, apparently satisfied all was well.

"How do I get to the fortress?" Sharkey asked.

"It will not be easy," Andola replied. "Perhaps you might want to—"

"Uh, excuse me?" Shelby interjected abruptly. "What was that?"

"I'm sorry?" Andola said.

"The eye on that book just opened," she stated. "It was looking around the room."

Andola glanced at Sharkey as if silently asking how to reply. Their leader hesitated for a moment.

"The Books of Light can see what's around them, but they can also see everything in a certain area of the world," Sharkey replied. "When they are in close proximity, they can see what each other sees. When they are all together," he continued, "they can see everything on Earth."

A million questions immediately flooded Cody's head, but all he could get out was, "Cool".

He glanced at his siblings as they all apparently tried to wrap their heads around Sharkey's words. Meanwhile, the two men resumed their discussion.

What does that mean? What can they see?

The men spoke about Drangarnir and Tindhólmur, some kind of rocks, as best Cody could determine, and the difficulty associated with gaining entrance. He tried to focus on what they were saying, when suddenly another voice filled the room. Turning his head, Cody nearly gasped. A woman stood in the archway. She was tall and lean with hair the color of autumn leaves and the biggest green eyes he'd ever seen.

"Darwon," she said, rushing toward Sharkey.

He stood and gave the woman a warm embrace.

"Alizia," he said. "It's wonderful to see you." He turned toward the teens. "I'd like you to meet my friends, Shelby, Charlotte, Martin, and Cody."

Each of them stood and shook the woman's hand. Cody blushed when his turn came. It was hard to look at her and not have a reaction. She was breathtaking.

"Would you care for some refreshment?" Alizia asked.

"I-uh..." Cody stammered.

"What Cody is trying to say," Shelby said, giving him a quick smack, "is that would be lovely. Thank you."

Alizia disappeared, only to return a few minutes later with a tray of glasses containing an aqua liquid and a plate covered with some sort of pastries.

While the teens drank their buddleberry juice, enjoying it as much as during their trip to Silver Citadel, Sharkey and Andola huddled together in a private conversation. Alizia set down a tray of what tasted like angel food cupcakes with a luscious blue fruit center and a sweet fruity drizzle across the top, then sat between the men.

"I get that last one," Cody whispered, reaching across the table.

"You already had three," Shelby said, slapping his hand.

"So did you," he replied.

"No, *I* had three," Martin added, grinning.

"I only had two," Charlotte said with a pout.

"Well, you girls need to watch your figures," Cody muttered with a chuckle.

Alizia suddenly got up and disappeared through the archway. She returned a few minutes later, setting down another tray. Cody wondered if she'd heard their squabbling.

"Uh, Mrs. Alizia?" Shelby asked.

"Shelby, please, just call me Alizia,"

"Alizia, what are these absolutely delicious things called?"

The woman laughed. "Thank you, Shelby. We call them bartlets."

"Well, count me in as a bartlet fan," Shelby said, grabbing another.

Cody suddenly realized, while they were swooning over the bartlets, Sharkey and Andola had left the room.

They teens waited for what felt to Cody like hours until finally Andola and Alizia returned.

"Mrs. Alizia?" Shelby said softly. "Do you by any chance have a bathroom I could use?"

"Of course, Shelby. This way," she replied.

"Where's Mr. Sharkey?" Cody asked.

"Darwon had to leave unexpectedly," Andola said. "I'm sorry."

"But how will we get home?" Charlotte blurted out, her eyes the size of saucers.

"He asked that I get you back to the bridge. From there he said you will know how to get home."

"We will?" Cody asked.

"We do?" Martin added nervously.

Chapter 27: The Cave Troll

Andola led the teens back to the edge of Alfheim.

"I can go no farther than the bridge," he said, stopping.

"But, what should we do?" Charlotte asked. "Mr. Sharkey – uh, Darwon – led us through various tunnels to get here. Suppose we can't find our way back?"

"I am sorry, my friends," Andola replied. "Eons ago, we visited your world frequently. However, as your people became more sophisticated, The Darvidian Council ruled our visits were too disruptive and had to cease. Only guards are allowed to advance, and even that is under the strictest rules of non-contact."

"You said bridge," Charlotte began.

"Yes, you crossed the Shimmering Bridge to get here."

"The bright lights we passed through on our way in," Cody began. "That was a *bridge*? Here in Iceland?"

Andola smiled. His expression reminded Cody of the same patronizing look they'd seen from Radianna. It wasn't mean, just lofty.

"Yes, the Icelandic bridge leads to Alfheim," he said. "Some bridges lead directly to Silver Citadel, what you used to call, Asgard. Others can be used to visit any dimension."

"My goodness," Shelby said. "It's a bridge super highway system."

"We have a bridge in Maine called Rúndyrr," Martin said. "Can this bridge connect to that one?"

"Perhaps. You could try. How did you get here?" Andola asked.

"We used our bridge to get to a place about an hour outside Reykjavik," Charlotte replied. "Then, we hiked the rest of the way."

"Can you go back the way you came?" the man asked.

"I guess we will have to," Cody said with a frown. He turned to his siblings. "I hope you guys can climb the rope."

"I hope we can find our way back to the rope," Shelby added.

"Be safe, my friends," Andola said as he disappeared down the path.

"Well, this is lovely," Martin said, frowning.

"Shelby, please tell me you can repeat that poem Sharkey used to open the doorway."

"I can try. Hopefully I don't mess it up and send us into outer space."

As Shelby spoke, a heavy wooden door appeared on the gnarled tree trunk.

Cody sighed, then looked upward. "Gatekeeper? Can you bring us home?"

"Were you expecting a response?" Martin asked.

"Obviously, not," Cody replied. "Well, let's go."

He stepped through the doorway into an array of shimmering colors. As the brightness subsided, Cody recognized the darkness of a lava tube. Shelby, Charlotte, and Martin appeared behind him.

"How are we going to get back up the rope?" Charlotte asked.

"One thing at a time," Cody said. "Let's find it first."

He started down the lava tube, making his way carefully across the stones. They got down on their bellies and crawled through the small opening, emerging in another lava tube. After a few minutes, they reached an intersection.

"Which way?" Cody asked, shaking his head.

"I think we turned right coming in," Shelby said. "So, I think we should go left."

As they headed along the dark tunnel, Cody began to feel less and less confident.

"What's that?" Charlotte asked, pointing toward something reflective on the ground.

"It's the piece of wrapper from my granola bar," Shelby said excitedly.

Cody was relieved but his optimism soon began to wane. He kept hoping they would find the chamber around the next turn. Then light on his flashlight gave out.

That's what I get for dropping it.

"How long were we walking on the way in?" Charlotte asked.

"About twenty minutes," Martin replied. "Remind me to set my watch back to the correct time when we get back. I forgot last time and was running around like a chicken getting ready for school."

"It's been almost a half hour," Charlotte said anxiously. "I think we're lost."

"Oh, no!" Shelby cried. "The batteries on my lamp are dying."

"That's not good," Martin said. "Hope all our flashlights didn't get new batteries at the same time."

As they continued through the cave, Martin and Shelby's lamps gave out. It became increasingly difficult to see with Charlotte's providing the only illumination. Darkness made the thump of Cody's heart seem all the louder. Finally, the rocky tunnel opened up to a chamber.

"Charlotte, look that way," Cody said, scanning the area for a doorway. "Hold hands and make a chain," he added, "so we don't get separated."

"Did you hear that?" Charlotte whispered anxiously.

"It sounds like..." Shelby began.

"Breathing," Martin whispered. "And it's coming from right—"

Shelby's scream echoed throughout the cave as an enormous creature emerged from the shadows, roaring like a Kodiak bear. It was too dark to see much, but the headlamp reflected its long white fangs. The creature stopped, screaming angrily as Charlotte's flashlight appeared to blind it.

"RUN!" Cody yelled.

"My foot is caught!" Shelby cried.

"Charlotte, keep the light pointed at its face!" Cody said, reaching down to pull Shelby's leg free.

"It's stuck!" Cody yelled.

"Can you move that rock?" Shelby whimpered.

"Martin," Cody said, glancing up at the creature. "Help me."

It was about the size of a bear, but that's where the similarity ended. It had a huge head and a big nose but very tiny eyes, and was nearly hairless.

"What *is* that thing," Shelby whispered.

"I don't know," Martin mumbled, "but it won't be winning any beauty contests. It's about as pretty as the trolls we met in the forest."

As the light from Charlotte's flashlight began to flicker, the beast took a few steps toward them.

"Uh-oh," Martin whispered. "We better hurry."

Cody and Martin tugged on the rock, but it wouldn't budge.

"UH, CODY!" Shelby yelled as the creature got a few steps closer.

"Come on!" he shouted. "Give it all you've got!"

I've got to get Shelby free! If only this rock would move.

They pulled with all their might until finally the rock shifted.

"GO!" Cody yelled, grabbing the flashlight from Charlotte.

Shelby and Charlotte took off down the tunnel. Martin hesitated a second then followed. Cody tried to run backwards, but it was almost impossible on the rocky surface. He waited a few seconds, letting his siblings put some distance between them and the creature, but as the flashlight dimmed even more, he took off after them.

"CODY!" He could hear Shelby scream. "HURRY!"

He ran as fast as possible, knowing the troll was at his back. It plodded so close behind, Cody could smell its horrible breath. A solid wall loomed ahead, then the flashlight died. They were trapped.

Cody stopped, blindly checking the wall for a loose stone, but there were none. He could feel saliva dripping on his neck as the beast hovered over him. He turned and slammed the flashlight into the side of its head. The troll's angry bellow reverberated throughout the cave.

"IT HAS *CODY*!" Charlotte's anguished cry echoed in his head.

He punched it in the midsection with all his might. Unphased, the beast lifted a massive arm and knocked Cody across the cave. His body hit the stone wall and dropped like a sack of potatoes.

I've got to get up. Guardian, help us!

Cody climbed groggily to his feet, feeling the beast standing over him. As he brought his arms up to cover his face, he spotted something else. It was too dark to see clearly, just a tall shadow.

Help!

The last thing Cody remembered was pain, as the creature's mouth clamped down on his forearm, snapping it like a twig. The troll pushed him against the wall, its angry roar filling the cave. The next sound Cody heard was a thud as both he and the beast hit the ground.

Chapter 28: The Way Home

Cody's first sensation was a throbbing arm. He sat up and tried to scramble to his feet.

"WHERE IS IT?" he yelled.

"Whoa, easy!" He heard Shelby's voice and felt a hand on his shoulder, pushing him down.

"What happened?" he asked, wincing in pain.

"We climbed through the small tunnel leading back to the main chamber," Charlotte said.

"Yeah, I'm not sure how we found it," Martin added. "Someone was looking out for us."

"Thankfully, when that *thing* threw you across the cave, you landed right in front of the entrance," Shelby added. "So, after you fell, we pulled you through."

"Nice job," Cody said, closing his eyes. "Thanks."

"There was something else," Martin offered, "something on the other side. It kept the troll busy until we could pull you out."

"Maybe it was one of the Alfheim guards Andola mentioned," Charlotte replied.

He glanced down at the strips of cloth wrapped around his forearm. Shelby had torn the bottom of her shirt to make a tourniquet. Cody almost grinned, realizing what a sacrifice she'd made for him. He wondered briefly whether he would ever be able to play football again. At least he was alive.

"How are we going to get back up those ropes?" Charlotte asked.

"Obviously, Cody's not going to be able to climb," Martin replied. "It's going to have to be you and me, Shelby."

"Oh, joy and rapture," she muttered.

"I think there was a radio in one of the backpacks we left up there," Charlotte said. "Unfortunately, you'll have to get back to the entrance to use it."

Cody was feeling a bit dizzy, maybe from the loss of blood, but something caught his eye. A shadow loomed against the far wall. It seemed strangely familiar.

You're seeing things Cody Hawke.

He blinked but it was still there.

"By any chance, do you guys see The Guardian standing over there?"

"You took quite a wallop on the head," Shelby replied. "Let's do this before I change my mind."

Shelby walked over and tugged on the rope to make sure it was securely tied, then began to climb. Cody rested his eyes for a moment. When he looked back, Shelby was about ten meters off the ground.

Good girl, Shelby.

Suddenly Shelby froze, apparently feeling something wasn't right. The rope spun out from the rock above. Fear choked him as she began to fall. He leaned forward and lifted his good arm.

SHELBY! NO! Do not let her fall! SAVE HER! SAVE US!

Cody watched with horrified eyes as Shelby plummeted downward. But before hitting the ground, she disappeared into thin air.

Chapter 29: The Awakening

The Guardian grabbed Cody's arm and closed his eyes. Suddenly the pain was gone.

"Thou could do this thyself," he muttered.

"What? Me? Heal *myself?*"

Cody glanced around and counted faces, one, two, three. All present and accounted for. He let out a sigh of relief.

"How did we get—"

"Doorways are not for The Chosen," The Guardian said crossly. "Thou can move at will."

"I . . . *WHAT?* When were you going to tell me that?" Cody asked.

"Now you know," The Guardian said.

"Is that what you were trying to tell me? I mean, that shadow was you, right?"

"Are you ever going to give him a user manual?" Martin asked with a cheeky grin. "You know, count to three for this and spin two times for that."

The Guardian gave Martin a steely stare.

"So, you're saying I can go *anywhere* I want, *anytime* I want?"

"Do not get too full of thyself," The Gatekeeper offered, joining The Guardian. "There are limitations."

"What kind of limitations?" Cody asked.

Both men turned and headed off into the dark.

"Well, that was helpful," Martin muttered.

"Tell me about it," Cody said, frowning. "They give me no information, yet they get disappointed when I can't do things myself."

"Martin's got a good point, why can't they make a Tube video or something," Shelby said as they headed out. "Let's go through the maze. I've had enough of caves to last a lifetime."

"Maybe you just need to practice," Charlotte said.

"Practice how?" Cody asked. "Things happen, but I have no idea what I did."

"I'm totally confused," Martin mumbled.

"Join the club," Cody added, flexing his healing arm.

"Well, how did you send us back here?" Shelby asked as they crossed the lawn.

Cody shrugged. "I saw you falling and, I don't know . . . prayed for you to be safe."

"Maybe there's a clue in there somewhere," Charlotte mumbled. "Could it be emotion?"

Shelby put her hands on her hips. "Well, you better figure out how to control this stuff or who knows what could happen. Don't be sending me to school without my makeup on," she said.

"Or, send me somewhere while I'm sitting on the throne," Martin added.

Cody grinned. "Don't worry. At this point, I'm completely useless."

"Try something," Martin said as they entered the foyer. "How about moving that big brass plate."

"I doubt I can," Cody said, shrugging, "but I'll try."

He focused on the plate and tried to imagine lifting it off the table. Clenching his fists and grimacing with extreme effort, he concentrated with all he had.

"Be careful you don't poop your pants," Martin said with a silly grin.

Cody frowned at the motionless plate, mocking his inability to make it budge.

"It's useless," he said with a sigh. "I'm never going to be The Guardian."

He turned to walk away, feeling frustrated.

"You'll get it eventually," Shelby said.

"It's probably good I couldn't move the stupid plate." He smirked. "With my luck, I'd make it whizz around the room like a flying saucer and end up taking someone's head off."

"LOOK OUT!" Shelby yelled suddenly.

The teens dropped to the floor as the plate hurled itself around the room.

"Holy Hannah!" Martin screamed.

"Keep down!" Cody yelled, as it passed overhead.

After about ten revolutions, the plate slammed into the wall above, embedding itself in a mural.

"The Guardian is going to be ticked at you!" Martin said standing shakily. "You ruined his favorite painting."

"Forget The Guardian," Shelby said, standing up, "Heather's going to kill you."

"Try to move something," Cody growled, imitating Martin's request.

"Hey, how was I supposed to know you can transport four people across dimensions, but can't make a plate hover for a few minutes."

Chapter 30: The Accident

"Where's Shelby?" Cody mumbled, swallowing a forkful of mashed potatoes.

"It's Jenna Conway's birthday," Charlotte replied. "Her parents took a few kids out to dinner."

"Oh, right," Cody nodded. "She mentioned it."

"By the way," Jack said, stabbing another slice of pot roast with his fork, "I wanted to tell you when you were all together, but it can't wait any longer."

Cody glanced up, waiting for him to continue.

"This sounds serious," Martin said.

"Yes, but in a good way," Heather replied.

"We are hoping to foster one more child, maybe two, before we get too far into the school year," Jack announced.

"What?" Cody knew his expression reflected a lack of enthusiasm. "Why?"

"Why *not?*" Jack asked. "We've got plenty of room and unfortunately there are plenty of children who need homes. That's why we're here. This is what we wanted to do."

"Why do we need to have so many kids," Cody muttered. "Isn't six enough?"

"You're not being fair, Cody," Jack said, his tone reflecting disappointment. "Suppose you were one of those—"

218

Cody jumped up from the table, his heart suddenly pounding.

"Really, Cody?" Heather said. "Stop being so dramatic. I agree with Jack. You're not being fair."

"Something's happening," Cody said, his throat feeling constricted.

"What? Are you okay?" Heather jumped to her feet. "Are you choking?"

"No..." Cody stared at her. "It's Shelby. Something just happened."

Please let her be okay.

"Like *what?*" Jack also stood up.

"I don't..."

He glanced at his foster siblings concerned faces.

"Sit down, honey," Heather said reassuringly. "I'm sure everything's fine."

Cody couldn't finish his dinner. He felt queasy. Something was wrong, he just didn't know what. Heather dished out plates of vanilla ice cream with blueberry sauce and whipped cream on top. Cody gave his to Terrell.

Afterward, they started on their homework. Open books were scattered across the kitchen table when the old rotary phone on the wall offered an anemic ring. Jack stared at Cody for a second, then hurried over to answer.

"Yes? Yes, it is."

Cody heard a muffled voice on the other end.

"Okay. We'll be right there."

Jack hung up the phone. He turned to face the group, concern permeating his expression.

"There's been an accident," he said.

The emergency room was filled with people. Some wore bandages or had bloodied clothing, others hobbled around trying to locate an empty chair. Many were rushed in on gurneys. The line to check in extended out the door. Medical staff stood by the entrance, ready to triage patients as they arrived.

"What the heck is taking so long," Cody grumbled over the slow-moving line.

"The 'waiting room'," Martin added impatiently, "is appropriately named."

Heather held Jess' and Gabby's hands. Cody worried the pot roast might come up, trying to escape the knot in his stomach. Charlotte glanced at him with red eyes. Martin kept looking up, as if praying. No one said a word until Jack broke the silence.

"Shelby Long, please," Jack said as he approached the desk.

"Are you her father?" A large woman with straight hair and long pink fingernails glanced up.

"Uh, her legal guardian," Jack replied.

After what seemed to Cody a ridiculous waste of time, Jack was finally directed to Shelby's location. Cody led the group down a hallway lined with gurneys. They reached a large open room flanked by medical stations, each encircled by a privacy curtain.

"Shelby?" Cody called softly from outside the third curtain.

Hearing a muted response, he popped his head in. There she was, unmoving. His chest felt like it might explode as he stared at her pale face. Scratches covered her face and arms and the area around her right eye looked dark. As the family filed inside the curtain, Cody saw Shelby's eyes flutter.

Thank God.

Struggling to sit up, she winced slightly, the pain apparently related to a sling on her right arm.

"Well, it's about time you all got here," she said, attempting a smile, but it didn't last.

Cody took a deep breath, relieved to see she was conscious.

"I'm so glad you're okay," Charlotte whispered tearfully. Cody and Martin nodded.

"Me, too," Jessica added tearfully.

"Honey, what the heck *happened?*" Heather asked in a shaky voice.

"I don't know. We were driving to dinner, when suddenly everything went dark."

"What do you mean?" Jack asked. "You passed out?"

"It was like a . . . black fog," she replied hesitantly. "No one could see where they were going. Cars started hitting each other and spinning out of control. It was terrifying," Shelby whispered.

"Oh, my goodness," Heather responded.

"Our car flipped over and rolled. I had my seatbelt on, otherwise I would've been thrown all over the place," she added.

"Are you alright?" Charlotte asked, taking her hand.

"I-uh, think so. Something hit my face," Shelby said, touching her swollen eye. "The doctor said I have a concussion. They were concerned about internal bleeding, but everything came back negative. I need an x-ray to determine whether my arm's broken, but I think I fared better than most."

"I'm so glad you're okay," Cody said softly.

"Mr. Long?" a male voice called.

"It's Quitmeyer. I'm Shelby's guardian," Jack said, turning to face a man wearing a white lab coat.

"Can I talk to you, sir?"

Jack nodded and stepped outside the curtain. Shelby's eyes suddenly opened wide.

"Where's Jenna?" she asked anxiously, "And, her parents? Jenna's friend Lisa wasn't wearing her seatbelt. I hope she's okay."

"Let me see what I can find out," Heather said softly, then joined the two men outside.

Cody watched their faces through a slit in the curtain. The doctor said something that made Heather's hand come quickly to her mouth. Jack looked away, running a hand through his hair as he stared off in the distance. A few minutes later, his parents returned.

"Did you find out about Jenna and the others?" Shelby asked.

"Uh, not really," Jack said with a seemingly forced smile. "They aren't allowed to discuss other patients. Let's just worry about getting you better and I'll ask around."

"Are they here?" Shelby asked, panic creeping into her voice.

Cody glanced at Charlotte and Martin. Their expressions spoke volumes.

Jack knows something and he's not saying. It can't be good.

Shelby knew it too.

"Are they…" her face became twisted. "I heard someone mumble DOA when they were getting me out of the car."

Shelby put her face in her hands and began to cry like Cody had never heard her cry before. The girl he cared about, maybe more than anyone on the planet, was broken, physically and emotionally. He stepped away for a minute, trying to get control of his emotions.

"The Darkness," Cody whispered with a scowl, clenching his fists. "I'm coming for you. You're going to *pay* for this!"

Chapter 31: The Fog

"Thank you all," Shelby said softly as the teens gathered around her bed. "I truly appreciate your thoughtfulness."

Her words sounded tired and rehearsed, as if she'd memorized them for just such an occasion. Except for a broken arm, she was fine, but she wasn't Shelby.

Cody sat on the edge of her four-poster bed, dodging the 'get well' balloons. The magazines they brought were stacked neatly next to her pillow.

"I can't believe you've been wearing that same old football jersey and workout pants since you got home," Cody chided. "What would Kala Bennington say?"

"They're just clothes," Shelby mumbled. "Nothing important."

"Your outfit doesn't even match," he added.

Shelby shrugged. He glanced at Charlotte and Martin, silently expressing his concern.

"I have an idea," Charlotte offered perkily, "Let's listen to John. I know you *love* his music."

Shelby shrugged again. "Whatever you want."

When will the old Shelby be back? Where's the spunky attitude? Is it gone forever or will it just take time?

Cody was immensely relieved to have her home, but he couldn't rest. Shelby was not the same person who had gone to dinner that

223

night and neither was he. The pile of untouched fashion magazines was a testament to her grief, as if part of Shelby had died that day. He, on the other hand, had a fire burning inside him, one that would not be extinguished until The Darkness had paid for its evil deeds.

"Where's Sharkey?" Cody demanded as he, Charlotte, and Martin arrived at the Rúndyrr doorway.

"He is battling The Darkness," the old man replied with apparent hesitation.

"Send me there," Cody ordered. "I want to fight this thing with him."

"That is not wise," The Guardian called, appearing out of the shadows.

"It has to be stopped!" Cody snapped. "Look at what it did to Shelby and her friends!"

"We agree," The Guardian replied evenly. "However, without a plan, thou will die."

"I'm supposed to be The Chosen," he cried. "What good is it if I can't protect the people I care about. Help me defeat this thing!"

The two men looked at each other, communicating in some unspoken language.

"Where is Nidhogg? Maybe he can help. NIDHOGG?" Cody yelled.

The Guardian shook his head, but said nothing. Cody's anguish made him even more determined to get payback for what The Darkness had done to his family.

"Is Grýla behind this? Is she causing this black fog?" Cody asked, hoping to get more information while the two men seemed to have a willingness for disclosure.

"Animus is the embodiment of The Darkness," The Guardian said. "He swarms the land, fostering dissent, promoting animosity and unrest wherever he goes. His job is to pit human against human, highlighting their differences, however minute, and making them hate each other for it. Unfortunately, his job has gotten much easier of late." The old man hung his head.

"The ogress, Grýla, brings on the black fog," The Gatekeeper added. "She creates natural disasters like hurricanes, forest fires, and tornadoes to make people desperate, driving them toward anger. She spreads disease and lures wayward children into her fold."

"Lovely creatures," Martin muttered.

"However, Sharkey is trying to defeat the demon General Odium and rescue The Light," The Gatekeeper continued. "Odium and his army defend The Darkness' stronghold at Bulwark."

"An almost impossible task without a stout-hearted army," The Guardian added.

"So, let me go help him," Cody offered.

"It will take much to defeat the demon, not just warriors on the battlefield." The Gatekeeper peered into Cody's eyes as if reading his mind.

"You're suggesting I just wait here and do nothing while good people are killed and Odium keeps The Light imprisoned?"

The two men glanced at each other and frowned.

"Is Odium's army made up of demons like him?" Charlotte asked.

"They are called Dreds," The Gatekeeper replied.

"What are Dreds?" Martin wondered.

"Grýla and Odium search the planet for those with the darkness inside, then recruit them to join their army. Not that these individuals have much choice. They either join or get eliminated."

"Like zombies?" Martin mumbled.

"You're saying he's taking people from our planet and forcing them to join his army? Where does he find them?" Charlotte asked.

"Everywhere," The Gatekeeper said. "He takes them just as they die, then turns them into demons, or zombies as thou calleth them," the man shrugged, "whatever that is."

"Can they be killed?" Cody asked.

The Guardian frowned. "They can be eliminated for the moment, but the darkness inside lives on. He can summon them again and again."

Cody paced about, removing his cowboy hat and running a hand through his hair.

"It doesn't matter," he said sharply. "I can't just sit here and let them take over."

"For now," The Guardian said, "that is *all* thou can do."

Chapter 31: The Fog

Heather and Jack drove the family to town for ice cream. It was unusual for them to spend money on something that, as Jack was fond of saying, can be had for a fraction of the price if you're willing to scoop it yourself. Cody was certain his dad's uncharacteristic generosity had to do with Shelby. It was clear even Jack had noticed the change in her demeanor.

Cody stared out the dirty window, watching the landscape flash by in a whir of golden hues, highlighted by a setting sun. The old van stopped at a traffic light. On one side of the intersection, a gas station and deli were locked up tight. Not unusual, Cody thought, for a late Sunday afternoon. On the other side, an abandoned strip mall seemed forgotten, it's graffiti décor the only sign of color.

Movement caught Cody's eye. He watched as a kid, roughly his age, broke the window of a car parked in front of the strip mall.

I've seen him before, hanging around school.

The boy checked his surroundings as if to ensure no one was watching, then reached inside to unlock the door.

Is he stealing that car?

The kid was fiddling with something under the dash when a balding man bolted out one of the mall doors, yelling and waving a dark object in his hand.

Is that a gun?

Cody pressed his face to the window. He couldn't hear what the man was saying, but he seemed very angry. As exhaust began to waft up from below the car's back bumper, the boy reached for the door handle. Before he could pull the door closed, the man lifted his gun and aimed.

Oh, no!

As the old van began pulling away, Cody heard a series of loud pops.

"Uh, Jack…" he cried.

The boy slumped over the steering wheel, then just vanished into thin air.

Huh? Where did he go?

"Is something wrong, son?" Jack asked.

"I-uh," Cody mumbled, staring back at the abandoned car.

The balding man searched the car, appearing equally confused.

"The demon takes them as they die," Cody whispered, recalling The Gatekeepers words. "Uh, it's nothing," he mumbled to Jack.

The kid may be a car thief, but he doesn't deserve that.

Shelby spent most of her time sleeping, while Cody spent his free time in the Rúndyrr cave. He had become obsessed with defeating this *Darkness.* It worked on him until all he could think about was his rage. He had to do *something* and was growing increasingly tired of everyone treating him like a child.

The three teens lingered absently in the cool dark near Rúndyrr's doorway. Charlotte and Martin let Cody be for a while, but were clearly growing weary of idly waiting for something to happen.

"Cody, let's go play a game or something," Charlotte said softly.

"We need to *do* something," Cody said testily. "I can't just sit around eating ice cream and playing games while The Darkness hurts people."

"Thy anger only strengthens The Darkness," The Gatekeeper muttered from a dark corner.

"What does that—"

Movement caught Cody's eye as Rúndyrr's stony façade dissolved into a swirl of activity. Sam Sharkey emerged from the doorway, breathing hard.

"Send me back to Drangarnir," he commanded, seemingly too preoccupied to notice the teens.

Sharkey's clothing was spattered with blood. Cody wondered whether it was his or someone else's. The Gatekeeper retrieved the scepter and uttered the words Cody had heard many times before.

Without hesitation, Cody took Charlotte's hand. Ignoring her look of concern, he motioned for her to take Martin's hand. As soon as the vision on the other side of the bridge began to materialize, he grabbed Sharkey's arm.

"*NO!*" he heard The Gatekeeper cry as they were pulled through the doorway.

Cody stood on a rugged hillside, a chilly breeze tugging at his shirt. He scanned the dramatic archipelago, gaping in awestruck silence. Chiseled crags blanketed with emerald carpet descended through the early morning haze, disappearing into a smoky bay.

"Whoa." Martin muttered distractedly.

"Well, *that* was brilliant." Sharkey's irritated tone brought them back to reality.

"I can't just sit at home and wait for The Darkness to hurt more people," Cody replied firmly. "I need to *do* something."

"Obviously not giving it much thought, and showing little concern for the safety of your siblings here, you just decided this on your own."

"Not giving it much *thought*? I've thought about it *every* second of *every* day since Shelby's accident," he cried.

"Well, you're in luck, Mr. Hawke. I don't have time to take you back. All of you," the man ordered crossly, "stay behind me at all times and do *exactly* what I say!"

Sharkey descended the grassy hillside with the teens close behind. Cody knew one slip and it would be easy to find oneself treading water in the silvery ocean that looked so deceptively inviting. He glanced at Charlotte and Martin, noticing the concern on their faces.

Sharkey's right. I should've left them home. What was I thinking?

At the bottom of the steep decline, a small boat bobbed on the incoming tide, tugging impatiently at its anchor line. Another rope tied to the bow encircled a rock jutting out from the coastline.

"Listen, why don't you guys wait here," Cody said, turning to Martin and Charlotte.

"That's a good idea," Sharkey interjected. "A better idea is why don't you *all* wait here."

"I'm coming with you," Cody stated firmly.

"Cody, we're not leaving you," Charlotte responded.

Martin's nod affirmed they were in agreement.

"Really," he said decisively, "I think it would be best if you wait here. I'll be fine."

"Give it up, Cody," Martin replied. "We're coming."

Sharkey shook his head and jumped into the small craft, appropriately named *Miss Sea Mist*. His weight and a heavy outboard motor pulled down on the stern. Cody helped his siblings aboard, then climbed onto the bow and pulled up the anchor while Sharkey started the engine.

They made their way up the coastline to an island the man called Tindhólmur. However, he added, to get to the *correct* Tindhólmur, they would need to pass through Drangarnir.

"Mr. Sharkey?" Charlotte yelled, trying to be heard above the engine's growl. "Where are we?"

"The Faroe Islands, Miss Charlotte, about halfway between Iceland and Norway."

Cody had the feeling they were trying to hide from something as they hugged the rocky cove. The ocean glittered like a jewel, a rising sun painting it with tangerine highlights. Just ahead, a breathtaking crag jutted out of the water. It angled up like a giant ski slope, its apex pointing toward the sky.

"Wow, that is a cool rock formation," Martin exclaimed.

"It's called Drangarnir, and it's a sea stack, Mr. Speck," Sharkey called.

He slowed down and put the engine in neutral. *Miss Sea Mist* bobbed gently on the rolling waves as Sharkey checked his watch.

"Are we waiting for something?" Cody asked.

"We are, Mr. Hawke," Sharkey replied. "We are waiting for the sun to appear in the center of Drangarnir's arch."

Cody stared at the shadow the enormous sea stack cast upon the water. The sunny swath at its center grew brighter and brighter. It took a few minutes for dawn to pull herself above the horizon, but soon a blinding sun poked directly through the middle. Sharkey shifted the boat into gear and headed for the stone arch at an unnervingly fast clip.

"Hold on," he commanded.

"Uh, Mr. Sharkey?" Martin called anxiously. "We don't, uh, want to *hit* that thing, right?"

I hope Sharkey can see where he's going in the blinding sun.

Cody pulled his hat down to shield his eyes. As they drew near the opening, the man pushed the throttle. Cody could feel his heart pounding, awaiting the impact he desperately hoped would not come.

"HOLD ON!" Sharkey yelled again.

Cody, Charlotte, and Martin screamed in unison, preparing for impact, then suddenly everything went dark. Cody felt a chill as they passed through Drangarnir's rocky arch, a fetid smell emanating from its mossy striations.

Chapter 31: The Fog

As they emerged through the other side, the warm sun had been replaced by a cold fog. Cody took a brief calming breath, but the boat was still moving at a high rate of speed with visibility barely a few meters. They reached a momentary break in the mist and all gasped at massive Tindhólmur looming directly ahead.

"Uh, Mr. Sharkey?" Martin called. "You do see that enormous rock."

"*SHARKEY?*" Cody yelled.

Sharkey powered down the boat, turning portside as they plowed through the murky soup.

"What just happened?" Cody asked, staring at the sunless sky.

"We passed into The Darkness' realm," Sharkey declared.

"Where *are* we?" Charlotte asked in a breathy voice.

"Approaching Bulwark Castle," the man replied.

The fortress was built into Tindhólmur's dramatic cliff face. Parapets lined the stone towers jutting out through the fog above. Cody grabbed the transom preparing for impact as a rock wall appeared just ahead. Sharkey pulled further back on the throttle and handed Martin a large flashlight.

"Keep the light pointing ahead," he ordered.

They made their way in and out of various craggy coves, finally turning into a dark cavern with no apparent way out.

"Uh, Mr. Sharkey..." Martin began as they headed directly toward the rocks.

"Not to worry, Mr. Speck."

The chamber narrowed to a cave that meandered under the island castle. About twenty meters in, a small beach spanned the cave's end. Sharkey jumped into the water and pulled the boat ashore. The teens followed him onto the rocky beach.

"Where to now?" Cody asked, scanning the solid cave surrounding them.

"This way, Mr. Hawke."

They followed Sharkey behind a rock abutting the cave wall and climbed through a small opening. The cavernous room on the other side was nearly bursting with metal pieces. It was either a junkyard or a stockpile of makeshift weapons, Cody thought.

"What's—" he began.

"Shh!" Sharkey hissed.

They made their way across the room, ducking behind a pile of scrap metal at the sound of voices. Sharkey's quick glare told Cody to remain still and silent.

"I say we eat them," a rough voice uttered, followed by a string of snorts.

"Wait! I smell something," another voice growled.

"It ain't nothing," the first voice responded.

Sharkey waited until the voices faded into the distance, then continued ahead. They entered another drafty room, this one circular in nature with a primitive staircase spiraling upward. An archway to the right, led to a series of rocky tunnels. Sporadic wall torches created pools of light, cutting through the prevailing gloom.

"In there," Sharkey commanded, pointing to a wooden door on the left. "Stay *absolutely* quiet and wait until I come back for you."

"But—"

"No buts, Mr. Hawke. That's an order!"

"Who does he think he is, giving us orders," Cody said testily as Sharkey disappeared down the tunnel.

"Let's *please* do what he says," Martin begged, following Charlotte into the small room.

Cody's anger only intensified as they waited in the near darkness.

"How are we going to free The Light and defeat The Darkness when he won't even let us—"

"Cody! Shush!" Martin hissed.

"Don't even *think* those words, Cody. That's how we lured Grýla to Rúndyrr," Charlotte said.

It was barely a minute later when a sickly smell filled the small room.

"Uh-oh," Martin mumbled, his frown apparent in the dim light

A low wail emanated from somewhere in the tunnel, getting louder and louder with each second. Cody opened the door a sliver and peered out.

"Oh, no!" Charlotte cried softly, peeking around him.

A black fog rolled toward them, consuming the light as it moved.

"COME ON!" Cody yelled. "RUN!"

Charlotte and Martin took off in the direction of the weapons room. Cody began to follow, but something made him stop. He turned, staring at the cloud in rapt silence.

Join me, Chosen. They treat thee like a child. Hate them for it. Let thy anger flow. Come with me and rule their miserable world like the king thou art meant to be.

"Who is this?" Cody shook his head, trying to rid himself of the voice echoing within, but the pull was too strong. "I'm, uh, listening—"

"CODY! *LET'S GO!*"

Martin's calling me. I should run, but maybe I'll listen a little longer...

"CODY!" Charlotte screamed.

The fog was just a few meters away, its foul smell filling Cody's senses. A chill permeated his body.

Join me, Chosen. They don't deserve thee. Together we shall command this pathetic riff-raff.

Suddenly Cody felt a hand on his shoulder.

"What art thou *doing*? Move!" the gravelly voice roared, pulling him back.

They hurried toward the scrap metal room, putting a few more meters between them and the black fog. Charlotte and Martin stopped and grabbed something to use as a weapon.

Hear me, Chosen. I'm calling to thee. Come back. Leave them.

Cody glanced over his shoulder.

I-uh, I'm listening...

He hesitated for a second, but the grip on his arm was strong, pulling him past the piles of scrap metal, everything from pipes to old swords.

"What was thy *plan*?" The Guardian growled, breathing hard. "Was it to get thyself *killed* or worse, *captured*? If so, it's working perfectly!"

"I-uh..."

Cody stared back, captivated by the cloud as it rolled along behind them. A hideous being became visible in the midst. It had a leathery red face, curled horns, and a spiked tail. The creature's torso was covered in metal armor. It sneered at Cody revealing long metal teeth.

General Odium.

Pillars of dense matter became apparent amid the swirling mist. The pillars quickly transformed into human-like creatures with hollow eyes and expressionless faces approaching in rows six across. The zombies staggered toward them, grabbing crow bars, chains, and tire irons.

"GO!" The Guardian yelled. "RUN!"

The sight of the Dreds approaching snapped Cody out of his fog. He bent down to pick up the remains of a car bumper, holding it out in a defensive posture. The first six demons surrounded them, waving their weapons. Cody tried to swing the bumper, but it was awkward and unwieldy.

The Guardian raised his staff and yelled words Cody didn't understand. A flash of light arced out from its top and three of the Dreds were thrown across the room. Cody dropped the bumper and tried to focus on doing the same, but nothing happened. He ducked as a tire iron narrowly missed his head, a length of chain surrounding his body.

"Charlotte, Martin," he yelled. "RUN!"

Cody unwrapped the chain and yanked it from a boy's hand. He stared into gray eyes, looking for some sign of life, but all he saw was emptiness. The boy appeared strangely familiar.

I've seen him before. It's the kid that was breaking into the car.

He recalled The Gatekeeper's words; General Odium takes people who have the darkness within and recruits them for his army.

Cody swung the chain and knocked the boy and two others off balance, then tried to use his mind to toss their weapons. The Guardian pointed his staff and threw a few more of the approaching Dreds across the room. Cody tried again, but nothing happened.

"Why can't I move things, like you?" he yelled in frustration. "Do I need a staff?"

"Thou are not concentrating. Learn to control thy mind," the old man replied gruffly.

Cody closed his eyes and imagined their weapons flying across the room.

It's impossible. I'm useless.

Suddenly, the sounds of metal hitting stone walls reverberated through the air. Cody stared for a moment in disbelief, then turned to check on his siblings. A group of Dreds surrounded them. Two raised their weapons, preparing to strike. Martin swung a tire iron to keep them at bay, but one approached Charlotte from behind and wrapped a length of chain around her throat.

Charlotte!

Cody ran toward them. Shoving the man away from Charlotte, he tried to loosen the chain, but a Dred hit him in the side with a crowbar. Charlotte tugged on the chain, gasping for air. Martin let out a painful cry as a tire iron hit him in the back, knocking him to the ground.

Martin!

"A LITTLE HELP HERE!" Cody yelled, as he grabbed the weapon.

Tossing the men across the room, The Guardian hurried in their direction. Cody glanced at the seemingly infinite army rushing toward them as he untangled the chain from Charlotte's throat.

"TAKE MY HANDS!" The Guardian yelled.

Martin and Charlotte each grabbed a hand and in an instant, they were gone.

"Let's go! You're next!" The Guardian yelled, appearing behind him.

Cody hesitated. Staring at the Dred's faces, he wondered what was going on in their heads.

"DO IT! *NOW*!" The Guardian commanded.

Cody reached back and took the old man's hand. The next thing he knew, they were standing in the Rúndyrr cave.

"That was foolish, *very* foolish!" The Guardian snapped, angrily pacing the floor.

"I had to do *something*…"

"Thou were told to wait until we had a plan," the old man's eyebrows angled up, dancing crossly in time with his words. "Thou could've been *killed*!"

He was right. It was foolish. Cody knew he had underestimated The Darkness' power. There was so much he didn't understand.

"Thank you for coming to help us," he murmured.

"Thou *don't*…" the old man began, appearing to soften. He took a deep breath and shook his head. "One thing is for certain. The Chosen is brave to the point of foolishness." He almost smiled.

Cody tossed stones into the fountain adorning the west side of Freya Manor's expansive yard, a variety of emotions choking his throat. He wanted to avenge what they had done to Shelby and the Conway family in the worst way, but he had to admit, he had no idea what he was up against.

How do I defend against Odium when he can control my mind?

Without a plan, he might very well die. The Guardian and Gatekeeper were, by their own admission, too old to fight the battle alone. Nidhogg had not responded to his calls since Grýla's attack. For all Cody knew, the dragon was dead, along with Pitaskog. Sharkey hadn't been seen for days. He couldn't ask his friends. It was just too dangerous.

It's up to me, but what can I do? The few tricks I've learned are not going to stop The Darkness.

Cody noticed a spot of light dancing in the air. He looked around, assuming it was a reflection, but couldn't determine its source. Suddenly, he realized the light was getting closer.

What is that? It's not a reflection. Could it be a hummingbird? No. It has a face...

A fairy, perhaps the same one that visited Shelby's room a while back, hovered just out of reach. She dropped something on the ground, then darted off. Cody picked up the tiny scroll. Carefully unrolling it, he perused the calligraphy adorning its stiff paper.

"The time has come, the need is clear,
For The Chosen to receive his Guardian gear.
To defend Rúndyrr and Earth herself,
Against the evil deeds of the darkest elf.
On the next full moon, at the fifth hour,
We will grant the defenders their rightful power."
It was signed *The Guardian.*

"What do you suppose it means?" Charlotte asked as the four teens meandered lazily about the grounds." It was the first time Shelby had been out of the house other than for school, in weeks.

"I have no idea," Cody murmured. "I'm hoping it means they have a way to help me defeat The Darkness."

"Well, tomorrow is the next full moon, so I guess we'll find out," Martin added.

"Do you think we're included?" Shelby wondered. "I mean, he said we're all part of the team and I, for one, want to rip The Darkness to pieces."

Cody was strangely relieved to hear Shelby's anger. Though uncharacteristic, it meant she was progressing through the stages of grief, as had he after his parents' untimely death. It meant she was beginning to heal, and he would be thankful to have the old Shelby back.

Chapter 32: The Gifts

Early the next morning, four anxious teens made their way down to the Rúndyrr cave. The Guardian and Gatekeeper were waiting when they got there, along with a guest they did not expect.

The Guardian approached them, black robe flowing as he walked. A golden sash covered his shoulders.

Is he dressed up for something?

The beautiful guest stepped forward wearing an ornate stole over an emerald green gown.

"Radianna," Cody said excitedly. "It's great to see you."

"And you, Cody," she replied with a smile. "How are you all? We were sorry to hear of your accident, Shelby."

"Thank you, Radianna. It's so good to see you," Shelby replied. "Can you stay for a while?"

"Unfortunately, no. I must get back, but I've been given permission to visit so I can be part of this special occasion."

"What occasion?" Martin asked.

A sound suddenly filled the cave, some sort of strange music Cody had never heard before. He wondered whether it was a ritualistic part of a Nimbusian ceremony.

Or, maybe it's required to block the dialog from unwanted listeners.

"We see now, as a part of the ongoing defense of Rúndyrr and protectors of The Light," The Guardian offered somberly, "we've been remiss in not giving thee a means to defend thyself."

"To that end," Radianna said with a warm smile, "we will now remedy the situation. Cody, please come forward."

He glanced at his siblings, unsure what this was all about, then took a few steps. Radianna held her right hand up, the other clutching some sort of golden star, much like the one on The Guardian and Gatekeeper's robes.

"Please place your right hand over The Star of the Æsir." Radianna took a deep breath. "Cody Hawke, The Chosen, Defender of The Light and future Guardian of Rúndyrr, the Shimmering Bridge, we have fashioned an ice sword that will respond to your commands. You must provide a name for your sword, one that is unique in your world and will ensure precise communication. Do you have such a name, sir?" Radianna asked.

"I-uh, no. I-I need to think about it," Cody stammered, glancing at his siblings.

"Very well. Martin, please come forward. Martin Speck, Defender of The Light and future Guardian of Rúndyrr, the Shimmering Bridge, we have fashioned an ice axe that will respond to your commands. You must provide a name for your axe, one that is unique in your world and will ensure precise communication. Do you have such a name, sir?"

"A name?" Martin asked, a silly grin pervading his face.. "How about Bob?"

The Guardian frowned. "Thou would like to call thy axe, *Bob*?" he asked dryly.

"Might I suggest runic names for your weapons," Radianna offered.

"Uh, that would be great," Cody replied sheepishly.

"Cody, might I suggest calling your sword, Tiwaz, representing the warrior god, Tyr. Tiwaz symbolizes honor, justice, and leadership, all traits that are strong within you. Please come forward."

Radianna closed her eyes and reached upward. An ice sword with an ornate silver hilt appeared in her outstretched hand.

"Tiwaz," Radianna said earnestly, handing the sword to Cody, "may it serve you well."

"Totally cool!" he whispered.

The end of the hilt was shaped like a god's head, an upward arrow carved into the glistening blade. Cody grasped the hilt, feeling a strong connection as the silver molded to his grip. Electricity flowed from his arm to the sword and back again, as if he and the weapon had become one, then it just disappeared.

Radianna smiled in apparent response to his surprised look. "You can call for it anytime by simply raising your arm and thinking its name."

She turned to Martin. "Might I suggest Uruz as the name of your axe. Uruz, the ox, represents strength, courage, and tenacity, something you have much of," she said warmly.

Again, she reached up and an ice axe appeared in her hand. The hilt resembled the head of a horned ox, an upside-down 'V' adorning the blade.

"Sweet!" Martin said as Radianna handed him the axe.

"Charlotte Cower, Defender of The Light and future Guardian of Rúndyrr, the Shimmering Bridge, for you we have fashioned an ice lance that will respond to your commands. You must provide a name for your lance, one that is unique in your world and will ensure precise communication. Do you have such a name, madam?"

"I-uh," Charlotte began shyly.

"Might I suggest Kenaz as the name of your lance. Kenaz, the torch, represents knowledge and inspiration, something you clearly bring to the world," she said with a smile.

Again, she reached up and an ice lance appeared in her hand. Its grip resembled a glowing torch with the shape of a 'less than' sign adorning its shaft. She handed the lance to Charlotte.

"Shelby, please come forward," Radianna said in a regal tone. "Shelby Long, Defender of The Light and future Guardian of Rúndyrr, the Shimmering Bridge, we have fashioned for you an ice bow and arrow that will respond to your commands. You must provide a name, one that is unique in your world and will ensure precise communication. Do you have such a name, madam?"

"Can I call it Gebo?" Shelby asked. "I feel like every day of my life going forward is a gift."

"Excellent choice," Radianna offered, smiling broadly.

"Teacher's pet," Cody whispered with a grin.

"Gebo, the gift, means sacrifice and generosity, something you certainly show the world every day," Radianna added.

Again, she reached up and an ice bow and quiver appeared in her hands. A carved 'X' adorned the bow, the grip shaped like an illuminated candle. She handed them to Shelby.

"These weapons represent our gifts to you from the people of Nimbus, honoring your efforts to defend this world and promote The Light. Wield them in good health."

"Radianna," Cody stammered. "I-uh, don't know what say . . . but thank you."

"Yes," Shelby reiterated. "How can we ever thank you?"

"These gifts are awesome," Martin added.

"Thank you so much," Charlotte whispered. "I feel so . . . special."

"I suggest you practice with them, get to know their unique qualities. May they serve you well, my friends," Radianna said, and with that, she was gone.

Chapter 33: The Question

The four teens spent the next week practicing with their weapons. Cody rigged an 'enemy' by strapping an old pillow to a tree. Even he had to admit their attempts to defeat the pillow were comical. Charlotte could barely carry her lance, dragging one end on the ground as she walked. Shelby couldn't even load the arrow in the bow, much less shoot it. Martin swung the axe with the same expertise as he did Taekwondo. And Cody, the one with the easiest weapon to wield, was certain the only enemy he could defeat, was a pillow.

"This is ridiculous," Charlotte said. "I'm going to take someone's eye out with this thing."

"Robin Hood made this look so easy," Shelby added. "I'd have more luck shooting it at myself."

"Yeah, stand back when I swing this thing," Martin quipped. "Otherwise, I might give you a *really* bad haircut."

"What do you suppose it does?" Charlotte asked, examining her lance. "Radianna and Sharkey used their swords to subdue the enemy by freezing them."

"Do you think our weapons do the same thing?" Martin wondered.

"Probably," Cody said. "But, is that all it does, or can you actually hurt someone with this thing?"

"I guess we'll find out at some point," Shelby added.

"You know," Martin yelled, glancing upwards, "an instruction book would be helpful."

Sharkey returned suddenly for a few hours, just to pack his things. Cody and the others followed him across the foyer and up the stairs, hoping for answers.

"Did you defeat it? Did you end The Darkness and save—" Cody began.

"Not exactly," was the vague reply.

"What does that mean, not exactly?" Shelby pressed as they ran down the hall leading to his room.

"It means that my actions are insufficient to defeat The Darkness," Sharkey called over his shoulder."

"Are you saying we're doomed?" Martin asked.

"The best I can do is slow it down," he replied, shoving a few shirts into his bag.

"So, what will it take to be rid of The Darkness forever?" Charlotte wondered.

Sharkey stopped packing for a moment. "We need to return The Light. Unfortunately, it is very weak right now."

"How do we go about doing that?" Cody asked. "I assume we need a strong army."

"Is there a way we could convince the military to help?" Shelby wondered.

Sharkey sighed. "You guys have it all wrong. It's not that kind of army."

"What does that mean?" Cody frowned, growing increasingly frustrated.

"You need to understand more about The Light and The Darkness," Sharkey said, hurling the strap on his duffel bag over his shoulder.

"I'm *trying* to," Cody could feel his face redden. "But you won't help!"

"Why can't you just tell us!" Shelby said testily.

"I've tried. It doesn't work that way, Miss Shelby," Sharkey said. "The Light is something you either understand or you don't."

"We don't even know what questions to ask," Charlotte muttered.

He strode down the hall toward the stairs with Cody and the others at his heels.

"So, you're just going to leave?" Cody yelled.

Sharkey stopped. The four teens nearly slammed into his back.

"Talk to The Gatekeeper. Perhaps he can help you learn. Keep in mind, the answer may not be what you want to hear, and when that happens, just remember I told you so."

And with that, he was gone.

Chapter 34: The Benningtons

"Why are the birds dying?" a girl in Cody's biology class asked.

"I heard they're just dropping out of the sky," another student added.

"Scientists don't know," Mr. Tallman replied, running a hand through his thinning red hair. "They are studying the air quality and other factors as well as the possibility of some type of virus."

"Aren't the fish dying also?" Jason asked, a boy Cody knew from football.

"Unfortunately, yes," Mr. Tallman responded, "along the Pennamaquan River. I've also heard about a strange virus going around that's making people sick and there is no cure or vaccine. Be sure to wash your hands every day when you get home . . . with soap."

"Then there's the dark cloud that seems to be parked over the northeast," Shelby added.

"An excellent point, Miss Long," the teacher replied. "That has scientists rather befuddled as well. And, let's not forget the California fires, the Oklahoma tornados, and gulf coast hurricanes."

"It's The Darkness," Cody mumbled. "And, there's more where that came from."

"Mr. Hawke, did you have something to add?"

"No, sir," Cody said, squirming a bit. "It's just, the things we're doing to our environment, well, they seem to be having a bad impact."

"Very true," Mr Tallman replied somberly. "As custodians of this world, we need to take better care of mother earth. We have only one option with regard to a home planet, at least right now, and at the rate we're going, it's not looking good for the future."

Cody glanced over at Shelby and Martin, noticing the look of concern on their faces.

"What do you suppose Sharkey meant by saying we should talk to The Gatekeeper," Charlotte asked as the school bus pulled away.

"Maybe we should take another trip," Cody replied, staring at the dark cloud looming to the west.

"To where?" Shelby asked. "How do we control the destination, if we don't know where to go?"

"Besides, we're *so* good at that anyway," Martin joked. "Maybe we just need to ask The Gatekeeper to send us someplace where we can learn."

"All that talk in biology class about the bad things happening in the world," Cody muttered.

"No one else seems capable of stopping these terrible demons. Maybe we should try." Shelby said.

"Yeah," Martin quipped. "Maybe Grýla will laugh herself to death, watching us try to stab her with our weapons."

"Or, we could be killed," Charlotte whispered, her tone far more serious.

"Maybe," Shelby said softly. "But I can't help feel there's a reason I was allowed to live."

"Besides, I doubt he'll send us anywhere truly dangerous," Cody added. "Even if it is dangerous, somehow we always get through. I wonder sometimes if he helps us."

"Dost thou wish to embark on a journey?" The Gatekeeper offered as the teens approached.

"Uh, yes," Cody said. "We have no idea where we want to go, but Sharkey said you could help us learn more about The Light and defeating The Darkness. Will you do that?"

"Very well," The Gatekeeper replied with a sigh, as if resolving himself to the fact that Cody would never stop trying.

"They make up a class of common compounds,
An aromatic list so long, it thoroughly abounds.
Names like acetate and butyrate are hard to say,
But they appear in things we use nearly every day.
A reaction that comes from acids and alcohols,
Encompassing everything from fruits to florals."

Martin smirked. "I may use them every day, but I have no idea what they are."

Cody grinned. "Charlotte, you're up," he said.

"Could it be…" she hesitated.

"Come on, honey. You've got this," Shelby said.

"Is it possible that it's…"

"Charlotte!"

"Okay, okay. Could it be *esters*?"

The doorway swirled its readiness. A sunny glow confirmed daylight on the other side as the four teens were pulled into its midst.

Cody watched people rushed purposefully in and out of a series of glass doors. The teens stood inside a large space filled with displays, everything from racks of clothing and shoes, to pots and pans.

"Well, at least we're indoors," Charlotte said.

"No freezing rain or molten lava pits. I like this place already," Martin added.

"We're in a department store," Cody said. "What could we *possibly* learn about The Light in here?"

"It's a beautiful store," Shelby offered, glancing around. "Could it be Saks or Bloomingdales?"

"Looks like we're in a big city," Charlotte added, peeking out the door.

Cody noticed the busy traffic outside, both cars and pedestrians, including a group of loud teenage girls assembling on the sidewalk. The girls entered the store like a flash mob, barreling past Cody and the others like they weren't even there. One girl bumped into

Charlotte as she passed, nearly knocking her down. Cody expected to hear an apology, but she just kept going.

"Nice," he whispered with disgust. "Are you okay, Charlotte?"

His foster sister nodded with a wry grin.

The last girl to enter the store let go of the door without holding it for the people behind her. It slammed into a baby carriage being pushed by a harried mom trying to get her family inside. A loud wail emanated from the pink bundle, apparently frightened by the force of the door hitting her carriage. The mom shook her head in silent anger.

"I'm sorry, ma'am," Cody called as he ran over to hold the door. "Let me get that."

"Thank you so much," she said with an appreciative smile. "It's nice to know there are still people with manners left in this world."

Shelby leaned over the baby carriage as the woman entered the store. "Don't cry, sugar," she said, smiling sweetly. "Everything is alright. Aren't you just the cutest little thing?"

The baby froze in mid sob, staring up at Shelby and breaking into a big toothless grin.

"That's my girl," Shelby said playfully.

The mom thanked them again and proceeded down the aisle.

"Do you think that teen mob has anything to do with why we're here?" Cody asked.

"Let's follow them and see where they're headed," Shelby replied.

The girls swarmed through various sections, heading purposefully toward something. They finally reached the makeup department and joined another mob already waiting there. Cody and the others got to the back of a long line, hoping for some indication as to whether this was the reason for their trip. One girl turned to him, a smirk on her face.

"I mean, like *really*?" she said, shaking her head in disgust. "What are *you* doing here?"

"I'm sorry?" Cody asked, lifting his cowboy hat, but the girl turned away.

"Excuse me," Shelby said, tapping a girl on the shoulder. "Can you tell me what this line is for?"

"*Really*? Do you live under a rock?" she frowned, glancing downward. "OMG, where did you get that hideous outfit, the dollar store?" she added and abruptly turned her back to them.

Shelby looked like she'd been smacked in the face. Cody thought he saw the glimmer of a tear in her eye. He clenched his fists, feeling his face get red.

"Don't pay any attention to her, Shelby," Charlotte whispered. "She seems pretty full of herself and obviously knows nothing about fashion except what she finds on the rack at Forever Selfies."

"I'd call her full of *something*," Martin said with a smirk, "but I'll leave it up to your imagination."

Shelby glanced at Cody as if waiting for him to say something. He knew this kind of thing generally got him into trouble so he chose his words carefully.

"I think your outfit blows hers away," he whispered.

Shelby smiled.

"Alright, everyone, please settle down," said a voice emanating from a loudspeaker perched atop a metal stand. "Let's get in an orderly line. Kala will be here momentarily."

"Kala?" Shelby immediately brightened.

Cody was sure he'd never seen a rowdier group of girls. The voice on the loudspeaker kept repeating words like 'orderly' and 'calm' over and over, but they seemed to have little effect. Shoppers stayed as far away as possible. Moms took small children by the hand and led them quickly past.

"I can't *wait* to meet her," a girl nearby uttered excitedly. "I want to show her my new handbag. Do you know what this *cost*? It was almost a *thousand* dollars," she said excitedly.

"I can't wait either," her friend replied, "I hope she's not still fat after her last kid."

"Who *are* these girls?" Charlotte whispered.

"I don't know," Martin said, "but they won't be winning any Miss Congeniality contests."

The line moved slowly winding its way around various counters until finally the four teens reached the front. There she was, sitting behind a table with two large men on either side, selling bottles of her new fragrance, *Queen Bee*, and copies of her recent book, *Being a Bennington*.

"Kala!" Shelby said with a gasp.

"Hello there," Kala glanced up. "Can I interest you in a bottle of my new fragrance? Or, perhaps you'd prefer a copy of my book?"

"Oh, Kala," Shelby said breathlessly, "I'm *such* a fan. I think you are so wonderful..."

Cody stood next to Shelby, her words fading into the background. He couldn't take his eyes off Kala. There was something odd about her, something he couldn't quite put his finger on.

"Are you going to buy something? If not, let's keep the line moving," a stern male voice uttered.

"But, I..."

"Please, sir, she just wants to talk to Kala for a minute," Cody said evenly.

The man gave Cody a smirk, as if to say, so do they all.

"Here," Cody said, pulling singles from his pocket, "how much?"

Martin and Charlotte also began searching for money.

"The fragrance is forty-two dollars and the book's fifteen," the man said offhandedly.

"Uh, we have..." Cody fumbled through the handful of singles. "Twelve dollars," he said with a frown.

"...I make my own clothes and I'd love to show you some of my designs," Shelby offered wistfully. "They would look *so* beautiful on you..."

"Sorry," the man said testily. "If you're not buying anything, let's move along."

Cody glanced at Kala, hoping she would intervene on their behalf, but she pushed back the dark hair surrounding her face and shrugged, as if to say there was nothing she could do.

Cody frowned and started to look away when he saw something that made him gasp.

"Move! NOW!" the big man growled.

He hesitated for a moment, then took Shelby by the arm and pulled her away.

"That was certainly accommodating of her," Martin grumbled as they returned to the main aisle.

"What would you like her to do?" Shelby asked. "We didn't have enough money."

"She's worth millions. She couldn't give you a discount on—" Martin began.

"Did you guys *see* that?" Cody interrupted.

"Her low-cut top?" Martin replied. "How could you miss it?"

"No, her *face*," Cody said. "The makeup hides it, but she has a gold tattoo on the side of her face, just like Radianna."

"Are you saying she could be..." Charlotte stopped, her mouth hanging open.

"Nimbusian? It would appear so," Cody replied.

"Well, as interesting as that is, it doesn't help us get out of here," Martin said.

"Shelby, give us the riddle one more time," Cody requested.

"The notes on top are small and go fast,
Fruity molecules known not to last.
Floral notes come from the heart,
They arrive soon after but not at the start.
Base notes are earthy and stick around long,
Heavy and musky, like a profound song."

"Any idea what that's about?" Cody turned to Charlotte.

"Unfortunately, no. It keeps referring to notes, so I assume it's about music, but there's nothing musical going on here," she said.

"Maybe this lady can help us," Cody said, heading over to a counter.

An attractive older woman wearing a black and white jacket smiled as they approached.

"Is there something I can help you with today?" she asked.

"Uh, maybe," Cody winced, trying to think of a way to ask without sounding ridiculous.

"We're working on a project for school and we were given this riddle." Martin jumped in. "We have no idea what it means. Maybe you could help us," he added.

"Shelby, can you repeat it again?" Cody asked as she stared at Kala. "Earth to Shelby."

"Huh? Sure," she said, reciting the riddle.

"Hmm," the woman replied. "It sounds to me like it's referring to how the notes of a fragrance unfold when sprayed on your skin."

"Interesting," Charlotte said.

"You see," the woman continued, "perfumes contain a mix of different scent molecules and these molecules have different weights. As the fragrance evaporates, molecules float up into the air. They get caught on tiny projections in your nose, called cilia, triggering receptor neurons that process smells."

"Wow, all that is going on when I smell a dead skunk at the side of the road?" Martin quipped.

"Yes," she laughed, "or when you smell something lovely."

"It sounds like different notes are processed at different times," Shelby said.

"Yes. The lightest molecules create what we call 'top notes.' They evaporate first so you smell them as soon as you put it on. The next group of molecules are 'heart notes.' These take a little while to evaporate, perhaps anywhere from fifteen minutes to an hour, so you smell these next. 'Base notes' are heaviest and are made up of earthy scents like musk. You might not smell them for a couple hours." The woman hesitated. "Does that answer your question?"

"Wow, you're amazing!" Martin said.

"Yes, that was awesome," Cody added.

The woman smiled. "You caught me at a good time. I just returned from fragrance training."

"If I might add, I *love* your fragrances," Shelby said, nearly swooning. "When I'm older, I plan to wear nothing but this perfume right here. Unfortunately, right now I can't afford it," she added with a rueful grin.

"I understand. Well, you four are delightful..." She hesitated, glancing over at the noisy teenage mob. "Unlike *that* group," she said, stepping over to a nearby drawer. "Here are a few samples for you. I'm not supposed to give them out unless you buy something, but I'll consider it an investment in a future admirer," the woman added, smiling warmly.

"Oh, my!" Shelby said, excitedly. "Thank you *so* much!"

"Yes, thank you," Charlotte added. "You have no idea how much we will enjoy these."

"Fragrance notes," Cody muttered. "Who knew?"

Chapter 35: The Virtual Assistant

"What do you suppose it means?" Charlotte asked, twirling one of her many braids, legs draped across the arm of Shelby's bedroom chair. "Is that what The Gatekeeper wanted us to see?"

"Are you *sure* you saw a gold tattoo?" Shelby muttered. "It was probably just gold dust makeup or some new jewelry she was wearing. You're a bit of an oaf when it comes to women, Cowpoke," she teased.

"I know what I saw," Cody said firmly. "I could see the spiral pattern drawn beyond her hairline."

"I thought the council or whatever, forbid them from coming here without special permission," Shelby said absently, a pillow propping up her head as she stared at the laptop.

"I wonder what the punishment is for disobeying," Martin asked, tossing a ball in the air. "I mean how do you punish people who are practically perfect? Do they make them spend a month as a nerdy teenager, or turn them into a dodo bird?"

"Radianna said we could ask her a question," Charlotte stated, sitting up abruptly, "if we ever needed help."

"She did say that," Shelby added.

"I assume she was just being nice," Cody said, staring anxiously out Shelby's bedroom window.

"Out of all the millions of people on Earth and billions of noises going on, how could she possibly hear us?" Martin wondered.

"It can't hurt to try," Charlotte offered.

Cody paced about for a minute, then stopped in the center of the room.

"Radianna? Radianna, are you there?" he hesitated. "You said you would help us if we need it. Well, we have an important question. We met the TV reality star Kala Bennington in a mall. I noticed she has a golden tattoo on the side of her face, similar to yours and those of the Light Elves. Is she from Nimbus... or maybe Alfheim?

The four teens waited in silence. Cody held his breath part of the time, not wanting to miss any sign she might use to contact them, but nothing happened. The TV and the clock radio on Shelby's nightstand were silent. He turned to the others, knowing his disappointment was obvious.

"I guess she's not listening . . . surprise, surprise," he said, frowning.

Martin grinned. "I'm sure they have much better things to do than listen to our nutty conversations."

"I mean, how would she even know we're trying to contact her, unless they have software or something that listens for certain key words," Charlotte added.

"She said to call her name," Shelby replied offhandedly.

"I *did* call her name," Cody said.

"Otherwise, they'd have to be listening to us all the—" Charlotte began.

"Uh, guys," Shelby said abruptly, sitting up in bed. "I-uh, think you need to see this."

They gathered around the laptop. Cody watched with silent fascination as the words, 'Hello, my friends', appeared on the screen. Suddenly a voice emanated from the speaker. It wasn't Radianna's voice, but rather the virtual assistant.

"Hello, Shelby, Charlotte, Martin, and Cody. It is Radianna. Thank you for contacting me with your question. I understand how this could be a source of concern for you. It is certainly a concern for the people of Nimbus," she said. "Yes, Kala Bennington, as you call her, is Nimbusian. And yes, being on Earth is a violation of everything we stand for. Kala – and by the way, that *is* a shortened version of her real name – is the great granddaughter of someone you know and love . . . Loki."

The four teens all gasped in unison.

"As are her sisters," Radianna continued. "This is the very reason we forbid our people to visit Earth. The sisters – my cousins – love the attention afforded them by your people."

Charlotte leaned in, clearly not sure whether to speak into the air or the laptop.

"Uh, Radianna? This is Charlotte," she said a bit shakily.

The words 'Hello, Charlotte', appeared on the screen.

"We were trying to learn more about The Darkness and The Gatekeeper sent us to that mall to meet Kala. Does that mean the Benningtons are somehow connected to The Darkness?"

"Excellent question, Charlotte," the virtual assistant replied. "We've been looking into the very same thing. If that is the case, there will be serious ramifications when we get them back to Nimbus."

"I can't believe Kala would do anything wrong," Shelby stated emphatically. "Last month, she gave a half-million dollars to the people of that hurricane-ravaged town in Florida."

"Yes, she has a good side," Radianna replied, "or, at least she wants it to appear so, but Kala is not acting in the best interests of Earth's people," she added.

"Radianna?" Cody asked. "What exactly *is* The Darkness? Grýla, the demon ogress attacked Rúndyrr so we thought *she* was The Darkness, but then we saw General Odium and his zombie army at his fortress and now you're saying the Bennington sisters could be part of it as well."

"The Darkness has no physical form," Radianna replied, "at least not yet. It is a collection of all the negative energy that exists in the world. It grows ever stronger, feeding on hatred and animosity."

"Is The Darkness a *movement?*" Charlotte asked.

"That's a good way to characterize it," Radianna replied. "Yes, Cody, The Darkness, or Animus, as he's called, is much more than just Grýla. She and Odium are The Darkness' henchmen, if you will, but as Charlotte said, it's a movement, a plan to assume control of the earth and it's people by promoting anger, hatred, and intolerance."

"So, what can we do to stop it?" Cody asked.

"The Darkness wants to divide you all, identifying the smallest differences between you and magnifying them into big things, things that will foster hatred in humans."

Radianna paused for a minute, as if collecting her thoughts.

"I wish you all could see yourselves as we see you. It is human nature to identify with certain groups, to feel like you are part of something . . . anything from sports teams and political viewpoints to states, countries, or religions. However, to us, those things are just what make you all unique, not things that should divide you. To us, you are collectively the people of Earth, a place you should treasure beyond all else.

"So, how do we fight this . . . Darkness?" Shelby asked.

"And, how do we promote The Light?' Martin added.

"Excellent questions," Radianna replied. "You respond by standing with The Light, being a beacon for change."

"How do we do that?" Cody asked.

"You are exceptional people," Radianna added. "You will find a way. If anyone on Earth can bring back The Light, it is you four." Radianna hesitated, as if wrestling with whether to say anything more. "Now, I must go. Be safe, my friends."

The teens sat in silence, hoping to hear more, but after a few minutes, they knew she was gone.

"What does it mean?" Shelby asked.

"Maybe the answer will present itself along the way," Charlotte mumbled.

"Good, because I'm more confused now than I was before she started," Martin added.

Chapter 36: The Answer

"I don't understand it," Jack mumbled, setting down the newspaper and taking a swig of his morning coffee.

"What is it you don't understand, dear?" Heather replied, flipping pancakes on the griddle.

"There's some weird virus going around. Lots of people are getting sick, some are dying. And, it's been so dark lately. I can't remember the last time we had a sunny day. It's like we're being punished for something," he added. "If we don't get some sun soon, the plants in the conservatory will all die."

"Maybe we are," Martin said. "Being punished, I mean. Yesterday, all the toilets in the school backed up. Kids were actually barfing from the smell," he added, a twinkle apparent in his eyes.

"Yuck," Shelby said, wrinkling her nose. "It was *gross*."

"The odor was so bad, they let us go outside for lunch. Even Meany Sheeny said it would be hard to eat a liverwurst sandwich with the smell of ripening poop—" Martin began.

"Okay," Heather interjected with a chuckle. "We get the picture."

Jack grinned.

"Sharkey says it's The Darkness," Cody muttered. "Maybe he's right."

Jack frowned. "You think the earth is slipping into darkness because some toilets backed up?"

"Not just because of one thing," Cody replied, "but maybe because of everything."

"Maybe the evil in the world has gotten so bad, it's beginning to take over," Shelby said.

"That's a scary thought," Heather mumbled, placing a platter of pancakes on the table.

"Mrs. Kendrick said that Americans buy about 50 billion water bottles a year," Gabby said. "All a person has to do to keep their 150 bottles a year out of the landfills is buy a reusable water bottle. Maybe darkness is taking over because more people don't care enough to try."

"So, what do we do about it?" Jack asked, stabbing some pancakes with his fork. "The Darkness."

"We need to bring back The Light," Charlotte replied.

"And how does one do that?" Heather asked.

"That seems to be the big question," Cody said.

Jack stopped chewing and gave Cody a look somewhere between amusement and are you kidding.

"Maybe we all need to sing more kumbaya songs and hug more puppies and kittens," he offered sarcastically.

"Ha-ha," Cody said with a frown. "You might not be laughing after it's been dark for weeks."

"What do you mean?" Jack was no longer smiling.

"I'm just saying," Cody murmured. "Suppose it doesn't get better and The Darkness takes over."

Jack frowned. "I wouldn't have taken you for the gloom and doom type, Cody."

"On a lighter note," Heather said, "no pun intended. We need to go to town and get more school supplies later, so don't go too far. I can't figure out where you four disappear to, but sometimes I swear you're in another country."

"Maybe he's onto something," Charlotte offered from the inglenook bench, her arms wrapped around her knees.

"Who?" Cody glanced up from his video game and grabbed one of the sofa pillows, stuffing it behind his back.

"Jack," Charlotte replied, "when he said we need to sings happy songs and hug puppies."

"Huh?" Martin murmured.

"I think what Charlotte is saying," Shelby added, "is that maybe we need to find a way to bring the world together, focus on something positive."

"Maybe we just need to fight this thing until we defeat it."

"I don't think so, Cody. If The Darkness enjoys fighting and dissent," Charlotte offered pensively. "Then, maybe we need to beat it by being better than it. Maybe that's the answer."

Chapter 37: The Defense

Cody and Shelby unwrapped the peanut butter and jelly sandwiches Heather had made them for lunch. The cafeteria literally buzzed with activity as last period kids dumped their trays and this period kids picked new ones up. Cody preferred the relative quiet of a corner table, one not centered amid the din of teenage rabble.

"What *is* this?" he frowned.

"PB and J," Shelby offered distractedly as she took a bite.

"I see that. What is this jelly?"

"Tastes like marmalade," she replied.

Cody dropped the sandwich onto the baggie. "Doesn't she know kids like grape jelly?"

Shelby giggled. "It does make you wonder sometimes. Her heart's in the right place, I just think she tries to make her food seem more sophisticated. Instead, it comes out. . . odd."

"What's going on over there?" Cody nodded toward a nearby table.

"Are they picking on that poor kid?" Shelby asked woefully.

"What kid?"

"That girl from biology class, the one who sits in the back."

"What's her name?" Cody asked.

"I'm embarrassed to say I don't know. She keeps to herself a lot."

"Maybe, if she lost the purple hair, people wouldn't bother her as much."

"Having purple hair means it's okay to treat you bad?"

"I didn't say that."

Cody was silent for a minute, trying to hear what was going on. Three guys from the football team had surrounded the girl. They pretended to ask her out, then laughed like it was a joke. One kid took her lunch, squishing her sandwich with his foot.

"Oops, my bad," he yelled, grinning from ear to ear. The other guys laughed loudly.

"Oh, my," Shelby said. "That poor dear. Cody, *do* something?"

"What? *Me?* Do what?" Cody stared at her. "Two of those kids are defensive linemen."

"Stop them. Make them leave her alone."

"How do you propose I—"

"Well, if you won't do something, I will," she said, getting up and walking over to the table.

Oh, no. This has trouble written all over it.

"What's *wrong* with you three?" Shelby said loudly. "What are you, *five* years old? Leave her alone."

"Get lost," one of the boys snapped. "We're just having a little fun."

"Well, you're being total jerks!" Shelby replied.

One of the linemen got up and stood over Shelby, as if to say, I could squash you like a bug.

"Just great," Cody mumbled as he got up from his chair. "I knew somehow this was going to end with me getting my face handed to me."

He sauntered in their direction and stood next to Shelby. "Come on, guys," he said. "Let's get back to our lunches. Personally, I'm enjoying the subtle nuances of a squished peanut butter and marmalade sandwich and a bag of mushy carrot sticks. It's so yummy, I don't want to miss it," he joked.

"We're just having in a little fun, Hawke," one of the guys replied. "Get lost."

"Well, I don't think she's having anywhere near as much fun as you are," he said softly. "So how about we all get back to our lunches."

"How about you mind your own business," the biggest guy said with a snarl.

"Come on, Duke," one of the kids said, climbing off the table. "This just got boring. Let's go."

"Who do you think you *are*, little J.V. quarterback?" Duke came over and bumped Cody's chest.

Silence prevailed in the previously bustling cafeteria. All eyes were on them.

"Who do you think *you* are, talking to him like that?" Shelby said crossly.

"Come on, guys," Cody said. "She's not going to let this go," he motioned toward Shelby. "Which means I can't let it go. Now come on, what do you say? Let's just—"

Duke stepped forward and pushed Cody hard, slamming him into the cinderblock wall. The impact made Cody wince, though he tried not to show it.

"Come on, sugar," Shelby said, grabbing the girl's hand and leading her away.

Cody could feel his face redden. He stepped forward and knocked Duke backwards into the table. The lineman scrambled to keep from losing his balance. A confused look permeated Duke's expression, clearly wondering how Cody was able to push someone his size. He lunged angrily at Cody, trying to wrestle him to the ground.

"COME ON, BREAK IT UP!" Principal Howard yelled, running in their direction. "I *SAID*, BREAK IT UP!" Neither boy responded. "Duke, how would you like to spend the rest of football season watching from the bench?" the principal roared.

Duke hesitated, then backed off, scowling at Cody.

"Duke, Cody, in my office! NOW!"

Cody felt like he might explode as he and Duke glared at each other.

"I'll get you for this, you little a—" A smirk crept across Duke's face. "Teach you some respect!"

Cody's face was hot with anger. He glanced up at the sprinkler head above.

Maybe a little cold water will wipe that arrogant look off your face and teach you some manners.

As Cody turned to follow the principal, the sound of spray was followed by a choked yell.

"What the f—" he heard the boy yell. "YOU'RE *DEAD*, HAWKE!"

He glanced over his shoulder at a soaked and very angry Duke, standing in a puddle of water. The cafeteria erupted into hysterical laughter.

"Cody Hawke, I can't *believe* you! Getting suspended the second week of school!" Heather cried, setting two plates down on the kitchen table then walking back to the stove to grab two more. "What were you *thinking*?"

Cody glanced over at Terrell absently chewing his food. He was sure the crooked little grin creeping across the boy's face was at his expense.

"Mom," Shelby said, fiddling with her chicken chow mein. "It was *my* fault."

"Yeah," Cody whispered in her ear, "now we're *even*."

"What do you mean, Shelby?" Heather asked.

"These kids from the football team were bullying this poor girl during lunch. I tried to make them stop, but one of the guys came at me and Cody stepped in to protect me. He tried to reason with the kids, but the big jerk pushed him and it went downhill from there."

Heather looked at them both, suddenly unsure what to say.

"Great job, kids," Jack offered, his eyes twinkling.

"Jack!" Heather replied crossly. "We do *not* condone fighting."

Their father let out a big sigh. "Honey, sometimes it's important to stand up for what's right. Cody didn't start it, he just defended Shelby against a bully." He glanced at Cody and Shelby. "I'm proud of you both and I bet if the truth be known, Principal Howard is also."

"The sun's shining," Martin said, grabbing his bookbag off the sunlit floor. "I almost didn't recognize it."

"Was that you?" Charlotte asked as the four teens headed upstairs to do homework.

"Was what me? Cody asked.

"We heard that big jerk got a little wet," Martin said.

The four teens let out a brief chuckle.

"It's nothing he didn't deserve," Shelby said. "By the way, it's Melody."

"What's melody?" Cody asked.

"The girl's name," Shelby said softly. "And she's very sweet. I took her to the ladies' room so she could fix her makeup . . . after she finished crying her eyes out."

Chapter 38: The God's Eye

The sweet scent of maple syrup lingered from plates piled high in the sink. Jack and Heather rushed out the door, late for some town meeting. Heather yelled a reminder on their way out for the teens to clean up the kitchen. Cody was relieved to see the three troublemakers tag along.

"You scrape and stack the plates," Shelby said to Charlotte. "I'll wash them."

Cody swept the kitchen floor while Martin wiped down the table, seats, and countertops.

"Do these kids get *any* food in their mouths?" he mumbled, sweeping under the table.

"Let's go." A man's voice broke the silence. "You wanted to help, now here's your chance."

Cody stopped sweeping and turned toward the door. Charlotte quickly dried and put away the last dish. Shelby looked over her shoulder, adjusting the rollers in her hair. Martin slid behind the table to wipe the far side. Cody wondered whether it was an attempt to hide his Thor pajama pants from Sharkey's view. For a moment no one moved, they just stared in his direction.

"Any day now." The man's expression motivated Cody to return the broom to the closet.

After a brief detour to get dressed, the four teens headed to the foyer where Sharkey waited with two backpacks and obvious impatience. Cody shivered slightly as they rushed out the side door, a dense fog enveloping the landscape. The trees had not yet begun to put on their fall wardrobe, but the heady aroma of a distant fireplace wafted on the slight breeze.

"So, where are we going?" Martin asked, as they followed Sam Sharkey through the maze.

"The Sacred Valley," Sharkey replied. "Specifically, the Cusco Region of southern Peru."

"Oh, good," Martin replied somewhat sarcastically. "A nice relaxing vacation. And *why* are we going there? You know, they have beetles the size of your hand, and anacondas that can squeeze you until your eyes pop out."

"Oh, the drama, Mr. Speck," Sharkey mumbled.

"What's in the Sacred Valley?" Shelby asked.

"They're filming the next episode of Live or Die Jeopardy," Martin replied, "starring yours truly."

"Incan ruins . . . *and* book number four, Miss Shelby," Sharkey replied, ignoring Martin's comment.

"And, what's so special about this book?" Cody asked.

"It's the Fourth Book of Light," Sharkey said. "We need to find it before The Darkness gets it."

"And why are bringing this gold?" Charlotte asked.

"You never know, Miss Charlotte, when you'll need it. Gold has a rather ubiquitous fan club."

"And what do we need with these ropes and metal clips?" Cody asked.

"You'll see, Mr. Hawke."

"Oh, goodie," Martin muttered.

The Gatekeeper waited somberly in the dark as they approached. He and Sharkey exchanged a brief but silent conversation after which the old man retrieved the gilded scepter. The Gatekeeper seemed uncomfortable with Sharkey's plan, but said nothing. Cody watched as the impenetrable arched doorway began to swirl with activity. On the far side, he could see only darkness.

They stood in a narrow alley flanked by stone walls that reached up to clay-tiled roofs. Cracked mortar conveyed the walls' age, reminding Cody of the tunnels beneath Freya Manor. The crisp night air carried a variety of suspicious odors throughout the old city, some pleasant, others not so much.

The teens followed their leader down various cobblestone alleys, some edged by gutters filled with rushing water. Cody was thankful for the soft moonlight to help them avoid the narrow alleys' pitfalls.

"Nothing but stone everywhere, stone walls, roads, and buildings," Shelby said.

"They used what was available to them, Miss Shelby," Sharkey said with a shrug. "Ahead are the ancient ruins of Ollantaytambo," he added.

"Does it have another little fun house like the one at Weaver's Needle?" Martin asked dryly.

Sharkey took a deep breath. "We will find out, Mr. Speck."

"The Coldswells of South Carolina will *never* find me here," Shelby mumbled. "I certainly hope you're not planning to abandon us like last time, Mr. Sharkey."

"It's not in my plan," Sharkey replied. "Well, maybe just for a minute. Wait here," he directed, grabbing a few gold coins from Cody's backpack and stepping into a nearby shop.

"That didn't take long," Martin muttered.

Sharkey returned a short time later with two hooded robes.

"Put these on," he ordered, handing one to Shelby and one to Charlotte. "It will be easier to do what we need to do without you two getting thrown in jail."

"Did you steal them?" Cody asked. "The shop isn't open at this hour."

"The owner was paid quite handsomely in gold," Sharkey replied.

"So, what's in Ollantaytambo," Charlotte asked, lifting the garment over her head.

Shelby stared at the robe's rough dark cloth for moment as if trying to decide which was worse, wearing it or going to jail. After a few seconds, she appeared to opt for the former.

"This was a strategic Incan stronghold, built to defend the entrance to the lower Urubamba Valley," Sharkey replied. "However, we are not here to visit the ruins themselves. *That* is our destination," he said, pointing ahead, "the Pinkuylluna mountain on the opposite side."

Cody squinted at a series of dark peaks dominating the horizon.

"What year is this?" Charlotte asked. "Obviously not the current one."

"June twenty-first in the year 1842," Sharkey said.

"Why now?" Cody asked.

"We need to get our hands on the fourth book before The Darkness finds it."

"What's so special about June twenty-first?" Charlotte inquired.

"The summer solstice," Miss Charlotte," Sharkey replied.

"I should've guessed that," she mumbled, nodding sheepishly.

The small town of Ollantaytambo, with its center marketplace and tiled rooflines covered in the soft glow of a waning moon, offered rustic charm. Cody tried to focus on the bumpy road, however it was easy to become distracted as they made their way through the living museum.

"What are we looking for?" Martin asked.

"About halfway up the mountain is a representation of the god Viracocha," Sharkey replied.

"What kind of representation?" Charlotte wondered.

"On the rock face of Cerro Pinkuylluna is the 140-meter face of Viracocha, overlooking the ruins. That is our destination, Miss Charlotte."

"140 meters?" Charlotte replied nervously, obviously doing the math.

"I can take a picture with my phone instead," Martin offered lightly. "Then we can go right back through the doorway and be home for lunch."

"We do not need a picture, Mr. Speck. We need what's hidden behind his left eye."

"That's about 420 feet of rock wall. How do propose we get to it?"

"It's an easy climb, Miss Charlotte."

"Oh, this is not good, not good at all," Martin mumbled.

"Who was Viracocha?" Shelby asked.

"An Incan god, deemed the *creator*, he was responsible for making the sun, moon, and stars. It is believed he made people from stones. Viracocha, like Odin, Glooscap, Oannes, Enki, and others, wandered the land in disguise, teaching his people the meaning of life, basically all they needed to know to thrive. Various miracles were attributed to him as he encountered the woeful plight of humans."

"What did he look like?"

"Well, Miss Shelby, according to legend, he was a tall man with short hair and a beard. He wore a white robe with a staff and book in his hands. The description is very similar to that of Quetzalcoatl, an Aztec deity."

"Was the book he carried the Fourth Book of Light?"

"Exactly, Miss Charlotte," the man replied.

"Were Viracocha and Quetzalcoatl from Nimbus?"

Sharkey turned and grinned proudly at Charlotte. His silence told them all they needed to know.

"Come, we need to make haste. It will soon be daylight."

A dark shadow lingered down the alleyway to the left. The figure sent a furtive glance their way.

"Is that guy watching us?" Shelby whispered.

"Hold up for a moment," Sharkey said, reaching into Cody's backpack for a few gold coins.

"What's that for?" Charlotte asked.

"Just keep walking," Sharkey said. "I'll catch up."

"Uh-oh, here we go again," Martin whispered.

Sharkey headed to where the man was standing. He said nothing but removed a pipe from his pocket and lit what Cody assumed to be tobacco, his smoky breath lingering on the early breeze. As the teens made their way up the street, Cody wondered if it might be some form of secret code. He couldn't picture Sharkey as a smoker.

"What do you suppose he's doing?" Shelby asked.

"It's probably best we don't know," Martin muttered.

They hadn't gone far when Cody heard footsteps. He was relieved to see Sharkey behind them.

"What was that all about?" Cody asked.

"Nothing," Sharkey replied. "Just needed a little information. Ah, here we are," the man exclaimed, "Lare Street."

"That's it?" Martin asked. "We can go home?"

"This is where our journey *begins*," Sharkey said, pointing to a crumbling narrow staircase, hidden between buildings.

At the top of the steps, a path Cody presumed would lead them to their destination, zigzagged up the mountainside. An eastern sky began offering colorful clues to the coming day, highlighting the buildings with a fiery glow. Cody couldn't stop staring at the surrounding mountains, hovering in the distance like vigilant gods.

Sharkey stopped suddenly. "Do you see it now . . . the face of Viracocha?" he asked, pointing toward the mountain.

"I see him!" Shelby replied. "He has a beard and he's looking out across the land."

"Whoa," Martin muttered, "he looks *really* angry. Are you sure you want to go up there?"

"That carved stone above his face makes it look like he's wearing a crown," Charlotte added.

"Fascinating, isn't it?" Sharkey asked, glancing at the ruins on the opposite side. "How these people were able to move granite blocks, some weighing as much as sixty-five tons?"

Cody stared at the terraced steps built into the mountainside and the temple beyond.

How did they move those massive stone blocks without the benefit of modern technology?

"What are the rows of buildings stuck into the mountain next to Viracocha?" Shelby asked.

"Those are ancient storehouses, Miss Shelby," Sharkey said, "It's where they kept their grain."

The climb wasn't as difficult as Cody expected, though he wondered how Charlotte felt about the elevation. About a half hour after leaving town, they reached the storehouses. The terraced buildings reminded him of ancient townhomes without roofs.

Making their way along one row of stone blocks, they paused for a moment to stare out through the opening. Far below, the Incan ruins dominated one side of the landscape and the town of Ollantaytambo, where their journey had begun, the other. A dizzying sun was just coming up over the top of a nearby mountain. All were silent, staring at the spectacular view.

"Come on," Sharkey ordered. "We don't have much time."

They continued up to the third and highest level in the storehouse, then climbed around to the back. Sharkey paced anxiously, periodically checking his watch.

"Are we waiting for something?" Cody asked.

"Give it another minute and hopefully you shall see," the man replied, then pointed. "Stand near the end and look directly between those stones."

Cody watched the sun appear just above the mountain, like a beacon, heralding things to come. Sharkey stepped forward to narrate the breathtaking sequence of events as they unfolded.

"The sun is the bandleader and it's rays are about to bring a golden orchestra to life," he began.

"How lovely," Shelby said dreamily.

"It's hard to see from here, but any second now the sun's rays will illuminate Viracocha's face. A jewel will emerge from his crown, deflecting the rays down and to his left, onto a golden effigy hidden in one of those carved stone steps," Sharkey said, pointing below. "The effigy will rise up when the light hits it," he added.

"How cool," Martin mumbled.

Just as Sharkey predicted, a golden likeness of Viracocha slowly emerged from the rocky slab, a three-meter figure of a robed man wearing a crown and gripping bunches of something in each hand.

"What is he holding?" Charlotte asked.

"Those are lightning bolts, befitting the earth's creator," Sharkey replied.

"What are they for?" Shelby asked. "And why are they angled back like that?"

"Keep watching," Sharkey whispered. "The sun's rays will deflect down off the lightning bolts and get channeled through the statue's jeweled crown. From there, the light will be deflected toward the storehouse, just below where we're standing. It will pass through that little window in the wall, then straight across toward another golden effigy on the other side."

Cody stared as the light illuminated the idol's gold crown like a perfectly choreographed dance and was then was diverted toward the storehouse. It passed through the window, just as Sharkey said, then illuminated a golden likeness of Viracocha that emerged in front of the opposite wall. A jewel in the god's crown began to radiate. The light reflected downward onto the stone floor, illuminating a golden plaque that glowed so brightly, Cody could barely look at it.

"What does it do?" he asked.

"You'll see," Sharkey replied.

A sudden loud scraping sound made him jump. The stone slab on the floor below slid slowly to one side, revealing a narrow entryway.

"Hurry," Sharkey ordered as the golden idols began their descent back into the ground.

Climbing down to the third level, the man stepped into the opening and proceeded down a flight of crumbling stairs. Cody followed, knowing the others shared his apprehension. As the stone slab slid back into place leaving them in total darkness, Sharkey lit the flashlight he'd taken from his backpack.

"Where are we going?" Cody asked.

"This tunnel will lead us to the area behind Viracocha's right eye," Sharkey replied.

"Okay," Martin added flippantly. "So far this hasn't been too bad. What could possibly go wrong?"

"What was that?" Shelby shrieked. "Something just landed in my hair."

Pointing the flashlight at her head, Sharkey grabbed something and tossed it to the ground. A dinner-roll-sized black beetle that looked like it was wearing a helmet, scampered off.

Shelby's mouth hung open and her eyes were wide as tennis balls. Cody wanted to laugh. He knew if Sharkey hadn't been there, a banshee scream, along with a string of loud expletives would've reverberated throughout the narrow tunnel. Instead, Shelby just stood there frozen.

"Keep up," their commander said impatiently as he headed off with obvious determination.

Shelby and Charlotte hastily lifted their robe hoods over their heads. The group followed the rocky tunnel for many meters with Cody trailing behind to keep an eye on his siblings. Shelby periodically swatted her head, checking for hitchhikers.

"Whoa!" Sharkey yelled, holding out his arms to make sure no one passed. "The God's mouth."

They stared down into a deep canyon. Light flooding in from a large crack to the left highlighted the obvious: there was no way across. Cody glanced out the opening, ruins visible in the distance.

"Well, that's it," Martin muttered, "the end of the road."

"Nice try, Mr. Speck. We can cross Viracocha's mouth using those steps," Sharkey said, pointing toward a series of narrow stone slabs jutting out from the right wall.

Cody counted forty steps about a half meter wide, encircling the chasm, each one higher than the last. Sharkey went first and after a few tenuous moments, reached the top of the opposite side. The teens followed in what Cody could only describe as agonizing silence. Charlotte held his hand the entire way, squeezing so hard he couldn't feel his fingers.

As they reached the top, Sharkey directed them to a short tunnel and another crude staircase leading up into Viracocha's head. A few minutes later a solid door spanned their path.

"Hmm, I guess that's it, door's locked," Martin said.

Sharkey located a small opening in the wall and inserted his hand. Shelby gasped with obvious apprehension. Cody heard a sound and the door began to slide revealing a rocky cavern with a high ceiling. Daylight poured in through a large eye-shaped crack, giving the room an eerie ambiance.

Below the eye, a series of pictures were carved into the wall. Each group of four pictures was etched into a large stone circle. There were four circles or wheels in total. The diamond shape in the center, encompassed four pictures, one from each circle. On the left wall, high above, a door flanked by ornate pillars had been carved into the rock.

"Cool," Martin muttered. "Nothing like a door you can't get to. What are those pictures for?"

"It's a puzzle, Mr. Speck," Sharkey replied.

"Of *course*, it is," Martin mumbled with obvious cynicism.

"In the year 1537, the Spanish conquest of the mighty Incan empire was well underway," Sharkey began. "Incan ruler Manco Inca Yupanqui, initially an ally of the Spanish, reigned from Ollantaytambo. He tried to retake the capital city of Cuzco, but the Spanish conquistadors were too strong. Their numbers and superior weapons resulted in his eventual withdrawal. But before leaving Ollantaytambo, Manco Inca hid The Fourth Book of Light, the one given to the Incan people, in the mountain where it would be safe."

"What's so important about these books anyway?" Martin asked.

"The Darkness has spent centuries trying to locate them all. Once he has them, his power will be all but unstoppable."

"They're just books," Martin replied. "How important can they be?"

"No, they are very special," Sharkey said with a scowl. "And, there are no *unimportant* books. Literature is the foundation of knowledge and enlightenment."

"Uh, what's that?" Shelby cried.

"That, Miss Shelby, appears to be a skeleton," Sharkey replied.

"It was a rhetorical question," she said with gulp.

"I see a few more over there," Charlotte said.

"I'd *really* not like to join them," Shelby said. "Did they die trying to solve your puzzle?"

"It's not *my* puzzle, but most likely, Miss Shelby."

"Perfect," Martin muttered.

"Exactly *how* did they die?" Cody asked.

"Well, Mr. Hawke," Sharkey mumbled, glancing around the room, "According to the instructions carved into the wall over there, I suspect there are multiple ways to die. Each time one moves a circle on the wall, they have roughly a minute to solve the puzzle. At that point, Supay – the god of death – will control their fate based on the combination of pictures in the diamond."

"So, what do the pictures mean?" Shelby asked.

"That is a picture of Inti, the Incan god of sun and fire," Sharkey said, pointing. "So, I suspect we will be burned to death if his pictures dominate the center diamond."

"Great," Martin mumbled. "That explains the scorched rocks."

"Paryaqaqa was the god of water," Sharkey said, pointing to another carving. "If his pictures are in the center region, I suspect we will be drowned. This picture is Pachamama, roughly equivalent to your mother nature. She was the goddess of fertility, however as I recall, she was thought to be responsible for earthquakes. Perhaps if her pictures are left in the middle, we'll be crushed by falling rocks," Sharkey concluded flatly.

"This just gets better and better," Martin added. "That explains the skeleton with his feet sticking out from under those rocks.

"Interesting," Sharkey mumbled, rubbing the stubble on his chin.

"What? What's interesting?" Shelby asked nervously.

"This picture appears to be of a fox. They were considered tricksters in Incan mythology."

"What does that mean?" Cody wondered.

"It means, Mr. Hawke, if *he* ends up in one of the center regions. I'm not sure what will happen."

"Right now, the four pictures of Paryaqaqa are in the diamond center. Which pictures should be there when we've finished turning the wheels?" Charlotte asked.

"Good question," Sharkey said. "I'm hoping the answer will present itself," he added.

"But you described all four options and none of them sound good," she replied.

"So, we will need to be focused and quick on our feet," Sharkey said with a grin.

"Lovely. How do we move the circles?" Martin asked. "They're five meters up."

"I suspect it has something to do with these things that look like ship's wheels," Charlotte said, pointing to four old wooden turnstiles centered on the rocky floor.

"Very good, Miss Charlotte," Sharkey replied. "I would agree. For clarity, let's refer to the four pictures in the center diamond as *north*, *south*, *east* and *west*. Shall we get started?"

He approached the rightmost turnstile and gripped the handles.

"WAIT!" Charlotte yelled. "What happens if we have a *mix* of the pictures?"

"Good question, Miss Charlotte. I suspect nothing . . . or everything, we'll see. Well, here goes."

Sharkey rolled up his shirtsleeves and began turning the rightmost turnstile. Age and time had apparently caused it to become stuck. The man pushed, arm muscles rippling, until finally the wheel began to move. The top circle, *north*, turned counter-clockwise, causing *west* to move clockwise. When Sharkey stopped, the fox and Pachamama, or mother earth, filled the two corresponding circle spaces.

Cody expected something to happen, but all was silent.

"So far, so good," Martin mumbled.

Sharkey quickly grabbed the third turnstile and pushed. It controlled the lowest circle, *south*, which also turned *east*. When both circles stopped, they also reflected the fox and Pachamama.

"Hmm," the man muttered while staring pensively, "two foxes and two Pachamama."

"I wonder…" Cody froze at the sudden sound of scraping rocks. "What was that?" he asked nervously.

The answer soon became apparent as boulders began to drop from the ceiling, one landing less than a meter from Charlotte.

"LOOK OUT!" Cody yelled.

A rock fell and hit one that was already on the ground, causing it to shoot out in Shelby's direction. She dove forward as it narrowly missed her leg.

"Get in close!" Cody commanded.

"Turn it again!" Shelby yelled.

They all huddled around Sharkey as he quickly turned the third turnstile. Cody decided to grab the first one and turn it as well.

"NO!" Sharkey yelled, but it was too late.

All four pictures changed and the boulders stopped falling. An uneasy silence prevailed as they stared up at four pictures of Inti in the center diamond. Fire suddenly erupted from each side of the cavern, blowing at least five meters out and scorching everything in its path.

"Get behind me!" Cody ordered. "The fire doesn't reach the very center of the room!"

He grabbed the turnstile while the others stood in single file at the center of the room, just inches from the scorching flames.

"STOP!" Sharkey yelled. "I'll turn this one."

As Sharkey turned the third turnstile, they stared up at the puzzle, now displaying two pictures of Inti, one of a fox, and another of Pachamama. Boulders began dropping from the ceiling while fire continued to blow out from the sides.

Shelby stepped back to keep from getting burned. Martin jumped to avoid a rock that would have crushed him, turning his body into the fire. He shrieked as the back of his shirt began to burn.

"MARTIN!" Shelby screamed.

Cody tackled Martin, smothering the fire as they landed. A boulder hit the ground next to them, trapping Cody's shirttail. He tried to jump up, but couldn't.

"TAKE IT OFF!" Shelby yelled.

Cody managed to remove one arm from the shirtsleeve and rolled over to get his arm out of the other. Sharkey pulled him to his feet just as a large rock landed on that very spot.

"That was *too* close," Shelby mumbled with a shaky sigh.

Charlotte cried, "It's so hot in here, I'm afraid our clothes will spontaneously combust!"

Sharkey turned the third turnstile once more, resulting in two pictures of Inti and two of Paryaqaqa. The fire stopped and no more rocks fell.

"Okay," he said, sweat dripping from his brow, "the good news is we now understand more about how this works."

"We do?" Martin asked, wincing from the burns on his back. "Maybe you can explain it to me."

"The fox," Charlotte said, "appears to be some sort of wild card."

"Exactly, Miss Charlotte," Sharkey replied, putting a healing hand on Martin's back. "I suspect each fox acts as wild card, triggering a reaction based on the other pictures. So, we do not want any foxes and we do not want four of any one picture."

"Great," Martin said. "So now what."

"We try other combinations, Mr. Speck."

"What happens when we move turnstiles two and four?"

"Good question, Miss Shelby. Let's give it a try."

Cody held his breath as Sharkey spun turnstile two, bringing up a fox on west.

"They move independently, having no impact on the other wheels," Charlotte yelled, as the force of water mixed with fire became hot spray, burning their skin.

"I see that, Miss Charlotte," Sharkey replied, turning turnstile one, changing north and west.

The water and falling rocks ended abruptly.

"Maybe we need to get back to the four pictures of Paryaqaqa," Sharkey mumbled, turning turnstile one again and two until west matched other three pictures.

A flood of water gushed from gated tunnels on either side of the cavern, filling the room so quickly, the teens were floating in no time.

"HELP! I can't swim!" Charlotte screamed. "Change something!"

"WHICH ONE?" Cody yelled.

"Anything that's not Paryaqaqa!" Shelby cried, grabbing Charlotte's hand.

Both Sharkey and Cody dove down. Sharkey turned turnstile two and Cody turned three, twice to avoid the fox. The water grew calm and began to recede. They rested for a moment on the wet floor.

"This is fun," Shelby muttered, wringing the water from her hair. "Let's do it more often."

Charlotte took a few steps back toward the door, staring pensively at the puzzle.

"Miss Charlotte," Sharkey said, turning around, "any ideas you have would be helpful."

"It's just..."

"Spit it out, Miss Charlotte," Sharkey said evenly.

"We now have three of the four pictures in the circle," she mumbled pensively. "Don't they seem to go together, making one picture?"

Cody stepped back. "Wow, you can't see it from up close, but you're right."

"Yes," Shelby added. "The images line up with each other, making a . . . face."

"The water is his hair and crown," Martin said. "The rocks are his left eye."

"The fire makes up his chin and beard," Cody added.

Sharkey turned, smiling from ear to ear. "Excellent, Miss Charlotte, all of you. Those three pictures together form Viracocha's face. Which other picture completes it?"

"Could it be..." Shelby hesitated. "The fox? We have Paryaqaqa, Pachamama, and two of Inti."

"You could be right," Charlotte replied. "I wondered why the fox would be depicted standing, but the side profile of its snout could form Viracocha's right eye."

"If you're wrong," Cody said, "We're going to get slammed by rocks, fire, *and* water."

"Mr. Hawke is right," Sharkey replied. "However, I think it's worth a try."

"Of course, you do," Martin muttered.

Sharkey gripped turnstile four with both hands and pushed.

"Clearly this one hasn't seen a lot of use," he said. "Let's all put our weight into it, shall we?"

Cody, Shelby, Martin, and Sharkey pushed on the four handles until it finally began to turn. For a moment, everything seemed fine. Cody glanced up at the image of Viracocha, then smiled at Charlotte.

Suddenly everything went terribly wrong. Rocks began to drop, streams of fire shot out from the sides, and water filled the cavern like a bathtub. The hot steam made Cody's face burn.

"CODY!" Shelby screamed.

Sharkey and Cody reached for the handle of the fourth turnstile, but all the turnstiles began moving on their own, resetting back to the beginning. Four pictures of Paryaqaqa now filled the diamond center. The fire receded and falling rocks tapered off, but water continued to fill the room.

"What..." Cody began, but was interrupted by Shelby's scream. He looked up to see a final boulder falling from the ceiling. As it hit the waist-deep water it deflected slightly, slamming into the side of Cody's head. That was the last thing he remembered.

Chapter 39: The Book

Cody's first sensation was someone touching his head. His second was dampness and a smell that seemed to emanate from antiquity. He sat up, rubbing his temple.

"Good to see you, Mr. Hawke." Sharkey's voice echoed about the chamber.

"Where . . . where are we?" Cody mumbled, glancing around the small room. He shielded his eyes from the light radiating through a large slit in the rock wall.

"We are behind Viracocha's left eye," Charlotte said.

"How did we get here?" Cody asked.

"We treaded water until the level reached that stone doorway on the wall," Shelby said. "The one Martin joked about being too high to reach."

The water triggered the door to open and we climbed into this little room," Charlotte added. "Then, the water receded and the door swung closed."

"How did I get up here?" Cody asked.

"Mr. Sharkey carried you," Shelby said.

Cody looked away so no one could see his frown.

I guess I should be grateful, but I hate the thought of him rescuing me.

"And here," Sharkey offered, "is where we found our quarry: The Fourth Book of Light."

He pointed to an unassuming rock bench below the eye. The top had been pushed to one side, leaving enough space to reach in and grab the prize.

"Okay, now what?" Cody asked, feeling his faculties beginning to return.

"Now, we go home."

"We can't go back the way we came," Charlotte said. "How will we get back to the storehouses?"

"The final test, Miss Charlotte," Sharkey mumbled. "We must climb across."

"Oh, no," Charlotte replied defiantly. "No, no, no!"

"Unfortunately, Miss Charlotte, there is no other option," Sharkey replied.

"I-I, uh, I can't. I'm afraid of heights."

"I agree, sugar," Shelby said with a frown. "I'm not crazy about them either."

"That makes three," Martin mumbled.

"You'll be fine," Sharkey said lightly. "I won't let anything happen to you."

Sharkey climbed out Viracocha's eye and began pounding stakes into the rock.

"You honestly think those little metal things will hold you?" Cody asked.

"Hopefully," Sharkey replied. "It's a long way down. Besides, they're not for me. They're for you."

As Sharkey hung from a rocky crevice to the right, Cody waited on a narrow stone platform just below the eye, trying to coax Charlotte out the window. She stared at him in blind terror.

"Miss Charlotte," Sharkey said. "There is no other way down. Your options are simple, die in this little room, or climb across. Besides, if you're still considering becoming an astronaut, you will need to get over your fear."

"You could have a little compassion," Shelby said testily. "We did not plan on hanging off the side of a mountain when we got up this morning."

"I understand, Miss Shelby. However, compassion will not get you to safety, only faith and a belief in yourself. Miss Charlotte can do this. It is not a difficult climb. It just takes a little confidence."

"You have the book. Why can't The Gatekeeper just bring us home from here?" Charlotte cried.

"The Gatekeeper must be contacted so he knows where we are," Sharkey said.

"Like giving him coordinates?" Martin asked with a snicker.

"Sort of. Unfortunately, there is only one person besides The Guardian who can do that."

"Who?" Cody asked stiffly.

"That would be *you*, Mr. Hawke."

"Me?" Cody felt his face redden. "What about *you*?"

"I," Sharkey replied dramatically, "am not The *Chosen*. Only *he* can move freely. I need to return at the appropriate time and place so The Gatekeeper knows where to find me. With you four, he hones in on the answer to your riddle."

Cody's surprised look was quickly quelled as he turned to three faces staring at him imploringly.

"What? Look, I, uh…" he stammered. "What I mean is, I *would* if I knew *how*. Trust me, I'd love to zap us home." He looked at their disappointed expressions. "This doesn't look so bad," he added lightly, glancing out over the landscape. "It'll be easy."

"Try, Cody," Charlotte whimpered. "Please. You were able to get us home from the Buri cave.'

"I don't know what I did," he said with a shrug.

"Hurry! I need to use the bathroom," Shelby whispered fiercely. "*Bad!*"

"*Again?* Just go in the corner over there," Cody replied. "I need to go also, but *I* can hold it."

Shelby made a face at him, as if to confirm the depth of her disappointment.

"Fine." Cody sighed, taking a deep breath and closing his eyes.

Focus! You can do this! Gatekeeper! Help us get home. Shelby needs to use the bathroom and so do I… really bad.

Something soft fell from the sky, smacking him in the head. He managed to catch the object as it rebounded off his forehead.

Sharkey and the others broke into hysterical laughter. Cody glanced down at the roll of toilet paper in his hand.

"Obviously, Mr. Hawke can only focus on his bodily functions right now," Sharkey said.

"I wonder where you got it," Martin quipped. "Hope you didn't leave some poor guy stranded."

"Give it to me," Shelby said, snatching the toilet paper from his hand. "Now I *really* have to pee."

"Let's just go," Cody said irritably, feeling his face redden.

He wrapped a length of rope around Charlotte's waist, then tied it around his own and helped her out the window. "Look at me, Charlotte. I promise I will not let you fall."

She glanced at him as if to say, how, by giving me a roll of toilet paper to hold onto?

Yes, you're right. I'm pathetic. I'm probably the worst Chosen there could ever be.

Charlotte followed Sharkey. Cody waited as Shelby tied the rope around Martin's waist, then her own and both joined them on the ledge.

The teens inched their way along, following Sharkey's lead as he strung rope though a series of metal squares wedged into the stone. Cody gripped the rope tightly, watching the man's movements so he could use the same footholds. Every meter or so, Sharkey wedged another bracket into the rock.

Things seemed to be going surprisingly well until something flew their faces. They had startled a bird, its nest hidden among the rocks. Charlotte let go of the rope and fell back, losing her footing.

"CHARLOTTE!" Shelby screamed.

She swung out then slammed back into the rocks, pulling hard on the rope around her waist.

"HELP! HELP ME!" Charlotte cried.

Cody glanced down at the length of rope. It was rubbing along a sliver of sharp rock, fraying as Charlotte swung back and forth.

"Charlotte!" Cody said firmly. "Keep as still as possible."

He and Sharkey reached down while Charlotte tried to get a foothold to lift herself up. They were inches from locking hands when the rope connecting her to Cody snapped. Charlotte dropped about two meters, again hitting the rock face. Sharkey struggled to maintain his position with Charlotte's weight pulling him down.

"Mr. Hawke, *now* would be a good time..." Sharkey began. "Forget it," he said.

Charlotte planted her foot on a ledge. She gripped a protruding rock and began to climb. Cody reached down. He could almost touch her hand.

"You can do it. Just a little further," he said.

Charlotte reached for a protruding branch to lift herself.

"I would not..." Sharkey began.

The branch snapped and Charlotte lost her grip. She glanced at Cody, a combination of fear and sadness in her eyes, then began to plummet.

"CHARLOTTE!" Shelby screamed.

NO! Stop! Please! Please do not let her fall. Bring her back!

Suddenly Charlotte stopped, suspended in air. Her eyes flew open. She glanced down, presumably to see who or what was lifting her, but there was nothing. A few seconds later, she locked hands with Cody and Sharkey.

"Well, well. Nice job, Mr. Hawke!" Sharkey said, beaming.

"Are you okay, Charlotte?" Cody mumbled. She nodded, her hands trembling as he retied the rope. "Where did you get this cheap rope," he asked Sharkey.

"From your barn," the man replied.

They made it to the storehouses without further incident. Cody's heart was still pounding as they stepped onto the path. Shelby, Martin, Charlotte, and Cody held hands as they headed down the path and stayed that way until reaching town.

Chapter 40: The Onion

The following day, after finishing their weekend chores, the group was off on another Sharkey adventure, this time, to retrieve the book belonging to the indigenous people of North America.

"Explorers found The Fifth Book of Light in a cave located in the Canadian province of New Brunswick," Sharkey explained as they crossed the yard. "Years later, it ended up in a Washington D.C. warehouse, along with thousands of other important lost and forgotten items."

"What is so important about getting these books?" Shelby mumbled.

"As I've explained, Miss Shelby, they were designed to offer immense power to the leaders who possessed them. The books are filled with all the knowledge and tools necessary to live well. It was the leaders' job to disseminate that knowledge to their people," Sharkey said.

"But how do they give The Darkness such power?" Charlotte asked.

"The books allowed each leader to not only watch over his people, but disseminate his acumen into their minds."

"Enabling him to control them?" Charlotte asked.

"Not exactly *control* them, but lead them toward The Light. If Animus is able to amass the entire collection, it will be able to lead all people blindly toward darkness. We are peeling back the layers of the onion. The fewer books it has, the less powerful it will be."

"How many of them are there?" Martin asked."

"There are nine, Mr. Speck. However, he has already managed to retrieve five. We are going back to get this one before he finds it."

"Please tell me it's not hidden in a jungle or a desert or back in prehistoric times."

"No, Miss Shelby," Sharkey added. "We are going to Washington D.C. in the year 1976."

"Hmm," Shelby muttered, "how dangerous could that be?"

The first thing Cody noticed was a series of heart-stopping booms. He glanced up at the source, fireworks like giant painted flowers, dripped down the night sky.

"What's the celebration all about?" Martin asked.

"As I said, it's 1976, your nation's Bicentennial, Mr. Speck," Sharkey replied. "The two-hundredth birthday of the United States. This way," he added, pointing down a nearby alley.

The low growl of an old tomcat made his dissatisfaction with their arrival clearly known.

"What's that awful smell?" Shelby muttered as they paraded past a series of garbage dumpsters.

Sharkey stopped, apparently assessing the viability of a large steel door. Turning the handle to ensure it was locked, he retrieved a small packet from his backpack. It contained a lump of what looked like clay. The man pressed it against the door near the handle and instructed them to stand back. A few seconds later, a small explosion, its boom timed in coordination with the celebratory pyrotechnics, filled the alleyway. A brief puff of smoke followed. As the dust settled, Cody noticed the door was ajar.

"Quickly," Sharkey commanded. "The silent alarm is notifying them as we speak."

"Great," Martin whispered. "You couldn't *do* something about that?"

They hurried along a main aisle past corridors of metal shelves stacked high with nondescript boxes. Each box had a typed label on the front containing a 12-digit number.

"There are millions of boxes in here," Martin muttered, "how are we supposed to—"

"Shush!" Sharkey said, stopping at one particular aisle. "The guards will be coming."

Cody noticed a glow coming from a box stacked atop a set of shelves. Sharkey appeared to notice it as well. He walked briskly toward it and removed the top, retrieving an ornate wooden chest from inside. As he lifted the lid on the chest, Cody saw a familiar eye on the gilded tome nestled within.

"STOP RIGHT THERE!" a man's voice yelled. "And, put down that book!"

Cody turned to see a young man in a navy uniform, his name stitched onto the white pocket. Behind him, a clearly winded older man clutched his chest.

"What the…" the second man muttered.

"Hello," Sharkey said in a friendly tone. "Sorry to bother you guys during the Bicentennial Celebration, but we need to pick up this book for our research."

"We were not notified about any pickups. And, you set off the alarm," the first man said suspiciously. "Put down that book and keep your hands where I can see them."

"How the heck did you get in?" the older man asked. "The doors are made of six-inch-thick steel."

"I've got some gold coins," Sharkey said, reaching into his backpack. "They're all yours."

The young guard ogled the gold for a moment, then grabbed the walkie-talkie from his belt.

"This is Tim Garlowski, Warehouse Seven," he said. "We've got a break…"

Sharkey reached out his hand. The man's eyes opened wide for a second then rolled back in his head. He appeared to faint, his walkie-talkie clattering to the ground.

"You're ready for a break?" a muffled voice asked.

The second man quickly reached for his walkie-talkie, fumbling with the buttons.

"HE *SAID*—" The man began, then he, too went limp and dropped to the ground.

"Grab their legs," Sharkey commanded, handing the book to Shelby.

"What? Why?" Cody cried. "And what the heck did you do to them?"

"They are just sleeping, Mr. Hawke," Sharkey replied. "And, we are saving their lives."

"From who?" Martin asked, as each one grabbed a limb and carried the men toward the main aisle.

"From Grýla," Sharkey said. "Hurry, we don't have much time. In there," he added, pointing.

They set the men down on the floor of a cramped office filled with piles of green-lined computer paper and stacks of rubber-band wrapped cards. The smell of beer wafted through the air. Suddenly Cody noticed a different odor, one that nearly made him choke, followed by a distinctive moan echoing throughout the warehouse.

"She's here," Sharkey said matter-of-factly. "Hurry."

They had just stepped into the main aisle when Cody heard an angry scream coming from down the corridor, near where they'd retrieved the book. He assumed Grýla came upon the empty box.

"Hurry! This way," Sharkey whispered, turning in the other direction.

"You can't just leave the guards on the floor like that," Shelby cried

"They'll be fine. Now let's go!" Sharkey replied.

Cody heard Grýla scream again. He glanced over his shoulder as the hideous ogress appeared at the end of the corridor, red eyes glaring out from beneath the hood of her cloak. Grýla launched herself with heart-stopping speed, clawed fingers visible beneath folds of dark fabric.

"RUN!" Sharkey yelled.

Cody took off while doing a quick head count.

Charlotte, Martin, Sharkey, Shelby. Where's Shelby?

He turned to see Shelby staring at the demon hag as if in a trance with Grýla closing in fast.

"SHELBY!" Cody screamed. "LET'S GO!"

Grýla reached her with long fangs exposed, but Shelby just stood there. Clawed fingers wrestled away the book she clutched tightly in her hands.

"Such sweet young flesh," the ogress screeched, ready to sink her teeth into Shelby's shoulder.

Don't you dare touch her.

Cody sprinted toward them, calling for his sword, Tiwaz. He was aware of a flash of light above as he felt his hand wrap around the sword's hilt. Just as the demon turned to face Cody, he plunged Tiwaz into her midsection. Grýla let out the start of an angry scream, then froze solid, her mouth wide open. Cody grabbed the book with one hand and Shelby's arm with the other.

"Come on!" he yelled, his words appearing to break her trance.

"Nice job, Mr. Hawke!" Sharkey called. "That's the second time you've impressed me. Let's go!"

They followed Sharkey out the main door, fireworks still dominating the night sky.

Two black and white squad cars raced toward them, sirens flashing.

"Come on, old man," Sharkey said with a growl, glancing upward. "Now would be a good time to get us out of here," he added.

Heather and Jack had gone out to dinner with friends. Cody was thrilled because they were allowed to order pizza . . . real pizza, not the frozen kind. He opened the front door just as a flash of lightning illuminated Freya Manor's frightening exterior. The delivery guy dropped the pizzas and ran. Cody watched him jump into his car and race down the driveway in a cloud of dust. He smiled, pushing the tip money back into his jeans pocket.

The seven kids devoured every slice of cheesy goodness like it was their last meal. Afterward, Shelby and Charlotte went upstairs to work on a school project. Martin headed to the living room to play a video game.

Cody sat by himself for a few minutes, reflecting on the events of the last few months. He thought about The Darkness hurting those he loved and how he'd almost lost The Guardian, The Gatekeeper, Charlotte, and Shelby.

He thought about the beautiful home he grew up in, the affluent lifestyle he'd enjoyed. It had bothered him once, leaving that all behind. But, not today. He knew with absolute certainly he'd trade everything for just one more minute with his family, his entire family . . . his new family.

"Marty Mole's glasses were covered with raindrops," Cody read aloud, "as the umbrella pitched and rolled, carried along by the blustery wind. His tiny hand slipped from the handle and he tumbled head over heels through the clouds. Marty was sure this was the end when suddenly he landed on Donny's back. 'I've got you,' the baby dragon said. 'Oh, thank you, Donny!' Marty cried. He gasped as the umbrella flew by with his friend Peter Possum still clinging to the handle…"

Cody felt eyes on him. He glanced up to see Shelby leaning on the living room door, watching him read to Gabby, Jessica, and Terrell.

"Don't stop," Gabby said.

"Yeah, keep going," Terrell added.

He winked, noticing the twinkle in Shelby's eyes.

Cody pulled the covers up to his chin and stared at the ceiling, feeling strangely peaceful. He thought about Charlotte's words regarding his anger toward The Darkness and whether it actually made things worse. Maybe vengeance, regardless of the target, is not the answer.

He also thought about his new foster siblings. The teens had been making a concerted effort to get to know them, spend more quality time instead of avoiding them. He had to admit the results were good.

As she began to feel safe with her new family, Gabby learned to listen more and talk less. The pressure she clearly felt to always keep the conversation going, to constantly entertain everyone and keep the mood light, began to ease. Being quiet became okay.

Terrell became less confrontational and more trusting, enough to let them occasionally see the person inside. He seemed to appreciate having big sisters and brothers around, family who would look out for him and never abandon him. Cody thought about Shelby's words.

When we take the time to peel back the outer layers of the onion, the ones that protect it from getting damaged, we get to the heart of things beneath. It's the same with people. They learn to trust one another, breaking down the walls they build to keep themselves from getting hurt. Defense mechanisms like talking all the time or hurting someone before they hurt you, begin to fade.

"Shelby knew that from the beginning," Cody said aloud. "I guess it takes me a little longer."

Chapter 41: The Invitation

Scattered papers nearly covered the kitchen table as the teens worked on their respective history reports. Jack and Heather left for town early, expecting higher than normal volume in the store due to Columbus Day markdowns. Jessica, Gabby, and Terrell were outside playing tag. Shelby had made frozen waffles for everyone, syrup-covered plates stacked high in the sink.

Cody often thought how ironic it was that while The Darkness was taking over the world, everyone just went about their business, oblivious to the danger. For now, trusting his mentors was all he could do.

Cody closed his book. "I'm done," he declared.

"Me, too," Shelby added, sitting back on the bench and pulling her knees up to her chest.

She removed wads of cotton from between her toes, apparently satisfied her nails were dry.

Cody glanced at her and laughed.

"What?" she said, giving him a silly grin.

"Your hair…" he began, glancing at the rollers. "Never mind."

"Oh, be quiet, Cowpoke," she said with a sniff. "It takes time and work for exceptionally beautiful people such as myself to get ready." He noticed the twinkle in her eyes.

"Time, work, gel, polish, *and* a bit of spit," Martin added.

"You're gross," Shelby replied. "Just because you boys don't know the first thing about how to…"

Cody looked up to see Sharkey standing in the doorway. The man glanced at Shelby and frowned.

"Get dressed," he said. "And get those *things* out of your hair. You're coming with me."

"We can't leave," Charlotte said. "We're watching the kids."

"Not you three," Sharkey replied. "Just her."

"And go where?" Shelby asked, appearing suddenly uneasy.

"Just get dressed," Sharkey repeated softly.

"Why me?"

"Because I want you to see something for yourself," he replied. "You've got five minutes."

"I-uh," Shelby began, glancing imploringly at Cody.

"Can you guys watch the kids?" he asked Charlotte and Martin.

"I-uh, suppose…"

"Do you want me to come with?" He turned to Shelby.

"Yes," she whimpered. "That would be great."

"Fine," Sharkey replied. "Both of you be ready in five and meet me in the cave," he commanded, then disappeared.

"What do you suppose he wants," Shelby whispered.

"I guess we'll find out," Cody said.

"Great," Martin mumbled, frowning. "For once, it's probably something cool and we'll miss it."

Cody and Shelby entered the cave about ten minutes later. Sharkey appeared agitated, but didn't say anything, instead directing his attention to The Gatekeeper.

"See if you can get her to come," he said to the man.

"Who? See if who can come?" Cody asked, but was ignored.

The Gatekeeper and Sharkey exchanged some silent correspondence. A few minutes later, the doorway lit up and a tall figure appeared on the bridge. It was Radianna.

"Hello, my friends," she said stepping onto the cave floor.

"Hi, Radianna," Cody and Shelby echoed excitedly. "It's good to see you."

Sharkey gave their friend a quick kiss on the cheek. A few seconds later, Radianna, Sharkey, Shelby and Cody stepped through the doorway. Cody could see daylight and hear voices laughing on the other side.

Chapter 42: The Disappointment

Cody stared at the back of a stately brick building that seemed to go on forever. An azure swimming pool dominated the yard, flanked by a spectacular bar and cabana. Various individuals, including some of the most beautiful people Cody had ever seen, congregated on nearby lounge chairs or drifted lazily on pool floats.

A woman Cody immediately recognized glanced in their direction, the smile quickly fading from her face. Cody heard Shelby gasp and felt her fingernails dig into his arm.

The woman jumped out of her chair and headed their way, stopping only to whisper a few words to a large man in a dark suit who looked completely out of place. It only took a few minutes for the previous bustle to become absolute silence as the loungers filed begrudgingly inside.

"What are *you* doing here?" the woman said testily to Radianna.

"Nice to see you, too, Kala," Radianna replied.

Kala frowned, stiffly crossing her arms. Two women Cody recognized as Kensie and Kyrie Bennington, joined them from inside the house.

"Oh, my," Shelby said with a breathy voice.

"I said, what do you *want?*" Kala glanced at Sharkey. "Hello, Darwon."

"Kallari," Sharkey replied, nodding. "Shalla, Wyndall," he added.

"You know why we're here," Radianna said. "The Elders have taken serious issue with your behavior," she added reproachfully.

"Well, good for them," Kyrie said crossly, making a face.

"Do you care at all for these people?" Radianna asked.

"We're not hurting anyone," Kensie replied.

"You're taking advantage of them," Sharkey said evenly. "You're doing nothing to help stop The Darkness. In fact, you're feeding it."

"Why?" Shelby blurted. "What are they doing that's so wrong?" she asked.

"They are better than this..." Radianna interjected, waving her arm. "Taking advantage of people who don't understand."

"We're not idiots," Shelby said with a frown. "And, they do a lot for charity."

"See?" Kensie added with a cheeky grin.

"Shelby, no one said you were idiots," Radianna replied, ignoring Kensie. "But *they* are not sixteen-year-old humans." She nodded toward the Benningtons. "They are individuals who should know better. We don't allow this sort of thing because they can manipulate you into following them blindly."

Kala crossed her arms. "You all sit up there in your ivory towers with smug faces and lock yourselves away. We're just having a little fun, that's all."

Radianna shook her head. "At their expense," she said.

"Whose expense?" Kyrie said peevishly. "They *love* us."

Sharkey stepped forward until he and Kala were standing face to face.

"The Darkness will win and there will be no fun left here, nothing but pain and misery."

"Says you," she replied sourly.

"I've seen it. I've engaged The Darkness in battle. I've tried to bring back The Light, but it's too far gone. He will destroy you, just like he destroys everything. As you know, it has happened before."

"We need your help," Radianna said firmly. "Perhaps together, we can defeat him."

"I doubt it," Kala replied. "Who cares, anyway? Maybe they're not worth saving." She shrugged, nodding toward Shelby and Cody.

"What?" Shelby seemed taken aback. "Are you saying you don't care what happens to us, your millions of adoring fans? Where's the

Kala who devotes all her free time to the children's hospital?" Shelby's voice became increasingly animated. "Where's the Kensie who talks about loving everyone and treating all people the same? And, Kyrie?" Shelby's voice cracked. "I-uh, thought you were so gung-ho on ending world hunger?"

"Come on, kid," Kyrie said, shaking her head. "It's all just a PR stunt to get more fans."

"I-uh, I c-can't believe that! You three are so wonderful. I can't believe what I'm hearing."

Cody could see tears well up in Shelby's eyes. Kala, Kyrie, and Kensie just stood there, looking at Shelby, frowning as if they were bored.

"What's *wrong* with you?" Cody snapped suddenly. "People put you on a pedestal. They love and care about you. And this . . . this is how you treat them? You're not *above* us," he said with disgust. "You don't even belong on the same planet as us."

Cody put his arm around Shelby and gently directed her away. She put her head on his shoulder, sniffling softly.

"Let's go," Radianna said with a sigh. "Clearly this is a waste of time."

"Ta-ta for now," Kensie replied flippantly.

"I hope you know what you're doing," Sharkey said patronizingly. "It's going to get pretty dark and cold around here and when they have no food or light, they'll drop you like yesterday's news. Then where will you go?"

Chapter 43: The Coming of Age

Heather and Jack purchased a new television with the extra money they made on Columbus Day. It was their first flat screen and it was a thing of beauty, even if it was refurbished. Cody didn't care what they watched, even the news was beautiful, at least for a while.

The evening news team covered one depressing story after another: random attacks and violent protests, a rampant virus, forest fires, hurricanes. Cody was relieved when the weatherman came on until he explained about the front that seemed to be 'parked' over the Northeast. He joked perhaps they had angered the gods. The news team all laughed. Cody glanced somberly at his siblings.

The teens gathered around the kitchen table, books and papers scattered about. Heather and the kids left to visit a thrift shop that had just opened in town. Cody stared distractedly at his math book, wincing at the thought of wearing someone else's used clothes. A pang of guilt washed over him as he noticed Sharkey standing solemnly in the doorway and realized how little his petty concerns mattered.

"Things aren't good, are they?" Cody asked.

"I'm afraid not, Mr. Hawke."

Sharkey sighed. "I just wanted to say goodbye. I may not be back."

"Where are you going?" Cody jumped to his feet. The others did the same.

"There is no time left for small victories," the man said.

"What are you going to do?" Charlotte asked.

"We are headed to Bulwark, hopefully to retrieve the books and free The Light," Sharkey replied.

"Let us come," Cody said.

"We can help," Martin added earnestly.

"It is too dangerous," Sharkey stated firmly. "As I said, we may not be coming back."

"I-uh, but—" Cody began.

"There's nothing to discuss, Mr. Hawke," Sharkey said. "Anyway, it has been a pleasure meeting you all." He shook each of their hands. "You are exceptionally bright, brave, and kind. You four have given us the impetus to fight this war. We are reminded there are truly good people in your world, people worth saving." Sharkey smiled disarmingly. "Wish me luck," he added, tipping his hat.

With that, he was gone. Cody stared at his siblings in doleful silence, a lump forming in his throat.

"What should we do?" Shelby asked with a sniffle.

"We have our weapons," Charlotte replied. "Not that we're any good with them, but maybe we should try," she added.

"I'm certainly in," Cody said.

"Me, too," Shelby added.

"Count me in," Martin said.

Cody put his hand in. The others reached in also.

"As Guardians of Rúndyrr," he said softly, "We ask the powers that be to give us the strength to defend our world and help our friends in this battle against The Darkness. If you're with me, say 'Defend The Light', on three."

"Defend The Light," they whispered solemnly.

The Gatekeeper shook his head as soon as he saw them.

"No," he said. "Go back upstairs. This is not a fight for kids."

"You sent us to ride an unfinished roller coaster and hover above a lava pit," Martin mumbled.

"That was different," The Gatekeeper replied.

"Regardless, we're not leaving," Cody stated firmly.

"So, you might as well let us go," Shelby added.

"The Bulwark is not a place people walk away from. I will not be an instrument in thy demise," the old man said, heading back to his dark corner.

"Then I'll do it," Cody said with determination. "You said The Chosen needs no doorways."

The Gatekeeper glanced back. A brief smirk crossed his face, as if clearly doubting Cody's abilities. Shaking his head, the old man resumed walking.

Cody held out his hands and the teens formed a circle. He closed his eyes, focusing on the family that had become such an important part of his life. Maybe they didn't share his blood, but they meant more to him than he could've ever imagined, even Sharkey.

The thought of losing the man was suddenly more than Cody could bear. He couldn't put it into words, but he felt a strong connection between them. If this Nimbusian was willing to lay down his life for them, then Cody would be there with him, shoulder to shoulder, until the end.

He worried about his siblings, but he had seen a similar steadfastness in their eyes. Sharkey had disarmed them all with his comments, however brief, about their goodness. It inspired something they were willing to fight for. Emotion welled up in Cody.

We need to get to Bulwark to help Sharkey and Radianna defeat this Darkness. I can't let them die.

He could feel the blood flowing through his body. An intense heat permeated his arms, passing through him and into his siblings. Cody felt as if he would explode from the warmth and pressure.

"I CAN'T TAKE . . . NO!" he screamed.

Just when he thought he would literally burst, everything went cold. When he opened his eyes, the four teens stood in a stone corridor, a distinctive moan emanating from somewhere nearby.

Chapter 44: The Dark Castle

"Whoa!" Martin said, his mouth hanging open. "You *did* it!"

Cody grinned, but his happiness was short-lived.

"Come on," he whispered, "we need to find Sharkey before The Darkness finds us. This way."

"How do you know?" Charlotte asked.

"I-uh, don't know how," Cody stammered. "But I'm pretty sure this is the way to go."

He headed down the dank corridor, an occasional torch providing the only illumination. They reached a large cavern with assorted weapons decorating the walls. A wide staircase dominated the left corner, winding down into shadowy darkness.

"Come on," Cody said, rushing toward the steps. "This way."

The tunnels at the next level down were even more inhospitable. Smells of mold and decay lingered on the foul air. Small rocks littered the ground, making passage treacherous.

"Watch where you're going," Cody murmured. "We don't want any sprained ankles," he grinned briefly at Shelby.

A few minutes later, they reached another large cavern. Five dark tunnels converged on the circular room like an enormous ship's wheel. Cody heard voices coming from one of the corridors. The teens hugged the wall until relative silenced resumed.

"Achoo!"

"Martin, shush!" Cody hissed.

"I'm sorry. I can't help it!"

He appeared ready to sneeze again. Cody glared at him until the urge seemed to pass.

"Ugh!" Shelby moaned.

"What's wrong?" Cody turned abruptly.

"Nothing," she whispered sheepishly. "It's just, well, I need to remember to go to the bathroom before we leave on these adventures."

Cody scowled. "Really?"

"I'm sorry! I get caught up in the moment," Shelby whined.

"Go over there in the corner," Martin said.

"No way!" Shelby replied.

"Listen, it can't smell any worse in here than it already does," the boy added.

"Kids?" Cody asked drolly as Shelby stepped away. "Anybody else have to sneeze or pee before the battle starts?"

"Very funny, Cowpoke," he heard Shelby mutter.

"What's that glow coming from the corridor across the room?" Martin whispered.

"It's very bright," Charlotte replied. "Could it be…"

"Maybe," Cody whispered, not wanting to speak its name.

He listened for a moment trying to make sense of the distant sounds. There were humanish voices, the echo of dragging chains, and something that almost resembled a lion's roar.

Suddenly a light arced across the room, exploding into a booming fireball. Part of the cavern's wall crumbled. Sharkey appeared as a group of Dreds approached from a corridor to the right. The man sported a white suit with the imprint of a dragon on the back. Radianna joined him wearing the same white jumpsuit they had seen during her battle with Loki.

The demons quickly surrounded them. Sharkey and Radianna stood back to back, swinging their weapons in large circles. Each time their swords touched a demon, the creature would freeze, then a quick stab would cause it to explode into a puff of dark smoke.

"Wait here," Cody ordered.

He called to Tiwaz and darted out into battle. Swinging the sword with all his might, Cody quickly took out three Dreds. He glanced around and realized Shelby, Charlotte, and Martin had joined as well.

"*NO!*" Radianna yelled. "GO! ALL OF YOU, GET TO SAFTETY!"

Cody hesitated, backing up slowly as perhaps a hundred more demons appeared from various corridors, quickly surrounding them.

Despite his black armor, Cody recognized General Odium approaching from the rear. Pencil-like metal teeth gleamed as he stepped into the cavern. Red claws extending from under his dark cloak gripped a curved lance. Odium pointed his weapon and another fireball arced across the cavern, its force knocking Cody to the ground.

"GO!" Sharkey reiterated. "We are expendable. You are *not*. Get to safety . . . my brother," he yelled.

"*What* did he just say?" Shelby asked.

"I-uh…" Cody climbed to his feet, staring at the man in silence.

"GO! *NOW!*"

"What should we do?" Charlotte asked, jabbing at the demons with Kenaz, her lance.

"The Books," Martin said, swinging his axe, Uruz. "Maybe we can find them while Sharkey and Radianna keep the Dreds occupied."

"Can you guys hold up the perimeter of that bright tunnel while Charlotte and I look for the books?" Cody asked.

"We can certainly try," Martin replied.

The teens fought their way to the other side of the cavern. Shelby took up the rear with Gebo, her ice bow and arrow in position. The distant light faded and grew bright like rays emanating from a beating heart.

"CODY! LOOK OUT!" Charlotte yelled.

A demon approached him from behind. Cody turned just as Shelby's arrow struck it in the back.

"Hmm," Shelby mumbled with a quick smile, "I might actually be getting the hang of this."

"Thanks!" Cody said, staring in awe as a quick burst of light indicated the appearance of another ice arrow in Shelby's quiver.

"Pretty cool, huh?" she grinned.

He nodded. "Somehow it fits you."

As they reached the entrance to the opposite tunnel, Cody glanced back at Sharkey and Radianna holding their own against General Odium and the Dreds.

"You guys stay here," he called. "Do what you can to keep the demons away. We'll try to be quick." Cody hesitated for a second. "And, uh, yell if you need us," he added.

Cody and Charlotte walked back-to-back as they made their way along the rocky corridor. The light flickered with such intensity it was difficult to look straight ahead.

Various open storage rooms lined the way. The two took turns darting into each one, searching for the books or something that might be used to hide them, but no luck. As they continued into the subterranean depths, the adjacent rooms became dungeons with chains anchored to the floor. Various rusty tools hung from the walls: loppers, pruning shears, and cultivators.

"What do you suppose those gardening tools are for?" Charlotte asked somberly.

"I'm guessing not for gardening," Cody muttered.

They reached another tunnel, one that headed left. At its end, a swarm of demons stood guard.

"If I were going to hide something valuable," Charlotte said softly, "I'd keep someone there to protect it."

"Are you up for this?" Cody glanced at her.

Charlotte opened her mouth, but appeared to change her mind. "Yes," was all she said.

"I'll do the fighting. You watch my back." Cody raised his sword. "We can do this, Charlotte."

He smiled at her, then ran down the corridor. Swinging his sword in every direction, Cody took out as many demons as he could while still having the element of surprise. He was grateful for his sports training, even so, his arms quickly grew heavy. The Dreds were so many and they were just two.

A sinking feeling came over Cody. The demons had surrounded him. Swinging Tiwaz in a circle, he tried to keep them at bay, but with limited success.

NO! I can't...

He felt himself losing consciousness from metal hitting his head. A wave of intense pain flushed over him as something penetrated his back. Cody dropped to his knees.

"*CODY!*" He heard Charlotte scream.

The Dreds stood over him, repeatedly beating him with their weapons.

Get up! Get up now! Fight!

He couldn't move. Then something slammed into the side of his head and he fell over.

This is it. Again, I've let everyone down.

"Charlotte," he mumbled, knowing his words were slurred, "get back to the…"

Cody was aware of the sound of fighting. He opened his eyes and saw three demons standing nearby. One after another, they dropped to the ground, a shaft of ice protruding from their chests.

Charlotte?

Suddenly silence prevailed. Cody realized the Dreds had disappeared. He focused on trying to heal himself, but it didn't seem to be working.

Focus! Why can't I do this? I'm going to die.

"Hold still," Charlotte ordered.

Cody groaned as she pulled something from his back. A wave of intense pain spread over him. He took a deep breath and closed his eyes, letting emotion build up inside. He felt the dragon burn on his palm, then the pain began to subside. As his mind began to regain focus, a voice echoed in his head.

CODY, HELP US.

"Find the books," he croaked to Charlotte, staggering to his feet.

"CODY?" she began.

"I'm fine, Charlotte," he said, staring at a bloody piece of metal on the ground. "Thanks to you."

As soon as he could steady himself, Cody headed down the corridor to help Shelby and Martin, swinging at anything that moved. Martin did the same with his axe. Shelby stepped back, picking off demons with her bow and arrow. Slowly, they pushed the Dreds back toward the main cavern.

"WHERE'S CHARLOTTE?" Shelby cried.

"Hopefully, she's coming," Cody yelled apprehensively.

As they neared the cavern, he could see Sharkey and Radianna, still barely holding their own. Another group of Dreds broke off and headed their way.

"Cody?" Martin called. "I'm not sure how much longer I can do this."

"CHARLOTTE?" Cody yelled. "ARE YOU COMING?

No answer.

I need to go look for her, but if I leave Shelby and Martin…

Then he saw someone approaching from down the tunnel. It was Charlotte, struggling with a heavy bag. Cody smiled, but his relief was short-lived. A dozen Dreds followed close behind.

"LET'S GO!" Charlotte screamed.

They were surrounded. Cody knew they would never survive the attack. He ran toward her with Shelby and Martin not far behind.

I've got to get them out of here.

He grabbed Charlotte's bag and flung it over his shoulder. Shelby and Martin joined them and the four locked hands. The Dreds were just a few meters away, running toward them with weapons drawn. From his vantage point, Cody could see Sharkey battling demons back in the cavern.

I need to help them.

With a heavy heart, he closed his eyes and thought desperately about going home.

Chapter 45: The Revelation

"What should I do?" Cody yelled as the teens stepped through the doorway. The two old men seemed relieved, clearly awaiting their return. "They're going to be slaughtered," he cried.

"Right now, you have helped more than you know," The Guardian replied earnestly.

He took the bag from Cody's hand.

"We will keep this safe," The Gatekeeper added.

"Are those…" Shelby's eyes were wide, "the rest of the books?"

The Guardian gave them a muted smile. "You four have rescued the remaining Books of Light, as has long been decreed in our scriptures."

"We were *supposed* to do that?" Martin asked.

Cody listened in silence, but his mind was back with his friends.

"I need to go back," Cody said. "Right now!"

"Then you will die along with them," The Gatekeeper said, his voice choked.

"Then I'll die," Cody said. "But at least I'll have done everything I could to help them."

"WAIT!" Shelby stepped forward. "Send me back to the Benningtons first. Please!"

She turned to Cody her eyes wet with emotion. "It won't take any time, but let me try. *Please!*"

Shelby stood alone in an enormous marble foyer. She heard voices coming from the next room.

"Here goes nothing," she whispered.

Kala, Kyrie, and Kensie looked up from their respective dinners and watched with obvious indifference as she entered the room.

"They're going to *die*," Shelby stated. The three women stared blankly in her direction. "They are going to die in a vain attempt to save our world, and here you sit eating dinner and drinking wine. They mean more to me than you three *ever* could. You're selfish, self-centered, and quite frankly, a huge disappointment," she said angrily. "I don't know how you came from the same world as them, but you're not worth the sand in their shoes."

Kala dropped her fork and gazed absently out the window.

"That's it?" Shelby hissed the words. "You don't even have a response? You care that little about anything . . . except *yourselves*, that is. No wonder you don't want to fight for The Light. You must be in with The Darkness. Maybe you've just got too much of Loki in you."

Kala glared at Shelby, rolling her eyes. "Do *not* bring him into this," she said. "We are *nothing* like him. And, stop being so dramatic. Not wanting to fight doesn't make you *in* with The Dark."

"It does if you're part of the problem," Shelby retorted.

Silence prevailed for a moment until Kyrie Bennington slowly stood, a frown crossing her face. She glanced at Shelby. "I've been thinking a lot about what you said the other day," she mumbled. "And, maybe you've got a point."

Kensie also stood, looking down at Kala. "Maybe we have gone too far," she said. "Maybe we've lost ourselves, lost our goodness. What *happened* to us? How did we get like this?"

Kala pushed her chair back, a smirk crossing her face. "You *know* how."

She stood, and for a moment, Shelby thought she would walk away. Then something happened. Kala froze as if a sudden vision came to her. She turned to Shelby, her expression changing.

"You four..." she began, "you went to Bulwark Castle to fight alongside our people?"

Shelby nodded. "How did you know that?"

"I can see things," she replied, then turned toward her sisters and sighed. "Perhaps it is time."

Kala raised her arm high in the air, a silver lance appearing in her hand. Her clothing became a white suit with the crest of a griffin emblazoned on the back. Kensie and Kyrie followed her lead.

Shelby gasped briefly, then whispered, "A griffin," in response to The Gatekeeper's riddle.

Cody stared at the Rúndyrr doorway, swirling with activity. It shimmered brightly as four people stepped across the bridge. She's incredible, he thought, grinning in Shelby's direction.

"Kallari, Wyndall, Shalla," The Gatekeeper said, nodding. "It has been a long time."

Kala, Kyrie, and Kensie bowed their heads in response.

"*Please* help them," Shelby whispered.

Kala nodded. "Send us to Bulwark," she ordered.

The Gatekeeper smiled briefly, winking at Shelby, then reached for the scepter.

"Thank you," Shelby said as the Benningtons stepped back onto the bridge.

Kala stopped, turning toward her.

"No. Thank *you*, Shelby," she said earnestly. Then they were gone.

Chapter 46: The Sacrifice

"Mr. Gatekeeper?" Shelby asked. "Sharkey reminded the Benningtons that this has happened before? Kala alluded to something similar. What were they talking about?"

"The Darkness has come close to overtaking this world a few times in the past," The Gatekeeper replied. "The Nimbusians stepped in to help, but…" he hesitated.

"But what?" Martin asked.

"There were four of them," The Guardian offered with an obviously heavy heart. "Four of your *Bennington* sisters. Gialla, however, didn't survive the last battle."

Shelby gasped.

"She tried to take on Grýla alone, but the ogress was too strong," The Gatekeeper added.

"Oh, no! All those things I said," Shelby cried.

"Why couldn't someone heal her?" Charlotte asked.

"Her body . . . it was too far gone. Our powers have limits," he replied.

"Do not lament, Shelby," The Guardian offered warmly. "Those words were long overdue. The sisters have spent years wallowing in their grief. Thou had the courage to say the things we should have said decades ago. The time has long since passed for them to rejoin their people."

Suddenly it all made sense, Cody thought, their unwillingness to help, their attitude toward family.

"The battle to save us cost them someone they loved," Shelby said softly. "The pain and anger drove them to a period of mourning that resulted in their isolation."

The Gatekeeper nodded.

"What can we do?" Cody reiterated. "We need to *do* something."

"It is best...". The Guardian froze, then faced The Gatekeeper. It seemed as if he had news and it wasn't good. The men conversed in some silent language, then The Guardian turned to Cody.

"Take this," he said, removing two books from the bag and handing the rest to Cody. "Protect these remaining books at all costs."

"Why? Where are you going? Where are you taking those?" Cody blurted.

The Guardian took a deep breath. "They are in need of my help. Grýla has joined the battle along with Odium. It is too much even with the Benningtons at their side. I will use these to lure Grýla away to The Blood Cave," he said, holding up the books, "in the hope that two fronts will spread their power too thin."

"But . . . you'll die," Cody yelled. "I'm coming with you!"

"NO!" The Guardian replied firmly. "I am expendable. Remain here and guard the rest of the books. If Grýla were to find them it would be catastrophic."

"I-uh, I can't let you do this," Cody cried. "You'll *die* fighting Grýla alone!"

"Then so be it," The Guardian said with rueful smile. "It is my time."

The old man put his hand on Cody's shoulder. "Thou art the future, my son. You've learned so much since your arrival at Freya Manor. Thou hast grown strong, but more important, thou hath demonstrated a steadfast mind and a stout heart, the heart of a leader."

"But, I-I could never fill your shoes. You're so much stronger and wiser," Cody cried, his eyes growing wet.

He looked to his siblings for help. Shelby and Charlotte's faces reflected their pain, tears trickling down their cheeks. Martin stared at the ground in an apparent attempt to maintain his composure.

"Thou will learn quickly. The Gatekeeper will be here to teach thee, for a while anyway," he glanced over at the aging man.

"NO! I'm coming with you." Cody wiped the tears from his face.

"The most important lesson thou can learn right now is to think of the greater good," The Guardian said sincerely. "That does not include sacrificing thyself for me. Thou still hath much to do in this life."

The Gatekeeper opened the doorway. Cody could see darkness on the other side. The two bearded men hugged briefly, then The Guardian disappeared.

"*NO!*"

Chapter 47: The Bad Decision

"The Light Elves!" Cody yelled suddenly. "They'll help us!"

"They will not leave their realm," The Gatekeeper replied. "It is forbidden."

"It's forbidden for them to interfere with humankind," Cody said, "but if they don't help, there won't be any humans to mess with."

"And what if The Darkness comes for the remaining books," The Gatekeeper said.

"We'll be right back," Cody replied. "Don't worry."

A few minutes later, the four teens gazed at the lush rolling hills of Alfheim. Their destination, the cozy cottage on the right, seemed peaceful, a sharp contrast to the events back home.

"Andola," Cody said, as the door opened. "I doubt you remember, but I'm—"

"Cody, of course," Andola said warmly. "Charlotte, Shelby, Martin, please come in."

The teens stepped into the foyer and nodded to the stunning woman waiting to greet them.

"Hello, friends," she called, "what can we do for you?"

"It's so good to see you, Alizia," Shelby said. "Thank you for inviting us into your home."

"Could we talk to you?" Cody asked. "Just for a minute."

"Of course," Andola replied, leading them to the sitting room. "I believe I know why you're here," he said soberly.

"You do?" Martin quipped. "That's makes one of us."

Andola sighed. "I believe I explained earlier that entering your earthly realm is not accepted by our Council."

"Yes, you did," Cody replied. "However, these are extreme circumstances. Mr. Sharkey, uh, Darwon, Radianna, Kallari, Wyndall, and Shalla have all gone to battle The Darkness. Our Guardian has also joined the fight, sacrificing himself to redirect some of Grýla's resources to the Blood Cave." Cody took a deep breath. "I am afraid the demons are too powerful and all our friends will die."

"We have nowhere else to turn," Charlotte added.

"We tried to help," Martin said. "But obviously, we're not warriors like them."

"We're supposed to be..." Cody hesitated, suddenly feeling a bit ill. "We're supposed to be guarding the books," he added.

Chosen! Help me.

Cody felt nauseous, his heart overwhelmed with dread. He turned to his siblings. "We need to return home . . . *now*. I've got a bad feeling."

"What's wrong?" Charlotte asked.

"I-uh, don't..." Cody began, standing up.

"Please," Shelby said earnestly. "We need your help. We're at the end of our rope."

"I am sorry," Andola replied ruefully.

"Please!" Charlotte cried. "They'll die!"

Andola sighed. "Very well. I will take it up with the Council when they meet tomorrow."

"Tomorrow? Tomorrow's not good enough," Shelby cried. "They need help now!"

"I-uh, I'm sorry," Cody said grimly, "we shouldn't have come. We need to get home quickly."

As the teens emerged in the Rúndyrr cave, Cody's worst fears were confirmed. The Gatekeeper was trying to ward off a small army of demons. They had beaten him into a corner and Grýla was about to go in for the kill. The old man swung his staff, but there were too many.

"NO!" Cody yelled.

The ogress glared at him as he reached up for Tiwaz. She turned to engage him in battle, then hesitated, possibly recalling Cody's attack in the warehouse. Martin, Charlotte, and Shelby called for their weapons as well. Scowling, Grýla grabbed the bag of books off the floor, then disappeared into a puff of black smoke. The demons followed.

"WHAT HAVE THEE DONE?" The Gatekeeper cried, trying to catch his breath. "I couldn't take them all on alone. Now the books are lost!"

"NO!" Cody screamed, hiding his face in his hands. "I've ruined everything! I'm so *stupid*!"

"How did they know the books were here?" Charlotte asked.

"Grýla can feel their presence," The Gatekeeper replied. "She senses their goodness."

Shelby and Martin helped the old man to his feet while Cody paced angrily back and forth. They left him alone, seeming to know he was inconsolable.

Cody felt responsible for losing the books. No, he *was* responsible. The Guardian said it was his duty to guard them, but as always, *he* knew better. Now all was lost because of his bad decision. He thought asking the Light Elves for help would be the answer. Another group of fierce warriors could make all the difference, but Andola dismissed the request with a wave of his hand and now Cody's stupidity had cost them their only advantage.

The Gatekeeper shook his head. "I know thou were only trying to help," he said walking over to put his hand on Cody's shoulder. "It was not thy fault. Thou..."

Cody began to pull away, anger getting the better of him, when suddenly he froze. The Gatekeeper's words faded into the background. Something clouded his thoughts, a dream of some sort.

It couldn't be, could it? I'm wide awake. But there it is.

"Cody? Cody, are you alright?" He could hear his friends calling.

Grýla's evil face filled his mind. The ogress grinned contemptuously as she handed the leather bag to General Odium. The general climbed one of Bulwark's sweeping staircases and headed to a large austere room. He placed the bag on a wooden table, then opened a gilded box and set each book inside. The demon sneered, closing the box, and Cody's vision ended.

He opened his eyes and turned to his siblings. "Stay here, please. I'll be back soon."

"Where are you—" Shelby began.

"I'll be fine."

Cody let the emotion of his failure wash over him. His face and hands turned red, hot blood pumping through his body. He closed his fist so the others couldn't see the light tattoo appear on his palm. The next thing he knew, Cody was standing in one of Bulwark's musty corridors.

This time, however, he hurried in the opposite direction. The passageway ended in a rocky cavern with a staircase leading up. A hallway at the top led to a room containing an enormous bed with a wooden table at the center.

That thing sleeps?

General Odium's long gilded box lay closed on the table. Resting his hand on top, Cody felt a tingling sensation, as if the box exuded some sort of force. He lifted the lid, relieved to see the books still inside.

The books are all here. That means Grýla took the two from The Guardian. God, please let him be okay.

Cody examined the box's interior, wondering whether the heavy metal construction and the strange forcefield blocked one's ability to sense the books' presence inside. If so, maybe the box prevented Grýla and Odium from perceiving their location as well.

He was about to close the chest when he noticed movement. The eye on the cover of Book One opened. It stared imploringly at Cody, as if silently asking for help. He felt its goodness and was certain it could feel his. One by one, the other eyes opened until all nine eyes stared back at him. For a moment, he couldn't move.

A bright light suddenly emanated from each book, connecting the eyes. Exhilarating warmth radiated outward, making Cody feel giddy, like the feeling one experiences during moments of incredible kindness. The light filled his head. He could see anything, just by thinking of it: The Great Wall of China, the Andes Mountains, the Parthenon, he could see it all. Scenes began to flash through his mind like streaming video.

I feel it... The Light... The love!

A policeman asked a young boy if he could be his big brother. The image of a nurse reading letters to an elderly woman in a hospital bed filled Cody's thoughts. A woman in a suit walked away smiling after donating dozens of toys to a shelter. A teenager rescued a dog that had been hit by a passing car. These and many more images flashed through Cody's mind until the emotion was too much to bear and he had to look away.

Are these just my imagination or are they all happening right now?

A sudden moan broke the vision and a smell so foul it could've come from the bowels of the earth. Cody turned to see Odium standing in the doorway. His heart pounded as he closed the case.

You should've joined me, Chosen, when you had the chance. Now you die. Your sweet young flesh will be very tasty.

Cody briefly closed his eyes, trying to keep the demon from invading his thoughts, then reached up to retrieve Tiwaz. Odium leapt toward him with teeth exposed. Cody pushed back, but those razor-sharp fangs slashed his arm, quickly drawing blood. As he focused on the throbbing agony, Cody's palm began to glow and the pain ceased.

You cannot win, Chosen. I will end you and feast on your entrails.

The demon grabbed Cody around the neck, lifting him off the ground, then knocked Tiwaz from his grasp. Cody watched helplessly as his sword slid across the floor.

Your little toys have no effect on me.

Cody punched and kicked, but the grip on his neck tightened. As he squirmed in an attempt to break free, his right foot reached the wooden table. Cody tried to push off, but instead knocked the table over. As it fell, the chest lid flew open, books scattering across the floor.

Ninth book.

Cody felt himself losing consciousness, Odium's grip closing his airway. Another voice invaded his head, but this one felt warm. Suddenly his mind filled with light.

Am I dying? Is this what death feels like?

Focus, Cody, he chastised himself.

Ninth book.

Cody managed to swing his body until one foot touched the ground. He pushed off in an attempt to break free, but Odium was too strong.

Can't breathe… Tiwaz, help me. I need my sword.

Suddenly, he felt something hit his outstretched hand. It was Tiwaz. Cody closed his grip on the sword's hilt and thrust the ice blade into Odium's midsection. The demon's scream curtailed as ice crystals permeated its body. Cody pulled the claw from his neck and fell to the floor, gasping for air.

Ninth book.

Glancing down at the leather-bound tomes with their brass clasps and tooled numbers, he realized books one through eight had landed with their covers facing up. The ninth book had flipped over.

He wasn't sure what made him scramble to the ninth book and flip it over, but he stared in awe as all the eyes opened. Again, a bright light spanned the books, connecting them to each other.

General Odium was beginning to thaw. Cody stabbed at him, but was too late. The demon knocked him to the ground, Tiwaz again slipping from his hand.

You have wasted enough of my time, pathetic boy. Now you die.

Odium bent over Cody, metal teeth inches from slicing his neck. Cody turned his body in an attempt to get away and found himself staring directly into the light radiating from the nine books. Incredible warmth spread over him as the light passed through his body.

WE ARE ONE, CHOSEN. WE ARE ONE.

Cody's first sensation was the general's teeth penetrating his neck. The next was his body on fire, pressure building inside. As he lifted his hands to push Odium off, a stream of light blasted out through his palm and into the demon's eyes. Odium screamed in apparent agony, the force of all that goodness knocking him across the room. He hit the wall hard and slid down its rocky surface.

Cody raised his head and saw the demon crawling around on the floor, hearing his anguished moans. Odium reached randomly out into the air, as if blind. Cody felt strangely sorry for him. That was the last thing he remembered.

When he came to, Cody was alone in the room. Shaking off the cobwebs, he climbed to his feet and set each book back into the chest.

"Oh, my, you're bleeding," Shelby cried as he stepped off the bridge.

"It's fine," Cody said, rubbing his neck. "Take this." He set the box down in front of The Gatekeeper and turned to his siblings. "All of you, please help him keep it safe. And whatever you do, do NOT open the box. I have a feeling it will keep the books hidden from The Darkness' view."

He glanced up in time to see The Gatekeeper's quick smile, pride apparent in the man's eyes.

"Where are you going?" Charlotte asked.

"I have to help him," he replied.

"Cody—" Shelby began.

"I'll be fine," he said, hugging his siblings. "Don't worry."

The next thing he knew, Cody was standing in a dark red tunnel, one he realized must be Blood Cave.

Chapter 48: The Blood Cave

Cody stared out into the melee, immense relief sweeping over him.

The Guardian!

Sharkey, Radianna, The Guardian, and The Bennington sisters were engaged in a battle of epic proportions in an enormous cavern located somewhere in the Icelandic cave. Grýla appeared in the fray, glaring back at Cody with her long teeth exposed. Sharkey swung his sword and the demon looked away.

How did they all get here?

His friends appeared to be growing tired. Each time they sent a Dred into a puff of black smoke, it was replaced by two more. The Guardian approached Cody, clearly worn from battle.

"I'm *so* glad you're okay," Cody said, choked by emotion.

The old man took a second to catch his breath.

"I lured Grýla here as planned," The Guardian said. "Once she had the seven books…" He hesitated, taking another deep breath. Cody winced, knowing his mentor was aware of his failure. "It was easy for her to overpower me and take the remaining two," he continued. "She then left for Bulwark with the nine books, returning shortly thereafter with the intent to end me."

"What happened?" Cody asked.

He smiled proudly. "The Darkness clearly underestimated The Chosen, a mistake I doubt it will make again. He had to send Grýla to search for the books, as apparently, Odium was blinded after a run in with The Chosen." He gave Cody another brief smile, then nodded toward the battle. "When she couldn't find the books here, she left briefly to look elsewhere, so Odium sent the Dreds after me. Sharkey and the others followed."

"Something happened at Bulwark," Cody said. "The nine books' eyes connected and somehow joined with me," he added, knowing it sounded crazy.

"Thou art The Chosen," The Guardian said earnestly.

"Earlier, when we were in Bulwark Castle, I saw a bright light at the end of the corridor. Was that—"

The Guardian nodded. "Sharkey tried to free it, but was not able. If by some remote chance we win this battle, perhaps The Light might free itself."

"Otherwise?" Cody asked.

The Guardian just shook his head. "Thou should go back home."

"I can't," Cody said.

The Guardian sighed, then turned to rejoin the battle. Feeling Tiwaz appear in his hand, Cody ran into the fray. He knew Sharkey and The Guardian's eyes were on him, he could feel their trepidation, but nothing was going to stop him from doing his part.

Much to Cody's surprise, he noticed something else. His clothing had transformed into a white suit. He felt something warm emblazoned on the back.

The battle went on for what seemed like hours, though nothing changed. In fact, there were so many demons, winning appeared impossible. He glanced at The Guardian on the far side of the room. The old man was getting beaten down. Radianna tried to reach him, but there were too many demons in her path. Cody swung with renewed energy, hoping to make his way across.

Suddenly a loud blast rocked the cave. He jumped out of the way as boulders and debris dropped to the ground, extinguishing handfuls of Dreds. When the dust settled, Cody could see a starry sky above. The explosion had taken out a huge chunk of the cave and earth overhead.

"Stay focused," he heard Sharkey yell, noticing the group of Dreds surrounding him.

Cody swung his sword in a circle until the area around him was clear. A gust of wind whipped through the cave. When Cody glanced upward again, he saw three white winged horses circling high above. As the horses folded their wings and dove down, he recognized the riders: Andola and two Light Elves.

Cody made eye contact with Andola, smiling his gratitude. The Light Elves turned out to be formidable masters in battle, each taking out multiple demons at a time. Andola and Grýla became engaged in a heated battle. For the first time in a while, Cody was hopeful.

Hours passed until Cody was so exhausted, he could barely lift his sword. Victory seemed to constantly elude them. Somehow, The Guardian appeared to be hanging on. He noticed Charlotte, Shelby and Martin waiting in the wings.

Oh, no! I asked them to guard the books! What are they doing? It's too dangerous here.

He ran to where they were standing.

"You need to go—"

"It okay, Cody," Martin replied, "The Gatekeeper told us to come."

"He said you were right," Shelby whispered. "That box makes them impossible to locate."

"We hid them somewhere, he'll *never* find them," Charlotte added, "in Shelby's shoe rack."

Cody grinned then slumped back against the wall, gasping for breath. "Still, it's too dangerous," he added.

"You're here," Martin said. "We're staying."

"I-uh…"

Cody was spent. He couldn't even respond as he attempted to heal the various cuts and aches occurring all over his body. The Guardian joined them at the sidelines, clearly needing a rest. Cody watched Sharkey fight, taking on Odium plus two or three demons at a time.

"Whoa," he whispered.

"He is incredible," Shelby added, obviously watching as well.

"He is a Drengr," The Guardian offered.

"A what?" Martin asked.

"Drengr," The Guardian replied. "Viking word for badass."

Cody wanted to laugh, hearing The Guardian – one so proper – swear. His amusement was short-lived as Sharkey hobbled over, various blood stains dotting his white suit.

"What are you doing?" Cody asked.

"I need to recharge," Sharkey mumbled, his flippant tone gone.

The man leaned against the cave wall and slid to the ground. He seemed to be trying to heal himself as well.

"Let me help thee," The Guardian said, placing his hand on Sharkey's arm.

"We're losing the battle," Shelby cried. "Every time you take out one demon, two more appear in its place. We can't win."

"Not true, Miss Shelby," Sharkey said, breathing hard. "We are just . . . resting. All is not lost."

"Call me a pessimist," Martin whispered, "but it's not looking good. Even you god-like guys can't keep this up forever."

"Where did you go?" Cody asked evenly.

Sharkey glanced up, a blank look reflecting his confusion.

"Back at Freya Manor," Cody said. "When you were leaving all the time. Where did you go?"

"I was planting seeds, Mr. Hawke."

"The world was ending and you were worried about your flower garden?" Cody frowned.

"Hey, gardening can be very therapeutic," Martin quipped.

The Guardian uttered a painful chuckle as he gasped for breath.

"Not flower seeds," Sharkey muttered. "I was planting the seeds of compassion and learning," he added.

"What does that mean?" Charlotte asked.

"You humans can find more ways to divide yourselves than anyone ever dreamed possible." Sharkey shook his head. "Especially you Americans."

"Hey," Shelby replied indignantly, "we're a potpourri of patriotic people."

Sharkey frowned "This one's too big. That one's too tall. She's got purple hair. He lives in this place, but she lives on the opposite side. This one's dark. That one's too light or talks funny." Sharkey hesitated, wincing in pain as he sat up.

"What's that have to do with anything?" Cody asked testily, feeling suddenly defensive.

"Ignorance and apathy, Mr. Hawke," Sharkey said. "The Darkness gains strength when people divide themselves and look down on others who don't look or feel the same."

"Are you saying we've been collectively feeding The Darkness?" Charlotte gasped.

"Not only have you been feeding it, Miss Charlotte, you're killing The Light." Sharkey stood on shaky legs and turned to them. "Over the course of many centuries, we gave your forefathers The Books of Light, one book to the leader of nine great civilizations: Egyptians, Aztecs, Incas, Vikings, Chinese, Romans, Greeks, British, and the indigenous peoples of North America."

"You went back in time?" Charlotte asked.

Sharkey nodded. "We decided to try and rewrite, or at least redirect, the bloody history of your ancestors."

"Did it work?" Martin wondered.

"These books, or Havamal, as we called them, gave each civilization all the keys to a good life. They contained details on what it means to live in peace: how to treat each other and how to be happy, plus the knowledge needed to thrive. We included the necessary math, language, and engineering skills to build irrigation systems, roads, bridges, etc., making life less demanding and allowing more time for leisure."

"What happened?" Cody asked.

"We checked on their progress periodically via the book's eyes and realized they had used this information for superiority in battle. Humans, we discovered were greedy and power hungry and there was little we could do to stop it." Sharkey turned, apparently to watch the current battle unfolding.

"But that was centuries ago," Charlotte offered.

"Maybe," Sharkey replied. "But things aren't much different today."

"How did the books get lost?" Shelby asked.

Sharkey looked back at them and took a deep breath. "The Darkness stole them. One by one, it amassed most of the collection, leaving little direction for humankind. Of course, it didn't matter anyway. The books were all hidden away in tombs, museums, or boxed up in some dusty warehouse. Each book holds a unique piece to the puzzle of life. Together, they are unstoppable."

"That's fascinating," Charlotte whispered, "but what does it have to do with planting seeds?"

"Ah, yes." Sharkey grinned. "The reason I started this dissertation. I've appeared in many places around the world in recent months, as a teacher, a pastor, a policeman, a child. I used the gold to procure food for those in poverty – humans have a difficult time feeling charitable when their stomachs are empty – and to do good deeds, planting the seeds of hope."

"What made you think that would help?" Shelby asked. "I mean, it takes time for seeds to grow."

"Very true, Miss Shelby," he rubbed his chin, "but sometimes the smallest of seeds can cause the biggest results. A group of us tried it in the past. It worked pretty well, but you are correct when you say it takes time."

"What group?" Martin asked.

Sharkey sighed. "Gandhi, Dr. King, Lincoln, Goodall, just to name a few."

"They were Nimbusian?" Charlotte asked with gasp.

"That they were, Miss Charlotte," Sharkey stated. "That they were."

He sighed briefly then, raising his ice sword and charged back into battle. The Guardian ran out to join him. Cody watched the old man swing his staff with the strength and intensity of a young man.

"Wish me luck," he mumbled, taking a few steps.

"CODY! WAIT!" Shelby yelled. He stopped, turning back toward her. "I have an idea," she said. "See if you can get the Benningtons to come over here."

Chapter 49: The Savior

Cody realized believing in himself had a big impact on how well he wielded his powers. Confidence made him a far more formidable warrior in the fight against The Darkness. He ran into battle, swinging his sword at any demon that came near. But hours passed and even confidence couldn't secure a victory. His arms ached. He wondered how much longer he could go on.

Shelby, Charlotte, Martin and, strangely enough, the Benningtons, had disappeared. Cody assumed they'd headed toward a less dangerous section of the cave to do whatever it was Shelby had up her sleeve.

"LOOK OUT!" Sharkey yelled, swinging at a demon that had approached Cody from behind. 'Stay sharp!" he added.

The Guardian continued to blast the demons with the power of his staff. White light arced out, extinguishing a handful of Dreds at one time. Cody glanced over at Radianna, wielding her impressive ice sword. The Light Elves had many weapons, including something that resembled hand grenades, allowing them to take out many Dreds with one blast. But they were so few and The Darkness had an infinite army. It took multiple strikes to kill a demon close up. First one had to stab them, turning them to ice, then after subsequent strikes, they would explode, but another would soon appear in its place.

Chapter 49: The Savior

Cody glanced upward. Darkness prevailed, literally and figuratively. He ran over to the side of the cave, needing a recharge. Thankfully, the Benningtons had returned and were about to rejoin the battle.

He watched his mentor, still keeping up the fight. The Guardian swung his staff, but it was all he could do to keep the Dreds at bay. Sharkey was engaged in combat with Grýla, clearly a formidable enemy. Five more demons appeared around The Guardian, beating the old man down. Sharkey tried to come to his aid, but Grýla followed.

"SHARKEY! LOOK OUT!" Cody yelled, but he was too late.

Grýla leaped onto Sharkey's back, sinking her six-inch long teeth into the man's neck.

"*NO!*" Cody screamed.

The Benningtons ran out to engage Grýla, but the damage was done. Sharkey sank to his knees and doubled over. The demons were becoming too much for The Guardian. Even with the Benningtons engaging Grýla and The Light Elves taking on Odium, there were just too many.

"COME ON!" Cody yelled to his foster siblings. "THEY NEED OUR HELP!"

The teens ran out into battle, swinging their weapons in every direction. Shelby had become quite proficient with her bow and arrow, hitting one demon after another. Charlotte had realized during their trip to Bulwark that her lance could fire icy projectiles. Martin's axe had the ability to levitate for short periods, thus allowing him to swing at multiple foes concurrently with limited effort.

Three demons stood over Sharkey, beating him repeatedly with their scraps of metal. Cody and Martin surrounded them, jabbing and swinging their ice weapons. As soon as the coast was clear, the teens grabbed Sharkey's limbs, dragging him to safety.

"What can we do?" Charlotte cried. "He's dying."

"He may already be dead," Martin said in a choked voice. "He's lost so much blood."

Emotion welled up in Cody. His face turned red. He glanced over at The Guardian. He too would soon share the same fate.

"What should I do?" he cried, staring imploringly at Shelby. "If I help Sharkey, The Guardian will die. If I help the Guardian, Sharkey will die. What should I do?" he yelled. "We need help! We need help," he repeated, his voice choked.

Nidhogg! Are you there? We could sure use your help!

Suddenly, Cody noticed something approaching from above. It was so fiery and bright he could barely look in its direction. Whatever it was, the object was coming at a fast rate of speed. Cody's hopes were dashed as he heard Charlotte confirm his suspicion.

"IT'S BURNING!" she yelled, staring upward. "It must be a demon."

Cody's heart sank. They were doomed. The Darkness was hurting his family and there was nothing he could do to stop it.

"WAIT!" Shelby yelled. "LOOK!"

The large beast flew through the hole in the ceiling and landed nearby, folding its enormous wings. Hesitating only a second, it drew a huge breath and forged into battle. The Guardian swung his staff, knocking a group of demons to the ground, while the beast released a stream of fire in their direction. The demons exploded into puffs of black smoke.

"NIDHOGG!" Cody cried with joy.

The dragon was still ablaze, the same as when Grýla left it to die, but somehow it seemed healed. Its body was no longer solid. It seemed almost gaseous, smoldering like the sun. At least it's bringing some much-needed light to this dark cave, Cody thought.

"Help Mr. Sharkey!" Shelby screamed, bringing him back to reality.

Satisfied The Guardian was safe for the moment, Cody dropped to his knees next to Sharkey. The man's body was limp, blood oozing from a line of holes along his neck and various wounds on his body. Cody's head was swimming. He still wasn't sure how to invoke his healing powers and there was no time to learn. Sharkey was dying.

"Do something, Cody!" Martin yelled.

"You've got to try!" Shelby said, sobbing. "He's bleeding out."

Emotion gripped Cody. His eyes filled with tears.

Cody's face got red. The anger and helplessness he felt swelled inside him.

Do something, Cody! You can't just let him die! Do something, or prove them right. You are helpless!

Chapter 49: The Savior

Suddenly, his arm felt like it was on fire. The blood rushed to his fingers. Cody's hand lit up, a dragon tattoo glowing on the palm. He glanced at his siblings. Shelby, Charlotte, and Martin appeared to see it as well, staring at him with wide eyes. Cody reached over and touched Sharkey's neck. He could feel the pressure build in his fingertips until he thought they might explode.

He held out his hand as long as he could, then pulled it back, half expecting it to blow up, but it didn't. The pressure began to subside and the light tattoo disappeared.

"Ugh," a man's voice uttered.

Cody watched Sharkey sit up, the wounds on his neck beginning to scab over. The man let out a painful groan, but he was alive.

"You *did* it!" Shelby said with a huge smile.

"Nice work, Mr. Hawke," Sharkey said, wincing slightly. "I take back every mean thing I've ever said about you."

Sharkey held out his hand. Cody noticed gratitude in the man's eyes as he pulled him to his feet.

"If you're going to learn to heal," Sharkey said, "you picked a good time to do it."

The teens all grinned, but their joy was short-lived as Sharkey and Cody returned to the battle.

Cody wasn't sure how long it went on from there, minutes, maybe hours. His arms felt like rubber. Whenever they appeared to be making headway, more demons would appear, as if Odium could create them as needed from an endless supply of bad people. Sharkey and Odium were engaged in a battle that seemed like it might last forever. Nidhogg was almost out of fire, using his tail as a weapon instead.

Radianna, Kensie, and Grýla circled each other in a deadly dance. The Guardian had disappeared. Cody's eyes darted around trying to locate the old man, but he was nowhere to be found. Curiously, Jezebel flew overhead, grabbing Dreds by the shoulders and tossing them against the cave wall. A few minutes later, he spotted The Guardian's head amid a group of demons.

As he swung his sword, Cody wondered if they had come this far only to lose in the final hour. How long could even the great Sam Sharkey continue to fight? It was a question he didn't want answered.

Shelby, Charlotte, and Martin had rejoined the battle, their ice blades glistening in the dim light, but it was too little, too late.

Suddenly Cody heard a choked scream. It was Shelby, staring off to the side. He looked just in time to see The Guardian fall, something protruding from his chest. Radianna did her best to hold off the onslaught, but it was too much. One demon sank a sword into her shoulder, another into her leg.

"NO!" Cody screamed. "HELP!"

Kyrie hurried in her direction. One of the Light Elves, a man they called Armally, engaged Grýla, but Cody could see he was out of steam. The man dropped to his knees as the ogress took a piece of his shoulder. Kensie and Kala hurried to his defense.

Sharkey turned just as Odium swung his lance, knocking him to the ground. The demon opened its mouth wide, clearly relishing the thought of tearing Sharkey to bits. Andola was barely holding his own against a dozen Dreds. Grýla grabbed Radianna and threw her battered body across the cave. As Cody rush to help, he saw Grýla glance in his direction and almost smile.

"The children are next," the ogress growled. "They will be *so* tasty."

"HELP US!" Cody yelled, as five demons surrounded him, but there was no one left.

A dark fog began to fill the cavern, descending from above. As it reached Cody, he felt a hollow chill, followed by feelings of dread and desperation. The cave grew so dark it became almost impossible to see their enemies much less fight them. Cody swung his sword at anything that moved, then he just stopped, despair filling his heart. He was unable to go on.

Is this it? Is this the end?

Hovering amid the gloom, Cody saw a devil-like figure with enormous horns, bat wings, and an oily dark complexion. It rode an ominous-looking black bull, snorting impatiently, pulling on its reins.

Oh, no! Who is that?

Images swirled about the demon, like snippets of videos streaming amid the darkness. They reminded him of the visions he'd seen emanating from The Books of Light, except these were horrible. People were fighting, beating and kicking each other with fury in their eyes. He heard violent outbursts conveying prejudice and bigotry, followed by senseless murders. He saw masses of bodies stacked high, some children, dying of apparent starvation in empty fields. It was so awful he had to look away.

The devil-like creature became clearer and more defined, growing in strength. It was hideous and Cody could smell the stink of its prevailing animosity.

Animus! The Darkness.

Chapter 50: The Battle's End

In a last-ditch effort, Cody raised his sword and swung with all his might, but he knew it only bought him a few seconds. This is it, he thought. This is the end. He couldn't see his Rúndyrr family but Cody's heavy heart told him they didn't have long. He sank to his knees, consumed by dread.

Then something changed. The gloom began to dissipate, it's dark mist swirling upward. Cody watched as a Dred, about to hit him with a tire iron, exploded into thin air. Animus growled angrily, its evil moan reverberating throughout the cavern. Odium and Grýla froze, grimacing as if in pain.

What's happening?

Writhing and squirming in its saddle as if in unbearable agony, Animus pulled on the reins. The snorting bull galloped upward along a winding trail of dark fog. A few seconds later, it was gone. One by one, the hordes of demons disappeared, without being touched.

Sharkey staggered to his feet and stabbed Odium with his sword. The general froze then fell over. As Cody watched, the demon began to thaw, snarling in a primal tone.

"FINISH HIM!" Cody yelled, jumping to his feet.

"No," Sharkey said, clutching his right shoulder, "he is already done. My mercy will render him more pain than anything I could do physically."

Chapter 50: The Battle's End

"If you won't do it, I will," Cody said with a growl, holding out his sword.

As he rushed toward Odium, the sky began to glow with a brightness that lit the cave like daylight. The general screamed, smoldering as if being cooked from within. He blazed for a few seconds, then imploded like a super nova and disappeared in a puff of black smoke.

As Cody shielded his eyes, a being appeared amid the light, hovering majestically above. It had the head of an eagle and body of a lion, powerful wings at its shoulders.

"Oh, no! Who's *this* now?" Martin cried.

"The *Griffin* has returned," The Guardian uttered reverently, his body propped up against the cave wall. "The Light is back."

Sharkey glanced up at the newcomer and bowed his head. Radianna pulled a shard of glass from The Guardian's chest and helped the old man to his feet, his robe still dripping blood. They joined Sharkey, bowing their heads as well.

"It is good to see you, my friends, The Griffin declared in a commanding voice. "The balance of power is restored. The Light of Nimbus shines once more."

"You have no idea how happy we are to see you," Kala said with a wide grin.

"Thank you all," he said, glancing at each of them. "Earth owes you a debt of gratitude. I am pleased to see we have a new generation offering their powerful light to this world," The Griffin added, nodding briefly at Cody, Shelby, Charlotte, and Martin.

Cody could feel his warmth radiating from above, exuding love and kindness. With that, The Griffin extended his powerful wings and took flight, disappearing like a shooting star into the night sky.

"It's over," Sharkey mumbled, still catching his breath. He turned toward Cody. "Great job!"

"Me? What did I do?"

"Not you," Sharkey replied. "Though you did a great job also."

"Miss Shelby," The Guardian added, wincing slightly as his wounds continued to heal.

"Shelby?" Cody turned to see her smiling broadly. "Did she take down Odium?"

"Miss Shelby realized the heart is mightier than the sword," The Guardian said.

"What does that mean?" Cody asked.

"She planted a seed, Mr. Hawke. And *her* seed took root quickly," Sharkey added.

"I don't understand," Cody said, frowning.

"Cody," Charlotte offered, "Shelby got the Benningtons to use their influence by addressing their millions of followers on social media."

"And, do what?" he asked.

"Kala, Kyrie, and Kensie held a live chat on the various social media platforms, prompting each of their fans to do something wonderful," Shelby explained. "They asked their school-age fans to find a person eating lunch alone in the cafeteria and go sit with them," she continued. "Ask about their hobbies or interests, something they had in common, something they could share."

"For their older fans," Charlotte said, "they suggested dropping in on a sick or lonely friend. Maybe go to the park and pick up trash or adopt a pet."

"We asked them to think of someone in their lives with different views and start a dialog," Kensie said. "Agree to disagree, but agree that their opinions don't define who they are as people, reminding them to always let their goodness shine through. Mean comments just promote anger and hatred."

"I was all Shelby's idea," Kala added, "She also suggested we ask our adult fans to grab a book. Read something magical or inspiring, learn something you didn't know, like a new language," she continued. "Or, just read to your kids for an hour or two."

"That's all cool." Cody shrugged. "But what does it have to do with a war against The Darkness?"

"Anger and apathy," Sharkey replied. "They are The Darkness' power, its food, if you will."

"Knowledge and compassion are its enemies," The Guardian added. "They fuel The Light."

"The power of all that compassion and enlightenment," Sharkey continued, "well, it gave The Light the edge it needed to break the chains of bondage and send The Darkness packing."

"As soon as The Light touched the Dreds, they were free," The Guardian added. "And when its radiance surrounded The Darkness allowing it to feel warmth and goodness, it was dark no more."

"Okay. But Shelby left hours ago," Cody mumbled, still not sure he was buying their explanation. "Why did it take so long to work?"

"Different time zones, Cody," Charlotte whispered. "It took time for different groups to get the message and make it happen."

"It was never possible to win this war by fighting. But, the net effect of all that compassion and enlightenment," Sharkey added, "was enough to beat The Darkness down and release The Light."

"You mean that . . . *Griffin*? He's The Light?"

"The Griffin is the embodiment of The Light, it's physical manifestation if you will, just like Animus represents The Darkness," The Guardian said. 'But like The Darkness, The Light is everywhere, everywhere there's goodness, knowledge, and compassion."

"I don't understand," he said with a shrug.

"Cody," Charlotte said, "don't you see? *We* are The Light," she said, tears welling her eyes. "But we, meaning humans, are also The Darkness, it just depends on each of us and how we choose to be, filled with hate or exuding love."

"All of you," Sharkey added, "you hold the key. Collectively, we push the balance of power from good to evil and back. The Darkness can't be defeated with weapons. Its power depends on us, how we treat each other and how we live our lives, in darkness or in light."

"Why didn't you tell me that earlier," Cody said, frowning.

"You needed to learn it on your own," The Guardian replied.

"I saw it," Cody mumbled, a sudden realization filling him with awe. "I *saw* The Light when I opened the case containing the nine books," he said. "It was all there, in my head. There was a policeman volunteering to be a big brother and a nurse reading letters to a dying woman."

"The Light has the power to encourage change," The Guardian said. "It's like a beautiful, bright beacon of hope, a snowball rolling down a hill, picking up momentum as it goes."

"And I saw The Darkness just now," Cody added. "I saw people fighting and killing each other."

Finally, Cody understood. They couldn't beat the Dreds because the world kept feeding The Darkness. It wasn't more swords or lances they needed, it was thousands, maybe hundreds of thousands of people doing wonderful things all at one time.

"At the risk of being nosey," Martin said, "I have a question." He looked at Sharkey. "When you called Cody brother, did you mean like, hey, bro, or did you mean like brother?"

"He means brother, as in sibling," Cody replied.

"When did you find out *that* little nugget?" Martin asked, staring at Cody with wide eyes.

"And why didn't you tell us?" Shelby added.

"I-uh, didn't know for sure," Cody said, shrugging, "until he said it." He looked around at his family and friends, shaking his head. "Who *am* I?"

Cody could feel the emotion well up in his eyes. He hadn't had the opportunity to dwell on it until now, but suddenly it hit him. His life before Freya Manor had been nothing more than a façade, a playbook, written to have a desired ending. Everything he loved was just there to serve a purpose.

Was any of it real? Who were my parents? Who, for that matter, am I?

"I'm ecstatic to have a brother, but at the same time I . . . feel so lost," Cody added in a choked voice. "Everything I thought was true, everything I believed in, was just a lie."

"That is not so," The Guardian said softly. "It is just, there was more to it than thou realized."

"When will I learn the truth?"

"In time," The Guardian offered. "Let us leave it at that, for now. I know thou hath questions, but thou hast been through much these last few months. It is time to be Cody Hawke, the high school student again, for a little while at least."

"I've been hard on you at times, Mr. Hawke," Sharkey said, rubbing the stubble on his chin. "I suppose on some level, I've been a little jealous."

Cody was taken aback. "Jealous of *me*? It's more like the other way around."

"We had different mothers, otherwise, I might've been The Chosen," Sharkey explained.

"You can have it if you want," Cody said. "I'm not good enough to fill The Guardian's shoes."

"No, quite the contrary," Sharkey replied. "You are exceptional."

"He is correct," The Guardian added. "Thou hast done more at a young age than either of us thought was possible. You are truly gifted," he said.

"I don't feel gifted," Cody muttered. "Most of the time I just get in the way or screw things up."

"Thou must understand," The Guardian said, stepping forward and putting a hand on Cody's shoulder, "there is a reason we call it *youth*. If individuals were born with all the knowledge they will have accumulated at the end, then what would be the point in living?"

"I guess," Cody replied, staring up at the starry sky.

"Is it gone for good, Mr. Sharkey?" Charlotte asked. "The Darkness?"

Sharkey shook his head. "Sadly, Miss Charlotte, no. We've not seen the last of The Darkness."

"Unfortunately, it will return," The Guardian said somberly. "As long as people feed their anger and focus on their differences. But for now, The Light is free to inspire and teach. The Darkness has lost much of its power. The nine books are back in the hands of those who support The Light. And *we* live to fight another day."

THE END

www.ingramcontent.com/pod-product-compliance
Lightning Source LLC
Chambersburg PA
CBHW030557180626
46816CB00005B/1583